THE SOUL COLLECTOR

"Johnston does an expert job
in this extraordinary mixture of police procedural,
head-banging vigilante lit, Agatha Christie (some splendidly
cryptic crossword clues), and Dennis Wheatley…Great stuff."
—*The Guardian*

"Captivating."
—*Daily Mirror*

"Clever in all the right ways:
its plotting is a little out of the box with its
mixture of all things serial killers; a touch of Golden Age puzzle
solving (Colin Dexter would approve); a large dose of machismo
bravado, and the emotional exploration of fledgling love."
—Mike Stotter

"A heady brew…the action is relentless."
—*Times Online*

PAUL JOHNSTON

MAPS OF HELL

MIRA

Recycling programs
for this product may
not exist in your area.

ISBN-13: 978-0-7783-2778-3

MAPS OF HELL

For questions and comments about the quality of this book please contact us
at Customer_eCare@Harlequin.ca.

www.MIRABooks.com

Printed in U.S.A.

In memoriam
Ronald Mackie Johnston
(1926-2009)

Novelist, ship master, bon viveur, and reader.
Dignum laude virum Musa vetat mori.

Work on what you have inherited from your fathers,
That you may possess it.
—Goethe, *Faust*

Prologue

The twins learned much about death before their tenth birthday.

Their mother wanted them to live with her parents, but their father insisted that the family stay together. It was unusual. None of the other doctors even had their wives with them, let alone their offspring. Special arrangements had to be made; permissions were granted, signed and stamped at high levels. Fortunately, the father's immediate superior approved of the children's presence. The experience would make them perfect citizens and perfection was the aim of all the nation's scientists, was it not? The fact that they were twins, thus providing many valuable points of comparison, was very much in their favor.

There was no school where the doctor worked, but tutors were easy to find. The place was teeming with them, even if they seldom lasted a whole year. Of course, the thin, nervous men and pale women could have been a bad influence, but the children were quick to see any deviation from the principles their father had taught them from the earliest age. They had complained about several teachers. Those undesirables were immediately removed and were not seen again.

As the boy and girl grew, they lost their puppy fat and turned into hard-bodied replicas of their father. The only thing that spoiled their flawless appearance—blond hair, ice-blue eyes, that remarkable nose—was the extreme pallor of their skin. They took one hour of exercise in the garden every day, rain or shine, but the atmosphere they lived in was hardly conducive to rosy cheeks.

After two years the children knew all there was to know about the human condition, especially that of the lower races. The doctor and his chief were pleased. That knowledge would stand the boy and girl in good stead when they became adults and continued the glorious work for future generations. Their mother was less enthusiastic. She sickened and died during the family's second winter in the East.

It couldn't be said that the twins were unduly affected.

One

I woke up in panic and felt pain all over my body—arms, gut, ribs, groin. I took a deep breath and turned onto my back. The searing light made me jam my eyes shut. Holding my hand in front of my face, I sat up slowly, finding it hard to balance, and looked at myself. I was naked and filthy, white skin rubbed raw in places from the rough blanket I'd been lying on. Suddenly I felt dizzy and pitched forward onto the cold floor. A rush of vomit surprised me, jerking from my mouth in successive surges. I felt like shit.

Then I realized something worse. I didn't know who I was. I had no memory. I had no past. I was no one.

I clenched my fists and tried to get a grip. Where was I? I looked around the room. It was only a little longer than the concrete platform I had been lying on, and not much more than twice as wide. One of the narrow ends was taken up by a metal door, and there wasn't a window in any of the other three walls. A long fluorescent light divided the ceiling, while the floor was concrete. I had no recollection of coming to the place. I had no idea, even, of what part of the world I was in.

I blinked and took in the room again. It was making my

head swim. The platform was at a weird angle to the floor
and it was wider at one end than the other. The walls, ceiling and floor had all been painted in the same dull gray
color, so it was hard to see where one ended and the next
began.

I realized I was sweating heavily. The place was roasting hot, even though there was no sign of a heat source.
The stench of my vomit was making me gag. I wiped the
floor with my blanket, then threw it into the corner. My
throat was parched and I searched in vain for a tap or
bottle. Apart from me and the stinking blanket, the room
was completely empty.

I wondered how long I had been there. I had lost all sense
of time and couldn't say whether it had been minutes or
hours since I'd woken. I went to the door and put an ear to
it. I couldn't hear anything. I seemed to be completely alone.
My empty stomach contracted and I clamped my arms
around my raised knees. Had I been left to rot in this hole?

At least my mind was working. I was able to think, but that
only made me feel more bereft. I yelled and listened for a
response. There was none. I felt my eyes dampen. I could
think and I could speak, but I knew as little as a tiny child.
Someone had stolen my identity, my very soul. I had never
wanted to see another human face so much. But no one came.

I inspected my body. There were yellow and black
bruises on my arms and abdomen, and lumps of dried
blood on my knuckles. I looked closer. Puncture marks
dotted the skin on the inside of my upper and lower arms.
I ran my fingers across my face. The stubble was thick. My
hair was short. I pulled some out and saw a mixture of
black and white. I felt scabs on my forehead. There was
nothing in the room that showed my reflection. I went to
the door and banged my hands on it. There was a narrow
space between the bottom of the door and the floor. I
dropped to my knees and lowered my head, but could see

nothing, not even a trace of light. I stood up again on unsteady legs, my eyes getting damp again as I realized I had no idea what I looked like.

I started to mumble, trying to find comforting words, words that would help me find out who I was. I took in my shrunken genitals. Man. I was a man. Muscles. My arms and legs hardened when I tensed them—I was in reasonable shape. I was thirsty, hungry. My throat hurt and my stomach rumbled. I stretched out on the floor, closed my eyes and tried to empty my mind of the here and now. Think. Remember. Who was I? Where did I come from? Who did I know?

For a time nothing happened. Then a name appeared unprompted in my consciousness.

Washington.

What did that mean?

I was suddenly aware of a dim figure, a man in a wig and a military jacket. Washington.

Wooden teeth.

What the hell?

Then, as if curtains had parted, my mind regained its visual function and I saw a wide, grass-covered open space with a tall, domed building in the distance. I seemed to know that the place was called Washington, but I had no idea where it was or what it meant to me. I was sure I had been there, though: the picture was too vivid to have come from a film or a book.

I said the word aloud, breaking it into syllables.

"Wash-ing-ton…"

…I am in a car driven by an impassive man in a dark suit. On the backseat beside me is a blonde woman, whose name I don't know. She seems to know me. She squeezes my arm as we pass, on our left, a white house with a colonnaded porch. She seems to treat it with exaggerated respect, as does the driver. The sun has almost set and its rays are casting a soft red light over the buildings. I'm in very good spirits.

"Hey, didn't you say you could take us wherever we wanted?" I say to the short-haired man at the wheel.

He glances at me in the mirror. "That is so, sir. But I suggest we go to your hotel so you can freshen up first."

I look at the woman by my side and laugh. "Oh, we're fresh enough. Why don't you take us to one of those rough places? I want to see the real Washington."

My companion shakes her head and leans forward. "Don't listen to him. He likes to think he's an expert on crime."

I laugh again. "And you're not? Come on, let's live dangerously. Let's go to Anacostia. That's where the drug dealers are in charge, isn't it?"

The driver nods. "Yeah, it's one of the places that's theirs. I really don't think—"

"Don't worry, we'll take full responsibility," I say, getting a frown from the woman. "Anyway, you've got a radio to call for help, haven't you?"

He twitches his head but then does as I say, turning to the right and crossing a bridge shortly afterward. The buildings change from stone to clapboard, and there are young black men on every street corner. They give the large car glances that combine interest with disdain.

"Seen enough?" the driver asks, after a few minutes.

"No," I say. "We want to get out and take the air."

"Speak for yourself," my companion says in a low voice.

I smile and kiss her on the lips. "Stop at the next junction," I tell the chauffeur.

"I really don't recommend this, sir," he says, but he complies.

"Coming?" I ask, as I open the door.

"Oh, all right," the woman says. "Idiot." She slides awkwardly across the seat and takes my hand. I feel her weight.

I lean down before I close the door. "Turn right and wait for us."

The driver gives me a disapproving look and then drives on.

We're on our own. For under a minute. The first boy—he couldn't have been over twelve—turns his bicycle toward us, pedals hard and then stops a finger-length from me.

"Watcha got in the bag, lady?" he asks with a wide smile, but I notice his eyes have narrowed.

My companion holds her shoulder bag against her abdomen. "Oh, just girly stuff," she says.

Another boy on a bike skids up. "Girly stuff?" he says, displaying gleaming white teeth. "We likes girly stuff." He looks at me aggressively. "How about you, mister? You like that shit?"

Over his head I see a fleet of medium-size bodies on bikes approaching.

"Give us a break, guys," I say. "We're just taking the air."

"Oh, yeah?" says another boy, wearing a baseball cap like the rest, but with sunglasses shielding his eyes. "How about we takes the bag, then? And everythin' you got in your pockets, big man?"

I puff out my chest and step toward him. "How about you guys go home to your mothers?"

The teenagers pull their bikes back and I grin triumphantly. Then I hear a deeper voice from behind me.

"You dissin' the youth, whitey?"

I turn to confront a tall, heavily built young man, his hair in cornrows and his tracksuit top open to display a large silver pistol in his waistband. I hear the woman beside me inhale sharply. Before I react, she hands her bag to the armed man and clamps her hand on my arm.

"There's our car," she says, pulling me toward the corner.

The limousine has appeared silently, the driver standing on the curb with a radio handset at the side of his head.

The boys pedal away, cheering, while the young man saunters away. He drops my companion's bag on the pavement. I go over and pick it up.

"Anything missing?" I ask, as I hand it over.

She checks. "Just my purse, with all the cash I brought," she says. "And my passport."

"Shit," I say.

"Yeah, right," says the driver. He holds the door open for my companion.

As we move off, I turn to her. "Sorry," I say, in a low voice.

"Sorry don't get you nowhere in this town, buster," she says, in an accent like the driver's.

I try to laugh, but I feel about two feet tall....

The scene stopped suddenly. I tried to bring it back, but there was nothing. I couldn't remember anything else. Who was the woman? I was obviously close to her. Where was she now? Where was I? I blinked and then banged my forehead against the wall. The pain was intense, but strangely I felt better for it.

Sometime later, there was a crash at the door and a tray appeared at floor level. I went over quickly, but the narrow hatch was instantly slammed back down.

"Hey!" I shouted. "Let me out of here!"

There was no response. I couldn't even hear any footsteps.

I examined the food on the tray. There was a cup of dirty-looking water, which I drank half of before I could stop myself. A hunk of discolored white bread and a piece of hard yellow cheese was all there was to eat. I wolfed them down, taking a small sip of water to soften each bite of the bread. When I'd finished, my stomach wasn't even half-full and my throat was as rough as it had been before. And the temperature in the room seemed to have gone up to scalding.

I went back to the slanted bed and lay down. I tried to

go back to Washington or to anywhere else that wasn't as confined as the grave, but my mind remained blank.

Then the music started—ear-shredding, grinding rock at terminal volume. Pressing my hands to my ears did little to shut it out. The light on the ceiling started to flash irregularly. I turned my head to the wall, but it seemed to be shaking to the thunderous beat.

I had no idea how long that went on. Soon after the noise finally stopped, there was another crash at the door. This time, a round hole appeared at waist level. Before I could move, the muzzle of a hose sprayed freezing water in at high pressure, soaking me instantly. The jets of water stung my skin and I was forced to crouch at the far end of the bed, not that it gave much cover. I cupped a hand and swallowed, but had to spit immediately. The water tasted like something had died in it. Quickly, the level rose to my calves and the soiled blanket started to move towards the door. I grabbed it and tried to rinse the vomit from it. Then the spray stopped as suddenly as it had started and the water flowed away under the door.

I soon noticed that the heat had been turned off. I began to shiver violently.

Draping the sodden blanket over me did little to help. Then, without warning, the light went out.

I sat in the total darkness, my head in my hands. Why was this happening to me? What had I done to deserve treatment like this? I tried to conjure up the woman I'd seen again, tried to find anyone from my past. Nobody came. Maybe the scenes in Washington, wherever the hell that was, had just been the fruits of my imagination. Maybe nothing meant anything and I couldn't even trust my own mind.

I fell away into an abyss, my breath rapid and my limbs locked by the chill.

The only thing I could hope was that I had died. Did that mean there was an afterlife? The idea was attractive. Perhaps I was in the underworld. Or in limbo. Or even purgatory.

Then the cold bit into me again and I was back in hell. It was obvious that whoever was doing this to me had a deep knowledge of cruelty and evil.

I had the feeling that I'd met more than one person like that in my unreachable past.

Two

I cowered in the dark for what seemed like an eternity. The cold grew even worse and I couldn't control my shivering. I tried to sit without the damp blanket, but soon found that I needed the meager insulation it offered. At least the music stayed off, though the silence became almost as disturbing.

Finally, the scene in the place called Washington came back to me. At least I had *some* memory function. I still couldn't remember who the woman was, or what we were doing there. What did the episode tell me about myself? That I was supposedly some sort of expert in crime. A policeman? A criminologist? In any case, I couldn't have been very smart, insisting on going to a notoriously dangerous district and provoking the robbery. I hadn't behaved in a very courageous fashion, either. In fact, I'd behaved like a major asshole. But the blonde woman didn't seem to think so. She had submitted to my whim and had accepted the loss of her valuables without much concern. What did that say about her feelings for me? And something made me think she was some kind of crime specialist, as well. Were we both researchers? Cops? I couldn't reach an answer that rang true and slapped the wall in frustration.

The blanket was making the skin on my shoulders and back itch. My nostrils were filled with the stench of vomit, which had somehow survived immersion in the water. I tried to breathe only through my mouth, but that made me cough heavily. Eventually I willed myself to sleep, but kept jerking awake in the darkness, my heart pounding. Finally, I fell like a stone into the pit, where scaly-skinned devils laughed at me in my nakedness, ramming rust-covered tridents into my flailing limbs...

Simultaneously the light came on and the door crashed open. Four men in gray uniforms covered by knee-length leather aprons burst in. Two carried long truncheons, which they dug into my armpits to raise me up against the wall. The others pulled a pair of what felt like paper trousers up onto my legs. I was lowered to the floor and a shirt of the same material was pulled over my arms. Not a word was spoken during the whole procedure. I opened my mouth to protest and one of the truncheons was pushed hard between my teeth. I got the message.

I was heaved out through the door and nearly collided with the wall on the other side of a dank corridor. The four men formed up around me and started to move forward. A truncheon in the small of my back made me stumble ahead, the muscles in my legs tingling from lack of use. I caught glimpses through open doors of other cells. Naked prisoners of both sexes stood with their legs apart and their arms raised to the side. They looked like they had been frozen in the middle of gymnastic exercises. But it was their eyes that were most striking—wide-open and bloodshot, staring across blankly at the wall above. Was that mindlessness the fate awaiting me—or could there be something even worse?

We moved on through more corridors, passing doors marked only with numbers. There was a faint smell of chemicals and the hum of machinery. The air seemed unnaturally dry. Then I was stopped outside a set of double doors. One of my escorts tapped the buttons on a touch pad and I was pushed through.

It was a large space, with lights shining at the far end.

My stomach clenched when I saw what I was being led toward.

The wooden post was taller than a man and about a foot wide. Ropes hung from it at neck, waist and ankle height. The untreated timber was stained a reddish-brown between the top and middle ropes. This was a place of execution.

I started shouting as I was dragged to it, demanding to know what was going on, but the men paid no attention. Two held me against the post, while the others tied the ropes tightly around me. They stepped away and I saw a line of men in the same gray uniforms moving toward me—these in berets, as well. They held old-fashioned rifles and stopped about fifteen yards away.

An officer with a pistol in his hand appeared at the side of the line. He gave me a contemptuous glance and then turned to his men.

"Ready!" he barked.

My heart was hammering and my eyes were wide. Even though the ropes didn't allow much movement, my whole body was shaking.

"Aim!" the officer shouted.

"No!" I screamed, my voice breaking like a teenage boy's. "No!"

"Fire!"

I was deafened by the thunder of the guns and blinded by the muzzle flashes. It was only when I opened my eyes that I realized I was still alive. I looked down at my chest and saw that the paper shirt was unblemished.

"Bastards!" I yelled. "What the fuck are you playing at?"

The line of men had turned their backs on me. They were marching into the dark at the far end of the room. The officer remained for a few seconds. He didn't speak, but fashioned his lips into a grotesque and chilling smile. Then he, too, turned on his heel and paced away, the pistol still in his hand. At least there hadn't been a coup de grâce.

"Bastards!" I yelled again, straining at the ropes. Then I dropped my head and started to sob. I had become aware of a warm dampness in the paper trousers. I'd lost control of my bladder when the blanks had been fired. At first I felt ashamed, then anger coursed through me. I had no idea why I was being treated like an animal, but the fuckers in the gray uniforms weren't going to get away with it. I raised my head and looked for someone to test my new resolve out on, but they had all gone. I was left on the execution post for what seemed like hours, my soaked trousers growing cold and uncomfortable. One thing I was sure of—I would pay my tormenters back.

Suddenly I remembered a face, that of a man, though it could have been a demon's: iceberg-cold blue eyes beneath short fair hair, a smile that made the firing squad officer's seem benevolent. The canine teeth, top and bottom, were sharply pointed and the tongue flickered between the incisors like a snake's. I knew who he was; he had remained despite my deficient memory. He called himself the White Devil and he had made a list of people to kill in revenge for what they had done to him.

I blinked hard and inhaled deeply. The face faded. The White Devil. I couldn't recall everything he had done, but I knew that I had resisted him. The irony made me laugh. My old enemy had inspired defiance in me, even while I was roped to the execution post. I was in the hands of ruthless men who could kill me—or pretend to—anytime they wanted, but I was still alive. I swore that they weren't going to reduce me to the state of the empty-eyed souls I had seen earlier.

The men in the leather aprons eventually came for me

and took me back to my cell. They ripped the paper clothes from me, their lips twisted in expressions of mockery and disdain, then shoved me inside. As soon as the door slammed shut, the nozzle was inserted and the cold water spray started again. I forced myself to take it full on and cleaned myself as best I could.

Later, a lump of bread and a piece of meat that I couldn't identify came through the hatch. I made myself eat slowly to stave off stomach trouble. The water that came with the food was less discolored than before. After I'd finished, I started to exercise, doing push-ups and sit-ups on the damp floor. My muscles burned, but I kept my breathing regular. I was in reasonably good physical condition, which made me feel better.

I knew what would be coming next—the loud music. I kept some of the bread back and dampened it to make earplugs. Then I closed my eyes and concentrated on recalling the music I had listened to in the past. After a while, some names came back and I concentrated on each one, making as many connections as I could.

When the industrial noise started, I blocked my ears and started to repeat loudly the strings of words I'd constructed.

"Page, Plant, Bonham, Jones.

"Jagger, Richards, Jones, Wyman, Watts, Taylor.

"Crosby, Stills, Nash, Young."

It was exhausting keeping the grinding music at bay and I often lost track of what I was saying. But eventually the constant repetition made me focus and I could remember particular songs and albums, which I fashioned into other strings of words.

"'Since I've Been Loving You,' 'Black Dog,' 'Hot Dog.'

"'Beggar's Banquet,' 'Let it Bleed,' 'Exile on Main Street,' 'Sticky Fingers.'

"'Woodenships,' 'Cathedral,' 'Almost Cut My Hair,' 'Ohio.'"

When the noise stopped and the light went out, I found that I was recalling rooms where I'd listened to the albums and faces of people who had been there.

Some of their names came back to me, too—David, Caroline, Andy. Names and faces, but nothing more....

They were enough. I was soaked and shivering, but I was still myself. I once had a life, and I was determined I was going to get it back.

Even if I still didn't know who I was.

When the light came on again, I turned onto my front and managed to get some sleep. The strange shape and angle of the bed no longer bothered me. I wasn't prepared to let anything get in the way of what was best for me, and I needed rest if I was to be able to fight my captors.

I awoke to the slam of the hatch at floor level. This time there was only a small cup of water. I wondered what that portended. I sniffed it, but didn't pick up any suspicious smell, so I drank the contents. That was a mistake. After a few minutes, I began to yawn widely and struggled to keep my eyes open. Whatever substance had been in the water was either flavorless or was concealed by the earthy taste.

Suddenly the door crashed open. The men in leather aprons came in again. I tried to resist, but I had little control over my arms and legs. I couldn't stop them from dragging me out, so I closed my eyes and tried to concentrate on something related to my past. If they were going to scare the shit out of me like they did with the firing squad, I needed a diversion. I looked down and concentrated on the scarring on my knee. Where did I get it? A car accident? A fall while skiing? I didn't even know if I skied. Another sport? That seemed suggestive. Which sport? I saw a muddy field and players wearing brightly colored shirts. That was it. Rugby league. I saw myself

holding an oval ball, breaking a tackle and then being hit
from two sides at the same time. Blinding pain as my car-
tilage went.

I opened my eyes as I was pulled into a clean and well-
lit room. People wearing green surgical suits were waiting.
At first I thought my knee was about to be fixed, then I remembered what was going on. Behind the people was a
bed with a long black box above it, cables and leads with
suction pads hanging down. I couldn't recall ever having
seen anything like it.

The silent men in the leather aprons lifted me onto the
bed and secured my arms and legs.

"Rugby league," I said to myself. "Try. Drop goal.
Penalty. Conversion." I noticed that the underside of the
box above me consisted of complex machinery—digital
devices, electrical circuits and the like. I got a bad feeling
about what was in store for me.

I smelled rubbing alcohol and felt a damp swab on my
arm. Then a needle was slipped into a vein.

"Try. Drop goal. Penalty. Conversion," I kept repeating.

I tensed myself to fight the loss of consciousness that I
was expecting, but it didn't come. I felt as if I were floating in the air, but I remained at least partly alert. The box
above the bed was lowered, stopping only a few inches
from my face. Then all the lights went out.

I kept silently repeating my rugby-league mnemonic. It
was effective in countering the panic I was feeling in what
had become a very enclosed space. Then lights came on
all over the base of the box and a whirring noise started up.

"Hello," said a soothing female voice. "Stay calm.
Nothing unpleasant is going to happen."

"Try. Drop goal. Penalty. Conversion," I continued saying to myself.

Suddenly I felt latex-covered fingers on my eyes. They
were pulling open the eyelids. Something metallic was

attached to them and involuntary tears flowed. I wondered if they were going to blind me and my heart started to thunder. I tried to cry out, but found that my voice had gone missing.

"There we are," said the woman. "That wasn't too bad, was it?"

She was lucky I wasn't able to tell her what I was thinking.

"Now, enjoy the show."

A screen was lit up above my face. Strident martial music began to play and images of men in suits and the occasional woman appeared. I tried to identify them, but recalled no names. I had the impression they were all politicians, but I couldn't be sure. Then the images started to change more rapidly and I lost track.

I went back to my rugby-league mnemonic, trying to ignore the pain around my eyes. But it was soon dashed from my mind as the brassy music rose to a crescendo and a picture of a hard-eyed man appeared. I knew I'd seen him before, I even knew he was the devil incarnate, but I couldn't place him or remember his name.

The whir of the machine became louder and the images on the screen started to move so fast that I could no longer distinguish what they were. Then every nerve in my body seemed to be energized and I felt my back rise from the bed. I was being asked an incomprehensible question repeatedly, in a tone that required an answer, but I couldn't speak, couldn't scream as my whole being seemed to take fire and my head throbbed.

Then I heard the words at last.

"You will obey every command that you are given, will you not?"

I fought against the urge to respond positively, trying to get the words of my mnemonic going again. Then I saw how to give myself a chance.

"Yes," I said, aware that the power of speech had returned to me. "Yes, I will obey every command."

But deep down I was still repeating *Try. Drop. Goal. Penalty. Conversion.*

Until a siren sounded and I fell into the deepest of holes.

When I came round, I didn't have a clue where I was. My head was ringing with strange sounds and I saw a blur of colors and shapes. Gradually my vision cleared, but my ears were still filled with discordant voices. There was a foul stench in my nostrils. I tried to move, but my arms and legs were confined. I looked down and saw that I had been tied to a wheelchair. I was wearing paper clothes again. I felt a twinge of alarm and glanced around. What I saw wasn't reassuring.

I was at the back of a long hall with no windows. In the dim light I made out a mass of people of both sexes, their limbs jerking about. Many of them were young and muscular. They were all naked and were crying out words that I couldn't understand. At the front there was a heap of large stones with a large upturned cross projecting upward from it. I began to get a very bad feeling.

Then a tall figure wearing a black robe appeared, hands raised high. I blinked and shook my head. I wasn't seeing things. The face was larger than it should have been and seemed to be carved out of stone. I remembered where I'd seen the like—on the sides of churches. An uglier… gargoyle…would have been hard to find, the features twisted, eyes bulging and nose spread wide as if having sustained heavy blows.

Another figure followed, this one clearly male—he was naked, a huge erection moving to and fro as he pranced about, cracking a short whip. But his head was not human. It was that of a carnivorous animal, its jaws open to reveal vicious yellow teeth, and without having to think, I knew immediately the word: *hyena.*

The gargoyle began to speak, the voice low and masculine. It sounded all around me, and I saw speakers on the walls. I also noticed the animal corpses hanging from the wooden panels—everything from rabbits and foxes to large creatures, bears. They must have been killed where they were suspended, as there was dark blood on the walls and pooled on the floor. That accounted for the stink. Looking closer, I realized that all the animals' eyes had been mutilated. Some were hanging from their eye sockets.

"Silence, my fellow worshippers," the gargoyle was saying. "Listen to the antiGospel of our lord and master. 'In the beginning was the word, and the word was with Lucifer, and the word was Lucifer.'"

The people in the hall broke into loud screams of approbation. A particularly crazed young man caught my eye—he dragged his nails down his bare chest hard enough to draw blood. I had seen him before. He had been in command of the firing squad.

The gargoyle spoke again. "Our lord Lucifer demands a blood sacrifice today, as he does every day. Bring on the victim!"

The man in the hyena head ran to the side, wielding his whip, but I was struggling to keep my eyes open now. Images were cascading before them, lines of men in uniform that went on and on. Then everything abruptly disappeared.

As I fell into the darkness, I heard a long, desperate scream.

Three

Hinkey's Bar was in a back street near the Washington Navy Yard, less than a mile south of the U.S. Capitol. It took up the ground floor of a crumbling building. The upper floors were home to a dope dealer, a producer of Internet porn, and several sad-eyed people who couldn't afford anything better. Hinkey himself was in his seventies. He'd been a minor-league baseball player in his youth and his exploits on the diamond were all he talked about. He sat in a corner with a bottle of cheap bourbon in front of him, while his son—known to regulars as Hinkey Part Two because, paradoxically, he bore no resemblance to his old man—ran the place with an attitude that veered between indifference and scorn, depending on the state of his hangover.

Back in the seventies, Hinkey had realized the place wouldn't last much longer on its clientele of working-class alcoholics and slumming students. He hit on the idea of hiring bands, particularly cheap and talent-free ones he could pay in beer. The old man was tone-deaf, so he didn't care if the musicians played rock, punk, post-punk, grunge or whatever shit was in fashion. Not blues or soul, though.

The black man's music wasn't his thing. He never got big crowds, but for three nights a week he made a half-decent profit. Hinkey Part Two wasn't tone-deaf, but he was into equal opportunity—he hated all music and all the people who came to listen. As for the bands, they featured the worst kind of lowlifes—tuneless, loudmouthed, thieving scum. The only time anyone saw Hinkey Part Two smile was when the audience threw glasses at the musicians.

Old Hinkey still handled the bookings, mainly because he had more interest in turning a buck than his 220-pound son. He didn't pay attention to the bands' names, but he kept up with D.C. scuttlebutt enough to go only for acts that brought in some kind of crowd. He'd heard that Loki and the Giants were popular with long-haired, highly tattooed kids who dress only in black, so he closed the deal with the lead singer—of course they didn't have a manager.

It turned out to be one of the worst decisions he'd ever made.

Loki was in what Hinkey called the dressing room. The proprietor had told him he used to take broads there back in the days when piss wasn't all that came out of a dick. That explained why there was an ancient bed with a rat-chewed mattress along one wall. Maybe the cracked mirror on the opposite wall dated from then, too. Hinkey had put a battered table and a light under it, and called it a dressing table. Pity he didn't pay more attention to his own dressing—the Hawaiian shirt he was wearing made Loki's eyes burn.

Still, the singer thought, the shit hole had some good points. The so-called dressing room had a door that opened onto the yard at the back of the bar. It had been asphalted and there was just room for the band's van to park there. That had saved them humping the amp, speakers and instruments through the front of the dive. It also meant that pussy could be checked in and out without anyone noticing.

Loki took out a Baggie and emptied some of the contents onto the table. That was another advantage to Hickey's—it had a resident dealer upstairs. He chopped out a couple of lines and bent low to snort them. The stuff had been heavily cut, but it still did the job. He sat back and twitched his head, feeling greasy strands of his waist-length hair slap against his cheeks. Since he'd turned forty, he'd had to start dying it black—gray hair didn't cut it when you were a thrash-metal Nazi satanist. He bared his teeth at the mirror. The lower part of his face was covered by a beard that reached his belly, while his cheeks and fore-head had been tattooed with Viking runes and whorls. His arms bore similar designs in red and black. His prize tats— the ones that would have gotten him beaten up in the street or even arrested in some of the more liberal states, includ-ing the hyper-politically-correct District of Columbia— were under his black T-shirt. There was a ten-inch swastika on his chest and an Iron Cross hanging from the bottom hook, while the words *I Am the Final Solution* adorned his back in six-inch-high Gothic letters. If the audience was the right kind, he'd take a chance and strip off to give them the full show. He'd had *Mein Kampf* tattooed on his lower abdomen, with an arrow pointing to his groin. He didn't think the Führer would disapprove.

Loki—born Duane Speckesser—had come a long way from Wisconsin. His parents were third-generation Ger-mans with a small farm. When he was a teenager, he got progressively angrier about their lack of interest in the Fa-therland. His old man had served in the Airborne and was proud that he'd kept the victors' peace in Berlin after the end of the Thousand Year Reich. As far as Duane was con-cerned, he should have hung his head in shame. A quarter of Americans had German roots, but very few of them showed any respect to the greatest German of all. Although the young Loki had little ability as a singer, he threw himself into the far-right music scene because he understood the power of songs to influence and inspire people. It also got him laid more often than his unprepossessing appearance would otherwise have merited. He had started off as a skinhead then found his real place in the underground metal scene that emerged in the eighties. He didn't even have to sing anymore, as roaring vocals out was the preferred style.

Loki did another line and stretched his muscular arms. He might have put on a load of pounds, but he still worked out with weights on the long drives between gigs. The Giants were the most popular Nazi satanic metal band in the South and Midwest, but the opportunity to play the capital, the seat of the Zionist Occupation Government, was not to be turned down, even if Hinkey was paying peanuts—the old fucker had tried to pay them off with a couple of crates of beer, but Loki had put him right. Maybe he'd put him even more right after the show. Then again, Loki was doing pretty well, what with album sales on the Internet—his songs were bought around the world, thanks to modern technology—and with donations from clandestine far-right organizations that approved of his agenda. Compositions like "Aryan Race," "Rise Up and Fight," "Smoke over Auschwitz" and "We Are Satan's Storm Troopers" had turned out to be real moneyspinners. He had to be careful how he presented himself in public, though. That was why he'd chosen the name of Loki, the Norse trickster god, and given the other musicians giants' names. He'd have preferred to have performed as the Children of the Führer, but that would have gotten the ZOG and its pinko pals jumping like scalded cats. He'd been inside more than once and he wasn't going back.

The singer stood up and slapped his black leather pants. They were getting tight; he could do with a new pair. Maybe he'd go shoplifting tomorrow. It was amazing how easy it was to rip things off when the rest of the band started brawling and threatening to throw up in shops. Which reminded him… Where were his sidekicks? There was less than an hour till showtime. The assholes had probably disobeyed his orders and gone into one of the black districts. It wouldn't be the first time they turned up for a gig covered in blood. Still, it was good for the image.

There was a double knock on the back door. Loki opened up.

"Look what we got!" said Bergilmir, the stick-thin bassist.

"Fresh as a Dachau daisy," added the guitarist Skadi, a podgy woman with dyed white hair down to her ass.

The drummer, Thiazi, pushed forward a young woman in a head scarf. "Guess what, big man? I reckon this one's a virrrgin." He smiled, revealing several missing teeth.

Loki grabbed the woman and pulled off her scarf. She had thickly curled dark hair. Around her neck was a gold chain with a small pendant. Loki pulled it off and let out a loud shout.

"A Star of David," he said, looking at the band. "You finally got one." He dropped the pendant and crushed it with his biker's boot. "Right, you guys get ready in here. I'm taking the dog to the van."

"Aw," Skaldi moaned. "Can't we watch?"

"Not this time," Loki said. "I've got something real special planned for this piece of Yiddish meat." He shoved the young woman toward the door. "No peeking," he said, staring at the musicians.

They nodded sullenly but cheered up when they saw the bag of coke on the table.

Outside, Loki opened the rear doors of the ramshackle white van and dragged his victim in. She was whimpering, but she hadn't given up struggling. When he ripped her blouse open, she let out a scream. The sound stopped abruptly when he slapped her cheek so hard that her head bounced against the sidewall. She slumped down, unconscious.

"Shit," Loki said. "I was going to ram Big Adolf down your throat." He unzipped his trousers. "Guess he's going somewhere even wetter." He grunted and pulled up the woman's skirt.

It was then that he heard a faint noise outside.

"Get lost, you assholes!" he shouted.

There was no reply, but the sound of footwear on asphalt came again.

Loki lurched for the door. "Will you get the fuck out of here?" he said, opening it.

A figure stepped into view.

"No," said a hoarse voice.

Loki took a punch to the face and crashed back onto the floor of the van. "Jesus," he said, raising his hand and feeling blood. "You broke my nose." He knew there was solid metal inside his masked assailant's glove.

The figure in black came in and leaned forward, then punched him again. There was a crack as Loki's left cheekbone broke and his head slammed back again. He screamed in agony.

"What is this?" he gasped. "I'll let the bitch go."

His assailant nodded. "Yes, you will. But I am not so merciful."

Loki looked up in the dim light of the streetlight. He saw the glint of polished steel in each hand above him. Then he opened his mouth in horror, unable to move as a skewer rammed through each of his ears. The lead vocalist didn't manage even a brief swan song before his brain shut down and he died.

The killer ripped open the dead man's T-shirt, then removed a transparent plastic file containing a single sheet of paper from a jacket pocket and smoothed it over the swastika tattoo, before securing it to his skin by pressing a pin into each corner.

After checking the still unconscious woman's pulse, the

killer got out of the van, then closed the doors and walked at an unhurried pace toward the street, cell phone in hand.

Hinkey's Bar wouldn't be having a musical evening after all.

Four

I woke up in my cell. The light was on and a ragged blanket had been thrown over my naked body. My head was aching and I felt nauseous. When a tray of bread and cheese was pushed through the hatch, I was able only to gulp down the water. Not long after that, I was violently sick, though what came up was nothing but liquid. I sat on the uneven bed with my legs drawn up, seeing the scarring on my knee at close range. It reminded me of something, but I couldn't remember what. My memory was very limited again. To my surprise, I found my heart beat fast. I was excited, alert, but I couldn't fathom why. Then I remembered the masked figures and the upturned cross. What the hell was going on?

The loud music came on and I sat motionless, letting it crash into me, all thoughts driven from my mind. I was seeing red, literally—it was as if I were immersed in a sea of blood. I felt sick again, but was only able to retch up a few mouthfuls of evil-tasting fluid. The room was suddenly very hot and I threw the blanket to the floor. It lay there like a tattered mat. I stared at it with mounting fascination, trying to understand why it was suddenly exercising such power over me.

At the same time, I was working on summoning up images, words, anything from my memory. Nothing appeared. I had the feeling that I had found some way of building up my identity, but I couldn't put my finger on it. All I could think of, in an attempt to stave off the blood that seemed to be flooding over me, was the blanket on the floor. What did it mean? A thin, scratchy covering that either kept me too hot or too cold, that was often damp from the flow of water that came through the door. The blanket lying on the floor. Like a rug. Or a mat.

A flash of clear white light drove the redness away. Mat. Why was the word so significant. Because the bastards in gray were trampling me as if I were a mat? No, there was more to the word than that. Mat. The blanket would act like a bath mat if I left it on the floor for the next spray of freezing water. No. What was the significance of *mat?*

My heart missed a beat and I leaped to my feet. Mat. It was my name. Matt, with two *t*s. I slapped the wall for joy and tried to dance a jig. My legs gave way and I dropped onto the blanket. My name was Matt. They hadn't taken away my identity after all—I had managed to keep something of myself from them.

I kneeled there with a slack smile on my lips. I was Matt. I was still what I had been before I arrived at this awful place.

Then I slumped forwards as the realization hit me—I might have known one of my names, but I had no idea of the others. Just as I had no idea of where I was or why I was here. And the next time I was put under the sinister box, I might lose the little that I had managed to salvage.

Time was running out for Matt, whoever the hell he was.

I didn't know how many more sessions under the machine I endured. Sometimes I could remember that my name was Matt, sometimes not. There were other occasions, the worst ones, when I doubted that I was called Matt at all, and that I was only hallucinating.

Then everything changed. I was dragged to the treatment room by the silent men in leather aprons. I remembered how asphyxiating it felt when the long box was lowered over me—and then, more quickly than usual, everything turned to black.

When I came round, I found that I was lying on a comfortable bed, one that seemed to be at the correct angle to the rest of a large room. I was hooked up to numerous machines. I felt as if I were floating, but my mind was sluggish, like it had been chained down. I tried to work out who I was, but failed. I was forced to lie back and look around.

To my left, beyond a desk equipped with an angled lamp and a computer screen, there was a window. The shackles on my mind immediately loosened at the sight of the trees in the middle distance, a great green carpet of them rising up a slope. This room was obviously above ground level. I tried to get up, but found that my arms and legs were secured. That darkened my mood. I had the feeling that I'd been in captivity before, though nothing specific flashed before me. My memory was sluggish.

A young woman wearing a white uniform came towards me, a warm smile on her lips. "Good morning," she said. "You've been asleep for a long time." She took a cell phone from her belt and pressed buttons. She spoke in a low voice and then turned her attention back to me. "How are you feeling?"

I shrugged. "Like my head's been filled with cotton wool. What happened?"

She gave me another smile and started checking the monitors. "The doctor will be here soon."

I let the evasive answer go. I could see I wasn't going to get anything else out of the nurse. A man with a goatee came in. He was wearing a white coat over a gray uniform.

I was sure I'd seen both him and his clothing before but, again, I couldn't come up with any specifics.

The doctor gave me a tight smile and took my pulse. He then looked at the clipboard on which the nurse had been recording readings from the machines. He gave her a curt nod.

"You are doing well," he said, looking at me but avoiding my eyes.

"Am I?" I said. "I don't suppose you'd like to tell me my name."

His expression went blank.

"Or what you've been doing to me here?"

He remained silent.

"Or even where *here* is?"

The two of them moved away. I decided to feign sleep in the hope that would make them drop their guard. That turned out to be a total failure. Not only did they keep their distance, but I fell into a profound slumber.

For some reason, the image of a bath mat filled my mind before I lost consciousness.

I woke up and looked around surreptitiously. The nurse was at her desk, head bowed. I closed my eyes again and tried to drive away the lethargy that seemed to have infected my thought processes. Then I remembered the bath mat I'd seen before I fell asleep. It seemed to mean something important, something more than "remember to put this down before you have a bath or you might slip when you get out." But I couldn't reach that layer of significance.

The machines around me were beeping and humming in random sequences. I found myself tapping my finger and thumb together and becoming aware of a rhythm. I kept my eyes shut as I discerned a melody. Music, it meant something, it was important to me. Suddenly, a string of words came to mind. I repeated them under my breath.

"Dylan, Young, Springsteen. Dylan, Young, Springsteen…"

The mantra gave me a warm feeling—it seemed to bring me closer to myself.

Then the words were changed by some opaque part of my brain.

"Pop, Hell, Rotten, Strummer. Pop, Hell, Rotten, Strummer…."

I didn't know what the words referred to, but I knew the person that I once was, the character that I'd lost, had paid attention to them. I was in the dark about my past, but there were still a few beacons lighting the way back.

At some point, the nurse roused me with a tray with the kind of food I hadn't seen for what seemed like months—fresh bread, bacon, eggs, fruit, orange juice, coffee. I ate and drank ravenously. It was hard to fend off real sleep after that, but I repeated my mantra again to stay surreptitiously awake.

Eventually—I had no idea how much time had passed—my patience was rewarded. I heard two pairs of footsteps approaching. The doctor and nurse were being very careful, keeping their voices low, but I heard one of the man's sentences clearly enough.

"Advise control center that L24 will be ready for coffining and psych-process closure tomorrow."

I took it that I was L24. The designation meant nothing to me and I had the distinct feeling I'd never heard it before. L24? It sounded like I was a machine rather than a human being. Screw that.

Then I started wondering about the other things the doctor had mentioned—control center, coffining, psych-process closure. All three of the terms were alarming. What was the center controlling? And what was the psych-process that sounded like it was almost completed? Worst, what was coffining? Surely they weren't going to kill me.

I tried to convince myself that if the people who were holding me had wanted that, they could have done it easily when I'd been comatose. But I wasn't going to take the chance. No way was I undergoing coffining.

I didn't have many options, so I quickly settled on a plan of action. I opened my eyes wide and started jerking my bound limbs as if I was having a seizure. I gasped for breath and thrashed my head around to add to the effect. All of that got the nurse's attention and she ran over to my bed.

I couldn't tell what the monitors were showing her, so I let out some screams, too. I didn't make them too loud in case that attracted other staff. But the nurse was either cautious by nature or the place was run with iron discipline. I caught a glimpse of her stabbing buttons on her cell phone. To my relief, she seemed unable to get through. She left a message, saying that L24 was convulsing and that the person she was trying to contact, presumably the doctor, should come immediately. I made even more of an effort with my act, thrusting my midriff into the air.

The nurse seemed to get the subliminal message. I felt her fingers on my wrists, then they were freed. Would she do the same with my legs? I sneaked a look and saw her trying to call the doctor again. I had to make my move. I sat up and grabbed her by the left arm, slapping the phone from her other hand.

"Untie my ankles," I ordered, leaning forward and transferring my grip to her waist. She gasped as I dug my fingers into her flesh. There was a pause as she struggled with the strap, then I was free. I took hold of her arms again.

"Where are we?" I demanded. "What have you been doing to me?"

The young woman's eyes bulged as I squeezed her forearms hard.

"What's my name?"

She shook her head, her lips pursed. She was obviously

trying to follow a procedure that she'd learned, but her wide eyes showed how scared she was.

"Tell me," I hissed, "or I'll break your arms."

"Please," she begged, "I can't. They'll...they'll kill me."

I could tell she wasn't going to talk. Without thinking about it, I swung my left arm. My fist connected with her lower jaw and she dropped like a stone. I got up and checked that she was breathing, then tied her to the bed and stamped on her cell phone. I knew the doctor might arrive any second, so I went to a cupboard against the wall. I found a gray uniform jacket and trousers, plus a pair of highly polished black army boots. The shoulders of the jacket bore red badges with the letters *NANR* in black. I pulled everything on as quickly as I could and headed for the door. On the way, I caught sight of the computer screen on the desk. I wondered if my details were visible and veered that way, but before I got there I heard footsteps outside. I ran to the door, the muscles in my legs tightening, and got there just before the doctor rushed in. I brought the edge of my hand down on the back of his neck and he joined the nurse on the floor. I considered going back to check the screen but decided it was more important to get moving.

I went out, surprised by my apparently instinctive fighting skills. I found myself at the end of a long corridor. Before I got more than five yards, I heard voices behind a closed door and ducked into an alcove. That was the right move. Two men in gray uniforms like the one I was wearing came into the passage and walked past the spot I'd been a few seconds earlier. They were wearing berets adorned with the NANR badge, making me wonder what the letters might mean.

I was about to go out into the corridor when I heard raised voices and a rush of feet moving towards the room where I'd been confined. Shit. Presumably someone was wondering why the doctor and nurse weren't responding.

I decided to make use of the staircase at the end of the alcove. It only went one way—down.

At the bottom, a short corridor led to an open door. I inched towards it and edged my head round the frame. Two men, again in gray uniforms, were sitting at an electronic control board, their eyes fixed on the scene that was being played out in the studio beyond. The men were separated from the action by a clear glass window. I followed the direction of their gaze, and froze. A man and a woman, both naked, were being filmed. What really made my heart pound was that the man had been tied to a wooden post, facing outwards. I had a flash of having been in a similar position and heard the crash of rifles. I remembered—the bastards had pretended to execute me by firing squad.

That wasn't what was happening to this man. He was being savagely whipped, his face and chest already crisscrossed by bloody stripes. The woman turned towards the cameras, her lips set in a tight smile. She held the position and I realized she was waiting for something. Then one of the uniformed guys leaned forward to a microphone and said words which boomed out through speakers.

"All right, that's enough. Kill him."

I could hardly believe what I'd heard, but the order was no joke. The woman in the studio had picked up a long knife with a wickedly curved blade.

It was time I made my entrance.

Five

The midafternoon sun was hardly strong enough to cut through the clouds over Iowa and a light drizzle was falling. Twenty miles east of Des Moines, Richard Bonhoff steered his ten-year-old Chevrolet pickup onto Interstate 80 and floored the gas pedal. He'd left the farm an hour earlier after a screaming argument with Melissa. Only now did it strike him that he'd failed to tell her where he was going. It was better she didn't know.

He passed a Winnebago with difficulty and went over to the outside lane. The pickup's engine had been giving him trouble for months. Chances were it would never get him to Washington, D.C., and then what would he do? Sit on the grass and weep, probably.

That had been the starting point of his disagreement with his wife. Melissa had come in tired from the yard and found him at the kitchen table with his head in his hands. She'd immediately told him how pathetic that was. Why couldn't he be a man and get on with his work? Lord knows there was enough of it to do now there were only the two of them. Richard hadn't replied. Then she'd said that he should stop moping over the twins' decision to leave home. Randy and Gwen were twenty-one years old. They were grown-ups, entitled to make their own decisions about their future.

"Yeah," he'd said, finally raising his head. "But we're entitled to know where they've gone, Mel. It's nearly three months now. How can you be sure they're okay? I mean, I come down at six in the morning and find them already gone, no note, no explanation—then a phone call in the evening, saying there's something they gotta do and not to expect them back soon. Since then, nothing. For God's sake, they could have been kidnapped."

"And the kidnappers held guns to their heads when they made the call? The state police told you what they thought about that idea. Anyway, where's the ransom note?" She gave a bitter laugh. "Not that we're gonna be able to pay. Get over it, Richard. They're not kids anymore. You have to let them go." His wife stomped into the utility room and started emptying the drier. "And, Richard?" she shouted. "If you don't fix the lights in the cattle shed today, I'm gonna get Ned to do it."

Melissa knew exactly how to get to him. She'd been screwing Ned Bartlett from the neighboring place on and off for ten years. He'd never had the balls to confront her about it, even though she hadn't been subtle. Well, to hell with her. If she was more worried about the livestock than her own children, she couldn't expect him to share his plan with her. He'd already put a bag full of clothes in the pickup. That was all he needed.

Fifty miles from home, Richard was still fixed in his resolve. The thing was, Melissa was right. Their beautiful kids were legally old enough to take charge of their own lives. That was why the cops couldn't give a shit about their disappearance. Oh, sure, they'd added their names to some list, passed it to the FBI, but according to Sergeant Onions, thousands of new names showed up every week across the country. It was up to Randy and Gwen to get in touch and that was all there was to it. Unless Richard had any evidence to suggest a crime had been committed?

Well, no, he hadn't—nothing that a policeman would understand, nothing concrete. But he knew something wasn't right. The twins had been weird ever since they'd won that newspaper competition last winter. They were both at college—Randy doing agricultural engineering and Gwen learning how to do accounts—when they'd gotten the news. They'd entered some competition in one of the supermarket tabloids and they'd won third prize. Third prize had been a weekend at a luxury hotel in Washington, D.C., with all expenses paid and a thousand dollars spending money to boot.

Richard tried to coax the pickup past an eighteen-wheeler and got honked at by an asshole in a Porsche. He went back into the slow lane and played it safe. So the kids flew off to the capital and had a great time, they said. Went to the White House, took in a concert, saw the Redskins get stomped all over. They were even spotted by a talent scout from some photo agency—apparently there was always demand for twins. But ever since then, they'd been different. They didn't come home from college at the weekends like most of the local kids, but they wouldn't say what kept them in town. They didn't come home during vacations for more than a few days. Richard had gone down to surprise them once and found them both away. Their roommates didn't know where they were, and Randy and Gwen wouldn't say where they'd been when they eventually came home. At least they still seemed to be close; if anything, they were even more involved with each other's thoughts and emotions. Neither of them seemed to have close friends.

Richard saw that he was low on gas. He didn't have much cash and his credit cards were almost maxed out. The trip to D.C. would leave him with zero funds. He saw a sign for a service station and took the exit.

After filling up the tank, he went to pay. There was an array of newspapers on the way into the store. He immediately picked out the *Star Reporter.* Even surrounded by the other tabloids, it looked cheap and nasty, the paper off-white and the print faintly smudged. Today the front page had a photo of a shrouded body on a gurney. The headline screamed Satanic Singer's Ears Skewered! He picked it up, not because he was interested in the story but because the *Star Reporter* was the paper that had paid for the twins' trip to D.C. and provided an escort. He was going to find out exactly what had gone on during that long weekend last winter, even if he had to camp out on the editor's doorstep.

Richard looked toward the pay phone. He told himself that he would hang up the moment Melissa started shouting, but he knew he wouldn't be strong enough to keep that resolution. If only Randy and Gwen hadn't gone. He used to be able to stand up to his wife when the twins were around. He turned away and went back to the pickup.

Six

I stepped into the control room, grabbed the two men by the ears and smashed their heads together. Then I pulled open the heavy door and went into the studio. The naked woman with the knife turned slowly towards me and I instantly saw that I was too late—the man was slumped in his bonds, a slick of blood over his chest. I shoved one of the camera stands aside and charged the killer, incensed by what she'd done and giving no thought to her gender. She raised her knife, but I pulled back my upper body and aimed a kick at her knee. She dropped with a scream. I stepped on the blade and got hold of her chin, forcing her head up.

"What is this place?" I demanded.

"*Fuck you,*" she gasped.

I gave another kick, keeping her head up. "Who are the assholes in uniform?"

She was panting, her eyes bulging. "Like…like I'm… gonna tell you." She obviously knew I was a runaway. Her lips twisted into a mocking smile. "You've got…no chance."

"Why did you kill him?" Up close, I could see that she'd slashed his throat.

"Ever...ever heard...of snuff movies?"

I lashed out at her with my boot, catching her on the other knee.

"Who's in charge?"

She stared up at me sullenly, her lips tightly closed.

I knew I shouldn't waste any more time. The temptation to turn the killer's own knife on her was huge. I managed to get a grip and satisfied myself with tying her to the dead man and gagging her with a rag from the floor. As I reached the door, it struck me that I should have taken the knife, but I wasn't keen on using the weapon that had deprived the defenseless man of his life. Then, as I heaved open the door, a loud and repetitive alarm began to sound.

The men in the control room were still comatose. They were wearing white T-shirts rather than uniform jackets. I looked around and saw a coat stand. Their jackets didn't interest me, but their sidearms did. I slipped a semiautomatic pistol into my pocket and then put one of the berets on. Now, I hoped, I looked like the real thing.

I went back upstairs. Perfect. There were uniformed people running in both directions. I stood in the alcove, then took a deep breath and joined the crowd. No one seemed to notice. Heading down the corridor away from the ward I'd been in, I saw a stairway ahead that led upwards. I took it, hoping that I'd find some sign of an exit. So far, I hadn't seen any directions I could understand.

I was in luck, at least to start with. I made it to the next level and realized I was in an entrance hall. The downside was that two assholes in gray were stationed at the heavy steel door marked Exit, and they were carrying assault rifles. It was only a matter of time before I was spotted. Without hesitating, I walked towards the door as confidently as I could. The alarm must have entailed some kind of lockdown because one of the guards took a step forward and leveled his weapon at me. If that was the way it had to be...

I smiled, then grabbed the rifle with both hands and rammed the butt into the guard's abdomen. He crashed to his knees. I had control of the weapon now. Taking another step, I drove the butt into the other gorilla's face. The back of his head thumped against the door and he fell down, unconscious. I looked for keys on their belts but found none. Then I saw a touch pad beyond the door frame. Jamming the muzzle of the rifle into the face of the first guard, who was now gasping for breath, I demanded the code.

"No fuckin' way."

So discipline was pretty strong in the gray ranks. I moved the rifle a few inches and fired a shot past his ear.

"Screw you, pal," the man said.

I heard a clatter of boots on the stairway behind. I had a few seconds, at most. I pointed the rifle at the touch pad, then thought again and loosed off some rounds at the lock mechanism. One of the doors remained where it was, but the other swung back a few inches. I put my shoulder to it and was out. I heard shouts and then a rattle of shots hit the door that I'd just pushed shut again. The glass was obviously bulletproof. The ricochets would have peppered the guards I'd taken out; it seemed that the escape of patient L24 was being treated more seriously than the health of the people who staffed the place.

Breathing in cold air, I rapidly took in the scenery. A high razor-wire fence rose about thirty yards in front of me. Beyond it, tall pine trees covered a gentle slope beneath low, iron-gray clouds. I heard orders being yelled out somewhere to my right, so I headed left. Visibility wasn't great, but that could be to my advantage. Getting over the fence wasn't going to be easy, though. I looked back at the building. It was long and low, with very few windows. At one end there was a raised area—that may have been the room I awoke in.

Suddenly lights came on, lights set in the ground at

regular intervals along the inside of the fence. So much for my advantage. A pair of rifle-toting men in the standard uniform came round the end of the block. One knelt down and sent a volley of shots in my direction. I hit the ground and heard bullets cut through the air above me.

"Over here!"

I looked to my right and saw a black man standing behind one of the fence posts. It wasn't exactly giving him much cover, especially since he was a big guy. He was unshaven and wearing what looked like blue-and-white striped pajamas. When I crawled closer, I realized the flesh on his face was slack and he was much thinner than the loose clothes initially suggested.

"You ain't one of them," he said, squatting next to me.

"How can you tell?" I said, glancing at the uniform I was wearing.

"You'd already have shot my ass." He handed me a lump of bread, then put his hands together. "Now get the hell outta here."

I put one foot on his joined palms.

"I'm gonna give you as much of a lift as I can," the man said. "There's enough electricity in these wires to fry an elephant."

"Oh, great," I said, my heart pounding. Then another volley of shots flew past us. "Here, take this." I held out the rifle to him.

"What am I gonna do with that, boy? Throw it over there."

I did what he said.

"Ready?" he asked when both my hands were resting on the top of his head.

"When you are. And thanks."

I felt my legs move down slightly, then I was arcing over the fence, my belly missing the vicious barbs by a whisker. I bent my knees and landed and rolled toward the rifle.

"Run!" the inmate yelled.

I did what I was told. The tree line must have been seventy yards away. My lungs were heaving and my legs burning as I made cover.

I stopped and looked back. The guards had caught up with the black man before he got back inside. One of them hit him in the face. Then the other took out his pistol and without hesitation shot him through the throat.

I gasped and saw red. I raised the rifle and loosed off several rounds. The guards both dropped, but I wasn't sure if I'd hit them. The murdering pieces of shit. I almost ran back into the open to give myself a better shot. Then there was the roar of an engine and a gray pickup emerged with at least five men in the back, all of them carrying rifles. I had to go.

There was very little light under the dense branches of the pines. Although the forest floor was relatively clear of undergrowth, I couldn't make out any paths. Voices rang out behind me, so I pressed on as fast as I could. At first my throat became clogged with phlegm, but as I got into a rhythm with my running, it loosened up. The muscles in my legs weren't fully stretched yet, but I felt they could cope. I must have been a fit bastard in my previous life.

I didn't stop to look round, not that the trees would have allowed much of a view, but I reckoned I was increasing the gap between me and my pursuers. That should have made me feel good, but it didn't. The farther I went, the stronger became the feeling that I was leaving something important behind. No, more than that, something *essential*. I ran on autopilot as I racked my memory for what that could be. Nothing. I had no idea. I had very little memory. I could remember everything that had happened since I'd woken up in the comfortable bed, but things before that were locked securely away. All I was thinking about was the savagery I'd seen—the man tied to the post and slaughtered like an animal; the emaciated man summarily executed for helping me. What could have inspired such brutality?

Then I considered what I'd done. I'd knocked out the nurse, clubbed the doctor, smashed two men's heads together, beaten the hell out of the naked man's killer and laid into the two guards at the exit. And I'd shot at the black man's killers, perhaps killing them. I wasn't much better than the gray-uniformed scumbags. And now I was abandoning something vital back in that prison. What was it? And how had I come to be at the heavily guarded location? What had happened to me there?

All the time I was struggling to find answers to those questions, I was moving across ground that was gradually becoming steeper. The space between the tree trunks began to grow. Looking up, I saw that night was falling. That would make things much harder for the men who were after me. I'd run at several different angles, so I may already have lost them. But, as I came out of the forest and into tall grass, I realized I was the most lost of all. I didn't even know which country I was in, never mind where the nearest town was. I stopped and listened for any encouraging sounds—no cars, no music, no people, hostile or not. I turned a full circle. There were no lights anywhere. I felt completely alone. For some reason, that didn't frighten me, though I felt disoriented by the scale of the trees and the vast number of them all around. Either I had no imagination or I'd done this kind of thing before.

After checking behind me, I moved off again. I'd only been going for a few minutes when the moon, three-quarters full, appeared ahead of me. A jagged line of rock was caught in the white light, slopes without tree cover leading up to it. I was in the middle of a wide meadow. To my right were more trees and I headed for them. When I made the cover, a wave of relief washed over me. The pines weren't as tall as the previous ones, but they were closer together. I had to push my way past the lower branches but kept going. My throat was parched and my stomach was rumbling, but I didn't feel tired. I would get farther away from my pursuers and then settle down to eat the bread I'd been given by the doomed man.

Then I heard a sound that worried me. Despite the state of my memory, I had no difficulty in identifying the howl of a hunting dog. It wasn't as far off as I'd have liked. Had that been why I'd lost the men behind me? Had they stopped to wait for the hound to join them?

It looked like it was going to be a long, hard night.

Seven

After twenty years in Washington D.C.'s Metropolitan Police, twelve on the homicide team, Detective Gerard Pinker had gotten used to corpses. That didn't mean he found attending autopsies easy. His partner Clement Simmons never complained. In fact, Pinker reckoned Clem even breathed through his nostrils during the procedures—too dedicated for his own good.

"I suppose you'll be looking forward to this," Pinker said in the elevator on the way down to the morgue. He straightened his tie and shot his cuffs. "What with being into voodoo and all that shit."

The tall, heavily built black man beside him shook his head slowly. "I'm not into voodoo." He ran an eye over his partner's diminutive figure. "At least not in the way you're into rich men's suits, Versace."

Pinker grinned and slotted a piece of gum between his thin lips. "Right, Clem. So I was just imagining the goat's head and the little dolls you got in your den."

"Not the doll with your name on it," Simmons said as the doors opened. "Shit, man, you know my grandmother was from Haiti. I'm interested in my family's culture, that's all."

Pinker stepped into the morgue and was immediately swamped by the smell of chemicals cut with flesh and blood. "Well, I'm glad my family hasn't got that kind of culture."

The big man followed him down the corridor. "Your family hasn't got any culture, man. You're nothing but West Virginia white trash."

Pinker met the grin with a raised middle finger. They went through the swing doors and found the medical examiner looking at a clipboard. She was above medium height and he liked the way she was built—slim, but stacked in the right places.

"Gentlemen," she said, raising her eyes briefly.

The detectives' demeanor was suddenly much more formal.

"Dr. Gilbert," Simmons said, shooting Pinker a warning glance. His partner had come on like too much of a pussy hound the last time they'd encountered the striking red-haired woman. Not that she couldn't look after herself, as she'd proved by dropping a scalpel less than an inch from Versace's new oxblood wing tips.

"Morning, Doctor," Pinker said. "I'm betting you never had one done through the ears before."

The medical examiner finished what she was doing and looked at him, her blue eyes icier than a mountain lake. "You lose, Detective. I had a drug dealer three months ago, shot with a .45 bullet through the external acoustic meatus, destroying the tympanic membrane, as well as the malleus, incus and stapes." She smiled briefly. "The brain was pretty messed up, too." She inclined her head toward the autopsy room. "Shall we?" She stepped away, her head held high.

"What, dance?" Pinker said under his breath. "Yeah, baby, yeah."

As the detectives approached the table, a technician moved back and they got a full view of the body. The man's naked form—overweight and heavily tattooed—was striking, as were the skewers protruding from his ears. His waist-length hair was hanging over the end of the table like a black flag. His long beard had been parted to allow access to the chest.

"No problem identifying this one, I imagine," Dr. Gilbert said, taking in the tattoos. "There can't be many Nazis in Washington."

"You reckon?" Pinker said, with a laugh.

"I mean, *real* Nazis, Detective," the doctor said, coolly.

Pinker wasn't retreating. "We don't have much idea how *real* he was. Far as we know, he was a thrash-metal singer. Those assholes play at being tough guys—Nazis, satanists, Charlie Manson fans, whatever. Doesn't mean they actually believe in that crap."

"Is that so?" The M.E. didn't sound overly convinced. "We've already photographed, measured, weighed, x-rayed and fingerprinted the body. I've also searched for trace evidence and done the external examination." She glanced at them. "You were late. I have four more autopsies scheduled today."

"That's all right, Doc," Simmons said. He knew how tedious those procedures could be. "What did you find?"

"Without too many long words," Pinker added. He remembered floundering in a tidal wave of technical verbiage the last time.

Marion Gilbert raised a perfectly plucked eyebrow and glanced at the report handed to her by a technician. "Male Caucasian, aged around forty to forty-five, height six feet four inches, weight 267 pounds. Hair black, dyed. Eyes brown." She indicated the dead man's chest and arms. "Obviously the main identifying features are the tattoos."

Pinker took them in. "Swastika, Iron Cross, *Mein Kampf* and an arrow pointing to his crotch. Nice."

"You should see his back," the M.E. said, shaking her head. "It says 'I Am the Final Solution.'" She glanced at Pinker. "That makes him a real Nazi in my book."

The detective shrugged. "Maybe, maybe not. You gotta keep an open mind in our business."

Marion Gilbert rolled her eyes. "Moving on. His clothing has been sent for further analysis. I found hairs on his T-shirt that weren't his. They're black, but not so long—probably from the woman he assaulted. Or from—"

"The assholes in the band," Pinker said. "They're all as hairy as—"

"You've located them?" the doctor asked.

Simmons nodded. "They were the ones who called the MPDC."

"They're all crying like little kids," Pinker added.

The doctor gave him a frozen look. "There were skin and fiber traces under his nails. Analysis is being undertaken. The victim had knee surgery in the not too distant past. There's also an appendix scar, from prelaparoscopy days."

"I'm presuming the time of death squares with the parameters we've got," Simmons said. "The band members said he got into the van around eight-fifteen and they found him around eight-fifty."

"The gig was due to start at nine and the first patrolmen were on the scene at nine-oh-two," Pinker said.

"The M.E. noted the body and ambient temperatures, plus the fact that rigor mortis hadn't begun, suggest that death occurred no earlier than eight o'clock anyway."

"Any sign that the body had been moved?" Simmons asked.

"No abrasions or bruising to suggest that. I take it you're investigating the band members."

"Oh, yes," Pinker said. "As well as the bar owner, his son and a scumbag dope dealer who lives upstairs. Also some fans who were waiting in the bar."

"Speaking of drugs," Dr. Gilbert said, "there were traces of cocaine on the victim's nostrils. Though the condition of his nose made examination difficult."

Simmons looked down at Loki's flattened and bloodied nose. "The way I see it, the killer hit him in the face—"

"Twice," the M.E. said, pointing at the broken and swollen skin on the left cheek. "There are two contusions on the back of the head that I would say came from impact with a hard surface."

Simmons nodded. "And then he stuck the skewers into his ears."

"Correct."

"Do you think the vic was conscious when that happened?" Pinker asked.

"He might have been," the doctor replied.

"Real nice," Pinker said.

Simmons gave him an irritated glance. "So cause of death was..."

"Penetrating trauma to the brain."

"In stereo," Pinker added.

The other two stared at him.

He shrugged. "Am I wrong? And obviously the wounds weren't self-inflicted."

The M.E. looked at the skewers that were protruding from the victim's ears. "It's theoretically possible that he could have done it himself."

"But unlikely," Simmons said. "Given that he doesn't have any knuckle injuries to suggest he punched himself in the face twice, and we didn't find any blunt instrument in the van with his blood on it. How about the number of assailants? Could there have been more than one?"

"I'll remove the skewers shortly so they can be checked for prints and traces," the doctor said. "One person could have done it. But it would have needed a lot of nerve. I would think the back of the van would have been too confined a place for two killers, especially with the woman in there, as well. Is she all right?"

"She's been sedated," Pinker replied. "But before that she told us she hadn't seen anything. The vic knocked her out before he got his." He sighed. "So, capital murder it is, by person or persons unknown."

"I take it there were no witnesses?" Marion Gilbert asked. "Before, during or after the murder?"

"We haven't found any yet," Simmons said. "We're still looking, of course."

"Of course you are." The M.E. nodded at him with more warmth than she'd been extending to Pinker. She looked down at the dead man's chest and the swastika on it. "Time for me to dissect."

Pinker took a step back.

"Oh, aren't you staying?" the doctor asked.

"I'll leave you to it."

Simmons watched his partner go and shook his head. The little man was full of himself until things got ugly in the morgue.

At the door Pinker stopped and looked around. "Oh, Doctor?" he said, a smile on his lips. "I'm betting the tympanic membrane is in a bad way, to say nothing of the malleus, incus and stapes." He raised both hands and moved his index fingers. "Like I said, in glorious stereo."

Marion Gilbert shook her head. "He's got a smart mouth."

Simmons grinned. "But you can't fault his memory."

Later, Clem Simmons found his partner in the homicide squad room. Pinker was on the phone, a soda can in his other hand.

"Okay," he said, "I've got the address. We'll be around later in the afternoon."

Simmons sat down at his desk with a grunt. "Anything juicy?"

"Doubt it, Clem. Some kid who was at Hinkey's earlier in the evening. Says he didn't see anything suspicious, but we'd better check him out."

Simmons was looking at his notepad. "Anything from the CSIs?"

"Nothing to get hard about. They're gonna examine some fibers they found on the blanket from the van."

"Could be from the band members. Or the Jewish girl."

Pinker screwed up his eyes. "You reckon one of the band could have killed him?"

"Or more than one of them." Simmons stifled a yawn. "It's a possibility. You talked to them, Vers. Did they give you the idea that they could put a skewer in a kebab without stabbing themselves?"

"Not really. They're all dope heads. So who did it? Some anti-Nazi and anti-satanic-thrash-metal freak?"

"Obviously a line of inquiry we'll have to follow. I'll get the computer geeks to see if there were any threats on the relevant Web sites and discussion groups."

"What about Hickey and his fat-bellied son?"

"They can stew a while longer. You never know what they might suddenly remember.

"There's something we haven't talked about, Vers."

"I know."

"Want to talk about it now?"

Pinker raised his shoulders. "Sure, Clem."

"You aren't too enthusiastic."

"Not exactly my field of expertise."

"Meaning it's mine?" Simmons asked.

"Well, you are into—"

"This has nothing to do with voodoo, man. Where is it, then?"

Pinker handed over a folder. His partner removed a transparent evidence bag that contained a single piece of white, unruled paper. There were small holes in each corner of the page and dried blood on the edges. On it, several squares and rectangles had been drawn by hand.

"What do you reckon, Clem?"

Simmons looked up. "Black felt-tip pen, one of the most common brands, according to the CSIs. Same goes for the paper." He ran a hand over his thick gray hair. "I reckon we might be making a mistake keeping this from the media."

"Why?"

"Because by now we'd have had plenty of experts calling us with their ideas."

Pinker laughed ironically. "Self-appointed experts, you mean. With their completely insane ideas. We've got enough to do without chasing leads that go nowhere. Besides, it was Chief Owen's idea to keep a lid on it."

"I know. But we didn't say much to put him off the idea."

"Standard Op with murders—to avoid copycats, don't publicize the details."

Simmons glanced at him. "You think D.C.'s packed with people who'll start skewering ears? And anyway, we didn't keep that part confidential."

"True." Gerard Pinker stood up and straightened the creases in his navy blue suit trousers.

Simmons looked at his partner. "You gonna leave those pants alone or am I gonna have to call the Vice Squad?"

"Pardon me while I scream with laughter." Pinker frowned. "Who do you reckon's behind this murder, Clem? Some kind of anti-Nazi group?"

"Maybe. There's no shortage of people with justifiable rage about what that gang of assholes did sixty-plus years ago, and just as much rage against fools who idolize them nowadays."

Pinker tightened his tie. "So you don't think some kind of righteous anti-satanist type was involved?"

Simmons looked at him suspiciously. "You trying to bring my heritage into this again?"

Pinker smiled mischievously. "Well, maybe one of

your voodoo guys stuck the pins in the vic. They do that, don't they?"

"Voodoo doesn't have a beef with Satan," his partner said, shaking his head. "Besides, it's a bona fide religion that came from Africa—or an occult science, if you prefer."

"No, I surely don't," Pinker said, sitting down. "I don't know—maybe someone had it in for the vic because of his music."

"Now you're talking. That thrash metal is seriously ear-breaking shit. Give me the blues anytime."

Gerard Pinker took the file back and stared at the blood-stained sheet of paper. "Come on, Clem. Direct that great brain of yours at these squares and rectangles."

"I told you before—they don't mean anything to me." Simmons let out a long sigh. "Jesus, Vers, you really have a way of needling people."

Pinker said nothing. He knew his partner would come up with something.

Simmons said, with a sigh, "For what it's worth, I'd say the fact that the murderer took the trouble to attach the page to his victim's chest shows it has some pretty major significance. But search me what it is. We need an expert's advice."

"That's it?" Pinker said, underwhelmed.

Simmons grinned. "Yeah, Vers. Apart from the fact that satanists and neo-Nazis are notorious for fighting among themselves. Which means we'll have to check all the members of any group Loki was involved with, as well as their enemies."

"Oh, great," Pinker said, seeing the risk of their workload increasing enormously. "Clement, my man, you just made my day."

Eight

I dropped down behind a low bank in front of a line of trees. The dog's howling was getting nearer and I had to make a decision. Assuming the hound had picked up my scent, I wouldn't have much chance of losing it unless I crossed running water. I hadn't seen any of that on the forested slopes so far. But if I waited, I'd have to put the dog and the men with it out of action. I checked the rifle's ammunition clip. It was full, and there were another seventeen shots in the Glock I'd taken. Enough to do some serious damage, but did I have the stomach for it?

I thought back to the wired encampment. As far as I could fathom, the bastards who ran it had carried out some questionable medical procedure on me. I thought of the woman who had killed the bound man. Why had that been filmed? And then there was the poor guy who had paid with his life for helping me. I had to do something for the other innocent people I was sure were still in the place. If that meant meting out summary punishment to the men on my tail, I was ready.

Lying on the cold ground with the butt of the rifle to my shoulder, I waited for my pursuers. I seemed to be well accustomed to handling the weapon. I tried to remember times in my past when I'd fired one like it, but nothing came. Then a chilling possibility struck me. Was I a professional killer? That would explain my calm assurance. But what kind of killer? A policeman, a soldier, a secret agent? Or an underworld assassin? Or maybe I was just a madman, a psychotic who enjoyed depriving others of life.

I hadn't reached a conclusion by the time figures appeared at the far end of the meadow. There were three of them, the middle one holding the leash of a large dog. As they got closer, I made out their uniforms and berets, as well as the assault rifles they were all carrying. The men on the right and left of the handler were holding their weapons in two hands, muzzles to the fore. They had to be my first targets.

I filled my lungs and then held my breath, took aim at the leg of the man on the left and fired. Before the others could react, I shot the man on the right in the leg, too. Both stayed down. There was a chance that the shots would have hit the femoral artery, in which case they were finished. I found that I wasn't too concerned about that. All that mattered was that they stayed down. I drew a bead on the man with the dog, but he had also dropped. His animal was less disciplined, though. It slipped the leash and came howling towards me. As it got closer, I saw that it was a German shepherd. It would have had my throat out, so I had no option. I switched to automatic fire and loosed a burst. The shots went over the dog's head but were enough to make it stop. The animal let out a high-pitched whine and turned tail. I had bought myself some time.

I got up and ran into the trees. They soon became thicker and I struggled to make progress. The moonlight was almost shut out by the layers of needle-bearing branches. My nostrils filled with the resinous scent of pine and I had to breathe through my mouth. My throat, which had already been parched, was now hurting even more. But I forced myself to run on, my boots making little noise on the blanket of fallen needles. The ground dropped away quite steeply to the left and I headed that way, in what I was sure was the opposite direction from the camp. I seemed to have an instinctual knowledge of location; perhaps I'd been trained.

Eventually my breathing got ragged and I had to stop. I reckoned I'd put at least two miles between me and the meadow, but that wouldn't be enough if the dog-handler and his hound had resumed the pursuit. I cocked an ear. At first I heard only the light wind soughing through the pines, but I quickly realized there was another sound coming through the trees at a lower level. I walked toward it cautiously, trying to get my breathing under control. Then I realized what it was—water running over rocks. That was exactly what I needed.

The tree line was at the edge of a sharp drop. I scrambled down and stood in the middle of the narrow stream. Although it was only a couple of yards across, the water came up to my knees. It was ice-cold and I felt the muscles in my calves tighten. I bent down and dashed water over my face, then brought handfuls to my mouth. I wondered if I should immerse my whole body in order to obscure my scent completely, but decided against that. It was a cold night and without shelter I would be in danger of hypothermia when I finally stopped running. I filled the canteen that had been on the uniform belt I'd stolen, walked up the stream as far as I could, and then stepped out on the other side. I thought about eating the bread from the luckless inmate, but decided I would keep it till I was hungrier. The ground was less steep and the trees came right down to the stream. I pushed my way through the undergrowth and into the next expanse of pine forest. Then I moved on as fast as I could.

The trees petered out after what must have been about an hour. The ground ahead was open, as far as I could make out in the moonlight that was now filtering through the thin cloud cover. I tried to listen for sounds of pursuit, but my breathing was rapid and loud. I had to get some rest. I walked a few hundred yards from the trees and then headed back toward them at a wide angle. That way, anyone after me would be stranded in the open and vulnerable to my rifle, even if the dog had picked up my trail again. I looked for a tree with low branches and found a good candidate. I was able to get high above the ground and the branches were still wide enough for me to sit with reasonable comfort. I unhooked the strap from the rifle and passed it round both my abdomen and the tree trunk. Gradually my breathing slowed and I was able to hear properly. I didn't pick up any sounds of man or dog, but my stomach was now rumbling loudly. I ate half of the bread, forcing myself to chew slowly. I was desperate for more, but I had no idea where my next meal would come from. Then I closed my eyes and tried to clear my mind for sleep. But, as my body went into temporary hibernation mode, my thoughts went haywire and, at last, I found myself remembering more from my past life…

…I'm on a hillside in the rain, my head down in the bracken and my hands gripping a rifle.

"Don't make any rapid movements," whispers the man in the waterproof jacket who is lying next to me. "In fact, don't even blink."

We wait there, motionless, as the big stag chews away. He lowers his head to the ground and then raises it quickly. He's seen men with guns often enough to be extremely wary. But the wind is blowing into our faces, so he can't smell us.

"Right, line him up," my companion says under his breath. "Remember where?"

"Chest...above the foreleg," I gasp, my heart racing. I'm suddenly seized by horror at the prospect of killing the magnificent creature.

I look through the sights and zero in on the stag, then pause.

"What are you waiting for?" the man whispers, his eyes wide. "He'll bolt any second."

I take a deep breath and hold it, then tighten my finger on the trigger. I have a vision of the great animal coughing up a lungful of blood, his head with the great array of the antlers dropping as his front legs collapse.

"I can't do it," I say, letting the rifle sink into the vegetation. That movement is enough to alert the stag. He leaps away, kicking his hind legs high, and disappears over the ridge.

"Sorry," I hear myself say feebly. "I..."

"Pillock," my companion says. "It took us three hours to get up here and you blow it just like that."

"Sorry, Dave. I just—"

"You chickened out, didn't you?" He gets up and wipes drops of water from his trousers. Some of them land on my face. "It cost us a bleeding fortune, this weekend. Flights to Inverness, hiring the Land Rover, paying the estate an arm and a leg for the privilege of doing their culling for them. And you can't even fire one shot in anger."

I stand up and take in the enraged face. Dave Cummings. Ex-paratrooper, former SAS man, amateur rugby league player—my best friend and tutor in extreme outdoor activities. It was his idea to spend a weekend deer-hunting in the Scottish Highlands. And now I've wasted my shot.

"At least I got the practice rounds in," I say, avoiding his eyes. The day before, Dave and I had taken a rifle up on the moors and blazed away at targets. "At least I know how to handle a rifle now."

"Oh, you do, do you?" Dave says, grabbing the weapon.

He's been up here numerous times over the years and can hunt as well as any expert. Then again, he does have a talent for anything to do with weaponry and sudden death. "That's your problem, you know. A few hours and you reckon you're a professional. Jesus, killing isn't as easy as you think." He breaks off and grins. "Then again, you just found that out, didn't you, Matt?"

I came to with a start. Matt. That was my name. I had a vague memory of a blanket lying on a cell floor. I had remembered before, but I must have lost it. My name was Matt, short for…Matthew. That flashed back to me, too. But nothing more. I thought about the deer-hunting scene. Dave. My friend Dave. The recollection of him was strong, in the sense that I was convinced I'd known a Dave, that he had been close to me. But there was nothing else, apart from the facts that he'd been a soldier and had instructed me in rifle-shooting. I thought again. He'd been a rugby player, too. We'd been on the same team. I suddenly remembered the scarring on my knee. Fortunately, although I felt a dull ache, my leg had stood up to the pressure of all the running I'd done.

I was strangely glad to find that the scene had stayed in my memory. Dave had often talked about us going to the Scottish Highlands. Where from? I tried to bring back where I lived, where I'd been born and brought up, but there was no response from my damaged memory. Scottish. What did that mean? Scotland came to mind. A country. But it wasn't my home, even though it was connected in some way I couldn't put my finger on.

At least I knew my name. Matt. But I had the feeling I had other names. I wasn't just patient L24 from the camp. But Matt what? Matthew what? Again, my memory failed. Whatever had been done to me in the camp was restricting me to only a few glimpses of my past. I could only hope there would be more. In the meantime, where was I? I thought back to the hillside in the rain. I had the distinct feeling I wasn't in Scotland, even though I could remember pine trees alongside the fern-covered slopes where we'd tracked the deer. But they were much smaller than the ones I had so recently run through, and there was no way I could have spent the night halfway up one of those small Scottish pines. So where was I? And who was I? Matt, with no other names and no memories of other people except Dave, wasn't enough for me.

Eventually I dropped into a dreamless sleep, and woke to the sound of birdsong. There was a stripe of gray over the ridge that must have been to the east. Dawn was breaking. I surveyed the country from my high position and took in vast slopes covered in trees and mountain ridges running between isolated summits. I felt lost, not just geographically but spiritually. This was not my home. How had I got here? How was I to get back to civilization without food to sustain me? It looked like no one lived anywhere nearby. Besides, I couldn't trust anyone—perhaps the people who ran the camp owned the land and any towns on it.

I listened intently for a few minutes, but heard no indications of the armed men. Unstrapping myself and stretching stiff limbs, I clambered down to ground level. I drank most of the water in my bottle, leaving a few mouthfuls in case there were no more streams in the vicinity. Ahead, I saw a narrow gap between the slopes of two mountains and decided to head for it. Perhaps there would be a road there, a way out of the wilderness. I set off and was immediately aware of my stomach—the water had obviously woken it up. I stopped and ate the rest of the bread, aware that I might have been making a big mistake. Then I saw the rabbit.

I raised the rifle slowly to my shoulder. I was about to squeeze the trigger—with no compunction this time—when

I realized that firing would give my location away. I watched
helplessly as the rabbit hopped back into the undergrowth.
I swore quietly. Even though I'd have had to eat the flesh
raw, it would have given me some much needed protein. I
decided I'd risk the shot. I was waiting for the animal to re-
appear when I heard the unmistakable sound of a dry branch
cracking. Either there were larger creatures in these mountains or my pursuers had caught up with me.

I considered running, but from the sounds I could tell
they were too close. I had to choose a position and make
a stand. But not on the ground—I had to assume there
would be more than one of them. I looked around for a suit-
able tree and found one with a larger than average trunk.
I pulled myself up until I was just below the cover provided
by the top of a shorter tree before me. Then I pushed my
head slowly through the pine needles and scanned the area.

At first there was no movement apart from small birds.
Then I saw a figure in gray emerge slowly about fifty yards
to my right. Shortly afterward, another man appeared, this
one to my left. Both were carrying assault rifles like the
one I had. I was relieved that there was no sign of the dog.
A third man came into the open almost directly in front of
me. I'd chosen my spot well. All three would have to cross
the open area between the trees. I slipped the safety catch
off my rifle and brought the stock up to my right shoulder.
Then, looking down at the men, I saw something that made
my stomach clench.

The man in the center was looking at a small device and
making hand movements to the others. Those movements
were directing them right toward me. How did he know…?
Then I understood—there must have been a bug somewhere on me. I ran a hand over the rifle, but found nothing
obvious. Shit. The bug could have been anywhere, given
that I'd stolen everything I had. I considered stripping and

leaving it all behind, but quickly dismissed that idea. They were close enough to hear me move. If I didn't act soon, they'd be so close they couldn't help but discover me.

I brought the rifle up and trained it on the man with the receiver. He had to be dealt with first. Before I pulled the trigger, a vision of Dave flashed before me. He was smiling. I felt myself smile back, and then I fired. I missed the device, but hit the man's wrist. The receiver flew up in the air as he dropped to his knees. I turned to the man on my right. He had stopped halfway across the dead ground. I flicked the rifle to automatic and let off a burst that peppered the ground in front of him. He turned tail and ran, leaving his rifle on the ground. I shifted my aim to the third guy. He was already heading back into the tree cover. I went back to single fire and let him have one a foot behind him to send him on his way.

Slipping down the tree as fast as I could, I hit the ground and started running. I had probably bought myself half an hour at most. I needed to stretch that and then find a place to hole up. My next priority was to locate the bug.

After about half an hour of uninterrupted running, I slowed to a walk and looked at the rifle, pistol and water bottle again. Nothing out of the ordinary caught my eye. I ran my fingers over my clothes. Again, nothing was obvious. That left my boots. I stopped briefly to check the soles. They appeared normal, though there could easily have been something hidden deep down.

As I picked up my pace again through the pine trunks, an unpleasant thought struck me. Maybe the bug wasn't in my boots or clothing at all. Maybe it was under my skin.

Nine

Richard Bonhoff was in gridlock on the Beltway. It was late afternoon and the low autumn sun was giving extra color to the already spectacular leaves on both sides of the freeway. Richard briefly thought of the more subdued shades in the fields back in Iowa, then concentrated on making the next exit for central D.C. He'd already missed one. The battered pickup stuck out like a Model-T among the pristine limos and SUVs that the capital's inhabitants drove. Not for the first time, the farmer asked himself what the hell he was doing. He'd considered flying, even though he hated the dry air and unexpected bumps and bangs, but he wasn't sure if his credit cards would have accepted the charge. At least with gas he could spread the cost around different bits of plastic.

This time he saw the sign for the exit well in advance and had no trouble getting off the Beltway. Now the fun would really start. Richard had never been comfortable driving in unfamiliar towns. When they went into Des Moines, Melissa usually took the wheel—she had no problem imposing herself on other drivers. Even the twins were more confident than their father was, not that he let them sit at the wheel often. Randy had bent the pickup's fender several times, while Gwen always drove like she was drunk. Richard shook his head as he remembered the twins, then set his jaw. He needed to concentrate on what he had come to do in Washington. The twins. He glanced at his watch. It was a quarter after four. He still had time to make a start today.

To his surprise, he made it downtown without any problem. He was heading for Mount Vernon Square. He found a parking lot and left the pickup there, astounded at the rates he'd seen at the entrance. No wonder the politicians needed unofficial contributions to their income—then again, they no doubt got recompensed for their parking charges. He went onto the street and walked quickly down to New York Avenue. The newspaper office was only a few minutes away, perfect since it was nearly five o'clock. He was presuming they closed at that hour though, for all he knew, D.C. folks might work longer hours than people did back home.

Richard stopped outside a large office block. The sign above the entrance said Woodbridge Holdings, which meant nothing to him. He went closer and examined the list of companies in the group. The *Star Reporter* was there. He was at the right place after all. As he was walking toward the glass doors, he saw his reflection. For sure, he was the only person within a mile wearing a plaid shirt, faded jeans and yellow work boots. Not to mention a faded John Deere cap. He took that off as he went inside. The security guards scrutinized him as he went through the metal detector. Then he felt the receptionist's eyes on him as he approached the desk.

"Can I help you, sir?" the young black woman asked, a smile playing across her lips.

"I'd like to see Mr. Lister, please," Richard said, his cheeks reddening. "Mr. Gordon Lister."

The receptionist nodded and looked at her computer screen. "Your name, sir?"

"My…my name?" Richard stammered. He hadn't expected that he would have to identify himself so soon.

"Yes, sir. You do have an appointment, don't you?"

Richard made out that he was even more confused than he felt. He preferred not to give Lister any advance warning, catch him cold. Playing the hick out of his depth might just get the job done.

"Can you…can you ask him if he'll see me without an appointment?" he said, with a certain country drawl. "I've driven all the way from Iowa."

The receptionist gave him a puzzled look. It was obvious she had little idea how far away his home state was but, after a sigh, she tapped her keyboard and spoke into the microphone of her headset.

"Mr. Lister, there's a gentleman to see you. He says he's from Iowa." She paused. "All right, I'll tell him." She looked up at Richard. "He's just leaving, sir. If you wait here in the lobby, he can give you a few minutes."

Richard nodded his thanks and retreated to a nearby sofa. There was a selection of newspapers and magazines spread across a glass table. He picked up the *Star Reporter* and read the latest about the murder of the rock singer in D.C. It seemed the Metro Police hadn't much idea who had done it, though the guy wasn't exactly an upstanding citizen. There were grainy photos of the dead man's chest and back, taken from some thrash-metal Web site. Even though his own great-grandparents had emigrated from Munich, Richard didn't have any time for neo-Nazis.

"He was quite a piece of work, wasn't he?"

Richard looked up and took in a small man in a tan leather jacket and an open-necked denim shirt. He'd been expecting an expensive suit and tie.

"Mr. Lister?"

"Yeah. You the guy from Iowa?"

Richard nodded. This time he gave his name. It didn't seem to be familiar to Lister.

"All right. How about a drink?"

Richard shrugged. This was more in line with what he knew about people who worked in the capital: work hard, play hard.

"If you like," he said, without much enthusiasm. He wasn't teetotal like Melissa, but he rarely drank alcohol. It made his head throb.

Lister was already heading rapidly for the exit. The heels of his cowboy boots clicked on the marble floor. It struck Richard that the guy would pass for a local back home. Weird. He caught up with him outside.

"There's a place just around the corner," Lister said, turning to the right. "So, first trip to Washington?"

"Yes."

"Seen much of the sights?"

"I just got here."

"Oh, yeah?" Lister went down the steps beneath a sign for Amberson's Cocktail Bar.

Richard immediately felt out of place in the watering hole's plush surroundings, even though no one paid him any attention.

Lister sat on a stool at the bar. "The usual, Tom." He turned to Richard. "What's yours?"

Richard thought it would be better to join in. "I'll have a beer. A Bud."

When the drinks came, Lister picked the olive out of the cocktail glass and popped it in his mouth.

"The classic Martini," he said, grinning to show dazzling teeth. "A decent slug of gin and no more than a drop of Martini."

Richard had never had anything in a glass that shape. He sipped his beer and managed not to grimace.

"So, what brings you to me, Iowa?" Lister ran his hand over his thinning fair hair. It was hard to tell how old he was. There were dark rings round his blue eyes, though his face was unlined and almost babyish.

Richard took a deep breath. He'd thought hard about how to handle this and meeting Lister had only made him more certain. He wasn't the sort of guy who would react well to being strong-armed.

"Mr. Lister—"

"Call me Gordy," the other man said, signaling to the barman for another. "Your beer okay?"

Richard nodded. "Gordy," he said, uncomfortable with the strange name. "Last November, you were involved with a competition in the *Star Reporter.*"

"I oversee competitions for all Woodbridge Holdings publications. Which particular one are you talking about?"

"One about pop music—twins who had hits. And you had to write a line saying—"

"Why you love the *Star Reporter,*" Lister said. "That's standard."

"Oh, I get you. In this case, the prize was a trip to Washington."

"Usually is." Lister tapped his nose. "I've set up a good deal with one of the hotels."

Richard was beginning to realize that Gordy Lister was an operator. "Well," he said, "my kids won and you looked after them when they were here."

"Really?" the small man said. "Can't say I remember. What was your last name again, Richard?"

"Bonhoff. I think you might recall them, Gordy. They're twins themselves. Randy and Gwen?"

Lister looked blank. "Randy and Gwen," he repeated, peering into his almost-empty glass. Then he raised his eyes. "Yeah, I remember. Real lookers, the both of them. Nice kids, too." He swallowed the last of his drink.

"I was just wondering…" Richard broke off, a sudden wave of emotion crashing over him. He took a deep breath. "I…I was wondering if…if you'd seen them or heard from them."

Gordy Lister's face took on a serious expression. "What do you mean?"

"Mr. Lister, Randy and Gwen left home three months ago and we haven't seen them since. To tell you the truth, they were never the same after they got back from Washington."

Lister gave a sympathetic smile. "Kids, huh?" he said, getting to his feet. "I'm very sorry, Richard. I don't have any idea where your kids are. They certainly haven't been in touch with me." He glanced at his watch. "Now, if you'll excuse me, there's somewhere I have to be." He extended his hand. "So long, friend. Hope you get to see some of the sights before you head back home." He dropped some bills on the bar and stepped toward the door, his hand raised in farewell.

Richard stayed where he was for some time. He was thinking about what had just happened. Something about Gordy Lister's manner wasn't anywhere near being right. He had no idea who Randy and Gwen were at the outset yet, after he'd recalled them, he immediately knew they hadn't been in touch with him. It was too slick. And his departure had been sudden.

Richard might have been a farmer from the Midwest, but he knew when he'd been given the brush-off. So much for the soft approach. He wouldn't be making that mistake again.

Ten

It started to rain, not heavily, but enough to mess with my vision. Blinking every few seconds, I kept going for what I estimated was well over an hour. Then I came to a break in the trees. There was an outcrop of rock and an overhanging section that I took cover beneath, stripping off all my clothing. I examined everything that I removed, from boots to jacket, but found nothing that resembled a tracking device. I was still dubious about the interior of the boot soles, but I couldn't see any sign that they'd been detached or tampered with. So I concentrated on myself.

I ran my fingers over my feet and legs. I wasn't sure exactly what I was looking for, but I presumed I'd recognize a foreign object—unless they'd somehow buried a bug deep inside my brain. I wasn't inclined to discount that possibility, given the activities I witnessed back at the camp. I wondered why they hadn't managed to track me down when I was still inside the building. Perhaps the device didn't work underground.

I felt my chest and abdomen. Nothing. Then I ran my fingers down my left arm; about an inch beneath the armpit, on the inside of the upper arm, there was a small raised area. I pressed it with a fingertip and felt something hard and definitely foreign. It was about the size of a small insect. The question now was, what could I do about it? I had nothing sharp in my possession. I tried to puncture the skin with my fingernails, but they had been cut short. Those people thought of everything. Short of shooting myself, I was screwed.

I stared out into the drizzle. Beneath the green foliage, I saw rows of thorns on the thin branches. I went over to them and managed to break a stem off. Taking it back to the rock overhang, I pried off thorns until there were only four left toward the end of the piece of twig. They were very sharp and it struck me that the bush might have poisonous sap. Too bad: this was my only option.

I took a deep breath, then jabbed one of the thorns into the skin alongside the raised section. I bit my lip and started to dig around. It wasn't easy and I used up three thorns, but eventually I managed to remove a small metal capsule. I was about to smash it with the pistol butt when I had a better idea. Some snails had come out on to the wet rock. I picked one up and gently crushed the shell. Then I removed the slimy flesh and used the last thorn to cut into it. I put the bug into the hole I'd made and placed the un-protected snail body on the highest rock. If I was lucky, a bird would swallow the whole thing and lead my pursuers a merry chase away from where I was headed.

I got dressed and checked the rounds in the rifle's clip. There were only four left—I had used more than I'd realized. At least I hadn't made any inroads into the pistol ammunition. I set off at medium pace as my knee was giving me occasional shafts of pain. They grew less frequent while I was running, so I didn't stop apart from once, at a narrow stream where I refilled my canteen and immersed my knee. The rain was heavier now, and I had to rely on whatever innate sense of direction I had, since the mountain peak I'd been navigating by what was now invisible. It was clear to me that I'd done this kind of exercise before, but whether as army training or as a sport remained hidden in the depths of my unreliable memory. I tried to prompt images from the past to flash up, as had happened with the deer-hunting and Dave, but nothing appeared.

At least, nothing I was expecting. I was running up a gentle slope, feeling the breath catch in my throat and trying to ignore the growing pain in my leg, when I suddenly remembered another tight spot that I'd been in....

...I push against the ropes, but there's no give in them. I try to speak, but the gag allows my tongue no movement. I can only moan and groan.

"You're wasting your strength, Matt," the woman in a blue police uniform says. She comes over to the chair I'm in and lowers her face to mine. "But I'll play fair." She laughs ironically. "Besides, no one can hear you." She raises a large knife with a partially serrated blade to within an inch of my left eye, then lowers it slightly and cuts the tape round my mouth. She smiles and rips it off my cheeks.

"Jesus!" I yell. "To hell with you, Sara!"

Instantly the knife is back at my eye. "We don't use the names of the underworld deities lightly, Matt," she says icily, then nicks the skin between eye and eyebrow. The drops of blood make me blink.

"No," I say, bitterly. "Not now that you're the famous Soul Collector. Self-appointed, of course."

She looks down at me, a smile on her lips that from another person would have been comforting, even loving. But her brown eyes are cold and unwavering.

"You didn't really think you'd escape me, did you, Matt?" she says, moving the blade down to my throat. "You must have always known that one day it would end like this."

She's right; deep down I've always been convinced. She was my lover and now she would be my death. I blink hard and get a grip on myself. Whatever else she does, she isn't going to break me.

"It can't be very satisfying," I say.

She looks puzzled; I've succeeded in breaking the patina of confidence.

"I mean," I continue, "after all the spectacular killings you've pulled off, cutting me to pieces while I'm tied up isn't much of a test for your skills, is it?"

Sara is far too smart to be fooled completely, but even a slight distraction may be enough for me.

"What do you suggest, Matt?" she says, bringing her lips close to my ear. "You want to play games?"

I have a flash of when we were lovers—her wrists tied to the head of the bed and her backside in the air... I thought we'd been as close as any couple could be, but she betrayed me, handed me over to the White Devil. I twitch my head and banish the image of the heartless murderer who had been my first tormentor. I have to stay focused.

"Give me a chance to get away," I say. "Make it a fair contest."

She laughs, the sound as empty as the grave. "According to the headlines, I'm a psycho killer, Matt. But I'm not a congenital idiot." Then she stands up straight and looks around the room. "All right, I'll give you a chance." She leans over me again and jabs the knife into my right knee.

I yell over and over as the blade is twisted around, and then slowly withdrawn. Ropes fall from my ankles, stomach and wrists and I try to get up. I collapse onto the floor.

"How's that?" she asks. "Let's say, if you make it to the door, I'll let you go. Fair?"

I force my thoughts into some kind of order, telling myself that I've had pain on the rugby field often enough. I bite my lower lip till my chin is slick with blood. The only thing I can think of is to make it appear that I've lost my nerve.

"No," I sob, "please, Sara...don't do this."

She steps back, out of the light.

"Go on, Matt. I'm not in your way."

"No," I squeal. "I can't...I can't move. My knee..."

She loses her patience and stamps over. Then I see her boot heading toward my injured leg. I scream the instant it makes contact and keep screaming.

"Shut the fuck up, you pathetic shit," she says.

I disobey the order, keeping my voice as high as I can.

Sara's face looms over me, but she keeps too far away for me to strike at her. "No one can hear you. All you're doing is pissing away what's left of your strength." She bends nearer. "Strong man," she says with bitter irony, launching spit onto my face.

I let out a long moan, then close my eyes and do the best impression I can of fainting. She doesn't buy it and lands her boot in my gut. I expel air rapidly, but stay supposedly comatose.

"Asshole," she says, her breath on my cheek.

I reckon she's as close as she's going to get. I think of the training I had from Dave. He always said, "Decide on a course of action and follow it through—no hesitation." Without looking, I whip my head forward and hear a crunch as my forehead smashes into her nose. I don't risk getting up but grab the knife that drops from Sara's hand and start crawling to the door. When I get there, I look back and see her trying to get to her feet, blood trickling between the fingers of the hand covering her nose. I should go back and finish her, but I'm committed to getting away.

In agony from my knee, I find an elevator at the end of a long corridor. I press the button, but before the doors close I see Sara coming toward me, her nose still fountaining blood. She empties the small pistol in her right hand into the elevator. I'm on the floor as the bullets narrowly miss my head. At last the doors close and I head down. When it stops, I haul myself up and stagger to the exit door. I find myself on a city street, all the buildings around as derelict as the one I've just left. But, amazingly, there's a taxi approaching. I stumble out into the road and force the driver to stop. He's wearing a turban.

"My God, sir," he says, after I've told him to take me to the nearest police station, "what is it you have been doing?"

I'm struggling to catch my breath. "Fighting...fighting with my girl," I say, stowing the combat knife in my pocket. Then there's another stab of pain in my knee. I wonder if I should go to a hospital first, but decide against it. The police need to know where the Soul Collector is, though she's probably already on her way out of the place.

I look out the window and catch a glimpse of an immensely tall building covered in silver light, an elegant needle pointing to the night sky....

It comes to me that this encounter with my former lover took place in New York City and she was dressed as a member of the New York Police Department...

I reached the top of the tree-covered incline and stopped behind a pine. The forest continued down the slope on the other side, and the narrow valley between the mountains wasn't far ahead now. My foot was aching, but I could bear it. The injuries that Sara had given me must have been several months back, if not more. I tried to remember more about the scene I'd just relived. What had I been doing in New York City? Where was New York City? I had the feeling it wasn't in the country that I lived in, nor was it in Scotland. I kicked the ground in frustration. I had been hoping that the longer I was out of the camp, the more frequently memories would return. That was happening, but it was taking too long. I needed more information about what had happened to me if I was to stay free.

I drank from the canteen and listened out for sounds of pursuit. The rain was heavier now and it was hard to distinguish individual noises. If the transmitter had been consumed by a bird or animal, maybe I really was on my own. I should have been encouraged by that thought, but instead I felt a terrible sense of isolation. The forests and mountains were huge and I was on my own against a ruthless enemy whose numbers I didn't know. If I failed to find food and shelter soon, I'd be easier prey than the snail I'd unshelled.

I moved off and achieved a reasonable speed going downhill. The trees thinned and I came to a track of sorts. The wheel ruts were covered in grass, so there obviously hadn't been any traffic along recently. I decided to risk using it—the day was almost over and I wanted to find shelter before the light faded completely. I jogged along the side of the track, prepared to dive into the undergrowth should anyone appear. I knew I was making a target of myself, but the trees on both sides were fairly high. Besides, my strength was almost drained. Taking risks was the only option.

I made it to the beginning of the narrow pass, rock faces rising up sheer to my right and left. I drank the last of my water and looked around. I didn't see or hear much apart from the fading light and the sunset song of the birds—my eyes were continually wet with rainwater. I had to hope that my pursuers hadn't gotten ahead of me. Maybe they had gone around the mountains by some other way. I took the rifle in both hands and stepped on down the track.

Heart pounding, I made it to the far end of the defile. There was an outcrop of rock on the left and I dropped down behind it. Wiping the rain from my eyes, I looked around the edge at the country ahead. The ground opened out from the narrow pass and sloped downward more gradually than on the other side. There were still plenty of trees, but I made out gaps between them. Then I blinked and stared. About a mile ahead, at the side of a clearing in the forest, was a low wooden building. There was no sign of activity in the vicinity and no smoke from the chimney. It was too good to be true. I told myself to be even more careful and set off again, following the line of trees and ready to slip between them.

After about half an hour, I made it to within three hundred yards of the building. It looked like a hunting cabin or the like, the eaves of the roof covering a railed veranda at the front. The windows were shuttered, which was a good sign. I waited for as long as I could in the wet, but saw no other signs of occupation. I had to go for it.

At the edge of the clearing around the hut, I turned to the right and approached from the rear. I leaned against the log wall and listened. Nothing. Creeping around to the far side, I checked that no one had been lurking out of my view. It was clear. At the front of the building, I saw tire tracks that were hard to date. They definitely hadn't been made in the last day or so, as the muddy surface caused by the rain wasn't churned up. I looked up at the sky. The light was almost gone, the clouds low and black, and I was shivering. It was time I got inside.

The door was locked, a heavy padlock fastening it to the frame. I smashed the rifle butt against it, but it held fast. I could have shot it out, but that might have attracted attention. Arms aching, I pounded away. Eventually cracks appeared around the metal panel the padlock was attached to. I slid the barrel of the rifle in and wrenched the panel away. It sheared off with a crack, leaving a patch of wood that was more lightly colored than the rest of the door.

I put my shoulder to the door. There was a loud crack

and then I was in. I slumped to the floor, panting for breath. I was soaked, cold, exhausted, starving and on the run. Surely things couldn't get any worse.

Eleven

The shop wasn't much more than a five-minute walk north from the U Street-Cardozo Station in northwest D.C. When talking on the phone to potential customers Monsieur Hexie played up his proximity to the hip bars and clubs on U Street, omitting to mention that his own street was less then safe after sunset. Not that he'd ever had a complaint. After all, he was in the business of selling supernatural power.

Monsieur Hexie's Voodoo Supplies had been in Shaw since 1977. Before that, the owner had gone by his given name, Francois Robiche. His parents had originated in New Orleans and later had worked themselves to early death in the kitchens of the capital's tourist hotels. In his teens, Francine had been a street hustler, his exotic looks and lithe body getting plenty of work. Eventually he saved enough to set himself up in the shop. He'd always been interested in what his *maman* called *"les pouvoirs secrets"*—the secret powers—and all he'd needed to do was read a few books to know more than his customers. A talent for self-advertisement had helped and soon Monsieur Hexie became a local character. The shop was in several D.C. guidebooks, as he'd paid the compilers under the table.

He sat at the back of the shop in the early evening, having closed up early.

Wednesday wasn't usually his day for private business, but this client had been insistent—as well as amenable to the inflated price he'd quoted. Even though he was now sixty, Monsieur Hexie was still powerfully attractive and his involvement in the occult was an extra turn-on for many johns.

There was still half an hour before he had to shower and prepare himself. He spent that time reviewing inventory. His Monsieur Hexie dolls were doing well, as usual—the wax men and women, both black and white, came with a set of long, sharp pins. Candles were always a good sell, too, especially the ones in red wax. And, of course, the traditional herbs that he concocted into his own mixtures were trusted by many customers to solve problems of a sexual nature. All in all, things were going well, despite the prevailing financial climate. He had paid off the loan on the shop years ago and lived in the small apartment above, so he didn't have many expenses. His only regret was that he'd never found a lover to settle down with, but he lived in hope.

Shooing away the stray black cat he'd named Satan— how the customers loved it when he called to the animal in the shop—Monsieur Hexie went to get ready. The apartment upstairs was cramped because a king-size bed took up much of the main room's space. It was surrounded by black candles and incense jars, and above the pillows hung an expressionless face mask. Men got a big thrill from screwing beneath the zombie's glassy-eyed stare. On the table by the window was the head of a moray eel that he'd had preserved. The fleshy jaws were wide apart. Monsieur Hexie slipped the wad of bills he'd removed from the till between them. It would take a brave thief to run the gauntlet of those needle-sharp teeth.

Sitting naked on the bed, Monsieur Hexie rubbed aromatic oil all over himself. The aroma was sweet and cloying, with a hint of rotten leaves. He knew from experience that johns couldn't resist burying their noses in it, so he made sure that there was plenty on his chest and lower abdomen.

Monsieur Hexie glanced at the clock in the shape of New Orleans. He had timed things perfectly. The chime from the street door rang out. He told people it was the repeated clang of the single-note bell that sounded at the beginning of the voodoo service to raise the zombie king. The electrician had been instructed to set the device to keep ringing while visitors climbed the narrow stair to the apartment. The snake skeletons and goat skulls on the walls of the stairway were all part of the trip; they also made sure that the advantage was Monsieur Hexie's, a state of affairs he did everything to sustain. More than once, Monsieur Hexie had been confronted by trembling men who had lost their nerve.

He slipped on an almost transparent silk robe over his sequined briefs and put on his high priest's headdress: three black ostrich feathers attached to a snake skin that circled his head twice. Then he went to the spy hole in the door. It had been a long time since anyone had dared lay a rough hand on him, but he was too smart to take unnecessary risks. The white guy he peered out at looked normal enough. He was probably in his thirties and of average height, brown hair, possibly dyed, a face that was smooth and rather girlish. His leather jacket and the pale green shirt were smart enough, even if at odds with the john's mild-mannered expression. If pressed, Monsieur Hexie would have said he was an office worker—an accountant or bank employee—trying to look cool in his free time.

He opened the door and extended a long leg. "Well, good evening, honey," he said in his most come-hither tone. "Ready for the trip of your life?"

The john looked at his bare thigh with a show of interest. As he moved a hand toward it, Monsieur Hexie stepped back.

"What's your name, darling?" he asked, smiling.

"Um…Pete," came the unconvincing reply.

"Uh-huh," Monsieur Hexie said. He grabbed his shirt-front and pulled him close. "And would you like a drink to warm you up on this chill evening, Pete?"

"Um…yeah." The guy looked at him and then cast a glance around the room. He seemed less impressed than most johns by what he was wearing, and the crocodile heads didn't make his eyes open wide, either. As for Satan, sitting on a cushion with his eyes half-closed, well…Pete was ignoring him completely. Monsieur Hexie wasn't concerned. The liqueur he made from rum and herbs had never been known to fail. He handed the john a generous measure in a heavy crystal glass.

"To the powers of darkness," he said, raising his glass.

The man stared at him like he was some kind of freak and eventually chinked glasses.

"Drink, child," Monsieur Hexie said, licking his lips. "It'll make you last all night."

Pete lifted the glass to his thin lips and took a sip. "Nice," he said, screwing his eyes up.

Cold fish, Monsieur Hexie thought. Sounds different to what he did on the telephone. Much less eager. He stepped close and started to unfasten the john's shirt buttons. He then shivered terminally as two sharp points pierced the skin of his back and ran through each of his kidneys.

The last thing Monsieur Hexie heard was a loud hiss from Satan as he scurried under the bed.

Twelve

Inside the gloom of the hut, I could make out very little. I felt around for a light switch before realizing there wouldn't be power lines in the middle of the forest. My head bumped into a metal object. I stretched up, feeling a stab of pain from the wound I'd made in my upper arm, and found a hurricane lamp. I shook it and heard the splash of liquid inside. Now all I needed was a match.

After I'd banged my shins against a heavy wooden chair, I thought about opening a shutter to let in the last of the daylight. I stopped myself before I got to the nearest window. I couldn't risk attracting attention. So instead, I started running my hands over all the surfaces, eventually finding matches in a wall holder. Putting a flame to the lamp's wick, I looked around the single room that composed the ground floor. There was a kitchen on the rear wall—gas stove, plate holders, no fridge. There was also a waist-high cupboard. I strode over and pulled it open. Bingo. The shelves were stacked with cans and packets. I reached a hand down.

The sudden crack made me jump backward, and I yelped at the sudden pain. I held my right hand under the lamp. The index finger was in a trap, the size of which suggested that rats rather than mice were the local pest. I pried the spring-loaded wires apart and examined the livid welt across the finger. It hurt even more when I bent it, but I didn't think it was broken. Then I remembered what I'd thought about things not getting any worse.

My stomach clenched and I realized I had to eat before I did anything else. Then I saw the wooden ladder that led up to a platform in the back half of the cabin. I clambered up it, my finger throbbing. A mattress covered most of the surface, and it was piled with discolored pillows, quilts and blankets. I dragged two blankets over and let them drop to the floor below. Although there was a fireplace with a pile of chopped wood next to it, I couldn't risk lighting a fire. The only way I was going to get warm was by wrapping up well.

I pulled off the outer layers of rain-soaked clothing and hung it across chairs, then wrapped one blanket around me and the other over my shoulders. Fortunately, the material was thick and the shivers that had plagued me since I'd stopped running gradually disappeared. I went back to the food cupboard and rummaged around: canned tuna, chili and several different kinds of beans. I found a can opener in a drawer and settled down to a cold feast. It was one of the best meals I'd ever eaten. After I'd finished, I looked for something to drink. There were cans of beer and a bottle of whiskey. They were no use to me as I couldn't risk blurring my senses. Then I found some sodas. I got through a couple before it occurred to me to examine them.

I checked the cans and bottles. The whiskey was from somewhere called Lynchburg, Tennessee, the tuna had been canned in Fort Lauderdale, FL, and the beans were from Pittsburgh, PA. I looked at the whiskey again. It was Jack Daniel's. The black label and name rang a bell deep in my memory. I opened the bottle and took a sniff. A subtle aroma flooded my nostrils and suddenly I retched.

I remembered—I had got horribly drunk on Jack Daniel's, and I knew where. In a bar with a view of a great storied building with colonnades and a high dome. The name of the city flashed into my mind. Washington. Washington, D.C. Capital of the United States of America.

I rocked back on my heels and tried to come up with more. I caught glimpses of a scene in a bar, people laughing and cheering. But I couldn't think who they were, or what I had been doing there. The only thing I knew for sure was that the bar was in Washington, near the seat of government. Did that mean I was in the United States now? I looked at the cans I'd emptied. Fort Lauderdale, FL. I sounded the letters *FL* together and immediately thought of the name Florida. Pittsburgh, PA, didn't register, but the letters on some other products I took from the cupboard prompted names—IL, Illinois. CA, California. It wasn't overwhelming proof that I was in the U.S.A., but it certainly seemed likely.

I stood up, feeling twinges in my knee. I needed rest badly. As I was heading for the ladder, I caught sight of a newspaper under the table. I picked it up and looked at the front page. It was a tabloid—that word popped into my brain instantly to describe the small newsprint pages— called the *Star Reporter.* The paper was dated May 12, 2008. I wasn't sure if that was recent, but I had a feeling it was. A photo took up most of the front page, showing an underdressed woman standing by a horse. The headline was Senator Bares All to Stallion. According to the story, the forty-nine-year-old politician had been seen riding naked on a ranch in New Mexico, an allegation she strongly denied. I flicked through the paper. It was full of what I suspected were either invented or hugely exaggerated scandals.

I put the newspaper back where I'd found it and unhooked the oil lamp. As I headed for the ladder, I caught sight of my face in a small cracked mirror on the wall. My hair was cut short, under an inch in length. It was mainly black, but when I looked closer I saw some white hairs. My face was haggard, the skin tight over the cheekbones. I tried a smile and saw straight white teeth. I tried to imagine how an unbiased observer would have described my appearance. The best I could come up with was craggy.

I scrambled up the ladder, gripping the lamp's wire handle in my teeth, and buried myself in the quilts. At last real warmth returned to my body, but it didn't make me much happier. It wasn't just that I was on the run from armed men, but the fact that I felt so alone. If I was in the U.S., as seemed likely, I was in a foreign country—I knew without being able to say why that I wasn't American. I didn't know if I had any friends here. Why had I been in the camp? What had been done to me?

I was a man without a past, running into a future I couldn't predict—far from home, on my own, in despair. I put the lamp out and laid the pistol on the bare wooden floor. If I'd been more in control of myself, I'd have gone back down the ladder and opened the door. That would have given the impression that I'd been and gone—no one in their senses would have stayed in a cabin with the door ajar when the rain was pouring down and the temperature was low. But I couldn't make myself get out of the warm cocoon.

Soon I fell into an uneasy and haunted sleep....

...The dark-haired girl is laughing.

"Come on, Dad," she says, pulling my hand. "We'll miss the film." She starts running down the street and I'm forced to follow, shortening my stride so I don't crash into her. We cross the road after a red double-decker bus passes. The cinema is lit up, people crowding the entrance. There are posters up for three screens.

I laugh.

"What?" the girl says, giving me a stern look.

"Nothing, Lucy," I say. "It's just that there are two Hollywood blockbusters on here and you want to see the Slovenian art-house film."

"So?" she says, her cheeks suddenly on fire. "Not every thirteen-year-old wants to sit through rubbish."

"You're the world's only such exception," I say, and buy the tickets. We are directed up narrow stairs to a small screen that was obviously an afterthought. There must be all of three other patrons. As it turns out, there are five minutes before the program starts.

"How's school?" I ask, offering her some chocolate-covered raisins.

"All right, I suppose." She twists her lips. "The others don't take it seriously enough."

"You're turning into a real little bluestocking." I dig a finger into the flesh behind her knee.

"Stop it, Dad," she says, pushing me away. "I'm too old for that." She looks around in embarrassment. "Especially in public."

"I'm sorry," I say, suddenly solemn. "I'll put in a call to the Metropolitan Police and have myself arrested."

"Ha-ha." She isn't able to resist the raisins. "Anyway, you know everyone who counts in the police. You'd just get off, like you always do."

I laugh. "Like I always do?"

"You-know-who looks after you," she says, smirking.

I change the subject rapidly. "What's so great about this film, anyway?"

Lucy puts on the horn-rimmed glasses she insisted on—the truth is, she loves the bluestocking look—and takes out a notepad and pen. "Well, it's supposed to be a penetrating examination of peasant life in contemporary Slovenia and—"

I fake a yawn. "Oh, great. Listen, I'll double your pocket money this week if we can change to the Tom Cruise film."

"No," she says firmly. "You watch far too many cop films. You need some proper culture."

I fumble for a response. "How's your mother?"

She looks away. "As if you care."

"That's not fair, Luce," I say. "You don't know everything that I feel about Caroline."

"Oh, I do beg your pardon," she says, giving me a superior glance. "Deep down you still love her, do you?" She snorts angrily. "The only time you show any concern about her is when we get targeted by one of the killers who keep chasing you."

"Don't be ridiculous," I reply, staring at a middle-aged woman a couple of rows in front of us. She keeps looking round and seems to be fascinated by Lucy. "I see your mother every weekend," I say in a lower voice.

"Yes, and you hardly manage to say two civil words."

I suddenly notice that her eyes are damp. "Oh, Luce, I'm sorry. I'm doing the best I can." Guilt crushes me. I know very well that the acrimonious divorce and the double nightmare of the White Devil and the Soul Collector have been far too much for her to cope with over the past five years. I put my arms round her. At first she resists, then she softens.

"It's all right, Dad," she whispers. "Come on, let's go to the other film."

I stay in my seat. "Oh, no you don't. You wanted this movie and you're going to sit through it to the bitter end."

She jabs her elbow into my ribs and smiles, then looks avidly at the screen as the lights go down.

I lean toward her. "Be gentle if I start snoring," I say in her ear.

My ribs take another pounding...

* * *

I woke up and found myself sweating beneath the heap of quilts. For a few moments, I had no idea where I was, then I remembered the cabin. I got my head clear and listened intently. There was nothing, not even any birdsong. It was obviously still night. I relaxed and started going over the dream. I knew for sure that the scene with me and the girl called Lucy, the girl who'd addressed me as Dad, had really happened. So I was a father. The realization hit me hard. I felt a tenderness well up. Now I knew there was something for me beyond the hell of the camp and the desperate chase through the forests. The idea that there was someone to stay alive for made me feel much stronger.

I thought about other things I'd remembered. I had been married to a woman called Caroline and was now divorced. Lucy referred to a "you-know-who," which I had the strong feeling meant some woman I was now involved with, not that I could come up with any recollection of her. Was she in the police? Was that how she could protect me? I felt a wave of desolation break over me.

I got my breathing under control. At least I knew there was someone else in my life besides Lucy and an ex-wife. All I could hope was that my memory would work better with every day I spent away from the camp. I thought of the scene with Lucy again. The red bus. The name of the location flashed into my mind. London. I immediately knew the city was the capital of Great Britain. That was where I lived, I was also sure. But, then, what was I doing in the U.S.A.? Maybe that was just an illusion. Maybe the people in the camp had programmed me to remember things that weren't true.

Sitting up, I slid my hand down to my knee. It was aching dully, but I couldn't feel any external pain. Then my right index finger gave a twinge. I remembered the trap and moved the digit gingerly. If it didn't function as it should,

I'd be at a serious disadvantage when I had to pull the trigger, as I was sure I would have to. I couldn't see what I could do. Splinting it would mean I couldn't fire the rifle or the pistol at all.

I sank back into the inviting warmth and softness of the quilts and drifted back to sleep. This time I saw a man's body peppered with bullets; a young woman hanging from the ceiling, her entrails touching the floor; an underground chamber painted to show all the horrors of hell; and a savage beast with yellow fangs leaping up at me—

I woke with a start. It wasn't the dream that had roused me. I had heard the unmistakable sound of an ammunition clip being pressed home. I felt for my weapons and slid silently to the edge of the loft.

Thirteen

Detectives Simmons and Pinker had been at the murder scene in Shaw since 2:12 a.m. They'd been contacted by a friendly MPDC dispatcher, who had thought there were potential links to the rock-singer killing they were already investigating. Before they went up to Monsieur Hexie's apartment, they spoke to the patrolman who had discovered the body.

"Neighbor called it in," the heavily built, middle-aged officer told them.

Simmons raised an eyebrow. "How'd that go, Max? Get over here quick as you can, I got a full description of the killer?"

The uniformed officer grunted. "In your dreams, Detective. Old lady across the street, she woke up and noticed the door here half-open."

Pinker looked over and made out a white-haired woman next to a uniformed female officer in the back of a cruiser. He went to get a preliminary statement.

"That it?" Simmons asked.

"We rang the bell, Detective," said the patrolman's

partner, a young man whose expression was avid. "No answer. So Max went up and found…"

"And found the vic," Max completed. "Facedown on the bed, two knife handles sticking out of his lower back."

"Lovely," Clem said under his breath.

"And that wasn't all." The young officer had found his voice again. "There was—"

"Shut the fuck up, O'Donnell," Max said. "You keep a grip on your dinner, you get to tell the story." He turned to Simmons. "There was a piece of paper on his upper back."

"It had been nailed there," Officer O'Donnell put in, his eyes wide.

"Squares and rectangles in black?" Simmons asked.

The patrolmen nodded.

"Looks like you got yourselves a serial killer, Detective," O'Donnell said.

Simmons gave him a weary look. "According to the FBI, three victims are required before that term is applied." He stepped closer to the young man. "You pay attention, now. Number one, we don't know if it's the same killer, even if the M.O.'s been repeated. Number two, nobody's using the word *serial,* not if they want their balls to stay attached. Number three, the Chief of Detectives banned disclosure of the paper found on the dead rocker. Just how the hell do you know about it, Officer?"

Simmons wasn't expecting an answer. He watched as Max dragged his partner back to the cruiser. He didn't think there would be any more leaks from the rookie. It didn't surprise him that the disclosure order had been ignored—beat cops always found out stuff in record speed. But the last thing they needed right now was someone blabbing to the media.

"Neatly done, Clem," Pinker said from behind him. "Shall we?"

They accepted overshoes and gloves from a CSI and

went up the stairs to the dead man's apartment, avoiding the areas flagged up for closer inspection.

"Your kinda place, Clem," Pinker said, taking in the voodoo mask above the bed.

"Screw you, Vers," the big man said, moving farther into the room. He had his eyes on the uncovered body lying facedown on the bed. Two handles protruded above the waist, one on the right and one on the left.

"Skewers, you reckon?" Pinker said, leaning over the body.

"Yup." Simmons looked at the piece of paper inside a plastic file on the victim's upper back. "You got the copy of the last one?"

"Yup." Pinker unfolded a sheet. "Same idea, but the shapes are in different places."

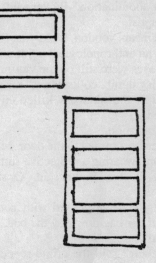

"If you were to put them together, would they make any sense?" Simmons asked.

Pinker tried that. There was no obvious overlap, so it was impossible to say if the squares and rectangles were supposed to fit against each other.

"Who knows?" the smaller man said. "Maybe numbers go in the shapes. Or letters."

"We got to do a crossword now?" Simmons said, with a groan. "Where are the clues?" He raised a hand. "And don't even think about saying 'Haven't got a clue,' if you want to do anything creative with your dick in the future."

Gerard Pinker grinned. "You sure the shapes don't mean something in that weird religion of yours."

"Last time I looked, I was a Catholic," Simmons said, looking at the black candles that surrounded the bed.

"Not that abomination," Pinker said. He'd been raised Southern Baptist.

"Oh, you mean, voodoo. I told you, I'm only interested in that from an anthropological point of view."

Pinker's eyes were still on the victim. "Say, what?"

"Don't play dumb, college boy," his partner said.

"You think the skewers killed him right away?" Pinker asked.

"A good question."

Both detectives turned to the door. Marion Gilbert was standing there, wearing a protective suit and overshoes.

"Evening, Doctor," Pinker said. "Or should I say *morning?*"

"I notice you've dispensed with *good*." The medical examiner put her bag down by the bed. "Is the photographer finished?"

"Yes, ma'am," said the crime-scene supervisor from where he was dusting for prints.

"Let me see if I can answer your question, Detective."

The M.E. set to work, measuring temperatures and filling in a checklist. Simmons and Pinker went over to the CSI.

"Anything for us?" Pinker asked.

The bespectacled man raised his shoulders. "Nothing very striking so far. We're collecting traces and fibers, of course. The main light was on. There's a dimmer switch and, assuming the beat guys didn't touch it as they say, then it was on low. That red bedside light was on, too. And the candles."

"Romantic atmosphere, huh?" Simmons said. "Windows closed?"

"And locked," the CSI replied. "The killer left out of this door and the one on the street."

"Leaving the latter half-open," Pinker said. "He was either in a state of panic or he didn't care."

"Nothing here that wouldn't belong to the vic?" Simmons asked.

"Not obviously so."

"Oh, Detectives," Dr. Gilbert called.

"That was quick," Pinker said, walking over to the bed.

"A preliminary report only," the M.E. said, with a tight smile. "To help you out."

"Kind of you, Doctor," Simmons said, giving his partner a blank look. Pinker got the message and kept quiet. "Time of death?"

"Rigor mortis has been developing for several hours. Calculating from the temperature, I'd say between six and, say, nine hours ago. As for cause, Detective Pinker, yes, the victim could well have died from his wounds. Until I see the internal damage, it's impossible to be sure. It looks very likely that the weapons punctured his kidneys. There isn't much blood loss, so I'd be inclined to think he died from shock."

"Not surprised," Simmons muttered.

Marion Gilbert pointed at the sheet of paper. "What's that all about?"

The detectives exchanged glances.

"Haven't a clue, Doc," Pinker said, stepping away from his partner.

The M.E. looked at them and shook her head in what looked like disgust. "Well, I wish you luck in finding one, gentlemen. No doubt I'll see you at the autopsy later on today."

Simmons and Pinker moved to the door.

"Asshole," the big man said. "What's with the clues shit? You reading Agatha Christie?"

"No," Pinker said, grinning. "I'd like to look for the doctor's clue, though."

Simmons scowled at him. "Pussy hound. You'd better start wearing out your expensive calfskin loafers. We need witnesses. You heard the doc. Between six and nine hours takes us back to between six and nine last night. Get canvassing."

"What about you?" Pinker demanded.

"I'm going to look for someone to ID the victim. But before that, I'm calling the Chief of Detectives. He is not going to be happy."

While interviewing a nearby shop owner, Simmons was called back to Monsieur Hexie's apartment. He went upstairs and found a fair-haired, middle-aged man and brunette young woman talking to the CSI supervisor. "Can I help you?" he asked.

"Peter Sebastian," the man said, studying him dispassionately. "FBI. I'm deputy head of violent crime."

"…you slumming?"

"Unfortunately not. I've spoken to your chief."

Simmons knew what that meant.

"This is Special Agent Dana Maltravers, my assistant," the FBI man said, glancing at the woman. She gave Simmons a tight smile. "No, Detective, we aren't slumming.

This is the second murder in D.C. in rapid succession. You can understand the Bureau's interest, given the large number of VIPs in the district."

"But they're not your problem, are they?" Simmons said. "You're a violent-crime man."

Sebastian looked at him icily. "Can we have some cooperation here, please?"

Versace chose that moment to make his entrance. "Cooperation?" he said. "That's my middle name."

Dana Maltravers looked at him. "And your other names are Gerard and Pinker?"

The detective laughed. "On the button. Give the lady a coconut."

The agent's lips started to form into a smile, then she saw her superior's expression. She ran a hand through her short brown hair and looked away.

Peter Sebastian introduced himself and his colleague again, then turned back to Simmons. "So, Detective, about that cooperation?"

Simmons raised his shoulders. "Sure. Tell us how this particular cooperation is going to play."

"Very well. You remain in primary control of the investigation into this murder and that of the rock singer, but you inform us of every development immediately." The FBI man smiled, showing gleaming and perfectly straight teeth. "And we reserve the right to take over if and when we deem that appropriate."

"Oh, right," Pinker said, stepping forward. "We do the legwork and you step in at the end to get the applause."

Sebastian's gaze hardened. "Let's face it, Detective, you and your partner haven't exactly covered yourselves in glory so far."

Simmons put a hand on Pinker's arm.

"If you're unhappy," the blond man concluded, "ask your chief about the terms. He agreed to them."

"No need," Simmons said. He and Versace had shown they weren't pushovers; now they needed to get on with the investigation. "What do you need to know?"

Sebastian inclined his head toward Maltravers.

"Has the victim been identified yet?" she asked, looking at her clipboard.

"Not officially," Simmons replied. "But the CSIs found a brochure for the shop downstairs. The photo of Monsieur Hexie matches the dead man."

Dr. Gilbert's initial impressions were then passed on. After hearing about their canvassing, Dana Maltravers looked at them both.

"What are your thoughts about the modus operandi?"

Versace shrugged. "Musta hurt something awful."

Clem gave a weary shake of the head. "I guess you mean the fact that both this victim and Loki were killed with two weapons?"

"Very good, Detective," Sebastian said. "I'm glad one of you has been paying attention." He ignored Pinker's glare.

"Oh, we both noticed that, all right," Clem said, rescuing his partner. "We're just keeping an open mind about it."

"Yeah," Versace said. "After all, most murderers have got two hands."

Sebastian and Maltravers looked at each other.

"You don't think the number two might have some symbolic meaning?" the female agent asked.

Simmons screwed up his eyes. "You mean, some kind of binary significance? A pair, that kind of thing?"

Maltravers shrugged. "I guess. Or maybe there were two killers."

Pinker glanced at Simmons. "We haven't excluded that possibility."

"There were no footprints on the street at the first murder," his partner added. "But the CSIs should be able to get prints from the rugs here."

"Let's leave that for now," Sebastian said. "We'll leave you to your work, Detectives. Perhaps we could meet at your office, say, midday?" His tone made clear that the issue wasn't negotiable.

After the agents had left, Pinker nudged his partner.

"Binary significance?" he said, ironically. "What the hell has that got to do with anything, Clem?"

"Search me," the big man replied, with a soft grin. "I just wanted to show off my lack of a college degree." He turned away from his partner. "Now it's time I worked on the voodoo connection."

Pinker gave a hollow laugh. Then he realized that Simmons was serious.

Fourteen

I flattened myself beneath the quilts, leaving a small space to see through. Unfortunately, my ears were still well covered, so the first sound I heard was the crash of the door being kicked open. I saw a figure in a gray uniform and beret, with a leveled assault rifle.

"Base, unit eleven at loggers' cabin. Door has been forced. Fugitive not present. Over."

I watched as his eyes moved up to the platform.

"Base, eleven. Wait one. Checking bedding. Over."

The man slipped a walkie-talkie into a holder on his belt and slung the rifle over his shoulder before taking out a pistol like the one I was holding. Then he started up the rungs.

I considered what to do. Killing the guy would be easy enough, but I was less keen on that than I had been the day before. I didn't want to be reduced to their level. Which didn't mean I wasn't going to get even with the shitheads in the camp at some stage, but I needed to get away first.

The man's head gear appeared, then his face. I had to act quickly, while I still had the advantage of surprise. I moved forward and reared up from the bedding, head butting him squarely in the face. The contact was good and he lost his grip on the ladder and crashed to the floor. I slid down the ladder and held my pistol on him. That wasn't necessary. He was out cold.

The walkie-talkie squawked before I could do anything else.

"Eleven, base. Confirm status. Over."

I had to answer—if I kept quiet, more people would be sent after me. At least I'd heard the unconscious man speak. I took the device from his belt.

"Base, eleven," I said, copying the accent as best I could. "Bedding clear. Stand by." It suddenly occurred to me that, if I held my nerve, I could sell the bastards a dummy. I removed a leather strap holding a compass from his neck then looked cautiously out the open door. There was no one else in sight. I went out onto the veranda and decided on a direction that I wouldn't be taking. "Tracks outside heading into forest. Bearing, thirty degrees. Over."

"Roger, eleven. Return to RZ point Charlie. Confirm. Over."

"RZ Charlie confirmed. Over and out."

I waited for a response, wondering if I'd said anything wrong.

"Roger, base out."

I exhaled hard, then looked down at the man by my feet. He hadn't moved, but I wasn't taking any chances. I checked the guy's belt. There was a sheathed combat knife at the rear. I pulled off his jacket and hacked it into strips. Tying his wrists, I ran the material round the top of the heavy table and secured it. After binding his ankles, I reckoned he was there for the duration. I took the watch from his left wrist. The time was seven forty-one, but there was no date or month display. The cold at night and the relatively short days, along with the yellowing leaves on the occasional deciduous tree, suggested it was autumn.

I removed a couple of full ammunition clips from the

young man's belt and pulled on my jacket. After I'd laced my boots, hung the compass round my neck and stuffed my jacket pockets with cans of food and drink, I was ready to leave. I took the man's rifle and pistol with me, as well as my own. They would be stashed in the forest where no one would ever find them. Finally, I dropped the walkie-talkie to the floor and crushed it with my boot—after the bug in my arm, I wasn't taking any more chances of being located than I had to.

Going to the door, I had another look around, and then set off. From the heights the day before, I'd seen an area where the forest seemed less dense. If there was any civilization in this godforsaken land, it was that way. The bearing was 170 degrees, well away from where I'd sent my pursuers. I ran across the open ground at medium pace. Sprinting might have attracted attention and, besides, I didn't want to put too much pressure on my suspect knee. I had an anxious minute before I made the tree line—I was panting more from apprehension than fatigue.

When I was about fifty yards inside the forest, I stopped and buried the second rifle and pistol under a thick layer of pine needles. I was on my knees with my head bent when I heard the male voice.

"Keep very still or I'll drill you a new asshole."

I did as I was told, cursing myself. The man I knocked out had identified himself as "unit eleven." A unit consisted of more than one person. The best I could hope for was that there weren't more than two.

"Get your hands up! High!"

"All right," I said, my tone as reasonable as I could manage while I slipped the combat knife from my belt.

"Shut up or you're dead!"

I considered pointing out that his superiors might not want me dead, but decided against riling him further.

"Stay on your knees and turn around. Slowly!"

I obeyed, feeling the forest mulch soak my trousers. The first thing I noticed was that my captor didn't have a walkie-talkie or a compass, at least not anywhere obvious. The second was that he was very young, his face dotted with pimples.

"What did you do to Hans?"

I played dumb. "I don't know any Hans," I said, the knife now up my sleeve.

"A guy dressed like me?" His tone was less aggressive. He took a step forward. "What's that you were burying?"

I ran through the permutations quickly. He obviously hadn't seen me at the cabin or with his partner, assuming Hans was the guy I'd jumped. If he hadn't seen the rifle and pistol, he must just have come upon me by chance.

"Shit," I said apologetically. "No, really. I always go early in the morning."

He stared at me, taking in the compass round my neck. "Where did you get that?" he said, jabbing the rifle's muzzle at me. "Is it Hans's?"

I decided to jack up the pressure. "Oh, now I get it. Hans was the pussy I kicked the crap out of." I gave a harsh laugh. "You won't be seeing Hans again."

The youth's cheeks flared and he moved closer, the rifle thrust even closer toward me. One more step...

"If you've hurt Hans, I'll cut your balls off," he said, a malevolent glint in his eyes.

I suddenly realized that, even though he was very young, someone had worked hard to bring out the worst in him.

I grinned. "You sure that won't seriously piss off your superior officers?"

"You can live without balls." Then he took the step forward that I'd been waiting for. I grabbed hold of the rifle with one hand, wrenching it out of his grip. At the same time, I let the knife slip into my hand. In a second, I had the blade at his throat.

"But *you* can't live without your throat," I said, breaking the skin above his Adam's apple.

"Fuck you, you piece of shit," he yelled, spraying my face with spittle.

"Keep your voice down," I warned, jabbing deeper.

After a few more seconds, the resistance went out of him and his body slackened.

"What's your name?" I asked, my voice softer.

"Fuck you."

"Rank?"

"Fuck you."

I laughed. "Serial number. No, don't bother, I've got the message." I looked at the letters on his cap badge. "How about this? What's NANR?"

This time I'd pressed the right button. "North American National Revival," he said with undisguised pride.

"What's that?"

He stared at me, but kept quiet.

"Bad move," I said, pressing the blade against his neck. Blood began to drip.

The young man whispered something and I leaned forward to catch it. The first word began with *f* and the second with *y*.

I made good progress through the forest after I'd gagged the young man and tied him to a tree with strips from his jacket. I'd buried the rifles, pistols and other equipment I'd taken from him and from Hans in a heap of needles a good distance from where he was. I wondered how long it would be before he was found, and was thinking that perhaps I'd finally got out of the zone controlled by the men in gray when I was distracted by the sudden sounds of a large animal crashing through the trees.

A German shepherd came pounding around a tree trunk, its jaws wide and worryingly speckled with foam. I went into automatic response mode and ran straight at the dog rather than waste time trying to bring a weapon to bear. The creature blinked its eyes, but it was too late for it to alter course. With a flick of my hips, I slid past it, having a flash of performing the same maneuver on a muddy pitch with an oval ball in my hands. I kept on running till I came to a thick tree trunk and took cover behind it.

Looking around the trunk, I saw the dog coming back in my direction. Then its ears pricked as a low voice came through the forest.

"Prince!"

I estimated the man to be about twenty yards to the animal's left. It ran toward him with a yelp. I wasn't clear whether the handler was aware of Prince's recent engagement with the enemy. I waited where I was, finger on the trigger. It was still aching from the rat trap, but I reckoned I could take out man and dog if I had to.

The German shepherd was leaping about, trying to make the dumb human understand what was going on. A gray uniform came into view. I stared. The handler was a woman. And she was stunning, with auburn hair in a plait beneath her cap and a full figure beneath the uniform, which fitted more tightly than did the men's. Her voice was deep and hoarse, the kind that raises hairs on necks. Shooting her in cold blood wasn't an attractive prospect.

Then I heard a crackle of radio static. She had her walkie-talkie turned up loud.

"Base, unit seventeen. Report, over."

She put the device to her ear. "Unit seventeen. All clear. Over."

"Proceed to loggers' cabin. Unit eleven nonresponsive. Confirm. Over."

"Unit seventeen, confirm heading to cabin, over."

"Exercise extreme caution, seventeen. Remember, target is to be immobilized, not terminated. Base out."

I watched as the young woman left in the opposite direction. Pity. Then again, I hadn't had to terminate her or the German shepherd. It was only after I'd been under way again for about a quarter of an hour that I remembered what had also struck me about the beautiful young woman. She bore a strong resemblance to the guy I'd dealt with in the cabin—the one called Hans.

Something else occurred to me: I seemed to have a very well-developed sense of self-preservation.

Two hours later, I was striding down a slope through the trees. The idea that I was leaving something important behind had filled my mind again. Although I hadn't heard any pursuers since the woman had turned back, my mood had darkened when it should have done the opposite. I remembered Lucy, my daughter. Where was she? Could the bastards at the camp have her? I stopped in my tracks. Then I thought of the words she had used in the cinema—*you-know-who*. The problem was, I *didn't* know who. I closed my eyes and tried to call up that mysterious individual, my assumed partner. I caught a glimpse of blond hair and—

The roar of the engine rang through the forest. It was directly ahead of me. I immediately started running in that direction. The sound of revving continued as I got to the tree line. There were only a few yards between me and the rear of a trailer loaded with massive tree trunks.

A bearded man in blue overalls and heavy boots was lashing the last of the ropes that secured the load. He stepped back and raised his hand to the truck at the front.

"All right!" he yelled. "Let's get the hell outta here!" He shifted his large frame toward the cab's open door. I made out the words *Woodbridge Holdings* painted over an image of an open newspaper.

I had only a few seconds to decide if I was going with them. I looked at the back of the trailer, then slung the rifle over my shoulder. There was an even louder noise from the engine and black exhaust streamed from the pipes behind the cab. When I heard the gears engage, I went for it. There were several ropes tied to a steel ring, so I had plenty to grab hold of. I was making a fine target for any gray-uniformed marksmen in the vicinity, but no shots rang out. As the truck bumped down the uneven muddy track, I pulled myself higher and toward the tarp covering the top of the load. With difficulty, I managed to crawl under it, the muzzle of the rifle banging against my head as the trailer rolled to the side alarmingly.

There were two problems with the place I'd found to hide. The first: if the load overturned on the track I'd be crushed to a pulp. The second: I couldn't see a thing from beneath the tarp. I managed to take the compass off my neck and check the bearing. Maybe—if I was very lucky—I'd be able to navigate my way back to the camp once I'd found help. I was still gripped by the feeling that I was leaving a vital part of my life behind. I caught another glimpse of blond hair, but recalled nothing else.

Fifteen

Richard Bonhoff woke up much later than he did on the farm. The budget hotel he'd found was in the eastern outskirts of Washington, near the beginning of the freeway. He had expected to be kept awake by the traffic noise, but he'd been exhausted when he turned in and had slept deeply. After Gordy Lister had walked out on him in the cocktail bar, he'd spent hours tramping the Mall. The nation's grandest sights—the White House, the Washington Monument, the Capitol, the Lincoln Memorial—hadn't impressed him much, even though they were lit up spectacularly. He kept looking at the photo of the twins he'd brought to show Lister, their smiling faces beaming up at him. That didn't make him happy. Rather, he had struggled to contain his anger. He hadn't even needed to show Lister the photo. He'd known who the twins where immediately, and he looked guilty as hell. Richard knew exactly what he was going to do.

After drinking a cup of vile coffee from the machine in his room, he headed out. Now that it was charged, the temptation to check his cell phone was great, but he resisted it. There would be a string of voice messages from Mel, each nastier in tone and content than the previous one. He didn't need the hassle. But then it struck him that the twins might have been in touch. He checked, cutting off the three messages his wife had left as soon as he heard her voice. As he'd suspected, there was nothing from Gwen and Randy.

Richard retrieved the pickup and headed down New York Avenue to the center. He left the vehicle in a multi-story lot around the corner from the newspaper office. The parking charges were killing him.

He took a seat at a coffee-shop window and kept his eyes on the Woodbridge Holdings building. There was no sign of Lister. The place filled up and he was told he had to buy something else if he wanted to keep the table. After four hours and a selection of overpriced drinks and snacks, Richard was down to his last ten dollars in cash, but he couldn't risk leaving to find an ATM—he couldn't even risk going to the can. By four o'clock he was getting desperate.

Then Gordy Lister came out of the building. He was wearing the same tan jacket, and high-heeled cowboy boots. He looked to right and left, and Richard realized the small man was nervous. Could it be that he'd spooked him by asking about the twins?

Richard got up and headed outside when Lister went left. He felt a stabbing in his bladder, but ignored the pain. Keeping about twenty yards back, he did his best to merge into the crowd of people in expensive clothes. When his target took another left turn, it struck him that maybe he was heading for the car park where the pickup was. That was how it played out. Richard decided to make a dash for his vehicle. He had no way of knowing which level Lister had parked on, so he could only hope they would reach the exit barrier around the same time.

His pickup would make a very obvious tail, but there was nothing he could do. He paid the ticket, using his credit card, and gunned the engine. The suspension strained as he took the narrow corners too fast, but he was in luck. Lister, driving a dark blue BMW roadster, was only one car ahead of him at the barrier.

Richard tried to drop back when he hit the street, provoking a horn blast from a young woman in a Japanese sports car. There was nothing for it but to keep closer to Lister than he'd have liked. He was relieved to see that the newspaper man was talking animatedly into his cell phone.

The roadster headed north. Richard was surprised at how quickly the smart buildings of the city center were replaced by dilapidated tenements. A few minutes later, a sign told him he was in Shaw. He'd heard the name on the local TV news back at the hotel. There had been a murder here last night, some guy who ran a black-magic shop, according to the overexcited reporter.

The traffic in the narrow streets was heavy and Lister had no chance to exercise the horsepower under his bonnet, meaning that Richard was still close behind. He was sweating, under attack from his bladder and worried that he would be spotted. He glanced around and saw a trio of young black men on the sidewalk. They were pointing at the pickup and laughing.

The line of cars hadn't moved much farther when Lister made a right and drove down a side street. By the time Richard had followed, the roadster had vanished. He pounded the wheel and drove on, looking desperately to right and left. Then he saw the BMW in an even narrower street to the right and slammed on the brakes.

Richard turned, then left the pickup in the middle of the road—it was a dead end and there were no spaces at the curb. He walked toward Lister's car, which was parked at the end of the street. When he got there, he saw it was empty but then noticed that the door of the neighboring house was ajar. He heard his target's voice.

"No!" Lister screamed. "Don't hurt me!"

Richard went to the door and listened. The screams continued. He went in and took some stairs that led downward at the end of the hall. There was a smell of fried food and dope, cut with a stink like the cattle shed back home. He made no sound as he went down. There was a single door to his left. It, too, was half-open.

"Jesus, don't hit me anymore." Lister was pleading. "I'll get the money for you, I promise."

There was a heavy slap, followed by a pathetic squeal.

Richard shoved the door open and stepped into the room.

He was instantly grabbed by two large men in white T-shirts. They had shaven heads and tattoos on their thick arms. Lister was sitting in a battered armchair, cleaning his nails with a tooth pick.

"Hey, Iowa," he said, looking up. "What the fuck are you doing on my ass?"

Richard stared at him. "But…but I thought…"

Lister laughed. "You *thought?* I wasn't sure folks did that out there in Hicksville."

The big men laughed.

"Give him a couple," Lister said, casually.

Two heavy fists smashed into Richard's solar plexus in rapid succession. He dropped to one knee and felt a warm gush in his crotch.

"Oh, Jesus, Gordy," the hulk on the right said, "he's pissed himself."

All three men laughed, Lister almost hysterically.

Richard felt a blush of shame ignite on his face. He blinked hard and struggled to contain himself.

"Pick him up," Lister said, stepping closer. "My, my, Mr. Farmer. Your missus ain't going to be pleased with the state of your pants."

The big men laughed again.

"Let him go," Lister said. "Iowa and me need to chew the fat."

Richard took a deep breath as his arms were released. Then he ducked down and crunched his elbows into the groins of Lister's muscle men. They both keeled over. He smashed his knee into each of their faces as they dropped. Then he pulled the matte black pistol from the belt of the unconscious man on his left and racked the slide.

Lister had retreated to the far wall at speed. He was fumbling in his waistband, but gave up when he saw Richard bearing down on him, pistol raised.

"Put it on the floor."

Gordy Lister removed his snub-nosed revolver and laid it down carefully, a finger in the trigger guard. "Jeez, Iowa. Where'd you learn those moves?"

"Marine Corps," Richard said, picking up the revolver. He went back to the comatose forms and patted them down. He stuck the semiautomatic he found in his belt, along with Lister's weapon.

The newspaper man's face was pale. "How come you pissed yourself then?"

"I drank a gallon of coffee waiting for you, asshole."

"Yeah, well, if you're gonna tail people, you wanna get another vehicle."

Richard gave him a frozen look. "You reckon you're in a position to tell me what to do, dwarf?"

Lister raised his thin shoulders. "What's next? You gonna shoot me?"

Richard shook his head. "Nope. At least, not yet. You're going to tell me about my kids." He stepped closer. "And no more bullshit."

Gordy Lister shook his head. "You don't know what you're getting into, man. I'm telling you, back off. This thing's too big for you."

Richard Bonhoff glanced over his shoulder at the men on the floor. "Like they were too big for me?"

"No, Iowa, a thousand times bigger than them."

"Let's get started, then." Richard grabbed him by the arm and dragged him out of the basement. "We'll go in the pickup," he said, grinning. "I wouldn't bet on your wheels being here when you get back."

Lister's expression was slack. "You're a dead man, Iowa."

"I don't take kindly to threats, Gordy." Richard said, having a sudden glimpse of his wife. He wondered if she'd ever believe what he'd just done.

"I mean it. They'll do you and they'll do your kids."

The ex-marine opened the passenger door and shoved Lister inside. "You'd better help me find the twins." He jammed the pistol between the small man's thighs. "Or I'll give you back the voice you had when you were a kid. Free of charge."

Sixteen

After an hour and a half, the trailer's tires started to grind over gravel. According to the watch I'd stolen, it was ten to five. I had cut a small flap in the tarpaulin but, in the fading light, all I could see was pine trees. Although night had now fallen, I saw no lights and I could make out only more tree trunks ahead in the headlights. No other vehicles had passed, in either direction. The forest seemed to go on forever.

Despite the uneven surface, I couldn't stop myself from falling asleep. Faces flashed before me. One belonged to my friend Dave, as on the deer-hunting trip. The sight of him gave me a bad feeling, but I couldn't fathom why. I also saw my daughter, Lucy. Then I froze as the smiling face of the Soul Collector reared up before me. Sara Robbins. I knew she had been my lover, but I couldn't recall any details or images of that time. The only thing I was sure of was that she had sworn to kill me. Could she be involved with these people?

There was a crunching of gears and the vehicle slowed down. I looked out from the flap and again saw nothing but trees. Then we moved onto a smoother surface. I looked at my watch. Eight twenty-two. There was still no other traffic and no house lights, but the asphalt road suggested we were at last getting nearer to civilization. I lay back down as the speed increased. At least there was less chance of the load overturning on a flat road. I closed my eyes again.

"You-know-who" was still elusive, despite the glimpses of blond hair. Now it seemed to be tied back in some kind of clip. The impression I got was of severity. Could *she* have something to do with the camp?

The road might have had a flat surface, but it wasn't lacking in tight curves, not that the driver noticed. After a couple of sideways thrusts, the load finally shifted. I felt one of the ropes tying down the tarp give way as the logs jolted underneath me. I scrabbled with my fingers to find a solid surface and nearly got an arm stuck between the great lengths of wood. The brakes screeched as the men in the rig realized what was happening.

The trailer came to a halt. My heart was trying to break out of my chest, but I forced myself to concentrate. I heard the doors open upfront, and then the thump of boots as the men jumped down.

"Shit!" one of them said. "I told you you was going too fast."

"Shut the fuck up, Hal," said the driver. "Fuckin' smart-ass."

They moved around to the rear of the trailer.

"Coulda been worse." The driver's tone lightened. "Only one of the logs has moved. Reckon we can tie it down."

They were silent as they flung more ropes over the load and secured them.

"That oughta do it," the driver said, tugging on a rope that had come over the tarpaulin. It was tight across my chest and I could hardly breathe.

"I don't know, Jeff," said the man called Hal. "Don't look right to me. What if we spill the load on the highway? We could kill someone."

"We could kill someone," the driver repeated scornfully. "Shut the fuck up, you crybaby."

"Screw you," Hal said. I felt the rope tighten again, and then the log beneath me quiver. He had climbed up.

I watched through the flap as he approached, his flashlight illuminating parts of the tarp. Then I saw the long-barreled revolver in his other hand. I wondered if that was normal for a driver's mate and decided it wasn't likely. These guys had some connection with the camp. I was sure of it, even if they weren't wearing the gray uniform. I struggled hard to get a hand free and grip my pistol. It was useless. I kept still as he got nearer.

The light blazed in my eyes.

"Hey, Jeff, you notice a tear in the tarp?" Hal called.

"No, I didn't notice a tear in the tarp," the driver replied, his tone still derisive. "What do you fuckin' care, Hal? You didn't pay for it."

I screwed up my eyes as the tip of a boot poked into my groin. The flashlight was no longer in my eyes, but I saw plenty of bright lights. At least I managed not to cry out. The pressure remained as Hal kept up his examination. At last the boot was pulled back and I felt heavy steps moving away. Tears had filled my eyes.

Soon afterward, we got moving again. Jeff was a bit more careful with his speed, but the load still canted slightly on curves, which was enough to increase the pressure on my chest enormously. My ribs were being crushed and I began to panic. Then I remembered the combat knife. It was in its sheath on my belt. My right hand was close to it, but I could hardly move my arm. I felt the trailer edge back to the horizontal and waited for the pressure to lessen. It didn't. The load hadn't shifted back.

Now I really lost my cool. Mustering all the strength I could, I drove my arm downward. The tips of my fingers touched the haft. I shoved against the rope again and got hold of the knife, but I still had to pull it from the sheath. My ribs were about to shatter and I was gasping for breath.

For the first time since I'd escaped from the camp, I really thought I wasn't going to make it.

Then I saw her face. The blonde woman was less severe now. She was looking straight at me, her red lips forming into a smile. I still couldn't remember her name, but that didn't matter. I knew that she loved me and I her. That was enough.

I heaved my arm free and stabbed the knife upward through the tarpaulin, then dragged the blade toward my face. It stopped when it reached the rope. The pressure was still intense. I started sawing through the fibers, desperately forcing breath into my compressed lungs. The rope gave way and my ribs sprang outward; it was a few minutes before I got my heart rate back to something approaching normal.

I made longer cuts in the tarp and got myself out into the open air. The timber hadn't moved while I was cutting the rope. I could only hope it wouldn't do so at the next corner. Whatever happened, I wasn't going to let myself be tied down again. If I had to take on Hal and Jeff, so be it.

The truck and trailer moved on through the night. I could see all around me now, but that didn't help much. The road was still lined by pine trees and there was no sign of life. I glanced at my watch. It was coming up to nine in the evening. Maybe everyone went to bed early around here. Then again, I hadn't even seen any houses yet. There were telephone poles alongside the road, and the idea that at least there was a phone system gave me some encouragement. I lay back down, this time on top of the tarp, and tried to recall the woman who had inspired me. What was her name? I said my own aloud, trying to hear how we would have been as a couple. *Matt and... Matt and his partner... Matt and his wife...?* Nothing. At least I could still see the face, with its prominent cheekbones and gray eyes. She seemed to have a habitually serious expression. When it softened, the eyes remained intense. I heard the thrum of the engine fade and the wind on my face weaken.

Suddenly I found myself in a place I couldn't immediately identify, an area of rolling hills and deciduous trees, an idyllic safe haven....

...birds are singing and a light breeze is blowing over the surrounding slopes. We've driven through picturesque small towns, and past prosperous farms, old stone houses and outbuildings. There are the peaks of numerous hills to the left of the road, the trees on their flanks covered by leaves in shades of yellow, red and brown. We stop at several overlooks, as the guidebook calls them. We are in the Shenandoah Valley in Virginia: valleys, cliffs, banks of cloud rising up the slopes to reveal cone-shaped summits, rocky peaks, even a waterfall.

We find a parking place and take the picnic basket we've brought, following a path through the trees until we come to a meadow. There seems to be no one else around. We throw the blanket onto grass that the midday sun has dried, but the bite in the air means we keep on our fleece jackets.

"Isn't this a paradise on earth, Matt?" the woman says, sipping chilled wine from the plastic cup I passed her.

"Better than Washington any day."

She nods. "Too much work."

"Speak for yourself." I laugh and take the plate she hands over.

"I thought you were working, too," she says, raising an eyebrow.

"I am," I assure her, suddenly on the defensive. "I told you, Joe Greenbaum's giving me a lot of useful stuff."

"Good," she says. "I wouldn't like to think you're taking a holiday while I'm slaving away with the FBI."

We eat smoked ham, cheese and fresh bread that we bought in one of the pretty towns. There's fruit, too, and the pale brown pancakes I can never resist. When we finish, we clear away the plates and stretch out on the rug.

She takes my hand. "You know, Matt, I could almost give up work and come to live here."

"According to the book, it's a tourist trap every weekend and all summer."

She digs her elbow into my ribs. "Typical. Can't you let a girl dream?"

I laugh. "How long would you last without a juicy case to get your teeth into?"

"Work isn't everything, you know," she says, raising herself up on one elbow.

"Is that right?" I lean over to kiss her on the lips. "I'll try to remember that." I get up. "Excuse me while I go and look for the little boys' tree."

She laughs. "Keep an eye out for the little girls' equivalent, will you?"

I make a carefree skip as I head for the nearby glade.

"And, Matt?" she calls.

I turn to look at her.

"I'm ashamed to say it in the open, but I love you."

I grin. "And so you should be."

"Is that it?" she says, as I keep walking.

"I'm desperate," I say, over my shoulder.

"You're not kidding," she shouts.

I relent as I reach the tree line. "I love you, too," I shout back.

She raises her hand.

When I walk back across the meadow, I can't see her. At first I assume she's lying down, but as I get closer I see that she isn't there. The rug is as I left it, the bag of paper plates and garbage beyond undisturbed.

I see myself from above, shouting her name and running about like a deranged animal. I look at the grass around the blanket, I call her number on my cell phone, I sink to my knees and beat the ground in anguish.

That's the last time I see her.

I go back to the spot several times, with uniformed men and with people in plain clothes. Other times I return on my own.

None of us finds the slightest trace.

I was back on the load of timber, trying to make sense of what I'd remembered. The woman, what had happened to her? What had we been doing in Washington, when I had understood that I lived in London, Great Britain? And this Joe Greenbaum? What was it he had been giving me? I couldn't bring him to mind at all. I remembered the FBI, though. Why was the woman I loved working with the Federal Bureau of Investigation? Was she a police officer? A lawyer?

Then the engine revved and the truck and trailer slowed. I looked ahead and saw lights. Civilization. I had made it. I would be able to find help. I shouldered the rifle and crawled to the rear.

I took in a sign by the roadside. Sparta, Maine, it read. Population 2,360. Elevation 673 feet. If I was lucky, there might even be a police station. At least I had an idea of where Maine was—up by the Canadian border. What the hell was I doing up here? As far as I remembered, it wasn't anywhere near Washington, never mind Virginia. I needed to get hold of a map.

The truck reduced speed even more, and then slowed into a petrol station. There was a kiosk selling food and drink, but I still had some supplies and I needed to find someone in authority. I lowered myself toward the ground and took cover behind a garbage container. There wasn't much sign of life, but I was still hesitant about walking down the road with the assault rifle over my shoulder. Maybe I'd be taken for a hunter. Then again, I was wearing the gray uniform of the North American National Revival. It would be interesting to see how the locals reacted. What if the camp had people in Sparta? What if this whole town belonged to the NANR?

I compromised by taking off the jacket and draping it over the rifle. Although the night was cold, I'd been through worse recently. I started to walk toward the center of the town and some bright lights up ahead. Clapboard houses lined both sides of the road, some in decent shape and some not. The cars and pickups outside each place matched the building's condition. There wasn't much money being made in Sparta.

I could hear muted sounds of music, the sentimental country laments beloved of truckers. But before I got there, I heard a different sound from behind a derelict, unlit house to my right. I knew immediately that the anguished moan came from a woman in distress. The fact that it was cut off abruptly made me pull the jacket off my rifle and move into the shadows.

"Stop your crying, bitch." The loud whisper was followed by a dull slap.

"Yeah," came another voice. "You'll have your mouth full soon enough."

I got to the edge of the wall and looked around it cautiously. In the dimly lit area at the end of an overgrown path I made out a figure sprawled on the ground, bare white legs splayed. Two men bent over the woman, pulling at the remains of her clothing. There was a tearing sound and the upper part of her body was exposed.

"Shit, Billy Ray, she ain't wearing no bra," said one of the assailants with a cackle.

"Well, get your lips on those titties, man."

"Don't even think about it," I said, walking round the corner and holding the rifle on them. "Hands in the air."

They turned toward me and stared. When they saw the weapon, they complied, slowly.

"Look what we got here, Bobbie," said one of them, licking his lips and giving me a slack smile.

"Feels like we're back in Texas, Billy Ray. Ain't that a M16?"

I stopped about five yards in front of them. I wasn't too keen on firing the weapon in town and reckoned I could take them whatever they tried.

"You guys from Texas?" I asked.

They nodded. They were both heavily built and red faced, and substantially the worse for drink.

"Thought I smelled cow shit." I grinned at them. "You fancied swinging your tiny dicks at a woman for a change, uh?"

They came at me surprisingly fast. I turned the rifle sideways and raised it like a weight lifter pumping the bar. One of them got the muzzle in his throat, the other the butt. They hit the ground, gasping feebly.

"All done?" I asked.

The one called Billy Ray suddenly had a switchblade in his hand. I clubbed him with the rifle stock and then followed through to make contact with the other man's head. They went down again. This time they were unconscious.

I moved to the woman. She was sitting up, and wearing only socks and panties.

"Are you okay?" I asked.

She nodded. One of her eyes had already started swelling.

"Just a second." I ran back and picked up my jacket, then put it round her shoulders. "Can you get up?"

"Yes." Her voice was faint.

I held her under one arm and she got to her feet without too much difficulty.

I looked at her face and saw that she was fairly young, probably in her late twenties. Her short blond hair was mussed and her face was dirty, but I could still make out that she was a looker. She was holding one arm over her breasts.

"Who are you?" she said, looking at me intently.

I could smell that she'd been drinking, too.

"Just passing through," I answered. "You meet these fools in the bar?"

"They were in there, but I didn't talk to them. Guess they must have followed me out." She touched the skin around her eye and winced.

"Did you get hit anywhere else?"

She shook her head. "No, the assholes didn't get that far."

I picked up what was left of her clothing. "Don't know if this is much use."

She threw away a badly ripped shirt and pulled on her jeans. There was a tear under the waistband and dirt on the legs.

"Do you live here?" I asked.

She nodded. "Schoolteacher. But I'm from Portland. This hellhole is my first job."

"Is there a police station?"

She looked at me curiously. "Where are you from?"

"London."

"London, England?"

"Yes." I smiled.

"Nice," she said, still ill at ease but smiling back at me as she slipped on her shoes. "Always wanted to visit." She twitched her head. "Police? Yeah, there's a state troopers' station."

"Maybe we should head over there," I suggested, taking her arm.

She tugged it free gently. "I'm Mary Upson," she said, extending her right hand. "Thanks a lot."

"Matt," I said, instantly feeling half-naked, since I couldn't remember my surname.

She waited and then shrugged. "Mystery man, huh? All right, Matt, let's go. It's about fifty yards beyond the bar."

I was wondering what to do about the M16. I decided that slinging it over my shoulder was the least-threatening way of carrying it. At least Mary Upson didn't seem bothered by it. Hunters in the area probably carried rifles all the time. I glanced down at my belt. They probably didn't carry Glocks. I slipped the pistol round to the small of my back. At least it wouldn't look at first glance as if I was carrying out a frontal assault on the police station. Mary also didn't seem bothered by the gray uniform.

"What about...what about them?" she asked, glancing back.

I stopped in my tracks. "Good point. Want to take any private revenge?"

She looked tempted for a few moments, then shook her head.

"Hold this," I said, handing her the rifle. I kneeled down and unzipped the would-be rapists' jeans. Then I pulled them off, prompting a groan from one. I managed to secure their wrists and ankles with the trouser legs. I took the cell phones, wallets and keys that I found in their pockets, as well as Billy Ray's switchblade. No doubt the authorities would look after the valuables.

I got to my feet and turned toward the schoolteacher. For a moment I thought she was holding the rifle on me with intent to fire. Then she handed it back with a smile.

"Let's go and see the troopers," she said.

"Right," I said.

We both had pretty good stories for the representatives of the law in the small town of Sparta, Maine.

Seventeen

Detectives Simmons and Pinker were on one side of the conference table on the fifth floor of the Metro Police building in Washington, D.C., FBI agents Sebastian and Maltravers on the other. Chief of Detectives Rodney Owen, thinner than the most ascetic of monks, the pale skin stretched tight over the bones of his face, sat at the head.

"Clem?" the chief said. "You want to bring us up to speed?"

Simmons nodded, then started to run through what had been done in the Monsieur Hexie case. The victim had been officially identified by the woman who cleaned the shop, a Tennessee native who didn't seem too surprised by the murder. According to her, folks who played with fire ended up getting burned. It turned out she didn't have anything specific in mind but, as a devout Baptist, she thought that "voodoo and all that mumbo jumbo was an offence to the Lord." However, she was in her seventies and had cried when she saw the victim's face. Living with a daughter who taught grade school, she wasn't any kind of suspect.

"Canvassing hasn't gotten us much," Simmons went on. "You know how it is in Shaw. Nobody wants to talk to us."

"You think maybe she saw more than she's saying?" the chief asked.

"Doubt it, sir. But even if she did, I don't think she'll come out with it."

Owen sighed. "That neighborhood is supposed to have gotten better."

Simmons glanced at Pinker. He was tugging on his cuffs, displaying a pair of cuff links that must have cost him most of last month's salary. Clem nudged his partner; they'd agreed beforehand that they would share the presentation.

"Yeah, right," Gerard Pinker said, looking at the file in front of him. "You've all seen copies of the M.E.'s preliminary findings and what we've got from the CSIs so far."

"Which doesn't amount to much," Peter Sebastian said, narrowing his eyes. "Would you gentlemen care to put this murder in context with that of the singer who called himself Loki? Indeed, do you have anything further to report on that case?"

Simmons leaned forward, his eyes warning Pinker off. "Apart from the skewers, the most obvious common factor is the drawings." He paused as the others found their copies of the pages attached to the bodies. "As you can see, they're similar in terms of the shapes, but the layout is different."

"Is there some occult meaning, do you think?" Chief Owen asked.

"Voodoo?" Pinker said, smiling at his partner.

"Nothing strikes me," Simmons said, shaking his head. "I've checked my books."

"Do you have any inkling of what the shapes might mean?" The FBI man's tone was almost neutral, but the hint of authority was plain enough.

"Do *you?*" Pinker riposted.

"We're looking into it," Sebastian said, glancing at his assistant.

Dana Maltravers nodded. "Copies have been passed to

our Document Analysis Unit. They have a database of symbols and signs."

"A database, eh?" Pinker said with a grin. "That's great. When can we expect the killer's name, address and social security number?"

"Detective," the chief said sharply.

Pinker raised his hands.

"You bring up a significant point," Sebastian said. "Are we right to assume the same person was responsible for both murders? There were no fingerprints at the first scene, were there?"

Simmons shook his head. "No footprints, either."

"So even if the CSIs identify what they found at Monsieur Hexie's—and they haven't yet—we can't be sure that killer also dispatched Loki."

Maltravers looked at her boss. "Apart from the M.O.s, sir," she said, in a low voice.

Sebastian held his gaze on Pinker. "We've already talked about the double murder weapons."

"And what was the consensus?" Chief Owen asked, pen raised over his notes.

Pinker smiled. "Well, sir, Clem thinks maybe the killer has a thing about twosomes." He grimaced as his partner's boot struck his shin.

Dana Maltravers broke the subsequent silence. "It's rare for two weapons to be used, particularly in successive cases."

"It's also rare for ears and kidneys to be pierced with such a degree of accuracy," Owen said. "No practice cuts, no miscues." He looked at the FBI woman. "What does your database tell you about that, Special Agent?"

"We don't need a computer to tell us that this is a highly skilled operator," Sebastian said. "That's one reason why the Bureau is involved in the investigations."

Pinker gave him a suspicious look. "What, in case the killer is some kind of prize exhibit?" He looked around the table. "Has it occurred to anyone here that maybe the significance of the number two is that the guy's stopping after the second murder?"

There was another silence.

"That would be very gratifying," Sebastian said, giving the detective a tight smile. "But it would still leave you with the task of catching that individual for these two murders."

"Cool it, Vers," Simmons said before his partner could answer.

"Very well," the chief said, eyeing the detectives dubiously before turning to the FBI man. "Dr. Gilbert will be starting the PM shortly. Anything else we need to discuss?"

"Actually, there is, Chief Owen." Sebastian stood up and passed a sheet of paper to each of them. "I took the liberty of sending one of our crime-scene people to Monsieur Hexie's apartment." He shrugged. "No reason not to make use of the Bureau's resources. Anyway, he discovered a set of fingerprints on a candleholder under the bed."

"You saying our people missed it?" Pinker said.

The FBI man shook his head. "I'm sure they'll report it in due course. But I very much doubt that you will have any record of this person's prints."

"So who is this Matthew John Wells?" Simmons asked, looking up from the sheet.

"That's where the story gets interesting," Sebastian said.

"So, are you going to tell us?" Pinker asked, when the agent kept quiet.

Peter Sebastian frowned at him and then nodded. "Of course I'm going to give you the details. They're already being distributed to law enforcement agencies all over the country."

As he elaborated, the faces of Rodney Owen, Clem Simmons and Gerard Pinker took on expressions ranging from surprise to sheer disbelief.

Eighteen

When the siblings were brought to the U.S., their father said they should never forget where they came from—but also that they should never mention it. After a year of lessons at home from tutors, they were allowed to attend school. Not the local institution of learning, but a private school in upstate New York, where there were many twins. It was clear from the start that they were both exceptionally able.

In a reversal of the usual way, it was the girl who proved to be better at the sciences, while the boy excelled at the arts and, later, at business studies. By the time they left school—both in the top percentile of their year—they had decided what they wanted to do. Their father supported them in every possible way, taking them on trips to the universities they were considering, and even managing a week's holiday that summer. The three of them spent it in Washington, D.C., visiting their adopted nation's monuments and museums. Both twins were so enthused by the city that they vowed to set up home there someday.

In the meantime, they had their studies to pursue. The boy passed at the top of his classes in both literature and business, while his sister was declared to be one of the most promising neuroscientists to appear in years. Within a decade, the boy had established the company that was now one of the biggest media corporations in America, while the girl was a full professor at an Ivy League university.

And then the tragedy happened. They were driving home for Christmas after a weekend in the Catskills, the boy at the wheel of an Italian sports car, when he lost control on an icy mountain road. The vehicle broke through a barrier and fell over two hundred feet, before bursting into flames.

Their father took the news of the accident very badly. He buried his offspring in a cemetery in Washington, D.C., remembering how much they had loved the city. He also wanted to commemorate their lives in the capital of the nation he knew they would have brought great honor to. It was said that the twins' badly burned bodies were found hand in hand, the bones fused by the intense heat.

The old man, already suffering from prostate cancer, passed away three months after his children. He was buried in the same plot. The gravestones did not bear the names that any of them had borne in the land of their birth.

Nineteen

As Mary Upson and I walked down the road to the troopers' station, I felt her eyes on me.

"Is this some kind of uniform?" she asked, looking at the jacket round her shoulders.

I shrugged, unwilling to go into details with a stranger.

"All right," she said, "try this one. Why are you toting that rifle? It looks kind of military."

I glanced at her. "Hunting," I said. "Just caught me a pair of Texan bushwhackers."

Mary Upson smiled. "You English and your crazy humor," she said. "Is there anything you're serious about?"

The lights of the state troopers' station were close now. I was about to get very serious indeed, but taking the rifle in with me probably wasn't a great idea. I stopped and put it down behind a bush by the steps.

"Smart," Mary said. "Ready?"

I nodded and went up to the door. The building was a standard wooden house that had been converted. There were bars on all the windows. I shivered, remembering the wire around the camp—and the ill-fated man who had helped me get over it.

We rang a bell and waited to be admitted. I looked up and mugged at a CCTV camera. Then the door opened.

"Evening, folks," said a young man in uniform, a semiautomatic pistol holstered on his belt. "What can I do for you?" He took in Mary's face and clothes. "Ms. Upson, what happened to you?"

"Hello, Stu," she said. "I was hoping you'd be on tonight."

The trooper's eyes moved to me. They weren't friendly.

"This is Matt. He helped me out."

"Oh, right," the trooper said. The badge on his chest proclaimed his name to be Stu Condon. He had fair hair in a crew cut and his upper arms were trying to break out of his pale yellow shirt. "Come and sit down. Tell me what happened."

We followed him into what would have been the sittingroom. There was a scuffed leather sofa and matching armchair around a low coffee table. Mary and I took the sofa.

"I've just made a pot of coffee," the young man said. "You want some?"

We both nodded. When he was out of the room, Mary drew the gray uniform jacket tighter and started to sob quietly.

"Hey," I said, touching her hand. "It's over. Those guys aren't going anywhere. They certainly can't hurt you now."

She gradually got a hold of herself and calmed down. I looked around for the trooper, but he was still behind the security door that blocked us off from the station's interior. There was a box of tissues on a shelf.

"Here," I said, handing her one. "You'll feel better when you get some coffee inside you."

"Thanks, Matt," she said, after she'd dried her eyes. "It's just…it's just, those men were so horrible. Like animals. And I'm kind of isolated up here. I don't have any close friends."

I thought about Billy Ray and Bobbie. They might have woken up by now. It would be a good idea if Trooper Condon picked them up before they started making a noise. But producing coffee for citizens in distress seemed to be exercising all of his talents.

In the station office, Stu Condon was examining the pages he had just printed out. He was keen about his career and he wouldn't normally have kept people waiting outside. Before the bell had rung, he'd been going through the daily wanted notices. He always paid particular attention to those issued by the FBI, because he harbored ambitions of joining the Bureau once he had a few years' experience. His eye had landed on the photo of Matthew John Wells. It wasn't often that Englishmen appeared in the notices. But he hadn't immediately realized that the man with Mary Upson was him, even when she'd introduced him as Matt. He was dirty and unshaven, his clothes scruffy. There was no doubt in his mind now, though. The question was, did he call for backup? Sergeant Johnson lived ten miles away, while Denny Morris would have swallowed the best part of a crate of beer by now. Anyway, this was exactly the kind of arrest that would get him noticed by the Bureau.

Stu was on his way to the door with a tray of coffee, when it struck him that he should call the number on the bottom of the wanted notice. He thought about it, but there was no instruction not to approach the man, as there was with escaped murderers and the like. Still, this guy was suspected of two seriously violent killings in Washington. He made up his mind. He could handle Mr. Matthew Wells no problem.

To be on the safe side, he unfastened the strap on his holster. If Mary hadn't been there, he'd have gone in with his Glock in both hands. With any luck, there would be a chance to draw later on. His heart skipped a beat. Mary would definitely be impressed if he took in a man suspected of two murders. Mary. She was a real honey.

It was time for Stuart Bellingham Condon to show just how good a lawman he was.

* * *

The instant the trooper walked through the door, I knew he meant me no good. Although he busied himself with handing out mugs of coffee, there was something in his expression that hadn't been there before, an almost breathless excitement. When I saw that the strap on his holster was undone, I knew my intuition was right. I took a sip of the brew—surprisingly good—then pushed my gut forward and feigned a pain in the small of my back. Slipping my right hand round, I got the fingers on the grip of the pistol. So far, I'd only attacked people who had been a threat to me or, as with Mary, had been behaving like animals. Taking on a representative of the law was a big step.

I listened as Mary told the young man about the attempted rape. He seemed to be paying attention, but his eyes were continually flicking toward me. Mary told him that I had rescued her, so he had no reason to be suspicious. Then I thought about the gray uniform. Could the people who ran the camp have some sort of pull with the local law? I wasn't about to take a chance on that.

Trooper Condon nodded at Mary and then turned to me.

"Care to give me your full name, sir?" he said, taking some folded papers from his breast pocket.

That was a tester. I said the first names that came to mind. "Em, Matthew James Page."

"And where are you from, Mr...Page."

That brief hesitation, and the glance directed at the papers he'd just unfolded, were enough to tell me that he knew more about my identity than I did. Was I a criminal? All the thoughts I'd had about my shooting and fighting abilities came back in a rush. My memory was so full of blanks that I could have assassinated the U.S. president and not been aware of it. But my survival instinct overrode all those suspicions. Whatever my

previous actions, I hadn't deserved what had been done
to me in the camp—like the man at the fence hadn't deserved execution.

Trooper Condon's eyes opened wide as I brought the
Glock to bear on him. I took a step forward and relieved him
of his own weapon, sticking it in my pocket. Out of the corner of my eye, I could see Mary Upson's face. Her lips
were apart, but otherwise she seemed surprisingly calm.

"Sir, I would caution you—"

"Forget it, Trooper." I pulled the papers from his hand.
There was a photo of me on the top one that stirred something in my memory. Compared with how I'd appeared in
the mirror in the cabin, this image gave the impression of
a well-fed, well-groomed, slightly arrogant type. The
leather jacket I was wearing must have cost plenty.

"Sir—"

"I said forget it. Get hold of your cuffs."

"What?" The trooper was either playing dumb or had
been gripped by fear.

"Your handcuffs." I moved the Glock nearer to his chest.
"Slowly, Stu."

"Right," he said, moving one hand round his belt.

"Put one on." I waited till he'd complied, then took his
arm and pulled him across to the wall. There was a heating
unit there. I hooked the other cuff around a pipe and closed
it. Then I patted his pockets and removed his phone and a
set of keys. "You want me to hit you?" I asked.

"Huh?"

I smiled. "So it doesn't look so bad to your superiors."

The look he gave me could have felled a buffalo.
"You're forgetting something, Mr. Wells," he said slowly.
"Mary here's a witness."

He was right. I hadn't considered what to do about her.
"Stay here," I said to her. "Let me have as long as you think
I deserve." I knew that was a risk, but I had the feeling she'd

give me a break—at least for the time it would take me to find some transport.

Mary Upson didn't respond. She held her eyes on me, gaze unwavering. I couldn't tell what she felt about me. It was a risk cutting her loose, but I didn't want to make the evening even worse for her.

"Take care of yourself," I said, smiling.

Then I turned and headed for the door.

I picked up the rifle outside and ran down the deserted street, discarding the Texans' phones and other gear. There were cars and pickups outside the nearest houses, but I wanted to put some distance between myself and the station first—if Condon didn't know which vehicle I'd taken, it would buy me some time. As I ran, I glanced down at the page with my photo. Beneath it was printed a name. Matthew John Wells. Wells. That was my surname. I still didn't remember it, but it seemed to fit. Matt Wells. Yes, I was sure that was who I was. Then I saw the reason I was wanted—suspicion of a murder committed in Washington, D.C., on October 29, 2009. The notification had been issued by the violent-crime unit of the FBI. I slowed to a jog. Jesus. Assuming the date was recent, and it squared with the autumn climate and conditions, I was in the clear. Then again, the only people who could vouch for me wore gray uniforms and killed people. What the hell was going on?

Suddenly, in front and to my right, there came the roar of an engine and the shriek of tires. A dark green sedan shot out of a side road and slid to a halt. The passenger door swung open.

"Get in!" Mary Upson yelled.

Something whistled past my head, then I heard a loud boom. I looked back down the road and saw the trooper. He'd got free and armed himself with a rifle. Another shot whizzed past as I threw myself into the car.

"Bloody hell!" I gasped.

Mary had her foot to the floor. She laughed as she glanced in the mirror. "That what you English say when you're under fire?"

I had my head as far down the seat as I could get, waiting for the rear windscreen to explode. To my relief, it didn't. A few seconds later, the road went left and we were out of the town center.

"You can sit up now," she said, a slack smile on her lips.

"How did the Lone Ranger get free?" I asked, stowing the rifle in front of the backseat.

"Search me. I left not long after you."

I looked at her. "So you're in the shit, as well."

Mary Upson shrugged. "Never did like that scumbag Condon. He came on to me once in the bar and wouldn't take no for an answer."

I reckoned that was a pretty weak reason for helping a wanted man, but I didn't have any alternative means of escape right now.

"What does it say in those papers he had?"

I told her about the murder in Washington.

Mary glanced at me quizzically. "When did it happen? Yesterday night? You get the early morning flight up here?"

"Thanks for the vote of confidence. As a matter of fact, I wasn't in Washington yesterday."

"That's a relief," she said, grinning. "I'd hate to think I was on the road with a killer."

I looked at her. "Why are you helping me, Mary?"

She met my gaze briefly. "Because you helped me."

"Simple as that?"

"Sure. What you did wasn't a small thing, Matt. Those Texan shitheads would have raped me, might have killed me. You saw the knife."

I nodded. "Which is why we went to the state troopers."

She shot me another glance. "Which is why *I* went to the troopers. Why did *you* go? And don't say you—"

"Shit," I interrupted. "The Texans are still tied up."

"Like I give a flying fuck. Do you?"

For some reason, I did. Then I thought of all I had been through in the forest and let that concern go.

"You can let me out anywhere you like," I said. "You can tell the trooper I threatened you."

She laughed. "Yeah, he'll buy that. I left the station on my own and I picked you up on my own. What kind of threat are you supposed to have made? Bring your car or I'll shoot up the bar?"

I glanced at the pines lining the highway. "That would do. It rhymes, too." I gave her a serious look. "Come on, Mary. Go back while you still can."

"Ah, screw it," she said with a wild laugh. "I could do with a vacation." Then her expression got more serious. "Besides," she said, catching my eye. "You're no killer. You could have hurt those Texans much worse than you did. You could have shot Stu Condon, too. Plus, you wouldn't have come with me to the station if you were on the run." She laughed again, this time more softly. "Looks like I've got myself a genuine lost cause. Want to tell me what's going on?"

I considered that and decided that, given the risk she was taking with her liberty, she deserved some kind of an explanation. Then again, what good would it do? In addition to the people from the camp, I had the FBI after me. I should surrender myself to the representatives of federal law, but no way was I going to do that. Someone was framing me and I intended to find out who. Then a thought struck me. What if my memory was playing games with me and I really had killed those people in Washington? What if I was a killer with no awareness of my actions?

Eventually I concentrated on telling Mary Upson my story, basically just the part about the cabin. I was still confused about the camp and was hoping I'd remember more details soon, so I avoided that subject. I also avoided mentioning my limited recall of my past, and that glimpses of memory came and went.

"What *is* that uniform, anyway?" Mary Upson asked.

I had been watching her face surreptitiously. So far there had been no indication that she was playing a part. Ever since she'd picked me up, I'd been wondering about her motivation. Could the people who ran the camp have people working for them as far away as Sparta? Could she be one of the bastards?

"I'm not sure," I said. "Have you ever heard of the North American National Revival?" She was still wearing the jacket I'd given her. I touched her shoulder.

She shook her head. "What is that? Some kind of militia?"

"They're certainly keen on bearing arms."

Mary Upson glanced in the mirror and then took a right turn. Almost immediately we were deep in woodland.

"What's going on?" I asked, my hand immediately on the grip of my pistol.

"Time for a change of vehicle."

We came into a clearing, the moon shining through thin clouds. I could see a low building in the headlights. Mary pulled up in front of the house and opened her door. "Coming?" she said.

I got out, holding the pistol against my thigh.

Then a figure holding a shotgun appeared at the side of the house to my right. The weapon was at the person's shoulder before I could do anything with mine.

Twenty

"**Y**ou really sure you wanna go through with this, Iowa?"

Richard Bonhoff stared at Gordy Lister, and then nodded. They were in the pickup, outside a dilapidated warehouse in southeast Washington. The newspaperman had made several phone calls, saying it was better if Richard didn't listen in. The upshot was that he'd managed to locate the twins—or so he said.

"This isn't far from where that Loki singer was murdered, is it?" Richard said.

"True enough," Lister said. "We're about a mile away." He nudged Richard. "Hey, did you read about that in the *Star Reporter?* We did a big story."

Richard glowered at him. "I never read that rag," he said, deciding not to admit that he'd seen the story there.

"It was good enough for your kids, Iowa," Lister replied, grinning.

"Yeah, that's where their problems started. What exactly are we doing here?"

"You want to see the twins, don't you? Hold on. They'll be out soon."

"They in there?" Richard peered at the building. "Why can't we go in?"

"Because it isn't safe."

"How come you know where they are?" All Richard's various suspicions of Gordy Lister surfaced at once. He grabbed the smaller man by the throat. "Are you using them? Are you making money off them?"

Lister struggled free and gave Richard a scandalized look. "Of course not. I used my contacts to find them, that's all."

The farmer wasn't convinced, but he had no other leads.

"Here we go." Lister pointed and they watched as a door opened wide. A head appeared, scanning the vicinity. The pickup was scrutinized.

"Whatever you do, don't get out, Iowa. They won't talk to you—I guarantee it."

Richard's heart was thundering. He watched as young people came out of the warehouse. Most were black, dressed in the uniform of the street—basketball shoes, loose jeans hung low, oversize T-shirts. But the clothes were torn and dirty, and the kids didn't look healthy.

"Who are these people?"

Lister raised a hand. "Wait," he hissed.

And then Richard saw them. He strained forward as Randy came out. Gwen was right behind him. They both looked terrible, their faces drawn and their hair, longer than when he'd last seen them, lank and tangled.

"What's happened to them?" he said desperately.

Gordy Lister snorted. "What do you fucking think has happened to them, Iowa? They're junkies."

Richard grabbed the door handle and got out. He started to run toward the twins, shouting their names. They looked around, their eyes wide. As he got closer, it was the eyes that got to him most—the pupils were yellowed and blood-shot, the overall effect as icy and empty as the sky in winter.

"Gwen! Randy!" he called. "Let me talk to you."

But the twins looked away, linking hands. Richard saw that their arms were bruised and pockmarked. Then he doubled up as one of the black youths drove a fist into his midriff.

"Get away, old man!" the boy screeched. "Ain't no place for daddies here."

Richard raised his head and saw the twins walking away. He screamed their names again, and then took a heavy punch to the side of his head. He keeled over and the kicking started. He tried to shout, but soon he couldn't raise a sound. He could only mouth his children's names as a final blow to the head sent him lurching into the dark.

He woke up with his head pounding, unclear where he was.

"Don't say I didn't warn you, Iowa."

Richard blinked and took in Gordy Lister's face. There was a weak smile on the newspaperman's lips.

"Wha…?" He sank back. He opened his eyes again and realized that he was in the passenger seat of his pickup.

"Where are you staying?" Lister asked, starting the engine.

The name of his hotel swam up to the surface of Richard's mind. He managed to whisper it.

The pickup moved off, gears crashing. "Jesus, you actually drove all the way from Iowa in this?"

"Stop!" Richard gasped, remembering the twins. "I need to talk to my kids."

"Forget it," Lister said. "You saw the crowd they're with. You want to get yourself killed?"

"What's it to you?"

"What's it to me?" Lister said, shaking his head. "Exactly what do you think I am? Some kind of animal?"

Richard didn't reply. He was wondering if he had the strength to open the door and roll out when the pickup was still moving.

"Look, Iowa," the newspaperman went on, glancing at

his passenger. "Let me level with you. I feel bad about what's happened to your kids. I liked them, really I did. I even tried to set them up with some advertising work."

"Yeah," Richard mumbled, "there's always a market for good-looking twins."

Gordy Lister looked at him again. "That's right. You know more than I thought." He raised his narrow shoulders. "But they got sucked into the drug scene. I've seen it happen before with kids from Hicksville. No offense."

"Fuck you," Richard said to himself. A thought struck him. "Take me to the police, will you?"

There was a sharp intake of breath from Lister. "Whoa, man. What do you think the cops are gonna do? The twins are twenty-one, they're adults. The cops will just give you the brush-off."

Richard sat up slowly, looking out at the lights of the city. For someone who supposedly had only known the kids for a few days, and that months ago, Gordy Lister was very specific about their age. Richard decided against insisting. Tomorrow, he'd go to the cops alone.

At the hotel, Lister put a hand on his arm. "You all right, Iowa? Need any help getting to your room?"

Richard pulled his arm away, the small man's touch burning like a snake bite. "Get the hell out of my pickup."

"Okay, okay," Lister said, opening the driver's door. "Sorry I asked." He turned back and caught Richard's eye. "There's nothing you can do here. You have a good trip home, you hear, Iowa?"

The farmer watched him walk away, then hail a passing cab. For all the fake concern, Richard knew for sure that the newspaperman had a serious interest in the twins.

Twenty-One

"Drop it!" The voice was high and harsh.

I glanced at Mary. She raised her shoulders. I let the pistol slide out of my hand and fall to the gravel.

"Now step away!"

I complied again. The figure came nearer and I realized it was an elderly woman, her white hair pulled back to reveal a heavily wrinkled face.

"You all right, Mary?" the woman asked.

"Yes, Mom. It's okay—he's with me."

I turned to the woman next to me. "This is your mother?" She nodded with a sweet smile.

"What's he doing with a semiautomatic pistol in his hand?" the old woman demanded.

"You might have told me," I protested.

"She took me by surprise, too. She used to be a pretty good shot, but I'm not sure that still applies."

"You mind your mouth, girl," her mother said, lowering the shotgun. "I'll have you know I killed three crows yesterday."

Mary raised her hands. "All right, Mom, I believe you." She came round to my side of the car. "This is Matt."

"Pleased to meet you," I said, extending my hand.

The old woman took it after a pause, her pale blue eyes scrutinizing me. "Where you from?" she demanded.

"London, England. All right if I pick up my gun now, Mrs. Upson?"

She leveled the shotgun. "I'm watching you. And don't call me that—I'm not an Upson."

"Ms. Jacobsen," Mary whispered.

"Mary's father upped and left me for one of his fancy women when she was six," the old woman said, allowing her daughter to take her weapon to my relief. "Beats me why she uses his name."

Mary shrugged. "Whatever he did, he's still my father." She took her mother by the arm. "Come in. Let's get you inside. It's a cold night."

She was right. I had only the uniform shirt on my upper body and I was shivering. I followed them inside. We went into a cozy sitting room where the wallpaper was faded and the paint flaking, but it was clean. And it wasn't a concrete cell.

"You sit here, Mom. Matt and I need to sort out the cars. All right if I borrow yours?" She headed for the door without waiting for a reply.

"You do what you want, girl," her mother said. "You always did."

I went back outside and helped Mary.

Although her mother's dark green Ford pickup must have been over a decade old, it was in good shape and it started the first time. I drove it out of a ramshackle shed and watched as Mary drove her car in.

"Now we're as anonymous as you like," she said when she'd finished. "It'll take the cops some time to link me to this place. Mom's only been here a couple of months."

I looked at her. "Why are you doing this, Mary?"

She returned my gaze, her eyes wide. "Can't a girl do what she can for an innocent man?" The doubt I was feeling about myself must have been obvious. "You are innocent, aren't you?"

"I think so."

"You *think* so?" She laughed. "That makes me feel a whole lot better."

I grasped her forearm. "Look, I'm in deep shit and I have no idea why. You should steer well clear of me."

Mary's lips twitched. "Too late, Matt. Once I've bitten the hook, I don't let go."

That struck me as a strange way of putting things but she headed back inside before I could comment.

"Anything to eat, Mom?" she asked, back in the sitting room.

"You're in luck, girl. I made a pot roast today, your favorite." The old woman's face was split by an unexpectedly sweet smile.

Mary smiled. "Okay, I'll get things ready."

"Want any help?" I asked.

She shook her head. "Nope. You chat with Mom." She smiled mischievously. "Tell her what you've been up to in the woods."

Ms. Jacobsen watched her daughter walk out, and then turned to me. "Sit down, Matt. Well, what *have* you been up to in the woods? What is that, some kind of uniform?"

I shook my head. "Just hiking gear," I said, lamely. "I...got lost and couldn't get my bearings for a couple of days."

"You were safe enough, though."

"I'm sorry?"

"Your gun," she said, frowning. "You English boys always go walking with Glocks in your belts?"

"Em..."

"Never mind." She got up and came over to me. "I don't want to know the details. You listen to me, Matt—if that's your real name. My Mary's had a troubled life. She's too trusting. This isn't the first time she's got involved with a man most parents would have shot before he got inside."

"But I'm not your daughter's—"

She raised a hand. "Hear me out. I'm not overpossessive, but I have to look after Mary every time a worthless piece of shit turns her head and then dumps her. Men are assholes. I reckon that applies where you come from as much as here." She looked into my eyes. "So don't expect me to welcome you with open arms. If Mary's happy for now, that's okay. But remember this. The last guy who messed with her is still in hospital." She laughed emptily. "Unfortunate hunting accident. You make sure you treat her right."

I watched nervously as she went back to her armchair. Never mind the camp and its armed guards. I had the feeling I'd walked into an even more dangerous creature's lair.

With the food served, the atmosphere warmed up a little in the kitchen. Ms. Jacobsen's pot roast was superb and I made a pig of myself—I couldn't remember the last time I'd had a good meal. Mary was cheerful and her mother managed to converse without savaging me. I learned that the old woman had been a legal secretary in Portland and had moved up here when she retired recently. There was a map of Maine on the kitchen wall and I was finally able to orient myself. Unfortunately, the northern part of the state seemed to be mainly trackless forest and, despite the bearings I'd taken with the compass, I didn't have much idea where the camp might have been.

After coffee and a very good homemade blueberry cheesecake, Ms. Jacobsen said she was going to bed. Mary and I cleared up the dinner things and went back into the sitting room.

"You really haven't told me much about yourself, Matt," she said, her eyes on me.

"Well, I—"

"It doesn't matter. I can see you need some time to get perspective."

"No, it's okay. You've taken a big chance for me." I told her I'd been chased through the forest by the people whose uniform jacket I'd given her. I didn't say why—not that I was too clear on that myself. I said that I'd taken the uniform after I'd come round and found myself naked. I didn't feel up to telling any more lies and my memory was steadfastly refusing to provide any more information.

"So," Mary said, "what's our plan?"

Her mother's warning was still ringing in my ears. "*We* haven't got a plan," I said, keeping my eyes off her. "You stay here with your mother."

"Matt!" she said irately. "The troopers are looking for me, too, remember?"

"Like I said, go back and say I threatened you. You're a schoolteacher. Why should they think you're lying."

"No chance! I'm helping you and that's final."

I thought about it. I could certainly do with help, especially with the FBI doing their best to frame me. Besides, my journey though the forest had made me keen to avoid being alone again. But why was Mary so desperate? A few seconds later I got the answer—suddenly her lips were on mine, her body crushing against me. I had a flash of the woman with blond hair, and a feeling of guilt; I was sure the woman meant a lot to me, and tried to detach myself. But Mary was like a force of nature and pinned me against the couch.

"Stop," I gasped, managing to twist my mouth away. "You don't even know me." I could have added that I didn't know myself.

"I know this is right," she said, getting her lips back on mine.

I was going to have to distract her. "We've got to get out

of here," I said, after I'd slipped aside again. "I don't want to involve your mother in this."

"Don't worry," Mary said, smiling. "They won't link her to us. No one in Sparta knows where she lives—she doesn't go into town."

"But they'll find her soon enough. The FBI is after me, not just the local idiots."

"Mom can look after herself," Mary said.

I had a feeling she was right on that count. "Can I borrow her pickup? You can say I made you give me the keys."

"Forget it, Matt. If you want the pickup, I'm coming too." She nudged me in the ribs. "You'll need me—I know the back roads."

Shit. I didn't really have any option but to take her. She *would* be a big help and there was no time to argue.

"All right, Mary. But we have to go now."

She kissed me hard on the lips. "I take it Washington, D.C., is the final destination? You need to find out who thinks you're a murderer."

I nodded. "I don't suppose there are any old clothes I could borrow?"

Mary laughed. "That's how an Englishman asks politely, is it? Yeah, one of my old boyfriends was about your size. He left a suitcase behind."

I wondered if Ms. Jacobsen had made him an offer he'd decided to accept, her shotgun pointed at his groin. She went out of the room and returned with a pair of jeans, a checked shirt and a padded jacket.

"Here you are. I told Mom we're leaving."

"What about your work?"

"I'll call in sick." She didn't bother looking away while I undressed. "Won't be the first time. Hey, you could do with a shower, English."

She was right. I followed her to the bathroom and locked the door behind me. The hot water felt great and when I'd finished, I almost felt human again. Then I remembered how many people were on my tail.

To my surprise, instead of feeling helpless, I found that I was ready to take anyone on. I didn't know why I was being targeted, but I was going to find out. It occurred to me that it might be the last thing I did. Too bad. I would go down fighting.

Mary was waiting for me in the hall, a cooler bag beside her. "I took the rest of the pot roast," she said, her eyes glinting, "since you seemed to like it so much—and various other things. Where we're going, there aren't too many malls."

We went out to the pickup. I transferred the rifle and other weapons from her car, stowing them under the seat.

"I'll drive," I said.

She pushed me out of the way. "Me first. You can look at the scenery."

"It's the middle of the night."

"So it is." She laughed. "You can tell me all about London, then."

"Right." I wondered how much I would be able to remember.

A few minutes later, we were heading up a narrow road, back into the Maine woods that I loved so much.

Twenty-Two

Abraham Singer pushed his glasses above his forehead and rubbed his eyes. He had been examining the medieval text since seven in the morning. Getting up from his office desk, he went over to the window. The lights of Georgetown spread out beneath him, those of central Washington visible in the distance.

The university had put him on the top floor of the building. At first he'd considered complaining, as there was no elevator and his knees weren't as good as they had been, but he'd quickly realized the benefits. He got the daily exercise that Naomi had been nagging him about since the bypass operation, plus—even more important—there was very little noise up here. Not that it mattered. He'd be retiring from the department in under a year.

The elderly scholar ran his fingers through his beard and looked at his watch. He should have gone home hours ago, but the text promised some new insights into the kabbalah, and he couldn't resist working on it to the exclusion of every other consideration. Naomi would be annoyed, but she'd have gone to bed already. He'd get an earful at breakfast.

Abraham looked at one of the photographs on his

desk—him and Naomi on their wedding day all those
years ago in Jerusalem. He had been doing his military
service and hardly recognized his young self, his face
fleshless and his body rake-thin. Naomi's cheeks dimpled
and her dark hair glowing in the sunlight, even in black
and white. There weren't many people at the celebration
as both their families had been ravaged by the Holocaust.
The Singers had lived in Nuremberg and had been sent
to the camps early in the war. Abraham's parents survived, but both had been taken by cancer soon after they'd
arrived in the home country. Naomi's mother had also
returned from Auschwitz, but she never spoke of it. She
had still managed to be the most cheerful person Abraham
ever met.

He took in the shots of their children—David, a lecturer
in film at Berkeley, and Judith, a journalist in Miami. They
had given him great joy, as did the five grandchildren, but,
if he was truthful, he would have to admit that his work
had always taken priority.

Abraham Singer was that rare bird, a scholar of Jewish
religion with serious misgivings about the ancient faith.
The easy answer would have been that the fact of the Nazi
horrors had created an entirely justifiable skepticism. He
knew that wasn't the whole story. He needed to believe, he
needed to maintain a link with the past that was creative and
fertile, but he found much of the ritual primitive and obscu-
rantist. That was why he had established lines of academic
debate with Christian and Muslim scholars who harbored
similar attitudes about their own faiths. But it wasn't
enough. He was still haunted by the suspicion that somewhere in the mass of manuscripts and texts was hidden the
key to an intellectually rigorous traditional belief. He knew
that feeling was as deeply rooted in Jewish tradition as the
orthodoxy he distrusted, but it was irresistible.

And so he had turned to the kabbalah. The problem

was that the ancient and medieval texts contained as much contradictory information as the most dedicated controversialist could desire. Although he was a rationalist, he couldn't resist delving into the mystic wisdom that tried to link God and the universe with the individual mind and body. To his surprise, he even found the occult text of Cornelius Agrippa fascinating in its identification of kabbalah with magic and the mystic meanings of numbers.

Abraham Singer walked across to the mirror above the disused fireplace. The building had once been a town house and he supposed that this would have been a servant's room. The floorboards creaked and the windows, still in their original frames, were hell to open. He glanced at himself and shook his head. Sixty-five, but he looked much older. Perhaps that was the price you paid for ignoring ordinary life and burying yourself in books.

There was a soft knocking at the door. The professor was surprised. Normally he heard people coming up the stairs. Besides, who would be in the building after ten at night? It must be the cleaner.

Abraham went over to the locked door—he had taken the university's security instructions seriously ever since one of his colleagues had been robbed at knifepoint a few months earlier.

"Yo, Professor, I gotta take your garbage," came an accented voice.

Singer didn't recognize it. Then again, the cleaners changed all the time. He turned the key, expecting a young Latino. Instead, what he saw made him step backward in horror, his hands raised. He was pushed hard in the chest and fell to the floor.

Then the light was taken from his eyes.

Peter Sebastian climbed out of the helicopter onto a football field on the outskirts of Sparta, Maine. The nearest field office was Boston, so he was on his own up here. He had left Dana Maltravers behind to keep an eye on the Washington end.

At least the state troopers were making an effort. The area commander had driven up when he was advised Sebastian was on the way and they had coordinated checkpoints on the main roads in all directions. Although the wanted man had been seen leaving the town heading south, he could have changed direction on the back roads. Unfortunately there weren't enough officers to cover all the possibilities, but if Matt Wells was planning on crossing into Canada, he'd probably have to do so on foot.

"This woman who's helping him, who is she?" Sebastian asked after they'd got into the unmarked car.

"Name of Mary Upson," Major Arthur Stevens replied. "Grade-school teacher. Trooper Condon can tell you more."

"He can also tell me how he managed to lose the wanted man," Sebastian said sharply. "My understanding is that your guy had him at his mercy."

The major kept his eyes on the road. "Seems the suspect knows how to handle himself."

They arrived at the state troopers' station. The three men in uniform straightened their backs when they saw their superior officer.

Peter Sebastian swept up the steps. "I want to see Trooper Condon." He stopped inside the door and eyed the young man who had followed him. "Take me somewhere private. You don't want your bosses to hear this." He looked beyond him. "I'll handle it from here, Major," he called.

Stu Condon opened the office door and took him inside. "He pulled a gun on me," he said, before the FBI man could speak. "I couldn't—"

"What kind of gun?"

"A Glock," the trooper replied, his face pale. "Seventeen shot, I reckon." He paused. "He…he took mine, too."

Maps of Hell 165

"Another seventeen?"

Condon nodded, his eyes to the floor. "And…and he had a combat knife in his belt. On his back."

"Is that the full total of his arsenal?" Sebastian asked, acidly.

The trooper shook his head. "I saw a rifle on his shoulder before he got into the car."

The Bureau man's eyes widened. "A rifle?"

"Yes, sir. I think it was an M16."

"Jesus Christ! Where did he get *that?*"

"Couldn't say, sir."

Sebastian glared at him. "What can you say about the woman, then?"

"Mary Upson? Schoolteacher, sir. Been here a year."

"I'm looking for local knowledge here, Trooper. She married? Have a boyfriend? What kind is she—lively, reliable, depressive, what?"

Condon looked at him awkwardly. "Well, sir, I don't really know. She isn't married. I don't think she has a boyfriend. Don't know if she has *any* friends, actually. She goes to the bar at weekends. Sometimes leaves with guys." He looked away.

Sebastian laughed. "How about you, Trooper? I see you're wearing a ring. You try your chances?"

Trooper Condon shrugged. "Nothing happened."

"All right, I'm not interested in your private life. This Mary sounds like a bit of a live wire."

"Yeah, I guess she can be. Sometimes she gets raging drunk. Then she won't let anybody near her."

"What about at school? Is she popular?"

Stu Condon chewed his lip. "My…my wife is a teacher, too. She doesn't like Mary. Says she's a troublemaker, always trying to change procedures. The kids seem to appreciate her, though."

"She got any family here?"

"No, sir. I heard she was from Portland."

Sebastian called in the major.

"Have your people in Portland been notified about Mary Upson? Apparently she's from there."

Stevens nodded. "They're checking on her now. Shouldn't take long."

The FBI man glanced at Trooper Condon. "I take it your men know about the weapons Wells is carrying?"

"They do. Anything more you can tell us about this guy?"

"Yeah," Sebastian said. "He's a judo and karate black belt, he knows boxing and he's trained in rifle and pistol use. Oh, and he's killed at least one person before."

Major Stevens and Trooper Condon exchanged glances.

"Um, there's been a development," the major said.

"Spit it out," Sebastian said, instantly alert. "Has he been sighted?"

"No. But local troopers have found two men tied up behind a house not far from here."

"Who are they?"

"We're not sure. There's no ID on them. They'd been knocked unconscious and only recently attracted attention—one of the locals heard shouting and called it in."

"Wells," Sebastian hissed.

"But why would he have been involved with them?" Stu Condon asked. He ran his hand over his short hair. "There was something strange about Mary Upson. She was wearing a kind of uniform jacket, gray like the pants Wells had. And her jeans were trashed."

Peter Sebastian eyed him dubiously. "Anything else you haven't told us?"

The trooper pursed his lips. "No. But why did they come into the station house, if he's on the run like you say?"

The Bureau man gave him a tight smile. "Let us do the thinking, Stu. This uniform, what was it? Military?"

"I don't know." Condon glanced at the major. "I never saw it before. There were some letters on the shoulder, but I can't remember them."

Sebastian's cell phone rang. He answered it and then groaned. "Another one? Jesus, Dana, what's going on?" He held the phone tightly to his ear. "Yes, I realize that means Wells couldn't have done it. But he could still have killed the first two victims and got up here on the early shuttle. He's involved some—what's that?" He rolled his eyes. "Yes, *obviously using a false ID.* Have you checked the airport CCTV? Well, get on with it. Anyway, he could still have a confederate who did the latest one." He listened again. "Okay, I'll be back as soon as I can."

"Bad news?" the major asked.

"Yes," Sebastian said, "very bad news indeed."

He stepped past them, his expression thunderous.

Nora Jacobsen drove her daughter's Toyota out of the shed and down the driveway. It was a chilly night and the ground wasn't quite soft enough to register tracks. When she got back, she would rake the gravel. The place she was heading was a couple of miles up the road. The local farmer dumped his old machines in a clearing he'd made in the woods. She'd leave Mary's car there. Old Snodgrass wouldn't even notice. Better still, the law wouldn't, either.

It occurred to Nora that she shouldn't be helping her daughter—at least, not this way. She should have sent this latest man of Mary's on his way with the shotgun up his ass, like she'd done in the past. But she reckoned there was no point anymore. Mary was old enough to make her own mistakes. She laughed. The one who'd made the mistake was the man called Matt.

Nora turned down the narrow track. No, Mary would be all right. She always got herself together again after the flings. That was the good thing: her daughter fought her own battles—she wasn't one of those overgrown kids who were continually around the parental home. That was just as well. The Antichurch of Lucifer Triumphant didn't take kindly to snoopers.

Twenty-Three

There was no map in Ms. Jacobsen's pickup. Road signs were rare and Mary sometimes even took gravel tracks. I had no idea where we were going. I put my hand on the Glock, fearful that the vehicle would suddenly be surrounded by gray-clad figures carrying assault rifles. That didn't happen, but there was something about the schoolteacher I couldn't put my finger on. In the light of the dashboard, her face had taken on a weird hue—pale green like a ghost in a child's dreams. Her jaw muscles were set hard as she concentrated on the difficult road surfaces and constant bends. That only made her more attractive. I tried to forget the fire that had ignited in my veins when she'd kissed me. I had the feeling that the blonde woman who was haunting me wouldn't be at all keen on that.

I looked at the compass from time to time. We had headed west for several hours, but had now turned south. That made me feel better. I assumed the camp was in the north of the state and the farther away I was from it, the nearer I'd be to some kind of safety. Then I recalled that the troopers were looking for us all over Maine. No doubt the FBI would have alerted the law enforcement agencies in the neighboring states, too.

"Want me to take over?" I asked. "You should get some sleep."

Mary turned her head toward me. "I have to navigate, remember, Matt?"

"You don't *have* to do anything. This trek is all my doing."

"We've been over that," she said impatiently. "Okay, you can drive for a bit."

She stopped the pickup and got out.

I joined her. In the moonlight, the road was like a snake winding down toward a lake.

"It's beautiful country," I said. "If you don't have to stay alive in it."

Mary looked at me. "Why were those people after you?"

I shrugged, aware again how little I knew. We went back to the vehicle.

"How come you were wearing that uniform?"

"My own clothes disappeared." I felt her eyes on me. "I'm not one of them, if that's what you're thinking."

"What were they called again? The North American…"

"National Revival."

"The North American National Revival," she repeated. "They sound like a gang of crazies. What do they want? Removal of the Zionist Occupation Government, an end to income tax, forcible repatriation of foreign workers?"

I slowed as a large animal shambled across the road. "Christ, was that a moose?" Then I thought about her words. I glanced at her, an icy finger stirring in my gut. "You seem very well informed about groups like that."

She met my gaze and smiled. "I had an argument with some of the more shithead parents at my school. They wanted me to teach their view of history. It got heated. I told them to go fuck themselves."

"Good for you."

"Fortunately they didn't tell the principal." She was looking at me warily. "So how can I be sure you aren't one of them? How do I know they weren't chasing you because you—I don't know—dissed one of the officers?"

I managed not to laugh at the irony. There was I worrying that Mary had some connection to the camp and she was doing the same thing.

"As far as I can remember, I didn't do anything to piss them off."

She raised an eyebrow. "Seems to me your memory isn't the most reliable part of your mind."

I kept my eyes on the road. Mary had noticed that I wasn't telling her the whole story. I wanted to, but something was holding me back. Something…

"Matt!" There was alarm in Mary's voice. "Look out!"

I blinked. The road had disappeared and all I could see was a line of men in gray with rifles at their shoulders. I heard myself scream, but instead of the blast of guns, there was a shriek from Mary and then a sudden, bone-jarring smash that jerked my head forward into the wheel….

…images cascading past the eye of my mind, visions I'd seen before but that were buried deep—a cell with all the angles wrong, a thin blanket, freezing water gushing in, men in bloodstained leather aprons, a complicated machine that lowers over me, swallows me up…music that deafens me, words full of hatred drilling into my brain…

And then I see her—the naked man tied to the post, the woman tormenting him, torturing him…cutting his throat—the woman, I can't make out her face, blond hair concealing it, blond hair turned into rat's tails by the spurting blood. Then the hair parts and I take in the features, the broken lips and split skin over prominent cheekbones…no, it can't be…it can't be her, not the woman I love, the woman who disappeared from the picnic spot in the meadow, no…

…and then I find myself in another place, high above

a wide expanse of water, the white caps of the waves marching away to a horizon of low hills. The sound of high-powered machinery in the background. Jets. From an oval window I see a raked wingtip with a pod beneath, an engine nacelle. Now we are passing over a jagged coastline, the land cut by ravines, pine trees dotted around, but not the slightest sign of human habitation.

"That must be Newfoundland," a woman's voice says.

I turn and take in the blonde woman in the seat next to me, with an airline magazine open at the map page on her lap.

"Hello, calling Matt Wells," she says, with a tight smile. "Anyone at home?"

"Sorry," I hear myself say. "Pretty desolate country down there."

She laughs and her stern face is transformed. "You'd love it, Matt. Think how much work you could get done. No distractions, no nights in the pub, no me."

"No you?" I say. "I don't like the sound of that."

She gives my ribs a solid jab with her elbow. "Aw, Matt, that's almost the nicest thing you ever said to me."

"Is that right? What's number one in that chart?"

She feigns deep thought. "Well, I suppose it would have to be the time you admitted you were wrong and I was right."

"I don't remember that."

My ribs take some more punishment.

"What a surprise." She looks into my eyes. "No, seriously, Matt. It would be the first time you told me you loved me."

"I don't remember that, either." This time I gasped as her elbow made even heavier contact. "Shit! All right, I do. It was the night I took you back to my place, unzipped your—"

"Stop it," she said, looking around. "We aren't alone."

"Oh, forgive me," I say, with exaggerated subservience. "How could I behave in such an inappropriate way with a senior member of her majesty's Metropolitan Police force?"

"Kindly call me by my rank," she says, a smile quivering on her lips.

"Forgive me—Detective Chief Superintendent."

She relaxes. "That's more like it."

I give her a haughty look. "Now it's your turn to call me by my rank. That's more like it, *sir.*"

She laughs. "Sir! You're just an ordinary member of the public. Why should I address you like you're my superior?"

"Em, because I am?" I reply. "Intellectually, morally, physically…"

"Now you're just being childish," she says, opening a folder. "I've got work to do." Her expression is severe, but I can see she's suppressing laughter.

"Bullshit," I say, my elbow extracting overdue retribution from her ribs. "You've read your case notes at least twice since we left London. You must know Gavin Burdett's activities off by heart."

She gives me a warning glare. "Keep your voice down," she says, in a loud whisper. "You know how sensitive this is."

And suddenly my memory supplies the relevant information. Gavin Burdett—British investment banker, Eton and Cambridge—he has extensive contacts with American business and specializes in burying funds in untraceable offshore accounts. And the woman next to me has found the evidence to nail him. Since she was promoted to run the corporate-crime team at the Met, high-profile business figures have been falling like ninepins. No one expected a violent-crime expert to be so effective in the most complex investigation branch, but in her first year she's really shown her mettle.

She puts down the folder and sighs. "You're right, Matt.

But this is the big one. If we nail Burdett, the way will be open for us to nail corrupt companies all over the world."

"*If* you nail Burdett," I say. "What's the name of the company you think he's connected with in the States?"

"Woodbridge Holdings. If we can put the squeeze on it, that'll really impress the politicians. Woodbridge has got international media interests, as well as subsidiary companies all over the place. They're into everything from logging to high tech, radio stations and newspapers to pharmacological research and development."

"Yeah, but lobbyists are already working on their behalf in Washington and London, aren't they?"

She nods. "Which is why this trip's so important. You know the hoops I had to jump through to get the commissioner to sign off on it."

I smile. "Jumping hoops… Were you in full-dress uniform?"

Her eyes burn into mine. "Behave yourself," she says primly. "You're right, Matt. There are people in Congress under Woodbridge's thumb. American jobs are at stake and you know how important they are, given the state of the global economy."

"I don't suppose it's impossible that they've got friends in the Justice Department and the FBI, too."

"True. But I think Levon Creamer is solid enough."

"Crazy name," I say, accepting a food tray from the stewardess.

"Yes, but he's head of Financial Crime at the Bureau. He's the one who got me the meeting with the politicians."

I'm unable to stifle a yawn. That gets me another nudge.

"Sorry if I'm boring you." She concentrates on unwrapping her scone. "Of course, *your* business in Washington is much more important."

I spread clotted cream on the jam I've already smothered over my scone. "Oh, no, it's just a minor project—

international crime during the Cold War, illegalities at the highest levels of government, assassinations, regime change…"

"Quite," she says. "Of course, there isn't any hard evidence."

I raise a finger. "That's where you're wrong, my dear. Joe Greenbaum is an expert in the field."

"And he's going to open his files to you, free of charge?"

I shrug. "Well, I can offer him a small consideration. And some information of my own in exchange."

Her gaze locks with mine. "I hope you haven't sneaked a look at my Burdett files."

I shake my head. "Certainly not. But I'd advise you against leaving them open in my flat. The cleaner might be an undercover agent."

She stares at me. "You haven't got a cleaner."

"What do you mean? I clean every Tuesday afternoon—" I gasp. "Ow, that hurt."

She laughs. "Serves you right."

I'm laughing, too.

But I still can't remember her name…

"Matt! Matt!"

I moved my head and almost threw up. Opening my eyes wasn't any more enjoyable. My vision was blurred.

"Matt? Are you all right?"

Mary Upson's face swam into view to my left, blood on her forehead.

"Yeah," I said, pushing myself up from the steering wheel. "What happened?"

"Never mind that. Let's get you out." She put her arm round me and pulled me out of the pickup. I slumped down on the bumper in the vehicle's headlights. "Let's have a look." Her fingers were on my face. "Your forehead's bruised, but the skin isn't broken." She raised a hand to her temple. "Unlike mine."

"We might both be concussed," I mumbled.

She nodded. "Have you got pain anywhere else? Ribs? Chest?"

I touched myself gingerly. "No, I think I'm in one piece."

Mary sat down beside me. "You were lucky. Do you remember anything?"

"Not much." I was thinking about the blonde woman on the plane. Where was she now?

"It was like you had a fit," Mary said. "You started shaking and your eyes were rolling. You're not epileptic, are you?"

I shook my head, which was a bad idea. Then I had a vision of the camp. Had I really been tied to a stake to face a firing squad? The woman I'd remembered—Jesus, had she been imprisoned, too?

"Matt?"

I glanced at Mary, my mouth slack. They'd put me under a machine; they'd messed with my brain. Had anything I remembered really happened? Or was it just the tip of a very large iceberg?

"What is it, Matt?" Mary shook my arm.

They messed with my brain, I told myself again. *They screwed up my mind.* But I was fighting it. I wasn't going to let them drag me down.

"Matt!"

I shuddered and then got a grip on myself. The blonde woman on the plane, my lover, the senior police officer— the one who'd disappeared in the Shenandoah Valley. She had meetings in Washington. The answers had to be there.

"Is the pickup okay?" I asked, getting to my feet unsteadily.

"The nearside front tire hit a rock. That was what made

our heads whip forward. It's flat. The spare's in good shape. You stay here."

By the time she'd finished, I already felt better.

"I'm driving," Mary said, in a tone that didn't invite contradiction.

I waited while she started the engine, then I gave the pickup a shove. The rear tires gripped on the gravel and we were back in business.

"There's a small town about ten miles ahead," Mary said.

As we drove on, a gray light began to spread from the east. The tips of the trees took on a brighter hue of green and birds flew across the road. The trees began to thin and we ran down toward a narrow lake. The road took a sharp turn to the right before the shoreline.

The state trooper had set his roadblock about thirty yards after the bend. By the time Mary braked, we were almost on top of it. I didn't have any time to duck down, let alone slip out of the pickup.

All I could do was rack the slide of my Glock and prepare for action.

Twenty-Four

"**Y**ou boys want to tell me just what the hell is going on in this city?" Chief Rodney Owen said, looking around the top-floor room where early-morning sunlight was glinting through the windows and Abraham Singer's body lay still.

Detective Simmons glanced at his partner. Gerard Pinker wasn't showing much interest in replying. Two CSIs were working on different parts of the room, doing their best to appear cloth-eared.

"Well, sir," Simmons said, "the indications are that this murder is linked to the previous two."

"The indications being the piece of paper with the boxes drawn on it," Owen said.

Simmons nodded. "And the M.O."

The three men looked at the paper that had been attached to the victim's back with carpentry nails.

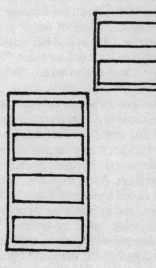

"It looks like the paper and ink will match the previous sheets," Pinker said. "The squares and rectangles are not in the same pattern, just as with the first and second ones, but they're broadly similar."

The chief nodded. "Go on."

"Then there's the M.O. This vic was killed by the insertion of wooden-handled skewers into each eye. The skewers match the Loki and Monsieur Hexie murders."

"Sweet Jesus," Owen said, shaking his head. "What does it mean, Clem?"

"We're working on that."

"Meaning, you're hoping the Bureau's experts come up with something."

Simmons raised his shoulders. "They've got the 'database.'" He recalled the first view he'd had of the old professor. He was lying on his front, the familiar transparent plastic file containing the piece of paper pinned to his back. Observing Marion Gilbert and her assistant as they turned the body over had not been pleasant.

"Any witnesses?" Chief Owen asked. "Who found the body?"

Pinker tugged on his cuffs and opened his notebook. "Another professor, name of Albert Rudenstein. He saw the vic's lights still on and came up. That was just after midnight. Rudenstein had been at a faculty dinner. No witnesses to an intruder so far. Apparently Professor Singer was often the last to leave. Apart from him, there was only a graduate student called Lawrence Jones in the building after seven last night, and he was gone by eight. He didn't notice anyone or anything out of the ordinary."

Rodney Owen was examining at the dark stains on the floorboards. "What does the M.E. think about time of death?"

Simmons glanced at his notes. "Provisionally, between nine and eleven."

"I don't see any sign of a struggle," the chief said.

Pinker had moved over to the victim's desk. "No, Professor Rudenstein said he didn't see anything out of place or missing. Not that we thought it was a burglary."

"What was this Singer's field of expertise?" Owen asked.

"Jewish culture."

"Oh, shit," the chief said, with a scowl. "Now every Jew in D.C. is going to be on my back." He glanced at Simmons. "Please don't tell me we've got an anti-Semitic serial killer on our hands, Clem."

The detective rubbed his cheek. "If he is, he's also anti-black and anti–thrash metal."

"Well, I can understand the second of those. The Loki murder doesn't fit the pattern in that respect. I mean, where does a long-haired, white vic come in?"

"Search me, boss," Pinker said, peering at the papers on the desk. "Jeez, this guy had small writing. I can hardly make out a word of it."

"Well, you better get used to it," the chief said. "Until we find out otherwise, the professor's specialization has to be our focus. What exactly was he working on?"

Pinker turned over the book that was lying open. "This is called *De Occulta Philosophia*, whatever that means." His major at college had been criminology.

Simmons swallowed a laugh. "On Occult Philosophy?" he hazarded.

"Not one of your voodoo books, is it?" Pinker smile sardonically. His partner hadn't been able to find anything linking Monsieur Hexie's death to his interest in the religion.

"Cool it, you two," their boss ordered. "That'll really get the tabloids going, another occult link. We've already had articles about witches' covens in Congress and satanic rituals beneath the Washington Memorial." He buttoned up his raincoat. "I'm going back to the office. See if I can keep dodging the bullets." He looked at each of his men. "You two need to find a good lead, and soon. Or the Feds will take over all three cases."

The detectives watched him leave.

"Fuck this shit," Versace said, in a low voice. "This guy's running rings around us, Clem."

"Just as well there's no woman in your life these days, eh, Vers? Since these murders started, you haven't had time to unzip your very expensive flies."

The smaller man gave his partner a scornful look. "When did you last get any, my man?" Then his expression changed. "Aw, shit. I'm sorry." Simmons's wife, Nina, had died of cancer a year earlier. They had been like a normal couple, with none of the strains of most police marriages. Pinker knew that Clem had never got the hots for another woman when Nina was alive, and he probably never would now she was gone.

"Forget it, Vers." Simmons headed for the door.

They met Dana Maltravers on the stair.

"Ah, Detectives," she said, enthusiastically, "I was hoping you could give me an update."

Gerard Pinker ran his eye over the young woman. Beneath the dark blue FBI jacket, her body was trim, and curved in all the right places. He might have made a move, but he knew he would never live it down at the MPDC building. Feds were the enemy, strictly off-limits.

"You were here a couple of hours ago," Simmons said, with a soft smile. "What do you think's happened since then, Special Agent?" He brushed past her, his partner close behind.

Maltravers followed them downstairs. "Tracked down any witnesses, Detective? How about you, Versace?"

The detective froze. His nickname was not for public use.

Dana Maltravers immediately realized her mistake. "I mean, Detective Pinker."

"Yes, you *do* mean Detective Pinker. Tell you what,

you tell me your nickname and I'll think about letting you use mine."

The agent's cheeks reddened. "Oh, I don't think…"

"Come on now," Pinker said. Special Agent Maltravers is quite a mouthful." He laughed. "So to speak."

The young woman didn't acknowledge the double entendre.

"Okay, what's *Sebastian's* handle?"

"I can't tell you that, Detective."

"Oh, well, there goes that update."

They had reached the hall inside the building's main door.

"Is that what you mean by inter-agency cooperation, Vers?" Simmons said. "I don't think the chief would approve."

Gerard Pinker looked at him as if he were a traitor. "I just think that knowing our colleagues' nicknames would make cooperation so much easier."

"Oh, all right," Maltravers said, looking away. "I'm known as Princess and he's called Dick—behind his back only, of course."

"Princess?" Pinker said. "Yeah, I suppose you do look kinda like that Diana woman. Apart from the hair color."

"Dick?" Simmons said. "By any chance, would that be followed by *head?*"

"So you are a detective after all," Dana Maltravers said, her eyes still averted despite her smile.

"Dick," Pinker guffawed. "I like it. Where is the man in question, by the way?"

"On his way back from Maine. He should be here soon."

Pinker's expression became more serious. "You realize the English guy Matt Wells has to be in the clear for this murder—assuming that was him up in lobster-and-moose land."

Maltravers nodded. "I've checked the airport security films. He wasn't in Reagan National. He would have really had to move to get up there by rail or car."

"Is it theoretically possible?" Simmons asked.

She nodded. "Yes, at least by train. Our people are looking at the Union Station films. Driving would be a real tester—it's over seven hundred miles."

"And why would he bother?" Pinker asked.

Simmons rubbed his chin. "But Wells is still in the frame for the Monsieur Hexie murder. He could have done Loki, as well, without leaving any prints there."

"Or he could have planned the Loki killing and the latest one," Maltravers said.

"You've really got a hard-on for him, *Princess,*" Pinker said. "I checked our files. He reported his girlfriend's disappearance back in late August, and then he vanished himself a couple of weeks later. Why suddenly turn into a killer?"

Maltravers stepped closer as a CSI walked past. "Maybe you didn't read the background documentation I sent over. He's killed before—in London."

"I know that," Simmons said. "But it was in self-defense. Just because he's capable—"

"He's certainly that," Maltravers put in. "A black belt in karate and judo, training in armed and unarmed combat from a former special forces sold—"

"So what?" Pinker demanded. "His girlfriend is a senior English police officer, for Christ's sake. She was over here to meet with your bosses."

"Among other people," Dana Maltravers mumbled, before straightening up.

"What about the Bureau's experts?" Simmons asked. "They come up with anything on the drawings?"

The agent's shoulders slackened. "Not yet."

Pinker moved closer again. "All right, Princess, let's hear your theory. What exactly is going on here?"

Dana Maltravers held his gaze. "It's…it's not *my* theory," she stammered.

"Oh, it's Dick the Dickhead's, is it?" Pinker said with a wide grin. "Never mind, lay it on us."

She took a deep breath. "Well, the idea is that Matt Wells's woman got picked up by the people she had in her sights—she was in charge of corporate crime and there are several companies that would love to see her dead."

"The Bureau been investigating them?" Simmons asked.

"It's not my department. But, yes—the financial-crime people are on the case. It's sensitive, though. These are household names."

"Who no doubt have a lot of pull on the Hill," Pinker said. "But what's that got to do with her man Matt Wells? Why would he suddenly hit on these particular victims? A metal singer with far-right connections, a voodoo huckster and a Jewish professor. They have anything in common that we're missing?"

Maltravers was chewing the inside of her cheek. "Not much," she said, in a low voice. "The drawings are the key, I think."

Pinker gave a bitter smile. "The very-hard-to-understand key."

Clem Simmons caught his eye. "Come on, Vers, we've got work to do."

"What about my update?" Maltravers asked.

"You'll get it when we do," Gerard Pinker said. "Hot off the press."

"I take it that means you haven't come up with anything new?"

"Correct," Simmons said. "You've got our cell-phone numbers."

Dana Maltravers did not look impressed.

Richard Bonhoff had gone back to the building the twins had come out of. Although the stone facade was crumbling, the door was secured with a heavy padlock and the windows barred. He hammered and yelled to no avail. After waiting for over three hours, he went back to the hotel to catch up on his sleep.

The next morning, after doing some writing, he went over his options. He wasn't sure how long his credit cards would remain unblocked, but he didn't care. He'd scavenge for food in garbage bins if he had to, but he wasn't leaving Washington till he found the twins. The obvious plan was to watch the building and approach them again. But he was outnumbered there and even his marine training would be little use against a gang of armed inner-city kids with their brains fried on whatever shit was popular these days. Better to concentrate on Gordy Lister. He was on his own most of the time, and when he had goons, Richard could handle them. Not that he expected Lister to repeat the mistake of underestimating him.

So what was he to do? There was only one option—tail Gordy Lister and squeeze him again. Now that the initial shock of seeing Randy and Gwen had faded, Richard had more questions for the newspaperman—such as, how had he known where to find them? And why did he have musclemen he could whistle up? Lister didn't seem to be a reporter. Richard reckoned he was more of a fixer.

He went out of the hotel to the store on the corner. He bought some bread and cheese. The usual tabloids were displayed in a rack. He picked up the *Star Reporter.* Today's edition led with a story about another murder—D.C. Prof Killed in Ritual Blinding? The article inside tried to link the murder in Georgetown to earlier ones with occult connections. Richard shook his head. At least they didn't have lunatic killers like that in Iowa.

On his way back to the hotel, he came up with a plan of action. He would head into the city center by bus and buy some different clothes, if his card allowed him. After that, he would follow Gordy Lister till he found out what he needed to know.

The blood was flowing fast in Richard's veins as he set out. He was doing something positive and he didn't plan on letting anything knock him off course.

A visitor to Joe Greenbaum's study would not have registered his presence behind the piles of books, folders and box files on his desk—until he lit one of the Cuban cigars, obtained from contacts in the intelligence world, and the smoke billowed up like a Native American signal.

Joseph Martin Greenbaum, doctorate from Harvard Business School, had grown up in Brooklyn. As the class genius, he'd been bullied at school until he'd put on enough weight to fight. Since then, he'd always had an interest in the underdog, which led him to investigate companies that mistreated their customers and workers. He had started writing the coruscating freelance reports that made his name during the Reagan presidency. His victims included a cigarette company that had paid for a whistle-blower to be run over, a bank that had used depositors' funds to finance cocaine smuggling, and a blue-chip accountancy firm that had signed off on an oil company's false tax returns. The magazines and newspapers who bought his articles knew they were always reliable. That was why Joe's apartment was in a secure block in Adams Morgan, his doors reinforced by steel and his triple-glazed windows impenetrable by all but the heaviest caliber weapons.

Joe loved his work, but he was the first to admit it had disadvantages. He could never make a relationship with a woman last more than a month, though wearing spectacles with bottle-lenses probably didn't help, either. He ended up staying in his apartment far too much. It wasn't that he was afraid of the scumbags who were out to get him, it was rather that he enjoyed digging in companies' entrails so much. And then there was his weight—250 pounds on a good day, more when he'd hit the Ben and Jerry's big-time.

Right now none of that mattered to Joe. First, he had seen the news of Abraham Singer's murder on the TV. He had only met the professor occasionally, but he'd liked his dispassionate take on Jewish culture and history. Joe himself had been brought up in the old ways, but he'd broken free of them at college. That didn't mean he'd lost all respect for the faith. Singer hadn't, either—he just put it under a more critical gaze than most believers. Joe's immediate feeling was that the horrible way the professor was killed had nothing to do with rituals, as some of the reporters were saying. Joe was as socially progressive as it got, but he remained old-school in one way: whenever a Jew was killed, he put it down to anti-Semitism—until there was evidence to the contrary.

That wasn't the only thing that was bothering Joe Greenbaum as he finished his morning delivery of doughnuts. Ever since his friend Matt Wells had disappeared—in fact, ever since Matt's partner, the high-flying policewoman, had gone missing in the Shenandoah Valley—Joe had been picking the brains of his FBI insiders. They had been unable to help in any conclusive way until earlier that week when, to Joe's amazement, he learned that Matt was a suspect in the murder of a black man who owned an occult supplies store. Apparently his fingerprints had been found in the victim's apartment; as far as Joe was concerned, that had to be bullshit of the finest quality. He'd known Matt Wells for years. They had first met at a crime-writing conference in D.C., had instantly bonded and had kept the bar open all night. Since then, they had e-mailed back and forth on a variety of subjects. Joe had also seen Matt several times since the policewoman disappeared. The Brit had been angry, overemotional and suspicious, but no way had he turned homicidal. Joe was 100 percent positive that both Matt and his lover had been kidnapped. He'd pulled every chain he had, but no one had a clue. And now Matt was a murder suspect? Screw that.

Joe Greenbaum shook his head. He had been looking into the D.C. murders and he had some ideas he wanted to bounce off Matt. Where the hell *was* his erstwhile drinking companion? If he didn't show up soon, Joe was going to have to make a move on the people the Englishman had been looking at. And that could have very serious consequences for all concerned.

Twenty-Five

I sat motionless in the pickup as Mary Upson slowed before the bulky Maine state trooper. The early-morning light wasn't strong enough to raise more than a faint glow on the waters of the lake, the dark green of the pine-covered mountains stepping back into the gloom.

"What next?" I asked.

"Cool it," Mary replied, keeping her eyes on the man ahead. "He's looking out for my car, remember, not my mother's pickup."

That was true, but I presumed our descriptions had also been circulated. I was holding the pistol out of sight, not that I wanted to use it. Something my friend Dave had said during some kind of small-arms training session in some desolate hills came back to me. "Bear this in mind," the ex-SAS man had said with a thin smile. "If you aim your weapon at someone, you've got to be 100 percent sure that you'll pull the trigger. There's no room for doubt."

And that was the problem. I had plenty of doubts about pointing my gun at an innocent law enforcement officer. For a start, what happened if he tried to pull his own weapon? Would I shoot him? The answer had to be no. I wasn't interested in injuring or killing people unless they harbored similar intentions toward me. Besides, firing a shot would get us noticed, even in the back of beyond.

Then I realized that my thoughts had run away with me—the impact of the wheel on my forehead was obviously still having an effect. Mary was already talking to the trooper.

"…my great-aunt Lucy Heaton. She's taken a turn for the worse and we're going to help her out."

The man was in his late forties, his cheeks and belly bloated. If it came to a foot race, I had the edge.

"Ah, right," he said, smiling back at Mary. "Got elderly folks in my family, too. You go ahead. Say, you haven't seen a green '98 Toyota Tercel, have you?"

Mary shrugged.

I leaned across. "As a matter of fact," I said, putting on what I hoped was a convincing American accent, "I did notice one of those. A man and woman inside?"

He nodded, his eyes wide. "That's right, sir."

"Now, where was it?" I said, prompting Mary. I didn't have a clue about the local place names.

"Oh, I remember," she said. "We passed them the other side of Rumford. Didn't look like they knew where they were going. They finally took the 108 toward Canton."

"Is that right?" The trooper stepped back. "Thanking you, ma'am," he said, turning toward the patrol car.

I watched as he got on the radio. "Nicely done," I said. "But I suppose there's a risk."

Mary glanced at me. "Why?"

"If our friend's bosses ask him for a description of us as witnesses, we may be shafted. Not all state troopers will be concentrating only on what people are driving." I thought about that. "On the other hand, we've both got injuries on our foreheads. He'd be justified in assuming they would have been mentioned." I looked over at the trooper.

He was talking animatedly into the handset. "Get moving. He hasn't got our names and, if we're lucky, he won't take note of the plates."

Mary took us slowly through the small town. There were only a few people around so early in the morning.

"Lucy Heaton?" I said, smiling.

She laughed. "Came up with it on the spur of the moment."

"What if he was the kind of cop who knows everyone?"

"Oh, I guess I'd have said she was staying with friends. If he'd asked me their names, I'd have lied again." She turned toward me. "And if that hadn't satisfied him, I suppose I'd have hit the gas."

There was a look in her eyes that was alarming. I remembered what her mother had said. It wouldn't do to get too close to Mary Upson. On the other hand, the more I knew about her, the better prepared I'd be.

"I wish I knew why you're helping me," I said, realizing I was still gripping the pistol. I put it on the floor beside my seat. "I mean, you're putting yourself at risk."

"Am I? You've been holding a gun on me since we left Sparta."

"Good story. It'll probably stick if you hold your nerve." I looked at the line of her face. She was determined enough, I could see that. "This is some kind of thrill for you, isn't it? Pretending we're Bonnie and Clyde, lying to cops—a lot more exciting than being a small-town schoolteacher."

Her cheeks reddened. "Screw you, Matt," she said angrily. "You just don't get it, do you?"

"Men are dumb," I said, holding my gaze on her as she swerved past a truck and accelerated hard.

"Yeah, you got that right."

I sensed that she needed to unburden herself. That could be tricky, especially if it created an intimacy between us, but I needed to find out more. I still had a suspicion that her presence was too good to be true. On the other hand, she'd already showed with the cop that she was a good liar. Would I be able to tell if she spouted a stream of bullshit?

I decided I'd give it a try. "Let me put it another way. Most men are dumb, but I'm not most men."

"You sure aren't, Matt Wells." She smiled sadly and drew her sleeve across her eyes.

"What is it, Mary?" I asked, resisting the temptation to touch her. She suddenly looked inconsolable.

Shaking her head, she didn't speak for some time. Her damp eyes were fixed on the road ahead.

"I'm sorry," I said, after she seemed to have calmed down. "This is getting to you, Mary. Stop the car, go back to your mother."

"No!" Her voice was shrill. "I'm not a child. I don't need my mother. I don't want my mother…" She hit the brake and turned without warning into a turnoff.

An eighteen-wheeler loaded with logs roared past from behind, the same logo with the open newspaper on the cab door as the one from yesterday. I started gathering up my gear. At least there was traffic on the road and hitching would be feasible.

"No!" she screamed again. "No, Matt. I don't want you to go. I want…I want to help you." She slumped forward, sobbing.

This time I did touch her, my arm going round her shoulders. "Listen, Mary, whatever's troubling you, I'm just making it worse."

"No…no, you're not." She tried to get her breathing under control. "You're…you're the best thing that's happened to me for a long time."

That was exactly what I didn't want to hear. Now it seemed that Mary wasn't helping me out of a sense of injustice. I'd engaged her emotions, which was flattering but dangerous. The blonde woman whose name still escaped memory rose up before me. I loved her and she

194   *Paul Johnston*

loved me—of that much, I was certain. Which meant that by leading Mary on in any way, I was exploiting her. That made me feel slimier than a worm.

She sat up and turned her red eyes and damp face to me, but she was smiling. "It's all right, Matt," she said, looking in the mirror and putting the car back in gear. "I'm going to tell you something, but you have to promise never to tell anyone else, okay?"

I looked at her as we moved back onto the road and picked up speed. "Okay," I said, wondering what I was getting myself into.

"I mean it, Matt," she said, her voice even. "The last person who talked had his tongue cut out."

My stomach did a somersault. Then I was taken on a walk through hell.

The Antichurch of Lucifer Triumphant was established in the town of Jasper, Maine, in 1846 by a logger named Jeremiah Dodds. Jasper was in the far north of the state, deep in the forest. Back then, there was no shortage of extreme religious sects, but the overwhelming majority were Christian. Jeremiah Dodds had no truck with Christianity, having been abused by a minister when he was a boy and savagely beaten by his father when he spoke about it. As a young man, he had consoled himself with the strong drink and the slack-jawed women ever present in logging camps. But, as he got older, those pleasures failed to divert him. One of the advantages of his enforced attendance at the church school was that he had learned to read and write. The only book that was readily available in the wilderness was the Bible and Jeremiah Dodds started to study it again in his thirties, but with a zeal possessed only by the true contrarian. The result was the antiGospel of Lucifer, a savage perversion of its New Testament prototype that set out a new faith based on violence and devotion to Satan. While Christians worshipped the blood of the Lamb that had been spilled for humanity, Luciferians saw holiness in terms of spilling human blood.

The Antichurch flourished in the great wilderness of the Maine forests, where the daily struggle to stay alive drained what little good there was in the loggers—they viewed themselves as nothing more than the timber barons' slaves. That mentality made them easy converts to Jeremiah Dodds's preaching. Anyone who objected was whipped from the settlements where he prevailed and hunted through the woods, ending up as a source of blood for the congregation's monthly rites. Soon there was no opposition and Dodds reigned supreme in Jasper and its neighboring towns.

So supreme was the Antichurch that it ran out of victims. That was the beginning of what was called the Great Trouble. For Jeremiah Dodds wasn't satisfied with the substitute blood of moose and bear. That, he proclaimed, would please Lucifer only for a short time. The congregations had to look for human victims in towns and camps where traditional Christian beliefs still held sway. So blinded were the faithful by the seductive power of the anti-Gospel and the subtle guile of Dodds that they covered huge distances, even in winter, to bring back living sacrifices. They preferred women and children because they were easier to carry—and because they provided the men with what were known as "virtues of the flesh" in the hours before they met the knife. The "virtues" were enjoyed in public and the lash was not spared, the only stipulation laid down by the antigospel being that the offerings to Lucifer were to remain conscious throughout. For it was said that the road to Hell was too splendid for even a second of the journey to be missed. However, their eyes were put out as soon as they were dead; to see the glories of the underworld was a privilege reserved for Luciferians.

The inhabitants of other places, those who retained some decency, resisted the unseen menace that haunted the pine forests as best they could. Initially, the disappearance of wives and offspring—the Luciferians never took whores, seeing them as fellow spirits—was put down to wild beasts. But finally the stories of the few Luciferians who broke free and survived could be ignored no longer. Parties of heavily armed men set out to confront the raiders in their base. For, rumor had spread that the town of Jasper was a sinkhole of corruption, a modern-day Sodom where the filthiest of unholy ceremonies were practiced, with victims being sacrificed on upturned crosses. With wholly justifiable rage and a less commendable desire for revenge, the true believers fell upon the abomination that Jeremiah Dodds had created. The Luciferians disappeared without trace. Jasper was burned to the ground and its name expunged from the maps. The arch blasphemer and murderer Dodds was hanged from the tallest tree, his face beaten to a pulp and his innards loosed upon the ground before his spirit went to its foul master below the earth. As a final, ironic affront, Dodds's eyes were torn out so that he wouldn't be able to see Lucifer's realm. For decades, people were reluctant to go within a hundred miles of where Jasper had been, lest a fearsome creature, its blinded face twisted and its feet tangled in its own entrails, should come upon them and drag them screaming to hell.

Such was the end of the Antichurch of Lucifer Triumphant, at least as far as the civic and religious authorities were concerned—in any case, they only heard the stories months after Dodds and his congregation had been eradicated by the mob. But the truth was that there were still people who enthused over the antiGospel. Despite strict repression of the text, it had remained in existence, circulated by subsequent generations of Luciferians with extreme caution—every copy accounted for, reproduction in any form forbidden on pain of death. Recently a Bangor man by the name of Regent, who had feigned devotion to the Antichurch, started to transcribe the text onto a Web site; he had never been seen again. He became the first human sacrifice in several years, his tongue and genitals sliced off while he was still conscious. His blood was drained and drunk by the faithful before the flesh and organs were stripped from his bones and burnt on the Antichurch's altar, beneath the obligatory inverted cross.

The word of Jeremiah Dodds was still alive in the ever-green forests of northern Maine and it was spreading. There was even a small congregation in the town of Sparta, one attended by a recent recruit to the cause.

"What?" I gasped. "Your mother is one of them?"

Mary nodded, her face damp with sweat despite the cold in the pickup. "I found her diary."

"But aren't you in danger? Do these lunatics have any idea that you know about them?"

"I doubt it." She glanced at me. "I'm not sure I'd be walking around in one piece if they did. I don't think Mom knows, either."

I thought back to the wrinkled old woman. She had alarmed me enough with her shotgun threats before I knew she was a member of the local satanist coven. Then I wondered about Mary. Was she more involved with the Anti-church than she'd admitted? Had she perhaps singled me out as a potential sacrifice? I twitched my head and tried to get a grip. She was driving me away from her mother. Then again, there might have been another altar in south-ern Maine. No, she would hardly have told me about the Antichurch if she were a member.

"Why are you telling me all this?" I asked.

She bit her lip. "Because I'm frightened, Matt. I needed to share the burden."

I reckoned she was being straight with me. But there was something familiar about the story, something hovering on the margins of my memory....

"How many members of this Antichurch are there?" I asked.

"Around ten, I think."

"Are there any other branches?"

She shook her head. "I don't think so. They're so paranoid about the antiGospel getting into the wrong hands that they prefer to limit their numbers."

"And what about Jasper? Have you any idea where that was?"

Mary raised her shoulders. "The congregation doesn't even know that. Mom wrote something about them asking their savior to direct them to what they call 'the field of glory.' I got the impression Lucifer hadn't obliged."

I thought about the camp I'd escaped from. Filming a man having his throat cut by a naked woman wasn't much different from the rituals Mary had described, but I didn't remember any devil worship per se.

I shook my head, wondering what I'd got myself into. Then I thought about the murders in Washington that I was supposed to have committed. Could they have some connection?

I was so caught up in my thoughts that I hardly noticed when we crossed the state line into New Hampshire. The minor road Mary had taken wasn't even under scrutiny. We had evaded the state troopers, but I had a feeling that the reach of the people at the camp was a lot longer than that of the Maine authorities or the FBI.

Twenty-Six

Peter Sebastian, perfectly turned out in a dark blue suit and striped tie, eyed the detectives on the other side of the conference table.

"Well, gentlemen. Over eighteen hours have passed since the discovery of Abraham Singer's body. What progress have you made?"

"We'd be making more if you hadn't called this meeting," Gerard Pinker said, shaking his head hopelessly.

"Nice," Sebastian said, smiling icily. "Very nice. Perhaps I should call in Chief Owen."

Clem Simmons gave his partner a long-suffering look and then caught Dana Maltravers's eye. He reckoned she'd have smiled if she hadn't been so in awe of her boss.

"That won't be necessary," Simmons said, flipping open his notebook. "As I'm sure you're aware, Special Agent Maltravers attended the autopsy with me. The report's not out yet, but the time of death isn't going to be much different from Dr. Gilbert's original estimate of between 9:00 and 11:00 p.m. Cause of death, major brain trauma caused by the skewers driven into each eye. There's no evidence of any other trauma, so it's likely the killer inserted them while the victim was still conscious."

"Meaning he knows what he's doing," Sebastian said.

Pinker gave a wry smile. "Kinda the impression we'd got from the first two murders."

"Quite," said the FBI man, holding his gaze on Simmons. "What about the significance of the M.O.?"

"Skewers again," Clem said.

"And two of them again," Dana Maltravers said. "So there's the same symbolism of the pair."

"Whatever that means," Pinker put in, smiling at her. "Maybe he just likes using both hands. Or maybe there are two murderers."

"I suppose that's possible," Sebastian said. "That's all we need. A pair of serial killers."

"Maybe they're twins," Pinker suggested.

The FBI man raised an eyebrow. "Let's not lose touch with reality completely." He glanced at Simmons. "Go on with your report, Detective."

"We've been canvassing the area. The problem is, the majority of buildings are university property, but offices rather than student accommodation, so there weren't many people around in the evening."

Peter Sebastian's expression was grim. "What you're saying, Detective, is that no one saw the killer."

"If anyone did, we ain't found 'em yet," Pinker said. Not for the first time, he reverted to the way he talked back home in Georgia when addressing the Bureau man.

"CSIs?" Sebastian said, looking at his notes.

"They're still comparing fingerprints with those we've taken from people who were in the professor's room recently," Clem Simmons said. "It'll take some time. There are students, other professors, cleaners. Same goes for fibers."

"Any suggestive background on the victim?" the FBI man asked.

"Suggestive?" Pinker repeated, smiling at Maltravers. "You mean, did he grope his students?"

Simmons frowned at his partner. "He was an expert in Jewish mysticism. That could be a connection with the other murders. He was studying a medieval book called *De Occulta Philosophia*. So—"

"So you think the killer has it in for people who dabble in the occult?" Sebastian said dubiously.

"That's what the dailies are saying," Pinker said.

"I pay no attention to trash like that," the Bureau man said.

Clem Simmons raised his heavy shoulders. "We haven't found anything else to explain the professor's murder. He seems to have been happily married…" He gave Pinker a long-suffering look. "And he didn't have a reputation as a groper. According to Professor Rudenstein, he wasn't one of those academics who stir up controversy."

"'Course, there is another possibility," Pinker said, eyeing each of the others in turn.

"Enlighten us, Detective," Sebastian said wearily.

"He was Jewish—could have been targeted by some far-right crazy."

"It's certainly a possibility." Sebastian looked at his subordinate. "Have you alerted the Hate Crimes Unit?"

Dana Maltravers nodded. "They're checking it. I've been through the victim's recent e-mail correspondence. There are no obvious threats. Of course, he could have deleted them. I've also spoken to his wife. She wasn't aware of anything like that."

"All right," Sebastian said. "Keep in touch with our people. What about the drawing?"

"The document-analysis experts are comparing it with the others," Maltravers replied. "There isn't much doubt that it was done by the same hand, and with the same pen and paper."

"And the meaning?" Sebastian asked impatiently.

"Um…unclear, so far."

"Anyone else have any ideas?"

"Could be building up to some sort of composite," Clem said. "The shapes are in different places on each page."

"True," the FBI man said. "The problem is, if it's not complete, then we can expect more murders."

Silence greeted that remark.

"Have you gotten anywhere with background checks on Loki and Monsieur Hexie?" Dana Maltravers asked.

"Not really," Simmons replied. "The band members are saying as little as they can. We've been looking at their activities. Loki got plenty of abuse on the band's Web site about his lyrics, but that seems normal in the circles he moved in."

"What about anti-Nazi and civil-rights groups?" Sebastian put in.

"Yeah, they thought he was a piece of shit," Pinker said, "but we haven't found any death threats. Same for Monsieur Hexie but Clem can tell you more about him."

"Thanks, partner," Simmons said. "The second vic actually seems to have been rather popular. People appreciated the stuff he sold. It made them happy."

"Woo-hoo for voodoo," Pinker said, with a sardonic smile.

Dana Maltravers looked up from her papers. "It seems he was still turning tricks, though, despite his age."

Simmons nodded. "From time to time. We tracked down the recent johns—Monsieur Hexie kept a client list on his computer. They were pretty upset."

"They had solid alibis, too," Pinker said.

"Could the list have been tampered with?" Sebastian asked.

Clem Simmons shrugged. "I guess. The list was a standard Word file."

There was another silence.

Gerard Pinker broke it. "What about your man Matt

Wells? The CSIs haven't found anything linking him to the latest scene."

Sebastian gave a tight smile. "They're unlikely to, given that he was in Maine last night."

"So you failed to catch him," Pinker said pointedly.

The FBI man stared at him. "The fact that Wells continues to evade arrest hardly suggests he's an innocent man."

"Oh, yeah? The way I hear it, the guy walked voluntarily into the state troopers' station. He wouldn't have done that if he was killing people, or even organizing their deaths."

Sebastian shook his head. "You aren't in possession of all the facts."

"Is that so?" Clem Simmons said. "We're the lead detectives on this investigation. You're not in a position to keep information from us."

Peter Sebastian got to his feet. "I'm in a position to do anything I deem appropriate," he said, picking up his notes. "Next briefing at midday tomorrow, please." He gave Pinker a malevolent smile. "Your presence isn't required, Detective."

"Right on, Dick," Versace muttered.

Richard Bonhoff was wearing a nondescript blue windbreaker and a Washington Redskins cap. For the past six hours he'd been in various locations with a view of the main entrance of the Woodbridge Holdings office—outside a shoe shop, inside a café, behind a van. There had been no sign of Gordy Lister and now, as the light faded, his stomach was rumbling and his feet were cold. But he was used to worse in the fields back home.

Richard knew he'd be pressed if Lister headed for the car park. He hadn't brought the pickup after the last fiasco, and he would have to rely on a taxi passing at the right time. Short of stealing a vehicle, there was nothing else he could do. He thought of the twins and their haggard faces. What wouldn't he do to get them back? Answer: nothing.

Then Gordy Lister made an appearance. He stood outside the office building for a while, looking around, markedly more cautious than before. Richard made sure the collar of his coat was up and the peak of his cap pulled low. Lister eventually started walking to the right. Richard moved out of the doorway he'd been sheltering in and kept to the sidewalk on the other side of the road. There were plenty of people around at the end of the working day, and he had to take care not to knock into those walking toward him. That was why he didn't immediately notice that Lister had company.

The man who had suddenly taken up a position beside the newspaperman was tall and wore what looked to Richard like an expensive gray coat. He had on a hat, the kind that men wore in black-and-white detective movies, and his face was partly covered by his own raised collar. When he turned, Richard saw a prominent nose. It occurred to him that Lister's companion was doing the same thing he was—trying to be inconspicuous. Interesting.

The two men continued down the street, Lister occasionally glancing over his shoulder. It struck Richard that maybe there were others watching the men, security men like the gorillas he'd laid out. He checked, but saw no sign of anyone, either on foot or in slow-moving vehicles.

When the men turned right into a side street, Richard got worried that he might lose them and ran across the road. Luckily, there was a gap in the traffic, but he warned himself to be more careful. If a driver had hit his horn, Lister's attention would have been attracted. The two men were still in sight, deep in conversation. They stopped outside a building for a few moments, still talking, and then went in.

Richard strode up the street, examining the building.

There was a panel of buttons and names to the right—
lawyers, accountants and the like. He waited until someone
came out. A blonde woman, speaking into her cell phone,
paid no attention when Richard slipped in past her. The two
men were by the elevators, the taller of them moving his
right hand up and down animatedly. Richard decided to get
closer, trusting his changed appearance. Lister's expression
was tense, his eyes locked on his companion's face.

"…the camp," the tall man said. "Everyone is in place.
What about your people?"

Lister's voice was barely audible. He lowered his gaze
as people came out of another elevator. Richard took out
a newspaper and opened it in front of him, trying to look
as if he was waiting for someone.

"You know they're ready." Gordy Lister's tone grew
sharper. "But what about the killer?"

"We can't risk the operation by taking everyone off it."

Lister shook his head. "So we run the risk of being
screwed by one of our own?"

"We have no idea of who might be the next target?"

"Same as before, I reckon—there's no shortage of occult weirdoes in this city."

"Gordon," the tall man said, lowering his voice. "The
company must be protected at all costs."

"What do you think I'm do—" Lister broke off when he
saw that his companion had turned toward the street door.

Richard heard the loud click of heels to his left. He
watched as a striking woman with short brown hair approached. She was wearing a sober pantsuit.

"Ah, there you are, my dear." The man in the gray coat
lifted his head. Richard saw that the skin on his face was
tight and unnaturally smooth. "I was wondering where
you'd got to."

"Sorry. A meeting ran late."

Lister pressed the call button. When the elevator came, the three of them went inside.

Richard Bonhoff watched the doors close behind them. He couldn't risk joining them in such an enclosed space. In the meantime, his mind was jumping hoops, trying to make sense of what he'd overheard. Gordy Lister had said people here were ready. Who? The twins? And who was the killer? Could that be the one the papers were calling the Occult Killer?

Jesus Christ, he said to himself. What have I got myself into? And what has happened to Gwen and Randy?

Joe Greenbaum was sitting in an interview room on the fifth floor of the MPDC building. He'd been there for half an hour and the plastic cup of thin coffee he'd been given had long gone cold. He was beginning to wonder if he'd done the right thing. He had tried to talk to one of the detectives on the Singer case over the phone, but the man had insisted Joe come to headquarters to give a statement. That was all very well, but he had work to do. The deadline for his article on high-level corruption in the U.S. automobile industry was only a week away and he hadn't even started pulling his notes together.

The door opened and a heavily built black man came in.

"Mr. Greenbaum? I'm sorry to keep you waiting." He sat down opposite Joe and eyed the untouched cup of coffee. "I've gotten used to it over the years. The good lord knows what it's done to my innards."

"Probably killed off all the bugs from the burgers in the cafeteria."

Clem Simmons laughed. "You eaten down there?"

"No, but I've heard stories."

Simmons's expression became more severe. "So, you've got some information on the Singer murder."

Joe Greenbaum raised his shoulders. "Information? I suppose you could call it that. It's just background, I'd say."

The detective opened his notebook. "I'll take anything you've got."

"First of all, I want to ask you about Matt Wells." Greenbaum shifted his bulk on the chair and grimaced. "Is this thing an instrument of torture?"

Simmons smiled briefly and looked at him with more interest. "What about Matt Wells?"

"He can't really be a suspect like they're saying in the papers. It's ridiculous."

"Why's that, sir?"

"Come on, Detective. I know Matt Wells. No way would he have killed that poor man."

"You know Matt Wells."

"Sure. I saw him several times in the weeks before he disappeared."

Clem Simmons kept his tone neutral. "You a friend of his?"

Joe Greenbaum smiled. "Yeah. I first met him at a crime-writing conference here a few years back. He can drink almost as much as I can."

Simmons narrowed his eyes. "Excuse me, sir. What exactly is it you do?"

"Freelance journalist. I specialize in corporate and organized crime." He could see what the detective thought about that. Journalists were only a few rungs up the ladder from mass murderers.

"So when you saw Matt Wells, was it business or pleasure?"

"Oh, both, I'd say." Greenbaum stretched backward and the chair creaked ominously. "We have similar interests. He writes a crime column for a British daily."

Simmons already knew that—he'd done an Internet search after Wells first became a suspect for the Monsieur Hexie murder. "Why are you so sure he's innocent? His fingerprints were found at the scene."

"Give me a break, Detective. We both know prints can be transferred. It's obvious that Matt's being framed. I mean, there's no evidence tying him to the other so-called occult murders, is there?"

"I can't confirm or deny that," Simmons said.

Joe Greenbaum smiled. "That's okay, Detective. I can see that you're not exactly sold on Matt's guilt. Is it true that he was spotted in Maine yesterday?"

"That's way outside my jurisdiction."

"All right." The reporter's expression grew more serious. "Listen to me now. Matt Wells's life has been under threat for three years. Have you heard about the Soul Collector?"

"His ex-girlfriend? Yeah, I read the reports."

"Okay. So you know she's gunning for him. I'd say you should be trying to nail her for these murders. She's been involved in that kind of thing before in the U.K. and she's likely to have samples of his fingerprints."

Clem Simmons chewed the end of his pen. He *had* wondered about the woman called Sara Robbins. The problem was, absolutely no evidence pointed to her involvement.

"It wouldn't surprise me if she was behind the disappearance of Matt and his policewoman lover," Greenbaum went on. "I know, there's no proof. But she's definitely capable of killing savagely and with the utmost precision."

"I don't suppose you've got any leads on her."

The reporter rubbed his unshaven cheek. "It's not really my area. I'm asking around, though. You can be sure I'll pass on anything I hear."

Simmons nodded. "All right, sir. Now, what about Professor Singer?"

"Oh, yeah. Well, it's nothing concrete, like I said, but you should check his e-mail correspondence from around a year ago."

"Why's that?"

Greenbaum's tone suddenly grew sharper. "Because some far-right assholes started threatening him and his family."

"How do you know that?"

"Because Abraham asked me to look into it, see if I could track the fuckers down. We weren't so close, but he was a friend of my old man—they were both professors at Columbia. We used to meet for a drink occasionally after he moved down here. He was a funny man—I mean, in the humorous way. He wasn't your typical dull-as-dust academic." He shook his head. "Fuck, Abraham didn't deserve to die like that."

Simmons noted the reporter's fury. "And did you find out anything about the people who threatened him?"

Greenbaum took a deep breath. "They weren't the usual boneheaded racist gorillas, I can tell you that. They called themselves the Antichurch of Lucifer Triumphant. I ran a check and found that they were founded back in the 1840s. Up in Maine, now I think of it—I wonder if that could tie in with Matt. They were supposedly wiped out ten years later, but it seems they've resurrected themselves recently. They spouted the usual crap about the Jews—how they're ripe for sacrifice, that Hitler was right, shame he isn't still alive. You know the kind of thing."

"What did you do with that material?"

"Passed it to the FBI. I know a guy in the Hate Crimes Unit, name of Harry Slater."

Simmons felt an icy finger run up his spine. He'd already wondered why Special Agent Maltravers hadn't mentioned the threats; he'd assumed the professor had deleted them. Now he was hearing that the FBI had received the information after all. What the hell were Sebastian and his sidekick playing at?

Joe Greenbaum shrugged. "I never heard anything and,

since the threats dried up, Abraham and I decided to let it go." He raised a thick-fingered hand to his brow. "I'll never forgive myself."

Simmons gave him a few seconds. "Anything else, sir?"

"Yeah, just one thing. The original Antichurch of Lucifer Triumphant was run by a lunatic called Jeremiah Dodds. He wrote a text called the antiGospel of Lucifer, which has never been found. There were strong but unsubstantiated rumors that people were sacrificed and their blood consumed." Joe Greenbaum looked up at the detective. "It was also said that, later in the process, they were blinded."

Clem Simmons blinked to dispel an image of the professor's mutilated face.

Twenty-Seven

I took a spell at the wheel as we followed the back roads through New Hampshire and New York. We didn't come across any roadblocks and the farther we got from Maine, the more relaxed I felt. After we stopped for fuel and to eat, Mary slipped into the driver's seat again, insisting she wasn't tired. The welt on her forehead wasn't as bad as mine. My need to sleep was suddenly overwhelming.

But what I got was hardly restful. I found myself in a wheelchair, my arms and legs bound. I was wearing weird clothes that seemed to be made of paper, and was in a long hall full of naked people, who were wailing in ecstasy. The walls were hung with animal corpses, bones showing through tattered skins. At the front I saw an upturned cross. A demonic pair was holding sway; a naked man with a hyena's head and erect penis whipped a terrified woman past a cloaked figure, whose ruined features were those of a terrifying gargoyle. Other naked men and women, none much more than college age, tied the woman to the inverted cross, her hands above her head. Her body was discolored with bruises and blood was running from cuts all over. She let out a long scream before a gag was pushed into her mouth. The congregation was chanting now. "Lucifer, Lucifer, Lucifer Triumphant." Then the gargoyle used a long knife to cut the sacrificial victim's throat, letting her blood spray onto the dark cloak. Her eyes were stabbed out. And then I recognized the woman hanging there lifeless. Her hair was blonde and she had been my lover—I had been on the plane to Washington with her....

I woke up with a jerk, my body drenched with sweat.

"Jesus, Matt," Mary said, her eyes wide. "What is it?"

I struggled to get control of myself. "Bad dream," I gasped eventually, settling back in the seat and feigning sleep. I didn't want to tell Mary what I'd seen. The Antichurch of Lucifer Triumphant was at the camp. Had I really seen that horror? It seemed real enough; I recalled a firing squad that had shot blanks at me. Why had they been messing with my mind? And still I couldn't remember my lover's name. I felt myself falling into the abyss again....

She was before me, the blonde woman, her expression one of wistful regret. It was as if she was forgiving me for failing to save her. But before I could reach out, her face disappeared and was replaced by one I was much less eager to see—that of Sara Robbins, the Soul Collector....

...I am in a well-lit place that I sense is home. My apartment is in London, on a new block in Chelsea Harbour, next to the river. The main room is big enough to play cricket in, something that my male friends and I have occasionally done when strong drink is consumed. Because of the threats that Sara Robbins made, I'm used to living in a state of siege. I've set up a daily reporting schedule with my friends and family—if I don't get the right form of words from them every morning, I press the panic button. It doesn't happen often, but Sara has struck in the past. That cost me one of my closest friends, but I can't...I can't remember his name. Months have passed, but I don't think she's forgotten me.

Then the Soul Collector strikes exactly at the least predictable moment. I'm in bed with my lover, the blonde woman whose name escapes me. I have finished giving her a massage and things are moving slowly to what will be a glorious climax.

"What was that?" she murmurs, opening her eyes.

On top of her, I stop moving. I also heard something, a faint but unmistakable thud. Even though the alarm system in the apartment is the most sophisticated on the market, I'm not taking any chances. I roll off the bed. There's a fully loaded, silenced Glock in a hidden floor safe in my walk-in wardrobe, but my senior policewoman lover doesn't know about that—there's a limit to what she will sanction, and handguns are seriously illegal in the U.K. So I'm reduced to grabbing the antique swordstick that I keep beneath the bed. She thinks it's only a walking stick.

"Stay here," I say after I've pulled on a pair of boxer shorts. I kill the lights and slowly open the bedroom door.

For some time, I hear nothing. I look cautiously round the chair and see that the heavy chain is still on the front door. There are three locks on it and all seem to be engaged normally. I breathe out slowly. That's good news. I brace myself and then crawl on all fours across the parquet floor, my feet slipping on the polished surface. When I get to the bar that separates the kitchen from the living area, I pause and take stock. There's no sight of anyone. That leaves the spare bedroom and bathroom beyond the kitchen. It's as I am heading there, still on my hands and knees, that I hear another thud, this one much more distinct. It comes from the spare bedroom. Jesus.

I scuttle across the floor and stand up by the full-length window. Then I press the switch and watch the blinds slowly roll up.

The bang on the glass is much louder at close range, and

it startles me. Then I realize what it is and stare in amazement. A large white bird—a seagull by the looks of the cruel beak—has been suspended against the window, its wings outspread and its head downward. The wind catches the carcass again and bangs it against the glass. Then I look closer. A red ribbon has been tied round the dead bird's neck. There's a label attached and on it are written the words *Death Flies by Night*.

Then mayhem breaks out. The floor shakes as an explosion comes from the front door. I dash toward it, into the cloud of dust that has immediately risen. My ears seem to be muffled and I put a hand over my mouth against the dust. I see a pair of figures moving quickly towards the bedroom. I shout. One of them stops and turns. A motorbike helmet is covering the head. That instantly brings to mind the last time Sara Robbins concerned herself with me—she rode a high-powered bike between the murders she committed.

The figure, which I now see is dressed completely in black, levels a compact machine-pistol at me and empties the magazine in a burst of sound. My dive behind the kitchen bar saves me, though I feel a heavy blow on one of legs. Then I see a round object bounce off the surface of the bar and drop by my legs. Grenade. I grab it and toss it back. There is a loud explosion and more dust comes over me in a wave. My ears are ringing. All I know is that my lover is in the bedroom and at least one of the intruders will also be there by now. I grab my blade and go round the end of the bar. A badly mutilated body is motionless on the floor. I don't waste time with the helmet and keep going.

But before I reach my bedroom door, a figure in black backs out, hands in the air. When the point of the swordstick pierces the leather biker's jacket, the intruder stops abruptly. I look beyond and see my blonde lover. She's naked and is holding a a ridiculously small pair of nail scissors.

I stare at her, my hearing gradually returning.

"What's that, Matt?" she asks, catching sight of my blade.

"I could ask you the same question." I slip the catch from the strap on the figure's neck and wrestle the helmet off. The intruder is a shaven-headed black man whom I don't recognize. I hear police sirens coming near. The occupants of my block aren't used to explosions at night.

"Watch him," I say to my lover. I go back to the prone figure and pull off the helmet. Another man, this one white and very dead.

"Who put you on us?" I shout to the other guy.

He doesn't reply. I know he won't ever reply. The Soul Collector will have made very clear what she'll do to his family if he talks. She'll also have deposited a large sum in a secret account for when he gets out of jail.

Afterward, when the police have finally gone, I sit with my arm around my lover's shoulders. We're drinking twelve-year-old malt whiskey, but it isn't doing much to fill the emptiness we're feeling. Sara Robbins will never let us live an ordinary life. Sooner or later I'll have to get her off my back for good.

Although my ears are still ringing, I can hear the seagull knocking from time to time on the spare bedroom window.

Death has flown away by night. But I know she'll be back….

When I came round, I insisted that I do some more driving. I'd had enough of what my memory had been dredging up, not least because I couldn't be sure how much of it to believe. I preferred to concentrate on the road.

Mary fell asleep and I carried on southward. I didn't know how long she was out.

"Where are we?" she said, yawning.

"Southern New York, not too far from New Jersey. I just saw a sign to West Point."

She smiled. "Did that mean anything to you, Mr. Englishman?"

Strangely enough, it did—one of the seemingly irrelevant pieces of knowledge my haphazard memory had clung on to. I must have watched too many trashy war films.

"Listen, Matt," Mary said, "you really need to get some sleep."

I nodded. My arms were tight and I was having trouble keeping my eyes open.

"It'll be dark in an hour or so. We should be able to find an out-of-the-way motel." She smiled at me. "We can make an early start in the morning."

"*We* don't have to do anything," I said. "I can hitch to Washington from here easily enough. You should get back to Sparta."

She gave a bitter laugh. "No, thanks. I've had enough shit from the law."

That caught my attention. "Really? That sounds a bit unusual for a primary schoolteacher."

Mary shot me a chilly look. "Curiosity killed the cat and all her kittens, Matt."

"Pardon me. I was just trying to get to know you better."

"And what would be the point of that?" she demanded. "You're making it very clear that you don't want me around."

I sighed. "It isn't that, Mary. This is going to get dangerous."

"Like it hasn't been already. Those weren't blanks Stu was firing at us."

"All right, all right," I said, raising a hand. "We'll talk about it when we stop."

An uneasy silence prevailed. It was Mary who broke it. "If you must know, those Texan assholes weren't the first men to take me around the back of the houses." She kept her eyes away from mine.

I recalled what Mary's mother had said about her daughter's emotional fragility.

"I'm…I'm not good at…at relationships," she said. "But sometimes I have…needs. I go to the bar and get hit on. I like it till it gets to the point where I have to…I have to get to it…then I can't go through with it." She let out a long sob.

I stretched out my hand, but all that did was make her cry even more desperately.

"You see?" she stammered. "You're no different from the others. I suppose you think I'm just some screwed-up neurotic."

I touched her shoulder. "No, I don't. I couldn't have got away without your help. Why should I have negative thoughts about you?" I framed what I said as carefully as I could. "Look, we need to break the journey. Let's find somewhere to sleep soon. We'll both feel better in the morning. Then we can decide what we're going to do."

The sobbing stopped and Mary looked across at me, wiping her eyes with the back of her hand. She smiled weakly. "Thank you, Matt. I knew as soon as I saw you that you were different from the others."

I couldn't argue with that. It would have been amazing if she'd ever encountered a partial amnesiac toting an assault rifle and two Glocks before. But I needed to be careful and not encourage her too much.

There was a sign for a motel not long afterward. The place was set back from the road with dense trees to the rear and not many vehicles parked outside.

"You'd better stay here," Mary said, rummaging in her bag. "I'll see if they can live without ID and pay in advance by cash."

I watched her go toward reception and then got out of the pickup, my hand on the Glock in my belt. I suddenly felt very vulnerable. I checked the area. There was no sign of anything suspicious. I watched Mary come out of the building, telling myself to be careful with her. I wished I'd specified that I wanted a room on my own, but I didn't have the means to pay for one and didn't want to antagonize her.

As she got closer, I saw she was holding up two keys. I gave a sigh of relief.

"We're in the corner rooms over there," she said, pointing to the far left of the building.

I drove the pickup over, parking it as far from the lights as I could, and front end out so we could make a quick getaway if necessary. We took the food inside and ate in the room Mary had taken. Mine was right on the corner.

"Right," I said when we'd finished the potato salad and cold cuts. "I'm going to have a shower and then crash out. I should be awake by daybreak. We'll get going then."

She nodded, watching me as I went to the door. "Is that it, Matt?" she said, with an uncertain smile.

"What?" I played dumb. "Oh, sorry. Thanks a lot, Mary. You saved my ass. Good night." I closed the door behind me and went to the pickup. I reckoned having the assault rifle in my room was safer.

I was still wet from the shower when Mary made her move. There was a soft knocking on the door. I groaned and wrapped a towel round my waist. She was a good-looking woman and I'd have happily frolicked with her if there hadn't been two problems—one, the blonde woman I loved and, two, the fact that Mary was emotionally fragile. Reluctantly, I took the chain off and opened up.

She slipped past me before I could react. I turned and saw her on the bed. She'd been wearing only a towel, too, but now it was on the floor. She was lying with her legs raised and slightly apart. The breasts that I'd suspected were spectacular turned out to be so. But it was her face I couldn't avoid, an expression that was a mixture of desire and anxiety. For all her physical allure, Mary was a sad spectacle.

"Please, Matt," she said, her voice breaking. "I…I want you."

I went over to the bed and picked up her towel. She grabbed mine and pulled it away. Her fingers moved on to my cock, which responded in a way I couldn't control.

"Mary," I said, before she locked her lips on mine. Her nipples, large and firm, pressed against my chest. I felt the blood burn in my veins as lust took command. I stopped resisting and fell gently forward. The hairs in her groin crushed against my belly.

"Matt," she said, the breath catching in her throat, "you know you want this."

I closed my eyes and let her guide my fingers inside her. She was wet, soft and yielding.

"Oh, Matt…"

And then I saw the other woman, the one I knew I loved. Her hair was spread out around her face and her lips were slightly open. "Matt," she whispered, her body arching as I entered her, "I…love…you."

In that instant, her name came to me. Karen, she was Karen. Karen Oaten.

I pulled rapidly away from Mary.

Her eyes sprang wide-open. "Matt? What is it?"

I had grabbed my towel and wrapped it round me again. Mary stretched forward, but I stepped beyond her reach.

"Please, Matt," she pleaded. "Tell me…tell me what's the matter."

I crashed to my knees, head to the floor. I hadn't just remembered Karen's name. I now also knew that she was over five months pregnant, carrying *our* son. My God— she had disappeared—she was lost. Had they killed her? Great sobs tore out of my chest as I banged my forehead on the thin carpet. I felt Mary's arms round my shoulders.

"Matt, please…don't be like this…please…Matt…"

I couldn't tell her. She couldn't help me find Karen. She didn't deserve to be caught up any deeper in my screwed-up world.

"I'm sorry," I said, wiping my eyes and pulling away from her. "I'm sorry, Mary. I can't do this. It's not you, it's me. I'm sorry.…"

I couldn't look at her as she shrank away. I heard the door close after her. I wiped the back of my arm across my eyes and stood up unsteadily. *Karen,* I was thinking, *Karen, where are you? What's happened to you?* At the back of my mind was the thought that I should get out of the motel now, get down to Washington as soon as I could. There would be leads to follow up—she couldn't just have vanished into the air. Then I saw images of offices, concerned people, some in suits, some in uniform, and I knew that I'd already followed everything up before I was taken to the camp. There had been no traces of Karen, either in D.C. or in the Shenandoah Valley. She really was lost. But I couldn't believe she was dead, I couldn't believe that.

I collapsed on the bed and fell like a stone into the empty darkness.

I woke up with a start. According to the radio clock, it was 5:43 a.m. I stood up, my arms and legs still half-asleep and looked around the room. Then I remembered the night before—Mary, and my remembering Karen.

Pulling on my clothes, I collected the guns. Mary had the pickup keys, but I wasn't going to deprive her of the vehicle. I would slip away and hitch a lift south. I went to the window and opened a couple of the blind's plastic strips.

Then froze.

A pair of police cruisers was pulling into the parking lot, their lights off despite the early-morning gloom. I looked to the left and saw Mary standing outside her door. She turned toward me and the cold fury on her face told me immediately that she had betrayed me. In truth, I could hardly blame her.

More police vehicles came into the parking lot. Among them were unmarked cars. All were pointing toward my room. I was caught like a rat in a well-deserved trap.

Twenty-Eight

Peter Sebastian was sitting in his office on the third floor of the Hoover Building. He had spent the night on the sofa there and was now compiling a report on the so-called "occult murders." The media, especially the evening TV news shows, had gone after the killings from every weird angle they could come up with. There had been theories that Professor Singer had been one of Monsieur Hexie's customers, that Loki and the Giants were a front for a far-right terrorist organization, and that the killer was a former cult member with a grudge against any and all mystic sources of knowledge and power.

At least the FBI's involvement with the investigation was behind the scenes and he hadn't been required to make a statement. That tiresome duty had fallen to MPDC Chief of Detectives Rodney Owen. In front of the cameras, he had been tight-lipped and decidedly non-user-friendly—which was unsurprising, given that his detectives had failed to make any progress with the three murders.

Not that Sebastian blamed them, despite his dislike of "Versace" Pinker. He had checked both detectives' records and knew that they were as good as anyone under Owen's command; the chief himself had made sure there were plenty of people backing up Clem Simmons and his partner. The problem was the series of killings itself. Sebastian had the feeling this was one of those once-in-a-lifetime cases—one that either made or broke the careers of the officers. Not that he or Dana Maltravers had been able to make any meaningful contributions. Not even the Bureau's experts had been any help so far. The truth was, they were up against a meticulous murderer with an impenetrable agenda.

Sebastian got up and poured himself another cup of coffee. He hadn't eaten anything apart from sandwiches for the past three days and his stomach was giving him hell. Too bad. Like his family, none of whom he'd seen for those three days, his body was going to have to take whatever was thrown at it till the case was solved. He looked at the notes he had made. With Matt Wells out of the frame for the professor's killing, building a case against him was hard. Sebastian asked himself why he was so sold on the Englishman. The fingerprints at Monsieur Hexie's place were a solid piece of evidence, but it was hardly conclusive. Okay, the guy was a smart-ass writer with ties to Detective Chief Superintendent Karen Oaten of the Metropolitan Police, and he'd made a lot of money from the book he'd done about the White Devil, but it was hardly his fault that he'd been chosen by that crazy killer as both scribe and victim. Nor was it Wells's fault that his ex-girlfriend, the one who called herself the Soul Collector, was a multiple murderer.

Still, Sebastian didn't buy everything about Wells. People who attracted trouble like the Brit had always had something to hide. It seemed likely that Matt Wells knew a lot more about the White Devil and Soul Collector murders in London than he'd disclosed in his book or newspaper columns, and Sebastian had read them all. It could also therefore be expected that he knew plenty about Karen Oaten's disappearance, as well as Monsieur Hexie's death. After all, why had he run from the state troopers up in Maine? Why had he still not come forward?

But right now, Peter Sebastian had other problems to deal with. The first was the pressure he was getting from the CIA. He'd been tapped by the Agency when he was in the Bureau's Puerto Rico field office. They wanted him to keep them advised on his activities. If he hadn't got himself in a mess with the wife of a local banker who worked for a drug gang, he'd have told them to suck their own dicks. As it was, the monthly deposit had been a big help over the past twenty years. And it wasn't as if the Agency had ever put him in a tight spot. Until now. They had an even bigger hard-on for Matt Wells than he did. He was beginning to wonder why. Could the disappearances of Karen Oaten and Wells have something to do with his number-two employer? The implications of that thought were making him jumpy. The CIA had a history of going to bed with people you wouldn't want your mother to meet.

Then there was Special Agent Dana Maltravers. He had picked his assistant with extreme care. Her record was spectacular—law and criminology at Columbia, a Yale MBA, top of her intake at Quantico and a four-year posting at the Miami field office that had her superiors singing "Halleluiah." Even when her brother committed suicide by jumping from his thirtieth-floor apartment in New York a couple of years back, she hadn't let him down. Until now. It wasn't just that she'd been incommunicado for two hours yesterday. She'd claimed her cell-phone battery was playing up, but he knew how unlikely that was—Dana was the kind of person who never had technical problems. No, she'd been strange ever since they got involved with the D.C. murders. He couldn't believe she was just squeamish. In the violent-crimes team, they'd seen the worst that America's sickos could offer, from skinned corpses in a Utah mining shack to piles of heads in a hacienda in New Mexico. By those standards, the occult killer was a pussycat.

Sebastian looked at his notes again. There were things he couldn't do till the other agents got in, like check on Harry Slater's Hate Crimes—he had passed them the details of all three murders. And he needed to push the document analysis about the drawings—those squares and rectangles weren't just random doodles, he was sure of that. He called up the three patterns of shapes on his screen once more. They meant something, either singly or in conjunction with each other. He moved them around, trying to make a coherent design, but again got nowhere.

Then his cell phone rang. He identified himself and listened, his jaw dropping. Some asshole captain in the New York State Police had waited until the operation was well under way to inform him that Matt Wells was being arrested.

The evening had gotten cold. Outside the office building in central Washington, Richard Bonhoff shivered. He was used to winters in Iowa, but there he always made sure to wear the right clothes. Right now, he wished he had bought another sweater and a woolly hat rather than the useless Redskins cap. At least it had shielded him from Lister successfully, though he wasn't sure that would happen again when the newspaperman reappeared. He looked at his watch. Over an hour had passed.

He had been thinking about the three people who had gone up in the elevator. The fifth floor was taken up by the offices of a partnership of lawyers. Richard had decided against following them up. He'd have stuck out even more among the sharks in suits than he did already. Then again, Gordy Lister's appearance—leather jacket and cowboy boots—didn't exactly conform. The woman in her plain suit was more like it, but she was young—he reckoned she couldn't be much more than thirty. Maybe she was a call girl whose job it was to service Lister and the tall man.

Richard shook his head. There was more to the woman than that. She was attractive enough to be a hooker, but too serious. The same went for the older guy—he wasn't out for a sexual jaunt. His eyes had strayed toward Richard once and they had made him avert his gaze immediately: they were pale blue and ice-cold. Who was the guy? He didn't look much like a lawyer, either.

Then it struck him that the three might go their separate ways when they came out. Which would he tail? Lister was the one who knew about the twins, but he didn't seem to be giving the orders. He didn't know anything about the woman. That left the tall man. Yes, he was the one, Richard decided. He'd wasted enough time with Gordy Lister. He fingered the screwdriver he'd bought earlier. As a weapon, it was better than nothing and, when he was young, he'd been trained how to kill with whatever was to hand. His gut flipped. He thought of the twins and pressed his lips together. He was ready to do what it took to get them back.

Twenty minutes later, the woman came out. She looked up and down the street before walking away to the left. Richard was in a darkened doorway, so she didn't spot him. A few minutes afterward, Gordy Lister appeared. He headed to the right, his head down. Richard's heart started to pound. The tall man was next.

He finished buttoning his coat, then adjusted his hat. He didn't pay any attention to the street, concentrating on taking a cigarette from a silver case and firing up with a matching lighter. Richard was struck by how self-assured the man looked, as if he owned the place. Maybe he did. After inhaling deeply several times, he strode away to the left. Richard gave him fifteen seconds, then slipped out of the doorway. He stayed on the opposite side of the road, his head bowed.

The tall man turned left at the next junction and walked with measured, long strides, never looking round. After he took another turn, Richard realized he was heading for the lot that Lister used. That was bad news. Once he'd got into his car, the tail would be over. Richard slowed down, wondering what to do. The best he could come up with was to continue tailing the guy. Maybe he would meet someone, or make a call that gave something away. He knew he was clutching at straws. This was bullshit. He should have gone to the cops. Tomorrow he would do that. He needed professional help.

The man dropped his cigarette outside the parking lot entrance and crushed the butt with a highly polished shoe. He still didn't look around. It struck Richard, out-of-towner that he was, that this guy wasn't exactly streetwise. A *stoned* mugger could have crept up on him. Richard timed another fifteen seconds and then followed. He was in luck. The tall man was still on street-level, moving toward the far corner of the parking area. Now it was easy. Richard bent over and used the vehicles to shield his approach. His target was standing next to a top-of-the-line BMW.

Richard got to within ten yards and was behind a dark blue Japanese SUV when he felt cold steel on the back of his neck.

"Hands on the floor." The voice was low and menacing. Strong fingers gripped his body and he realized that there was more than one man to deal with. The screwdriver was taken from his pocket and tossed away.

"That's it," said a second voice gruffly. "Get up, asshole."

Richard raised himself slowly, preparing to go into action as soon as the barrel moved away even slightly. Then he felt a sharp pain in his lower back.

"We heard what you did last time," the first man said. "We aren't scared of ex-marines, pal. In case you're wondering, this is a combat knife and I've used it to gut twelve people."

Richard knew immediately that the man was telling the

truth. He let himself go slack. Then he took a heavy blow to the head and crashed to the concrete. The last thing he knew was another hit. It cracked his skull from one side to the other.

The twins hadn't died in the wreckage of the Italian sports car in the Catskills back in 1972. They instead watched as two unconscious young people of matching gender and build were taken from an eighteen-wheeler loaded with lumber. Their bodies were doused with petrol and then the car pushed through the crash barrier by the lumber truck. Men were already waiting in the gorge below to check that the bodies were burned beyond recognition. The twins climbed into the rig and went on to their new lives.

In later years they sometimes talked about whether their deaths had really been necessary. Larry, as the male now called himself, tended to think they'd been overcautious, but reinventing himself as a rich man's son from Colorado had given him the opportunity for much creative thinking. His sister, now Jane, was less concerned with external appearances. She spent most of her time in the lab, developing drugs and treatments that brought in millions and had impressed several government agencies. Of course, their father would have been impressed by their daring and their subsequent achievements. They hadn't told the old man that they were going to start their lives again, so he had been forced to mourn their deaths before facing his own. It wasn't in them to regret his passing.

The twins trusted each other implicitly. Indeed, their interests were closely connected, both intellectually and businesswise. But they didn't often meet. They didn't feel any danger of their true identities being uncovered, even though there were people in the country's deep establishment, those who had real power in their adopted country, who were aware of what had happened in the Catskills. Rather, the twins felt at ease living apart. They met once a year, each time in a different place. Other than that, they spent their time in their chosen locations—Jane in her research facility in northern New England, Larry close to the seat of power in Washington, D.C.

Even the events of recent weeks hadn't brought about any change in the twins' activities. It would take more than a breach of security and the deaths of some insignificant people to worry them.

Twenty-Nine

I stepped back from the window and checked my weapons. I had the two pistols and the combat knife in my belt, and extra clips in my pockets. The M16 would make the cops keep their distance, even if I ran out of ammunition. I didn't want to get into a firefight; I was pretty sure that wouldn't be up to me, but I wouldn't shoot first. I looked through the slats of the blind again, screwing up my eyes. I could make out officers with rifles crouching behind the vehicles. Mary Upson was no longer on the boardwalk. It was time I made a move.

I went to the bathroom, keeping the light off. There was a small window that I reckoned I could get through. I opened it and looked out. There was very little light at the rear of the building. If the local commander knew what he was doing, he'd have deployed men at the rear. I sincerely hoped the FBI had not been called in yet. They would have covered all the angles.

"Matt Wells?" The loudspeaker distorted the man's voice. "Come out with your hands up! Leave all your weapons in the room!"

Obviously Mary had told them about my mini-armory.

I couldn't blame her. If I had any self-control, I wouldn't have let myself succumb to her charms. As it was, I had done the worst thing that a man could do to a woman—reject her at the moment of sex. Never mind "Hell hath no fury like a woman scorned"—hell hath no fury like a woman unfulfilled.

"Matt Wells! This is your final warning! Come out with your hands up now!"

I forced myself to concentrate on the siege. I had to give escaping a try. I was no use to Karen and our unborn son in a cell. They were alive—I had to believe that. They were alive.

Then there was a rattle of automatic rifle fire and the window disintegrated. The blinds flew about the room in small pieces. At least that saved me breaking the window. From the back of the room, I aimed my rifle above the roofs of the cruisers and loosed a sustained burst. That emptied one of my clips. I slapped in the last one, ducking down as more rounds blasted into the room. I took a deep breath and fired off half of the clip. Then I ran back to the bathroom, bending double as another hail of fire came in. Plaster dust filled the air and made breathing difficult.

I flicked on the M16's safety and threw it out of the window. To my intense relief, no one fired from the back of the motel. I stuck my head and shoulders out. For a few seconds I panicked, unable to get a grip on the window frame. Then I succeeded, propelling myself into the chill air. I hit the ground awkwardly and winded myself. The butt of the assault rifle was by my face. Gasping for breath, I got to my feet, picked up the M16 and stumbled forward. The ground was covered in some kind of prickly bush that tugged at my trousers. I drove my knees up and down, getting a flash of rugby training. Then the vegetation cleared and I found myself in a dip, the ground ahead sloping up to a fence. To my rear, the firing had finally stopped. Any second now, the cops would be in the room and would find me gone. My time was running out.

I clambered over the wooden fence. There was an asphalt road beyond, not much wider than a track and without traffic on it. I peered through the dawn mist and made out a barn about a hundred yards to my right. I slung the rifle over my shoulder and sprinted down the road, feeling the pistol grips jab into my belly. I slowed as I approached the building. A cow was by the fence. It stopped chewing, its large wet eyes on me.

Looking round the corner of the barn, I saw a two-story house close by. There were lights on inside, people round a table. The farming folk had got up early, but they either hadn't heard the gunfire or it somehow passed for normal around here. I glanced back and saw no sign of pursuit; an ominous silence hung in the damp air. I unslung the M16 and headed toward the building. There was a pickup parked beyond the front door. I would be in full view of the family, but I had no option. I kept to the dark spots in the yard as much as I could and made it to the vehicle without attracting attention.

I saw that the passenger-side door lock was up, but the keys weren't in the ignition. I opened the door quietly, sliding the rifle to the floor. Then I moved over to the driver's seat. My American friend Andy's face swam up in front of me. He'd been in a gang in New Jersey when he was kid and he'd learned all sorts of useful tricks, one of which was hot-wiring cars. I remembered some lessons he'd given me back in London, but it was one thing hot-wiring your own car with no pressure and an expert beside you, quite another a few yards from where the owner was eating and a posse of armed police about to come down the road.

I felt beneath the steering wheel and wrenched out the wires. I could make out the colors in the lights that were shining out from the house, but I wasn't sure they were the same in the U.S. Shit, my fingers were twitching like a kid's on a first date. I took a deep breath and tried to remember what Andy had shown me. Fortunately, that strand of my memory seemed to be working perfectly. I stripped the ends of the wires with my fingernails, then twisted a few together. The starter motor gave a dull hum and then the engine turned over. I hit the gas, engaged Reverse, and shot away from the farmhouse. As I moved toward the road, I saw an elderly man in a plaid shirt come out of the farmhouse, waving and shouting.

Looking to the right, I saw a group of police officers in Kevlar jackets, carrying a mixture of rifles, shotguns and pistols. They were about fifty yards away but didn't seem to notice I was the truck's driver. I swerved to the left and floored the gas pedal, keeping my pursuers in sight in the mirror. It struck me that a smart operator would have blocked the road in both directions. Then again, a smart operator would have stationed personnel at the rear of the motel.

As I drove, I fumbled under the seats for a road map. No such luck. The farmer would have known his way around blindfolded. Then I remembered the compass. I took it out of my shirt pocket and oriented myself. As soon as possible, I needed to head south, or better, southwest. That much my memory was capable of supplying. There was another junction ahead, with a sign to Interstate 87. I decided to take the smaller road that hugged it for a while and then go for a vehicle upgrade.

A few minutes later, I reckoned the time had come. There was a clump of trees to the right of the road, with a narrow track leading there. I made the turn and drove up the rough surface. There was good cover in the trees and I left the pickup in the most out of sight place I could find. If the farmer found it before the cops did, he could have the M16 with my compliments, though I threw away the half-empty ammunition clip. I made sure the pistols were secure under my belt and jogged back to the road. There was very little traffic and no sign of pursuit yet. I ran onward to the right, the interstate entrance ramp about half a mile ahead in the rapidly brightening dawn. It was touch and go. If an obliging driver passed, maybe I had a chance.

I got to the road that led to the interstate, my lungs straining and my knee beginning to protest. I stuck out my thumb and, to my amazement, the first vehicle slowed and then stopped. It was an eighteen-wheeler carrying a forty-foot container. I stepped up and grabbed the door handle on the nearside.

"'Morning," said the bearded figure at the wheel. "Cold enough to break a polar bear's balls." He grinned at me, running his eyes over me. "You one of those jogger assholes?" He engaged first gear and hauled the load up the incline toward the interstate.

"Uh…no," I said, putting on an accent that I hoped would pass for Canadian. "Just in a hurry."

"Where you heading, man?"

I decided to go for broke. "Washington."

"Well, I can take you as far as Baltimore. That do?"

"Certainly will." I remembered taking a day trip to the city from D.C. when I was at the crime conference. Joe Greenbaum and I had ended up in a waterside restaurant, eating crab and drinking a ridiculous amount of beer. Which reminded me. I needed to get in touch with Joe.

The driver extended a huge hand and grinned. "Name's Derek. But you can call me Bo."

"A perfect ten," I said, with a laugh, remembering the movie. My memory was behaving more strangely by the minute.

"You got it."

I decided to play safe in case he tuned into the local radio-station news. "I'm Pete," I said, suddenly having a glimpse of a completely bald man—my gay friend Peter Satterthwaite.

"You a Canuck?"

"Yeah," I said, taken aback that my attempt at an accent had hit gold.

"So you gotta like Neil Young." Bo's expression had turned grave. There were some things you didn't joke about.

"Oh, yeah," I replied.

"Gimme your top five songs."

This guy was serious about his music. I thought I was going to have to kick-start my memory, but it had things well under control.

"Let's see. 'Thrasher,' 'Cortez the Killer,' 'Ohio,' 'Powderfinger' and 'Heart of Gold.'"

"Yeah!" Bo shouted, holding up an open hand. "Four out of five ain't bad."

I made the high five and grinned. "No points for 'Heart of Gold,' eh?"

He grunted. "Middle-of-the-road bullshit."

I thought of the blonde woman called Karen. "The girlfriend likes it," I said.

"Oh, that's all right, then," Bo said with a grin. "Whatever the little lady wants…"

I swallowed a laugh. If Karen had heard herself described in those terms, the bearded man would have been wondering where his reproductive organs had suddenly gone.

"So," he said, passing another container truck, "what you got on in D.C.?"

I shrugged. "Meeting up with some friends."

"What is it you do, Pete?"

I went with what made the real Pete his first million. "Computers."

Bo glanced at me. "Is that right? I hate the fucking things."

That was good. He wasn't going to catch me out on

techie particulars. "Yeah, well, I guess you don't have much call for them in your line of work."

"True," he said, almost wistfully. "I just sit here all day driving other people's stuff, a slave to the machine."

I looked at him. I hadn't expected to come across a revolutionary in the cab. He deserved encouragement. "You need to make a stand, Bo. What's in the box?"

"Lobsters," he said, shaking his head. "Rich folks' chow."

"You could always turn the heating up."

He laughed bitterly.

I smiled. When he slid a CD into the player, I sat back in the comfortable seat as the unmistakable chords of Neil's *Rust Never Sleeps* rang out. In a few seconds, I was miles away. Way across the Atlantic, in fact....

...watching Gavin Burdett as he comes out of the investment bank where he works in the City of London and heads to Bank underground station. He's wearing one of those deeply untrendy gray coats with a black collar. The heels of his highly polished and doubtlessly ridiculously expensive shoes ring out on the pavement. I take up position about five yards behind him and start the tail.

I'm doing it for two reasons. The first is that effective tailing requires regular practice. Ever since Sara's first threat, I've acquired as many useful skills as I can. The second is that Gavin Burdett is the chief suspect in Karen's current major case—but she's run up against the buffers with him, stymied by his lawyers and the care he's taken to obscure his activities. I've been writing articles on transnational financial crime, so I have my own interest in nailing him. But I want to help my lover out, too. She's confined by the parameters within which the police have to work. I have no such problem. Of course, if I do anything to bring Karen's case into jeopardy, she'll tie my intestines round my neck. That adds to the challenge.

Besides, everything I've found out about Gavin Burdett suggests that he's a major-league scumbag. He has a reputation in his company for treating subordinates like dirt; his wife divorced him after she caught him with his dick in the Filipino maid; and one of his former business partners put his head under a train rather than face the charges Burdett had set him up for. Tailing a bastard like that will surely reveal something interesting.

Burdett sits down in the only available seat in the Tube carriage, beating a heavily pregnant woman to it and resolutely avoiding her outraged glare. I raise a newspaper and watch him surreptitiously. He takes a magazine from his briefcase. The multimillionaire investment banker gets down to *Big Babes on the Bounce,* indifferent to the scandalized looks on other passengers' faces.

"Pillock," I say under my breath, then get ready to leave the train when my target stands up.

Burdett comes out on street level at Bethnal Green and looks around. The bastard is handsome in a slightly raddled way, his hook nose, sallow skin and the thick black hair brushed back from his forehead giving the impression of a practiced lothario. I wonder if he is on his way to some woman—maybe he likes a bit of rough, something that wouldn't be hard to find on the Roman Road. But instead, he starts walking north up Cambridge Heath Road. I keep a discreet distance. Then he slows as he approaches a row of shops. He goes into the second one.

I stop about twenty yards away. This is interesting, but not in any way that I'd have guessed. Gavin Burdett has gone into an establishment called Black As Night. According to the door the shop supplies "Candles, Tarot Cards, Caribbean Herbs and Roots, Occult Books—Everything Wild, Wicked and Witchy."

Burdett comes out half an hour later with two heavily loaded plastic bags. I'd never have put him down as a devotee of black magic. Then again, he's about as satanic-looking an individual as I've ever come across. And that includes the White Devil and the Soul Collector....

"Hey, Pete, you still alive?"

I came round to the sound of Bo's voice and blinked away the vision of Gavin Burdett. "Where are we?"

"Between Philly and Baltimore. Some dream you were having, man." A radio presenter was rattling away in the background.

I nodded, my mouth dry. "Haven't been sleeping well lately."

"Not much sleep to be found down in D.C., neither."

I looked at him. "What do you mean?"

Bo grinned. "You know those occult killings?"

I felt a stab of unease in my gut. "Yeah?"

"Well, there's been another one."

Thirty

At MPDC headquarters, Clem Simmons logged off the Internet and leaned back in his chair. He wasn't happy with what he'd just found. Joe Greenbaum was right about the Antichurch of Lucifer Triumphant—its ravings had been reported on a site run by an occult enthusiast who called himself The Lord of the Underworld. Earlier, Simmons had got a techie to access the e-mail correspondence on Professor Singer's laptop. There were no threatening messages in the mail program, but the victim had made a folder for them in his documents file. He had named it "Filth." Dana Maltravers hadn't caught it—another disappointment. The virulence of the threats had surprised Simmons—the professor was going to have his throat cut with the jagged lid from a can of pork; the same weapon would be used to mutilate his wife and children; their bodies were to be dumped in acid baths.

The problem for Clem was what to do with the material. It was circumstantial in the extreme and, according to the Web site, no member of the Antichurch had been identified. On the other hand, those people were clearly inciting racial and religious hatred. The obvious course of action would be to ask Peter Sebastian to involve the FBI's experts, but Simmons wasn't sure how much he trusted him.

Gerard Pinker came up to his partner's desk, a wide grin on his face.

"What going on?" Simmons asked, looking up.

"Get this. The English guy Matt Wells got away from twenty-five New York staties this morning."

"What are you so excited about? Sounds like Sebastian was right about him."

"Give me a break, Clem," Pinker said. "Dickhead's been blowing smoke up our asses."

Simmons heaved himself to his feet. "Come on, we're going to be late for our very own deep throat." He grabbed his coat and headed for the elevator. After hitting the street, they walked toward the National Mall.

"You seriously think Gordy Lister's going to have anything on the murders?" Pinker asked, stopping at a kiosk to buy gum.

Simmons shrugged. "He's helped us before."

"Yeah, with a loony tunes dope dealer we already knew about and that vigilante pimp-killer the *Star Reporter* turned into a celebrity."

"We aren't exactly overflowing with leads, Vers."

Pinker tightened his silk scarf as the wind whistled between Capitol Hill and the Potomac. "All right, let's see what the slimeball has to say."

The newspaperman was where they'd asked him to be, in front of the Washington Memorial. He wore a thick wool coat. His hands were in his pockets and his back was toward them.

"Gordy," Pinker said, from the newspaperman's left side.

"Lister," Simmons added, from his right.

He gave them each an angry look. "What the fuck, guys? What's so important that I have to freeze my ass off out here?"

"If memory serves, you're the one who prefers meeting out of doors," Pinker said.

Lister gave a hollow laugh. "Yeah, well, I got my reputation to think about."

"You're going to have your nuts in a bag if you don't mind your mouth," Pinker said, baring his teeth.

"Cool it, Vers," Simmons said. "I'll get straight to the point, Gordy. You guys been running plenty of stories about the murders."

The newspaperman gave him a neutral glance. "You mean the occult killings?"

"As you call them," Clem Simmons said, twitching his nose. "So, we were wondering if you maybe had some angle you haven't come clean about."

"What do you mean 'some angle'? We aren't detectives, my friend."

"You got that right," Pinker said, stepping in front of Lister. "Hey, asshole, you forgotten the last time you tried to play cute with me?"

Gordy Lister looked at his cowboy boots. "No," he mumbled.

"I didn't think so. If you don't want me to stomp on your toes again, start talking."

Gordy's head stayed bowed for some time, before he raised it slowly and looked at Simmons.

"Call off your attack poodle, will you, Clem?"

Simmons laid a hand on his partner's arm. "Don't mind him," he said, smiling encouragingly. "What have you got?"

"What I heard, a writer from London is the man. Matt Wells, his name."

Pinker edged closer. "Come on, Gordy, you know that's bullshit. He could only have done Professor Singer if he used a private jet." He caught Lister's eye. "And he didn't."

Lister shrugged. "That's what our sources are giving us."

"Those sources wouldn't happen to be in the FBI, would they?" Simmons asked, poker-faced.

Lister looked down again. "You kidding, Clem? You want me to name our sources?"

"Rhetorical question. What else are you hearing?"

"Not much. 'Course, the guys who are working the stories might be looking at things they haven't told me yet."

Gerard Pinker shook his head. "You people are so hot for that sexy occult angle, aren't you?"

Lister raised his bony shoulders. "Sure. It sells papers."

"I bet it does," Simmons said, giving him a slack smile. "Speaking of demons, you ever hear of the Antichurch of Lucifer Triumphant?"

"Jeez, it's cold out here. The Antichurch of what? No, man, doesn't ring any bells." He shuffled his feet.

Clem Simmons held his gaze on him, then glanced at his partner. "He hasn't heard of the Antichurch of Lucifer Triumphant, Vers."

"No. No, he hasn't."

The newspaperman took out his cell phone and looked at the screen. "Look, guys, I got to go," he said, avoiding their eyes. "See you around."

Pinker waited till Lister was out of earshot. "What do you reckon?"

"Obviously he was lying about the Antichurch. The question is why. Is that the *Star Reporter's* next big story?"

They started to walk back to the MPDC building. They hadn't gone more than twenty paces when both their phones rang.

Peter Sebastian stood on the west bank of the Anacostia River, below the National Arboretum. To his left, a tent had been erected by the CSIs around the body of the middle-aged male Caucasian that had been found in the river. People had gathered at the barrier tape behind him and he could hear their voices. There wasn't much sense of shock—people in northeast D.C. were used to violent death—but they were still curious.

The FBI man's curiosity had also been piqued, and not just by the murder. He watched as Dana Maltravers showed ID, ducked under the tape and came toward him, her expression as resolute as ever.

"Sorry I'm late," she said, points of red on her cheeks.

Peter Sebastian gave her an icy look. "I've told you before that I need to be able to reach you at all times, Special Agent."

Maltravers recoiled. "I was over at Hate Crimes, sir."

"Really? And what took you there?"

"Those threats that were found in Professor Singer's e-mail program? It turns out Hate Crimes has logged the group that made them."

Peter Sebastian's face changed. "The Antichurch of Lucifer Triumphant? What do Hate Crimes know?"

"Very little, unfortunately. It was founded over a hundred and fifty years ago, up in Maine. But it only lasted a few years, till it was violently put down by the locals. There was no sign of it until the threats against Professor Singer late last year."

"So could they be the killers we're looking for?"

Maltravers raised her shoulders. "Apparently they used to perform human sacrifices."

"Shit." Sebastian looked at his subordinate. "Good work, Dana. I presume Hate Crimes is collating information."

"I asked them to. You may have to make a formal request. You know what they're like. They guard their data, even from us."

Sebastian watched as Detectives Simmons and Pinker arrived at the barrier tape. "Here come the soon-to-be-relieved investigating officers," he said in a low voice.

Dana Maltravers turned toward the tent.

Peter Sebastian put a hand on her arm. "Just a moment, Special Agent. Do not engage in any more flippant conversation with Pinker. He and his partner are about to become the enemy."

Maltravers nodded uncertainly, then followed her boss to the tent where the latest victim lay.

"Son of a bitch," Gerard Pinker said, standing by his Crown Victoria outside the barrier tape. "Who does ol' Dickhead think he is?"

"Someone who has more pull with the commissioner than you and me," Clem Simmons said.

"Not to mention Chief Owen."

Simmons shrugged.

Pinker scowled. "Shit, I've never been taken off an investigation in my life."

Simmons smiled softly. "Me, neither. Then again, we haven't exactly covered ourselves in glory here, have we, Vers?"

"You really think this is one of them?"

"I'm not sure."

Simmons thought about the male corpse in the tent. He'd been naked when he was found, so the pair of knives in his chest had looked like the obvious cause of death. It hadn't been until Dr. Gilbert had examined the skull beneath the dead man's hair that other wounds had been found. The M.E. reckoned that the larger of the two skull fractures would have been lethal. Although it was hard to tell because of the body's waterlogged condition, she thought that the knives had been inserted postmortem. The time of death was hard to calculate, but Marion Gilbert reckoned the victim had been in the water for at least twenty-four hours, and he had certainly been dead before he went into the river. Her initial evaluation was that the man was in his early forties, in good physical condition and in a profession that demanded substantial exposure to the elements—his hands and face had weathered, probably over the course of many years. The only distinguishing feature on the body was a tattoo on the upper right arm. It showed the Marine Corps insignia and the words *Semper Fi*.

"Let's get out of here," Pinker said, opening the car door. "I'll tell you what I think."

"Oh, yeah?" Simmons said, getting in the passenger side.

"Oh, yeah," his partner mimicked, reversing out onto the road. "That guy wasn't killed by the occult killer."

"And your reasoning is?"

"For a start, knives were used instead of skewers. Plus, he hasn't got a drawing pinned to him."

Clem Simmons nodded. "True enough. Even if it had been pulled off by the flow of water, there would have been puncture marks."

"Right. And we kept those collections of shapes out of the public eye. So whoever killed the floater didn't know about them."

"Mmm. You could be right. Or maybe the killer just ran out of time."

"Yeah, sure," Pinker said, shaking his head. "I'll tell you something else, Clem. The murderer of the first three is a class act. He didn't just toss his victims in the river. Why take the risk of being spotted when you're smart enough to leave no traces?"

The daylight had almost gone. Simmons eyed the lights of central Washington ahead. "You're forgetting the fingerprints at Monsieur Hexie's place."

"Matt Wells's? They're a ruse and you know it, man. The Brit isn't even in the city."

The big man closed his eyes. "Maybe," he said, rolling his head on the rest. "But who gives a shit, Vers? We're off the cases, remember?"

"Screw that," his partner said, spittle flying from his

lips. "Those Bureau assholes will come begging for our help in a day or two."

Clem Simmons laughed. "Assholes? There was me thinking that you had a soft spot for Princess Maltravers."

"Kiss my ass, big man. You know brunettes don't do it for me."

"I saw the way you've been scoping her."

"Unfortunately it takes two to do the horizontal tango, Clem. She wouldn't even look me in the eye back there."

Simmons swallowed a laugh. He reckoned Dana Maltravers might have been warned off by her boss. Not that it mattered anymore. He didn't trust either agent one little bit.

"Shame about Dr. Gilbert, though," Pinker said, starting the engine.

"How's that?"

"We won't be seeing so much of her. Now, there's a woman I could go for in a big way."

This time Simmons didn't hold back on laughing. "Jesus, Vers. You think you stand any chance with the M.E.? She's way out of your league, man."

Pinker shook his head. "See, that's where you're wrong, Clem. I've always had a good feeling about her." He looked to the left. Marion Gilbert was heading toward a black SUV, her head down. "You notice a change in her recently?"

"How do you mean?"

Pinker raised a hand at the M.E., but she didn't respond to the gesture. "I don't know. She's looks kinda stressed. Maybe these murders have been getting to her."

Simmons shook his head emphatically. "You lovesick fool. Dr. Gilbert lives and breathes homicide victims. She's got formaldehyde in her veins."

Gerard Pinker pursed his lips as he drove away from the crime scene. Sometimes, he thought, his partner was surprisingly unperceptive.

* * *

The blonde woman was lying on the bed and looking out of the window. Her eyes were wide as she took in the trees beyond the high fence and the mist rolling down them. It made her think of a wispy summer dress, but she couldn't remember ever wearing such a thing. She couldn't remember much about herself at all. All she knew was that she was in hospital, the doctor had told her so this morning. After he'd gone, the friendly nurse had said she was doing very well and that her treatment was almost finished. But when she had asked what she was being treated for, the nurse had just smiled and said the doctor would explain everything soon.

The next person who came into the room wasn't a doctor, though. She was dressed in a gray uniform with shiny black boots, and she wasn't like the nurse—she was stern. Her brown hair pulled back from her face in a tight grip, and she didn't smile once. She handed the blonde woman a file and told her to study everything in it. After she'd gone, the woman looked at the photograph and read about the man depicted in it. There was a lot of detail—where he lived, what he did when he wasn't working, his family. Then there was a separate section about his work. The blonde woman read the words and committed them to her memory, but she didn't understand all of them. They were written in her native language, but the writing was hard to follow in parts.

When the doctor finally came back, his questions made her even sleepier. He asked her for her name, her date and place of birth, her parents' names and what she did. Her mind was completely blank and she couldn't answer any of the questions. For some reason, she didn't find that in the least upsetting.

Thirty-One

Trucker Bo dropped me on the outskirts of Baltimore. The only money I had was a few dollars I'd got in change when Mary and I had stopped at a gas station—she had given me cash for gas when she went to the washroom. I had to assume the rail and bus stations in Washington would be being watched.

So I stuck my thumb out again. This time it took me longer to get a ride, but eventually a young man in a cargo van stopped. He was going to D.C. with a load of bathroom tiles for a house in Kalorama Heights. I played the Canadian tourist again and got him to explain where that was. My memory was playing games with me again—I had no recollection of where in D.C. my friend Joe Greenbaum lived.

The radio was playing and a news bulletin came on not long after I'd got in. I wondered if my name was going to come up, but the news was all local and the shoot-out at the motel in New York wasn't mentioned. I found out more about the latest news on the occult killings.

"Good old D.C.," the driver said, glancing at me and smiling wryly. "You get much of that kind of thing back home?"

I had a flash of the White Devil and the Soul Collector. "No," I lied. "It's pretty quiet where I come from…in Ontario."

"Well, it sure ain't been where we're heading." He laughed and lit a cigarette. "Go, you Redskins, go."

I tried to make sense of what was coming from the battered speakers. It seemed that a body had been found in a river, and there was evidence to connect the unidentified male Caucasian to the previous murders. My name didn't come up. Then I heard that the FBI had taken over the investigation. That was not good news.

The young man let me off in the area he identified as Adams Morgan and I went straight to a phone booth. I had enough coins to make a call. Fortunately Joe's number was listed. I got connected.

"Greenbaum."

"Joe, it's Matt."

There was a brief silence. "Jesus, Matt. Where are you?"

"In your town."

"I don't believe it," he said, the words coming in a rush. "The police…well, I'll tell you when I see you. Where are you exactly?"

I looked around. "Eighteenth Street and Belmont Road."

"Okay. Stay there. I'm on my way."

About fifteen minutes later, a yellow-and-black taxi pulled up and I saw Joe's heavy frame in the back. I got in the other side and punched his shoulder.

"It's great to see you, man," I said, meaning it. I suddenly felt emotional. Seeing someone I knew, someone I remembered, brought home how much I'd been through.

Joe smiled. "Yeah, this is a surprise—a great one, of course." He looked over his shoulder and said the name of what sounded like a bar to the driver. "I only hope I haven't landed you even more in the shit."

"What do you mean?"

"I went to the cops about you." He raised his hands. "All good, don't worry. But they may have thought it was worth staking out my place, in case."

"So they're still after me...." I said, my voice low.

"Not if they listened to what I said."

"I just heard on the radio that the FBI has taken over the investigation."

He nodded. "Yeah, I heard that, too. I'm not sure that's a good thing."

The taxi pulled up outside a run-down bar. After paying, Joe got out and scanned the area. "Don't worry. We're not going in. There's another place about a ten-minute walk from here. You up to it?"

I laughed. "Are you?"

"What do you mean?" he said, feigning outrage. "I'm at my fighting weight."

"I didn't know hyper-heavyweight had been recognized."

He thumped me in the chest. "Yeah, I've missed that classy English humor."

"Shall we split up for a bit? See if anyone's on our tail?"

"I forgot you were an expert at this. Okay."

I crossed the road and ducked down behind a van with high sides, while Joe kept walking straight ahead. I waited while a couple of people passed him, but neither showed any interest. I kept him in sight as he waddled on. When he went into a much more salubrious bar, I looked around again. There was no one suspicious, at least to my eyes, so I went to join him.

Joe had found a table at the far corner of the place, which was a cross between a neighborhood bar and a trendy young persons' hangout. The waitresses were wearing short black skirts, so it was bearable. Joe had already ordered us beer.

"So, let me look at you, man," he said, taking in my less than salubrious clothes. "Still buying your gear at Bloomingdale's, eh?"

I laughed. The oversize reporter had a comic streak that was at odds with his work outing corrupt businessmen and officials. "I see you're still on the sperm whale diet."

"Yup," he said, grinning. "Blubber three times a day keeps the doctor away."

I had come up with that jibe the first time I'd met Joe— he'd made a comment about how thin I was.

The beer arrived, accompanied by a platter of snacks. I suddenly realized that, although Bo had given me a bottle of water, nothing solid had passed my lips since last night at the motel. I actually managed to match Joe bite for bite. That seemed to impress him.

"All right," he said, wiping his lips. "Tell me what happened."

"I'll tell you what I can remember."

He raised an eyebrow. "Meaning?"

"Somebody wearing army boots has been stomping through my memory." I told him what I could about the camp and my escape. It would be fair to say he looked astounded.

"Jesus, Matt. What is this shit?"

I shrugged. "I was hoping you might be able to help me out there, Joe."

He smiled. "What, along the lines of 'Yeah, now you come to mention it, Matt, I know just the place you mean up in the Maine woods. It's a research center run by the CIA and—oh, look—I have the cell-phone number of the man in charge.'"

I laughed. "That kind of thing, yeah."

Joe's expression grew more serious. "Why would someone want to mess with your mind, Matt? Do you know something they want forgotten?"

"Good questions, both."

He rubbed his unshaven chin. "Can you remember anything about how you got up there?"

"No, that's one of numerous things that my brain is

steadfastly refusing to access. I've remembered Karen's disappearance, but…" I broke off, suddenly seeing the woman on the upturned cross whose throat was cut.

"What is it, man?"

I took several deep breaths. I wasn't going to let myself believe that Karen had been the victim. It must have been a trick. But why would anyone be so heartless? She was pregnant, for Christ's sake. Our son…

"Matt?" Joe's hand was on my arm. "Are you okay?"

I snapped out of it and gave a weak smile. I wasn't going to tell him—if I did, it would seem even more real.

"Just a bit wasted—not enough sleep."

"Not enough beer." Joe raised a hand for more. "So you don't recall you and me running around Virginia and D.C. after Karen disappeared? I pulled the chain of any law enforcement professional I thought might be able to help."

"No…. Doesn't surprise me that you did what you could, though."

"Yeah, well…" He looked away, embarrassed. "'Course, I had to do the same thing when you didn't show for our usual late breakfast. You must have been snatched somewhere between your hotel and my place. We were using it as base camp for *our* investigation—the Feds were getting nowhere fast."

"What about the local cops in Virginia?"

"Oh, they did all they could. I used a contact of mine in the Bureau to kick ass down there."

"Then you had to cope with me vanishing, too."

He nodded. "It was the same story as with Karen. I kept them at it, but there was nothing—no witnesses, no messages, no ransom demand. I even wrote an article about you both for the *Washington Post*. They stuck it on page twelve, so who knows how many people noticed. That was ten days ago. The story's died a death since then."

I gave an ironic laugh. "And I nearly died several more times in the camp and on my way here."

"Certainly sounds like the people in that camp were very unhappy that you'd gotten away. I wonder…" He broke off, for once not raising his glass to his lips.

"What?"

"Nah, it's just my suspicious mind. I was thinking that maybe those assholes in the gray uniforms have got some pull with the Bureau. I mean, I was always sure you weren't behind any of these occult killings, despite your prints at one of the scenes. Someone's gone to a lot of trouble to frame you, my friend."

"That much I'd worked out for myself, Joe. The question is, who?"

A spectacular waitress brought a fresh pitcher and Joe filled our glasses.

"Someone who had access to the scene, obviously."

"Which means either the killer or someone who knew his or her movements. Or, alternatively, one or more of the investigators."

He nodded. "The latter being the patrol cops first on the scene, the CSIs, the D.C. detectives on the case or the FBI—take your pick."

"How come the FBI was involved?"

Joe put his hand over his mouth and burped. "Because it's D.C. and there are so many VIPs around. That'll no doubt be behind the Bureau pulling rank and kicking the MPDC team off the case today."

I watched as the waitress brought another platter of food, then I picked up a buffalo wing. "So what's your line on the murders, Joe?"

"My line? Well, apart from the fact that no one seems to have a clue what's going on, I reckon that the occult shit is just a distraction from the real deal."

"Which is?"

"Come on, Matt. It shouldn't be too hard for a crime novelist like you to spot."

Joe stared at me. "Yeah. Jesus, Matt, you hadn't forgotten you were one of those, had you?"

"Em, no…it just hasn't seemed very important recently."

"No, I guess it hasn't. On the other hand, you've been right in the middle of a prime example of what I'm talking about."

"Of a…shit storm?"

Joe grinned. "Well, yeah, that. But what I'm getting at begins with a *c* and has four syllables."

I shrugged, being far from in the mood for word games.

"Come on, man," Joe said, spreading his arms wide. "This is the world capital of—"

"Conspiracies," I said, in a flash of enlightenment.

"You got it, Matt. And I know just the man to help us nail the fuckers behind this one."

That made me feel better, but not a whole lot. I had the feeling that time very much wasn't on my side, or on Karen's—if she was even still alive.

After I'd eaten and drunk enough to feel human again, we decided to go back to Joe's place. The fact that we hadn't seen a tail earlier suggested there probably wasn't surveillance on him. To be certain, we went the back way into his apartment, climbing over the fences between small yards. Joe said his neighbors used that route all the time for dope deals.

We made a plan for the next day and Joe went to crash, claiming that he'd overdone the beer. I sat at his desk with great heaps of printouts and files all around me, and logged on to the Internet—one of the things that my unpredictable memory seemed to have retained was how to operate a computer. I checked the reports of the D.C. occult killings in the American Press and brought myself up to speed. Then I checked the U.K. papers. I was glad to see that my own rag, the *Daily Independent,* had been suitably shocked by the disappearance of its crime columnist, though the story had quickly gone cold. There had been a degree of outrage when I became a murder suspect, though it was hard for my colleagues to argue against the fingerprint evidence. No doubt it would have helped if I got in touch with them, but I wasn't going to do so—at least not yet. Joe and I had agreed it was better that I kept my head down for the time being.

I looked at references to Karen in the Web pages, too. There was much indignation about the disappearance of a senior Metropolitan Police detective, but even that story had lost the news editors' interest after a couple of weeks. I leaned back in Joe's oversize chair and looked at the ceiling. It was so cracked that the people upstairs must have been ardent punk fans, though thankfully they weren't pogoing right now. I was thinking about Karen—the way her face turned from stern to amused to loving in the space of a few seconds; the way that, in the weeks before her disappearance, she had started to rest her hand on her belly.... God, how I missed her....

…and I'm in a luxurious hotel suite, watching CNN on a vast plasma TV attached to the wall.

"Matt," Karen says from the bedroom, "come and see."

I tear myself away from a story about Mormon marriages and go through, my legs still numb from the transatlantic flight. Karen is in the bathroom. It's twice the size of mine back in London, and I reckon I have one of the bigger bathrooms in that city. The fittings probably aren't real solid gold, though I couldn't be 100 percent sure. And, miracle of miracles, there's a normal-height bath in an American hotel.

"Neat, eh?" Karen says, laying her toiletries out on the marble runway behind the taps.

"Neat, yeah," I reply. "Can you leave room for my toothbrush and razor?"

She hits me with her toilet bag and that leads to a tussle, which leads to one of the beds. I am told to be careful. Strangely, that instruction, as well as the emperor-size bed, add a certain frisson to our lovemaking. If I'm not careful, she'll be wanting to be pregnant on a permanent basis.

"Is he all right?" I ask, resting a hand on her belly.

"Loving it," she says, her voice deep. "Apparently fetuses are stimulated by their parents doing it."

I find that vaguely disturbing, but don't say so. Shortly afterward Karen, being Karen, starts to talk about her big case. To be fair, she has a meeting at the Justice Department tomorrow and she wants to have all the facts straight.

"...nail that bastard Gavin Burdett," she says, her eyes flashing. "God, he makes me sick."

I smile at her. "Aren't police officers supposed to remain impartial and dispassionate?"

I get an elbow in my stomach for that.

"Take my word for it, he's a complete scumbag."

I remember the time I tailed Gavin Burdett to the occult supplies store in the East End. I still haven't told Karen about that, not least because I don't know what to read into it. Burdett is the kind of highly focused investment pirate who doesn't waste his time on anything that doesn't make him money.

"In fact," Karen continues, in an unusually forthcoming mood, "when he's in Washington, which he is at least once a month to meet with the thieving money men over here, he stays at a private house in Georgetown, near the university." She turns to me, an expression of disgust on her face. "Do you know what he does there?"

I'm tempted to reply that he summons up the devil, but hold myself back. "Do tell," I say sweetly.

"He has whores sent round. According to the FBI, they all look underage…"

"Why haven't they arrested him, then?"

She looks at me as if I'm an idiot. "Because he'll get off in half an hour with the lawyers he can afford. Besides, his hide is mine."

"You've been reading my Western phrase book again." I can no longer resist the urge to needle her. "And just how are you going to get the Justice Department to sign off on that?"

"Simple," she replies. "I'll ask them for everything they have on Burdett, and at the same time insist I have a right to arrest a British citizen back home."

"And you think they'll buy that?"

Karen gives me her most seductive smile. "Undoubtedly," she says, getting off the bed. "I'm going for a bath."

"Mind you don't drown under the weight of your own…the weight of my son," I say. When she's safely ensconced in two feet of warm water, I go over to the expansive dressing table. Typical Karen. Instead of facial unguents and hairstyling equipment, she's laid out her case files under the mirror. I cast a practiced eye over them and find the one on Gavin Burdett. The thing is, I'm going to have plenty of free time when Karen's at meetings. I've acquired a taste for tailing Gavin Burdett and it would be a challenge to do so in a foreign city. I find the relevant FBI report and note down the address of a house in Georgetown.

Thirty-Two

Joe Greenbaum was sitting on a bench in Rock Creek Park in northwest D.C. I was watching from behind the tree line through a pair of his binoculars, the midmorning air still chilly enough to make my nose twitch. We were about a hundred yards from the nearest road but, given time, it wouldn't have been hard for the cops to set up an ambush. So Joe had called Detective Simmons only half an hour ago and insisted on meeting immediately. He hadn't mentioned me.

When a heavily built black man came into sight, I scanned the area behind him, and to his left and right. It was a weekday, so there weren't many people in the vicinity. A female jogger passed Joe, but she was wearing skintight gear—no place to hide a weapon. Besides, she disappeared round the corner rapidly.

The cop approached Joe and, after shaking hands, sat next to him. I watched his face. It was rugged, with a slightly world-weary expression. He looked competent and, more to the point, reasonable. I gave them a few minutes, scanned the paths and woods one last time, and then broke cover. I had one of the Glocks and the combat knife under my belt in the small of my back. No doubt Detective Simmons was armed, too, but I wasn't going to let myself be locked up again, no matter what happened.

I joined the track about twenty yards behind them and started walking. Joe didn't turn round, and neither did Simmons, until I was almost on them.

"Jesus, Matt!" Joe said in surprise, as I sat down. I hadn't told him how furtive I could be. He looked at the detective. "Like I say, just hear the man out."

"Mr. Wells," the detective said, leaning forward and extending a hand. "Welcome back to D.C. I'm Clem Simmons."

I shook his great paw. He seemed friendly enough and not particularly interested in arresting me. "Call me Matt," I said. "Clem."

He smiled. "Okay, Matt. Joe here says you've got things to tell me. You've got to understand, I can't offer you any kind of assurance that I won't take you in." Furrows appeared on his forehead. "But, as you know, I'm not investigating the killings anymore."

I nodded. "But you don't think I'm guilty of them."

"It's up to you to convince me of that. Tell me, you got an interest in black magic, that kind of stuff?"

I raised my shoulders. "Interest, no. Involvement, yes. In the past I was chased by a pair of killers who played around with satanic names and imagery."

"The White Devil and the Soul Collector. I read about them. Seems you're pretty good at looking after yourself."

"I took precautions," I said, and then told him something about the training I'd undergone with Dave. Then I got on to the camp and my escape from it.

When I'd finished, Simmons glanced at Joe and shook his head. "Is this guy for real?"

Joe and I laughed, then saw the serious look on his face.

"It ever occur to you that the Soul Collector could be

behind these murders, Matt?" Simmons asked. "I mean, she's bound to have your fingerprints, isn't she?"

"Yup," I said. "But if she is, I've no idea how to nail her, especially off my home ground."

"She couldn't have got herself involved with this Antichurch of Lucifer Triumphant, could she?" Joe asked.

I didn't mention that they were at the camp—I didn't know him well enough to spill my guts completely. "Sara's capable of anything," I said. "But we'd be better off tracking the Antichurch itself."

The detective shook his head. "The FBI has got their Hate Crimes people involved."

"Any reason why you can't run a check, as well?" I asked.

"Apart from the fact that I'm off the case?" Simmons shrugged. "I guess I can do that."

I nodded. I liked the man, but he wasn't exactly buzzing with solutions to my problems. Karen was as lost as ever, while I was still suspect number one.

"Yeah," Simmons said, "I can check the Antichurch out, at least here in D.C., but that won't keep you out of jail down the line, my friend. And I've got other cases now."

"What about the latest victim?" Joe asked. "Any ID yet?"

The detective shook his head. "Not that I've heard of. The Feds won't be telling me anything, though."

"But he is another occult killing," I said.

"You tell me, Matt," Simmons said. "Personally, I'm not convinced. Could be a copycat."

"Oh, great," Joe said, with a groan. "Now we've got two crazies terrorizing the capital of the world?"

The detective caught my eye. "So, what are you going to do?"

I smiled. "You sure you want to know?"

"Probably not." He looked at Joe. "I'm trusting you to keep me informed."

Joe nodded. "Anything helpful you want to drop our way?"

Clem Simmons checked the area. There was no one near us. He slid his hand inside his coat and handed a brown envelope to Joe. "I must be out of my mind," he said morosely. "You didn't get these from me. The press doesn't know about them. Every victim's body except the last had a drawing pinned to it. See if you can figure out what these mean before the assholes in the Bureau do. And make sure you tell me first." He walked away at surprising speed for such a bulky man.

Joe and I looked at the photocopies. The names of the relevant victim had been printed on each sheet, along with an arrow pointing upward. I examined the different arrays of geometric shapes, but couldn't make a meaningful pattern out of them.

"Doesn't look particularly occult to me," Joe said.

"No," I agreed. "Then again, the Antichurch of Lucifer Lunatic notwithstanding, we don't think the murders really have too much to do with the black arts, do we?"

He shook his head. "In which case, what is this shit?"

"Joseph, I don't have the faintest idea."

We split up before we reached the paved road.

Clem Simmons was looking out of the office window. He didn't register the walls of the neighboring buildings or the pale blue autumn sky above. Instead, he was watching himself as he would soon be—a man in late middle age without a job or, most likely, a pension. Although he'd considered what to do carefully before the meet, after the event his thought processes seemed pathetically flawed. He'd been sure that slipping information to Joe Greenbaum would be an agreeable way of sticking it to the Feds, and perhaps garner some new insight. He had contacts that Clem could only dream about. But the reporter had blindsided him with Matt Wells. And, even more surprisingly, Clem had been convinced by the Englishman's crazy story.

He shook his head. Ever since the cancer had taken Nina, he'd been struggling. Until the occult killings, he hadn't really cared whether he and Vers caught murderers. The only thing he'd wanted was to get back to the house he and his wife had shared for twenty-four years, to take in her scent before it finally faded from her clothes. But these cases were different. He had a burning need to find the killer, no matter the cost. Perhaps it was because a voodoo believer had been murdered, but he thought it was more than that. If he could crack this case, if he could solve it before the Feds, he could retire happy. And now it was more likely he'd be sent packing without a penny to his name.

Gerard Pinker came up. "Where the hell have you been?" he demanded. "I got so bored waiting I went down to the coffee shop to check out the girls in uniform."

Clem Simmons handed him a sheaf of pages, each one in a transparent cover.

"What's this?"

"New information, a letter addressed to me by the guy in the Anacostia River."

"What?"

"Keep your voice down. We're off the case, remember?"

"Wait a minute." Pinker looked at his partner apprehensively. "You mean, you haven't shown this to Chief Owen?"

"Nope. He'd have to pass it to the Feds."

"What are we going to do with it?"

"Follow it up, of course. You'd better read it first."

Gerard Pinker went through the text, taking in the photocopied photographs that had been attached. When he'd finished, he dragged his chair over and slumped into it. "Christmas has come early for us this year."

Clem Simmons finished writing. "Could be… Okay,

here are the main points as I see them. The first photo confirms this is the dead man, right?"

Pinker nodded. "Hold up. Where did the letter come from?"

"The owner of the Travel Happy Motel brought it in. The maid found it on the bed this morning. The envelope was marked 'Urgent.'"

"He must have seen you on the TV."

"Yeah, that press conference after Monsieur Hexie was found." Simmons looked back at his notes. "So, the floater is Richard Bonhoff, a forty-three-year-old farmer from Iowa. He came to D.C. a week ago to find Gwen and Randy, his twenty-one-year-old twin children."

Pinker sat up straight. "Who won a competition in the *Star Reporter* last December that brought them here, and they were looked after by our friend Gordy Lister. No wonder that fucker looked shifty yesterday."

"According to the dead man, Lister tried to scare him off with a couple of heavies and Bonhoff, ex-marine that he was, dealt with them as only marines can. Then Lister took him to see his kids. They've apparently become junkies. When he went back to find them later, there was no one around."

Pinker stared at his partner. "What do you reckon? Gordy Lister's into dope? Or maybe he's running some kind of white slave ring."

"You reckon Lister's up to that, Vers?"

"Hell, yeah. That little prick would sell his mother if the price was right."

Simmons nodded. "Yeah, he probably would. But I think there's more to it than Gordy running a solo scam. I think there might be something in what Bonhoff says about Woodbridge Holdings being involved."

"Could be. They own the *Star Reporter,* so they aren't exactly scoring high in the ethical business chart. What else are they into?"

"I'm about to start working on that."

Pinker stood up. "So what do we do? Haul in Lister?"

"We could do." Simmons smiled wickedly.

"Oh-oh," his partner said, suddenly the apprehensive one for a change. "What have you got in mind, Clem?"

The big man stood up and moved close to Pinker. "Well, I was just thinking, we're off the case anyway, so why don't we keep this unofficial."

"*This* being?"

"We tail Gordy Lister."

The small man raised an eyebrow. "You forgetting what happened to this Bonhoff guy when he did that?"

"Um, we're cops, remember?" Clem Simmons took the pages back from Pinker. "By the way, there's something else I've got to tell you."

His partner's face went white as his partner described his meeting with Joe Greenbaum and Matt Wells. And Clem thought Pinker's eyes bulged like an impaled octopus's when he heard that the official prime suspect had been handed copies of the killer's diagrams.

Joe had made a prepaid Internet reservation for me in a cheap hotel on the other side of the Potomac. We reckoned that would keep me away from prying eyes, not that I was planning on doing anything except sleeping there. Joe also gave me five hundred dollars. I used a couple of hundred to buy some jeans, shirts and a thick jacket. No doubt the New York State police would have circulated a description detailing the clothes that Mary Upson had given me.

I took a shower and changed into my new outfit. The hotel was near the Rosslyn Metro station, within walking distance of Georgetown. I was about to set off when I felt a sudden pulse of pain in my head and staggered to the bed. Images flashed before me in rapid succession—a wire between the camp and the pine trees; a flat machine covered in wires and flashing lights lowering over me like the lid of a coffin; an explosion of sound from the line of soldiers with rifles to their shoulders...

I shook my head, trying to rid myself of the visions. I was sweating heavily and my hands shook. Then everything went blank and I felt the rough bedcover against my cheek. I gradually got my breathing under control and opened my eyes. The roar of the traffic on the freeways filled my ears and I sat up. What was going on? I had thought that as time passed the effect of whatever was done to me would wear off. My memory was getting better, even though there were still plenty of gaps. But I wasn't free of the place—there were still invisible chains tying me to it. That machine, its lights and the hum of sophisticated electronics, the things I'd been forced to see and hear—I couldn't recall them in detail, but I felt their weight. It was like a worm with sharp teeth wriggled in my brain, endowed with the power to extinguish my thoughts and personality at any time. I was going to have to be very careful when it came to making important decisions.

I stuck one of the Glocks out of sight under my belt, leaving the other one in the wardrobe safe. Worried about my erratic memory, I wrote the code on my forearm. In my pocket, I had a piece of paper with the address of the house in Georgetown that Gavin Burdett stayed in when he was in D.C. Although I'd remembered it once, I wasn't sure I'd be able to do so again.

It was a clear autumn day, the colors of the trees in the distance and the gray-blue water beneath the sky making the place feel more like a sparsely populated rural town than a great city. As I crossed the bridge, I looked at the gray walls and slate roofs of the university. When I'd attended the crime-writing conference in D.C., a seriously dull criminologist had given a lecture there. The only laugh was provided by a local detective who said that criminology was as much use in law enforcement as a liquorice night stick. I wondered if Clem Simmons knew him. What *were* his motives in sharing information with Joe and me? He must have been desperate to solve the cases he'd been taken off—or maybe he just hated the FBI. The latter wasn't exactly my favorite organization right now, either.

The diagrams—if that was what they were—flashed into my mind. I'd left the hard copies I'd made in the safe. There was something about them, something hovering on the margins of my consciousness. They had some esoteric meaning, even though they remained nothing more than collections of squares and rectangles. Random was the one thing they weren't—I was sure of that. But their significance continued to elude me. Could there be something mathematical about them, a code in the lengths and angles?

The bridge crossed a busy freeway and led down to M Street. The address I wanted was a few streets to the north. I found it easily—a well-maintained row house with a heavy black door and solid-looking windows. Even under cover of darkness, it would be hard to break in unnoticed. On the other hand, standing on the street for any length of time would attract attention, too. I was going to have to come up with a plan pretty soon—and I wasn't even sure that Gavin Burdett was on this side of the Atlantic. I walked back to Wisconsin Avenue, then went down to M Street and found a cell-phone shop. With a prepaid phone I went back outside and called Joe.

"Yeah, it's me," I said. "Any news?"

"Not much. I'm still looking at that Antichurch, but no hot leads yet. Oh, and the FBI's violent-crimes unit's giving a press conference about the murders at three o'clock. I'll be there. What about you?"

"I've located the house. No sign of G.B. I'm going to check the back."

"All right, man. Make sure your phone's on vibrate."

I heard a guffaw as I ended the call.

Walking farther down the street, I found a hardware store. I bought a collection of basic tools and a plastic safety helmet, so now I looked reasonably official. I headed back to the house, this time turning onto the street behind. I had counted my steps so that I ended up behind the right place. There was a large tree between two houses, its leaves an iridescent blend of red, yellow and green. More to the point, there was a narrow driveway leading inward. I walked confidently down it.

There were a couple of garages on the right and a high stone wall blocking my way ahead. I looked around. There were trees behind me, so I was pretty well obscured from the houses I'd passed. I considered the situation. If I was challenged, I would say I was a contractor. If the worse came to the worst, I had the Glock. I was thinking about Karen. Even if Burdett wasn't staying in the house, I might find evidence tying him or the owners to her—even to her disappearance, if I was really lucky. Maybe she was even in there. I had to go for it, but first I would check the front again. It would be dumb to break in from the back and find someone had recently arrived.

I retraced my steps. About fifty yards before I got to the house, a black limousine swept past me and stopped outside it. I slowed down and started rummaging in my toolbox. I looked up when I heard a door slam. A figure in a dark blue coat had got out of the car and was walking to the front door. When he got there, he looked round and nodded to the waiting chauffeur before going inside.

I recognized him immediately. It was Gavin Burdett.

Thirty-Three

Peter Sebastian glared at his subordinate. "When does the Marine Corps think its database will be operative again?" he demanded.

Special Agent Maltravers tried to smooth talk him. "It shouldn't be long. Not more than another two hours."

The blond man looked at his watch. "But that takes us to after three o'clock. What am I supposed to announce to the gathered press? That the victim was in the marines, but we don't know who he is?"

"You could always put the blame on the marines."

Sebastian looked at her unbelievingly. "Are you out of your mind, Dana? You don't fuck with the Marine Corps."

"Or alternatively, you could say that we're informing next of kin."

The anger faded from his features. "That's more like it. What else have we got?"

The young woman looked at her notes. "Not a great deal. No witnesses to the body being dumped in the river, no reports of anyone being beaten. Then again, the scene's location is hardly the safest in D.C."

"Nor are the residents likely to talk to us. Are we getting

full cooperation from the MPDC since we took the occult cases from them?"

Dana Maltravers shrugged. "I guess. The dispatch commander gave us access to all reported incidents. Nothing's squared with our man."

"No missing-persons reports that match?" Sebastian asked hopefully.

Maltravers shook her head. "I'm having them all checked."

"Shit. I'm walking into a bullring with no pants on."

His subordinate swallowed a smile. "Sir," she said tentatively, "are you quite sure that the man in the river is connected with the occult killings?"

Peter Sebastian looked at her thoughtfully. "Any particular reason why I shouldn't be?"

"Well, for a start, there was no diagram."

"Go on."

"I'm concerned by the lack of a specific locus. The other three victims were all killed in places where they worked."

"If you count Loki's van as a workplace."

"I think we can. The point is, the killer went to great trouble to study his victims and identify a time of attack. The guy in the water looks more like a straightforward homicide. Maybe he was just caught up in a gang scrap."

Sebastian's eyes moved off her. "Maybe... But the quickest way I could get control of the cases was by including the latest one in the series. The press doesn't know about the diagrams, anyway."

"You're going to maintain that policy?"

"I think so." He looked at the file in front of him. "What are the document-analysis people saying?"

"Still nothing. They're inclined to think that the killer's playing what they call 'diversionary games.'"

"They're just hedging their bets. Hate Crimes?"

"Still waiting."

Sebastian's eyes opened wide. "*What?* I sent the assholes

a formal request." He grabbed his phone. "Christ, if you want anything done around here, you have to do it yourself."

Dana Maltravers backed out of her boss's office. When he was in that kind of mood, he was impossible to handle.

I gave Gavin Burdett some time to settle in. A minute seemed long enough. Then I went up to the door and gave the bell a long push. There was a security camera above the top left corner. I made sure the safety helmet covered the upper part of my face. It was possible Burdett knew what I looked like—my photo appeared at the head of my newspaper column every Thursday.

The door was opened on the chain.

"You gotta problem with your icebox," I said, laying on an American accent.

"What?"

"Your icebox," I repeated, sounding as irritated as possible to put him on the back foot. "Excuse me, could we move this along? I got five more customers waiting."

"Oh, very well."

I heard the chain being removed. As soon as the door opened, I brushed past him. By the time he'd closed it again, I had the muzzle of the Glock against the back of his head.

"If that feels like a semiautomatic pistol," I said softly, "it's because it is one." I glanced around. There seemed to be no one else in the vicinity.

Burdett was swaying slightly, but was otherwise motionless.

"Right, then, Gavin," I said, dispensing with the accent, "let's be having you."

I grabbed him under the arm and threw him across the black-and-white tiled floor of the elegant hallway. He cannoned into the wall, shock on his face.

"You…you know my name," he said, kicking his legs as he tried to get up.

"Oh, yes. Don't you recognize me?" I took off my hat and smiled, but kept the gun on him.

"Wells," he said, clearly puzzled. "Matt Wells. What the hell do you think you're doing?" He sounded like the archetypal Brit abroad, appalled at the way he was being treated—except I was a Brit, too, and he hadn't seen anything yet.

"Empty your pockets," I said.

"You're joking, aren't you?"

I went over and kicked him on the knee.

His face twisted in agony. "Bastard! What was that for?"

"Your *pockets*," I repeated, glaring at him. It wasn't just that he was an arrogant piece of shit—I was sure he knew things about Karen.

Keeping one hand on his knee, he started pulling things from his jacket and trousers. I took his BlackBerry to examine later and glanced through the rest—keys, small change, wallet with several platinum cards, a gold fountain pen and so on. Changing hands, he emptied the remaining pockets—cigarettes, an expensive-looking lighter, chewing gum and an open packet of condoms. I remembered from the files that Burdett was married. Unless his wife was hiding upstairs, I had the feeling he was once again planning on sampling what D.C. had to offer in the underage flesh department.

"Up," I ordered, then pushed him roughly into a sitting room full of antique furniture. Whoever owned the place wasn't short of money or taste. There was an escritoire in the far corner with a wooden chair in front of it. I glanced at the windows. White net curtains obscured us from prying eyes. The main curtains, of an excessive floral design, were tied back with golden ropes. I wrenched the latter free and used them to tie my captive to the chair, then flipped him onto his back, making sure the telephone was well out of his range.

"Don't bother shouting. You'll no doubt have noticed that the windows are double glazed."

"This isn't the first time I've stayed here," Gavin Burdett said contemptuously.

"Congratulations. I'm going for a look around. If I hear even a squeak out of you, I'll take my boot to your other knee."

He stared at me with barely contained anger and then nodded curtly.

I checked the other rooms on the ground floor. There was a superbly appointed kitchen, with a heavy door that I guessed led to the backyard. There was also a dining room that would have done an English stately home proud. Upstairs there were three bedrooms, furnished in degrees of opulence that ranged from regal to imperial, each with its own bathroom. I checked the wardrobes and cupboards: no one.

Back downstairs, Burdett was coming nicely to the boil.

"Look here, Wells. You can't just assault me and tie me up like this."

"Is that right?" I asked, stepping closer to his undamaged knee. That shut him up. I looked at the painting above the fireplace. I reckoned it could have been a genuine Corot, but my memory was having a blank about nineteenth-century art. It was doing okay on Burdett, though.

"Is this your place?"

"None of your business," he replied, then watched my foot draw back from his knee. "No, it isn't. Associates of mine let me use it when I'm in town."

"Very decent of them," I said, wondering how close these associates were. Close enough to be listening to our conversation? I hadn't noticed any microphones, but that didn't mean there weren't any. It was time to hurry things up.

"Where is she?" I swung the muzzle of the Glock round so it was trained on the banker's face.

"Where is who?"

If he'd managed to keep his eyes on me when he spoke, I might have considered believing he was ignorant. As it was, he'd condemned himself as a poor liar—hard to believe for someone who was in international finance.

I kicked his good knee. That produced a gratifyingly high-pitched yelp.

"You know who I'm talking about, Burdett," I said, pressing the muzzle of the Glock into his temple. "Stop pissing about. You also know what happened to me, don't you?"

He tried to twitch his head to the side, but that was even less convincing.

"You piece of shit," I hissed. "Karen was getting close to you and your criminal friends, so you had her grabbed. Me, too, when I wouldn't let the dust settle. Where is she?"

"I…I don't…" Gavin Burdett broke off when I raised my foot over his groin. "I…they said—"

The sound of the key in the front door was almost inaudible. Curiously, despite thousands of hours listening to loud music, my hearing was still acute. I went out to the hall at speed and saw the door open slightly. I lowered my shoulder and charged into it, then slid on the heavy-duty chain. I'd made a mistake by omitting to do that earlier, but this was no time to court-martial myself.

"What the fuck…" came a deep voice from outside. "Hey, Mr. Burdett, you okay?"

I headed for the kitchen and unbolted the back door. Ahead was a stretch of paving stones surrounded by low bushes; beyond that was the wall I'd seen from the other side. I looked over my shoulder and saw a pair of bolt-cutters gripping the chain. Burdett's friends had certainly come fully equipped.

I sprinted down the yard and hit the wall. It must have been eight-feet high. I managed to get the toe of my boot into a gap in the mortar and drive myself up until my hands reached the top of the wall. Mistake. What I hadn't noticed from outside was a single strand of barbed wire alongside the touch pads of the alarm system. A loud honking started from the house. I gritted my teeth and hauled myself upward, feeling blood on my hands. Looking round, I saw two men in black suits spill from the back door. Both were carrying silenced pistols and raised them at me. I propelled myself over the wall and crashed onto the lane beyond. My knees took the brunt of the fall. They weren't in as bad a state as Burdett's, but they still hurt like hell. I ran down the lane and made it to the street. No one tried to stop me. I turned right.

And there was a screech of tires behind me. I dropped down between two large sedans. I had a few seconds to make a decision about how to play this. "Always attack," Dave used to say. That was easy to do when you were surrounded by your SAS comrades in full-destroy mode, but the advice had been good in the past. I stuck the Glock under my belt and took out the combat knife. The black car had slowed down and was keeping pace with the men on foot, whose steps I could hear approaching. I let the first one go past, then rose up quickly to grab the second round his neck, the point of the knife breaking the skin lower down his back. That was another of Dave's catchphrases—always shed blood if you want to gain control. I felt thick drops daub my hand.

"Tell them," I said to the man, who was standing stock-still in my grip.

"He's cutting me with a knife," he said. The unwavering nature of his voice told me he was a pro.

"Put the gun down," I said to the man in front. I watched as he complied, relieving my man of his weapon at the same time. A silenced pistol was much more use in a city street. I looked to my left. The large black limousine was a few feet away, the window at the front passenger's seat lowered. I saw two guys inside, both in suits. They looked like the president's detail, moonlighting.

"Out," I said. "Both of you. If you want your friend to keep his kidney, don't let me see any weapons."

They came out slowly, glancing at each other. I had a feeling they weren't meant to pay much attention to each other's safety, so I needed to get moving. I dragged my captive to the car and bundled him inside after I'd tossed another silenced pistol onto the floor. There was enough space for me to clamber over him before he could react. I dropped into the spacious driver's seat, engaged Drive and hit the gas. I heard a series of dull noises before we'd gone fifty yards—they must have had back up weapons under their jackets. The man next to me slumped forward. The car's glass was obviously armored, as the rear windscreen was hardly marked, but my captive had been unlucky. A bullet had ricocheted off the door frame and hit him in the head.

I knew for certain that the surviving pursuers would be phoning for reinforcements. It was also likely that some public-spirited resident had witnessed the scene and called the cops, so I dumped the limo three streets down and walked as nonchalantly as I could onto M Street. A taxi was passing and I immediately hailed it, telling the driver to take me to Union Station. I could melt into the crowds there and pick up the Metro. I was glad I'd studied the city map before leaving my hotel.

I took frequent glances over my shoulder and thought about what I'd done. Had showing myself to Gavin Burdett been worth it? On balance, I reckoned it had. I was now completely sure that he'd been involved in Karen's disappearance, and mine, too, most likely. Joe would probably be able to trace the owners of the house—they might not be too clean, either. As for the damage I'd done to the banker's knees and the accidental death of the man I'd taken hostage, I didn't waste time on remorse. I had the feeling that I hadn't always been as hard-edged as that. Then I recalled what had been done to innocent people at the camp. I could only hope that Karen was still alive and well. At least the bad men knew I was on their case now. That meant I was going to have to stand tall—and I wasn't sure if I was up to that.

Another thought struck me. Maybe what had been done to me in the camp was behind my ability to evade capture and get as far as D.C.—maybe I'd been turned into a callous killer. I'd killed before, as the FBI notification had indicated in Maine. But now I was really good at it.

Thirty-Four

Gerard Pinker was cold, hungry and seriously bored. He'd been in the cocktail bar around the corner from Gordy Lister's office for three and a half hours while the newspaperman got more and more drunk. The detective was wearing a mustache that came down to his chin and a suit that Chief Owen, the department's resident fashion critic, would have seen as way too preppy. Pinker had borrowed it from his younger brother Leonard, who worked for a D.C. lobbying company and was conveniently the same size.

If his man had done anything interesting, Pinker could have hacked the evening. It would also have helped if he'd been able to drink more than a couple of beers. But Gordy Lister had sat at the bar, talking to no one except the male barkeep. He'd used his cell phone a few times, but never for long; none of the conversations had made him noticeably happier, either. Pinker hadn't trusted his disguise enough to go nearer, so he hadn't heard what Lister had been saying. He was about to call Clem and ask him to take over early, when a tall guy with short fair hair walked in and stood next to Lister. Pinker decided to go for broke. When he got to the bar, he still couldn't hear much because of a couple of guys whining about the Redskins nearby.

Gerard Pinker ordered another beer and leaned forward, pretending he was scoping the female barkeep's ass. For a few moments he thought Lister had made him. The newspaperman caught his eye, but there was no sign of recognition in the bleary gaze. The tall guy was talking in a low voice more or less directly into Gordy's ear, his eyes never wavering from the other man's face. Pinker got the feeling that the verbal shit was being kicked out of his target. Then, with no warning, the other man and Gordy headed rapidly out the door.

Pinker threw some money on the bar and went after them, counting fifteen before he opened the door. When he hit the street, the pair was already moving away to his right. The detective waited another fifteen seconds—that had been the unit of time he'd been taught to stick to by a veteran cop when he was young—then set off after them. At the end of the street they stopped, forcing him to slip into a doorway. When he looked out again, he saw they had separated. It was decision time—should he follow Lister or the guy who'd been chewing him out?

In any event, Pinker never had to make his mind up. His cell phone vibrated against his thigh and he answered quietly.

"You better can the tail, Vers. There's been another murder," Clem said in a low voice. "There's been another murder."

"Shit. Our killer?"

"Sounds like it. The vic's a woman over in Lincoln Park. She read tarot cards for a living."

"What about the Feds?"

"If we get there first, it's ours till they start crying to Chief Owen."

"I'll drink to that." Pinker scribbled the address down in his notebook and looked around for a taxi.

Lister and his interlocutor had already disappeared.

* * *

I was sitting at the window of a coffee shop in Adams Morgan. When Joe Greenbaum came in, I looked down the street in both directions. There was no obvious tail.

"Jesus, Joe, that stuff will kill you," I said, when he sat down with an enormous mug of cream-topped coffee. "So, what have you discovered?"

"The house in Georgetown is owned by a company called N.E.W.S. Properties," he said, swallowing from the mug. "Mean anything to you?"

The reporter grinned. "Sure. It's a subsidiary of Wood-bridge Holdings."

That rang a bell. "Woodbridge Holdings?" I repeated. "That was the name on the logging truck I stowed away on in Maine." The logo came back to me, too. "The words were written on an open newspaper."

"You got it, Matt," Joe said, licking cream from his mustache. "It's kinda interesting. Woodbridge Holdings owns numerous papers across the country, including that rag the *Star Reporter.* They also own large stretches of forest and produce their own stocks of paper. Guess where?"

"Not Maine by any chance?"

"Bull's-eye again, Matt."

"The camp I escaped from—maybe Woodbridge Holdings owns that, too."

Joe gulped down the last of his coffee. "They certainly have enough of Maine under their belts. There's more. They also have interests in drug research and production. And, to advise them on their substantial foreign investments, they use a London-based bank by the name of—"

"Routh Limited. Employers of one Gavin Burdett."

"Correct. Did you never see Woodbridge Holdings in Karen's files, Matt? She must have known about them, since she was after Burdett."

I shrugged. "I may have, but I don't remember." I broke

off as a nasty thought came to me. "Maybe they wiped stuff like that from my memory at the camp."

"Doesn't seem to have been wholly successful," Joe observed.

"Not wholly." Then, suddenly, I felt as if the furniture in my brain had started to rearrange itself. Things I hadn't been able to connect came together. "Karen must have found evidence linking Woodbridge and Routh. So she was kidnapped."

"And so were you, after you kicked up such a fuss." Joe looked down at his empty cup. "But that doesn't explain the occult murders. I can't believe they're doing them just to frame you. Besides, the first one happened before you escaped."

I remembered the BlackBerry I'd taken from Gavin Burdett and handed it to Joe. "See what you can find in that. Back in London I tailed Burdett to an occult supplies shop. Maybe there's some link between him and the killings."

The reporter looked at me doubtfully. "You think he's the murderer?"

"He's a sleazy bastard," I said, then shook my head. "But I doubt he's capable of murder. Anyway, he's the kind of tosser who would pay somebody else to do his dirty work."

"He works for Woodbridge Holdings, so that puts the focus on them. And we're in luck there. They have their head office in this fair city."

"Is that right? What about the Antichurch? Did you find anything on it?"

Joe sighed. "A few references on the kind of Web site that's written and read by crazies. People seem pretty much in awe of it, though. Or scared shitless. I sent my e-mail address and asked them to contact me, but don't hold your breath."

"Jesus, Joe, that was taking a chance. You've made yourself a target."

He shrugged. "Not for the first time. They'll have to get in line."

I was impressed by his understated courage. "What happened at the FBI press conference?"

"Nothing much. They didn't release the dead man's name—they say they're contacting the family. They seemed pretty sure the occult killer got him. There's some evidence linking the victim to the others, but they didn't give details."

I stood up.

"What are you going to do, Matt?" Joe asked apprehensively.

I smiled. "Don't worry. I've kicked enough kneecaps for one day."

That didn't seem to reassure him much. "They'll really be after you now," he said.

"Give me the Woodbridge Holdings address, will you?"

Joe tore out a page from his notebook and scribbled some words, then handed it over. "Don't do anything rash, Matt."

I laughed. "What, like stand outside shouting 'Give me back my memory'?"

"That would fit the bill."

I squeezed his shoulder. "Don't worry, my friend. I'll be careful. I've got Karen to worry about."

I felt his eyes on me as I headed for the door.

Chief of Detectives Rodney Owen was standing outside an apartment building in southeast Washington. Although the lights of Capitol Hill were under a mile away, the area wasn't much of a picture. Apartments were gradually being taken by yuppie types, but the recession had made things hard for them and many of the buildings were still occupied by people with little to their names. Uniformed officers had strung barrier tape around the entrance and were keeping the curious at bay.

Clem Simmons arrived and saw the chief immediately. He sighed in relief when he saw no sign of Peter Sebastian or Dana Maltravers.

Owen came over. "I broke the speed limit."

"I was wondering," Simmons replied.

"Yeah, well, I want this case. Till we're sure it's the same killer, it's definitely ours. That asshole Sebastian can kiss my ass."

Simmons smiled. If he'd been a nervous man, he'd have felt bad about the meeting with Matt Wells and Joe Greenbaum, but that didn't bother him. He reckoned they were reliable. Whether this murder was in the series or not, law enforcement needed all the help it could get.

A taxi pulled up and disgorged Pinker, without his false mustache.

"Cool threads," one of the uniformed officers said, provoking a scowl from the detective.

Owen grinned. "Sure you aren't overdressed, Vers? I hear it's pretty messy up there."

"Do my brother good to get the real world's substances on his clothes." He accepted overshoes and gloves from his partner. "What do we know?"

Owen glanced at his notebook. "Patrolmen were called by a neighbor who heard a scream from the vic's apartment on the top floor. He looked through his peephole and saw a figure in a hooded jacket come down the stairs—didn't see the face. The call was logged at 8:26 p.m. Our heroic citizen stayed behind his locked door. He says he didn't look down at the street."

"Can't blame him for prioritizing his own skin," Simmons said. "You ready?"

Pinker nodded. The pair headed into the building.

"Check out the buzzer panel," Owen called. "Second button from the top."

"Crystal Vileda," Pinker read. "Diviner." He looked at his partner. "What the hell does that mean?"

"Means she read the future," Simmons said, walking into a hallway that had once been elegant but was now very shabby.

"Oh, yeah? Unless she had a death wish, she couldn't have been much good."

Clem Simmons shook his head. Sometimes he found Vers too much.

A CSI was working at the elevator, so they walked up to the fourth floor. The house was narrow, one apartment per level. The door at the top was open, another technician dusting the panels for prints. They went inside, stepping around a CSI who was on her knees, examining the rug.

"Gentlemen," said Dr. Marian Gilbert, stepping back from a large armchair. Her face was flushed. "I was wondering where you'd got to."

"Jesus," Pinker said involuntarily.

The detectives took in the naked body sprawled across the chair, arms wide and legs sprawling. The woman was white, though olive-skinned. She looked to be in her thirties and was in good physical condition. Pinker was reminded of poses taken by women in porn movies— except they didn't usually have chopsticks projecting from their nostrils.

"Quite," the M.E. said, glancing at the police photographer. "Are you done?"

The man nodded and stepped back.

"What do you see, Doc?" Simmons asked. He was trying to resist the temptation to throw his coat over the victim— he felt ashamed to be looking at her in such an exposed state.

"I see a very unusual cadaver," Marion Gilbert replied. "I—"

"Are those chopsticks?" Pinker interrupted.

She nodded.

"Are they the cause of death?" Simmons asked.

"I don't see any other." She pointed to broken skin on the left temple. "I doubt that blow would have done more than knock her out briefly. Assuming the chopsticks penetrated the brain, they would certainly have caused major trauma. I think they're ivory, which is strong enough to do the job. I suspect they were sharpened to ease penetration."

Pinker groaned. "Thanks for that, Doc." He looked at his partner. "Two murder weapons like the others…but not skewers."

Clem Simmons nodded. "And no paper with drawings on it. We need to turn her over."

Marion Gilbert nodded to her assistants and they slowly turned the victim onto her front, keeping her face off the chair.

"No diagram there, either," Pinker said, exhaling rapidly. "With the change in murder weapons, that gives us a chance of keeping the case."

The M.E. looked at him and then shook her head. "I rather doubt that, Detective." She pointed to the table at the far end of the room.

The two men went over. There was a pile of cards at one corner. They were larger than the ordinary playing kind. In the center were three more, arranged in a row, and next to them, in a clear plastic sheath, was a piece of paper. An array of squares and rectangles had been drawn on it in black ink.

"Shit," said Pinker. "More squares and rectangles."

"I'm guessing the killer didn't waste time attaching this to the vic after she screamed," Simmons said. He bent closer and took in the tarot cards. "Death, the Devil and the Seven of Swords."

Gerard Pinker squinted at the garishly colored and grotesque illustrations. "You know what they mean, Clem?"

"Not really," his partner said. "The Devil and Death are obvious enough."

"Actually, they aren't."

The men turned to find that Dr. Gilbert had joined them.

"Tarot is a hobby of mine," she said, smiling briefly. "The Devil may appear to fit the pattern of the occult murders, but the card actually has more to do with the subject being bound by fear and temptation, by material things or addictive behavior. Negative thinking is in there, too."

"There's nothing more negative than being murdered," Pinker interposed.

The M.E. shook her head. "No, that isn't it. I think this shows that the killer is rather ignorant of the tarot." She paused. "Assuming it was the killer who arranged the cards, of course. The victim might have laid them out before her death."

Simmons was watching the M.E. curiously. "What about the other cards?"

Marion Gilbert pointed at the skeletal horseman. "Death has to do with change, with new beginnings as much as with endings. As for the Seven of Swords, that suggests... could suggest greater knowledge on the part of the killer. The hooded man running off with the swords represents deception and subterfuge."

"Plenty of that around here lately," Pinker said. He looked at his partner. "So what are we saying happened here? The murderer hit the vic on the head and, while she was unconscious, arranged the cards?"

Simmons raised his shoulders. "Could be. Then Ms. Vileda came round and screamed before he could stop her. He left the diagram here and went to kill her, then ran out." He looked back at the dead woman. The M.E.'s people had put her on her back again, and the chopsticks protruded from her face like a pair of ill-fitting teeth.

Just then, Peter Sebastian walked into the apartment wearing a white protective suit, its hood over his head. Dana Maltravers was behind him in a matching outfit.

"Aw, hell," Pinker said, only partially muffling his voice. "Dickhead and Princess on parade."

Thirty-Five

I went to the Woodbridge Holdings office, but I only walked past, making sure I didn't attract attention. I wanted to take a look at the enemy's lair—not that I knew who the enemy was exactly. I was planning to do some research into that. Then my cell vibrated against my thigh.

There was a text from Joe: "New occult murder reported. Watch yourself!"

That took the wind from my sails. Presumably Clem Simmons or some contact in the FBI had let him know. I wondered if there would be any evidence linking me to the murder this time. I had to move things along. That took me back to Karen. The case notes she'd brought from London were either with the FBI or had been returned to her office, so there was no accessing them. That left me with one option—the Internet.

I headed for Union Station and found a café. I bought a large coffee then I sat with my head in my hands, trying to concentrate. There was information in the depths of my memory—I was sure of that—but it wasn't obliging right now.

I went back over the events since I'd escaped from the

camp in Maine. What hadn't I followed up? I remembered
the underground building, the violence, the armed men
and women in gray...and there it was—they had worn
badges bearing the letters *NANR*. I had asked one of my
pursuers what they stood for. What was the reply? It came
back to me after some thought. North American National
Revival. I typed the words into a search engine.

Thanks to the glorious lack of censorship on the Web,
I found the organization in seconds. The problem was, the
North American National Revival seemed to have nothing
to do with anything in Maine. Its headquarters were in
Butte, Montana, and its manifesto, riddled with spelling
and grammatical mistakes, didn't seem particularly
offensive—it called for reductions in federal taxes, a halt
to immigration, especially from Mexico, and more teach-
ing of traditional Christian beliefs in schools and colleges.
There was nothing overtly anti-government, and certainly
no references to an armed wing or camps ringed with
barbed wire. Then again, they would hardly have mentioned those in public. I went back to the site's home page
and clicked on "Local Centers." Glory be—there was an
address in Washington, D.C. I wrote it down and then
logged on to a city map. I found that the location on
Q Street was close to Dupont Circle Metro station. It was
well into the evening and the office would probably be
closed, but I decided to check it out all the same.

I got there in under half an hour. The building was a low-
rise office block. Most of the lights were either dimmed or
off, but it was brighter up on the second floor. A security
guard was standing outside the glass doors.

"NANR?" I asked.

The elderly black man gave me an impenetrable look
and then pointed to the elevators. "Second floor," he said,
with a brief shake of his head that attracted my attention.

I stepped closer. "What are they like? I'm a journalist."

The guard eyed me for a few moments. "Wonderful people," he said, the irony almost imperceptible. "Wouldn't say a thing against them."

"How about anything *for* them?"

"That neither," he said, his lips almost forming into a smile. "Are you really a reporter?"

"I write a weekly column." That wasn't a lie, though he wouldn't have heard of my London paper. Then again, I'd forgotten its name until recently. "On crime," I added.

That got him interested. "Is that right, son? Well, the NANR is always saying it isn't a criminal organization." He looked around—we were still alone. "Some might not agree."

"Why's that?"

The security guard leaned closer. "I'll tell you why. Because it's run by the worst kind of racist pig—the kind who's learned how to cover up what he thinks about people like me."

That was interesting, but I needed more. "You got any examples of racist behavior?"

He shook his head. "No, they're far too smart for that. I'm just going by my gut. The top man here, a guy called Larry Thomson, is the worst. He looks at me like I'm his best friend, but I know for sure he wants to hang me from the nearest tree."

"Is he here at the moment?"

"Yup."

"You wouldn't care to give me the nod when he comes out, would you?"

"What you going to do?"

"Just see where he goes," I replied. That seemed to disappoint the guard. There was a large concrete plant holder at the side of the steps that I concealed myself behind. Then I sent Joe a text, asking him to run a check on this Larry Thomson.

About an hour later, a group of people came out of the

elevator and walked toward the exit. They all nodded politely to the guard, especially the man at the rear. He was
tall and fair-haired, with a prominent nose and probably in
his late fifties. He was carrying a black leather briefcase
and had the bearing of a leader. I looked over at the security
guard. He briefly extended a finger at the tall guy's back
as he headed down the steps.

I followed at about twenty paces' distance and soon realized that Thomson was heading for the metro station I'd
come from—the others had all respectfully wished him good-
night and dispersed. I went inside and loitered on the Glen-
mont platform, then got on the same train that he did and
followed him off it at Metro Central. He exited the station and
headed north. I'd been thinking about asking him straight out
whether the NANR had an armed wing in Maine, but my
bravado had dwindled away. Now I was more interested in
where he was going. Then I saw we were on the street I'd
scoped earlier. As Larry Thomson approached the Woodbridge Holdings building, I started to walk faster and was only
about five yards behind him when he turned up the steps. I
whipped out my cell phone and managed to take a photo of
him without being noticed either by him or the security man
who opened the door for him. I saw Thomson go toward a
bank of elevators inside as I walked on nonchalantly.

At the next corner, I stopped and sent the photo to Joe,
telling him of the link I'd just established between the
North American National Revival and Woodbridge Holdings. I was hoping he'd manage to dig the dirt on the tall
man. Meanwhile, I'd be subjecting my memory to another
bout of the third degree.

Chief Owen was standing outside the apartment build-
ing in Lincoln Park, flanked by Clem Simmons and Gerard
Pinker. He was looking at the pavement rather than at Peter
Sebastian.

"No, there's no chance of this being a Metro P.D. case," the FBI man said firmly. "The pair of weapons and the presence of the drawings clearly link it to the series we've already taken over."

Owen raised his eyes briefly. "What about the floater, then? You haven't tied that to the other murders. I heard the vic was a farmer from Iowa."

"Actually, we're not sure he's connected, but we're holding on to him for the time being." He eyed the detectives wearily. "Haven't you got enough cases of your own to investigate?"

"What about Matt Wells?" Clem Simmons asked, ignoring Pinker's immediate alarm.

"Our people have found fingerprints that we expect to be his," Dana Maltravers said. "We haven't had any sighting of him. You?"

Simmons shrugged. "We aren't in missing persons, Special Agent."

"He's a murder suspect," Sebastian put in.

"He's a murder suspect in cases we've been excluded from," Rodney Owen said.

"Is that the level of cooperation we can expect from you, Chief?" Sebastian demanded. "Because if it is, I'll be on the phone to your superiors right away."

Owen gave him a haughty stare. "Cooperation is a two-way street." He looked at his detectives. "Besides, we haven't got anything to pass on, have we?"

Simmons and Pinker shook their heads.

The group broke up, the detectives heading for their cars.

"Nicely done, Clem," Pinker said in a low voice.

Chief Owen looked over his shoulder. "I hope you men have been fully open with the Bureau," he said, a smile appearing at the corners of his mouth. "No, I don't want to hear about it. Just get the job done." He got into his Buick and drove off.

"What job's that, Clem?" Pinker asked as they got into his partner's car.

"Don't ask me," Simmons replied. "Besides, we've got cases of our own to investigate."

Joe Greenbaum was at his desk, his desktop and laptop computers in operation. There was a large bottle of Pepsi on one side of the keyboards and an almost empty box of doughnuts on the other. He hummed tunelessly as his fingers rattled the keys rapidly, his eyes jumping from one screen to the other. He hadn't succeeded in finding another image of Larry Thomson yet, but he'd gathered other information.

Earlier he had taken a look at Gavin Burdett's Black-Berry. He'd tried to make sense of the limey banker's diary, but the guy seemed to keep names and places in his head—there were only times listed for each day. He was certainly having plenty of meetings, though the pages were blank four days from now.

One of Joe's failings was that he frequently got distracted by what he was working on. That was why he'd had a camera installed outside his apartment, showing not only the vicinity of his door but also the stairway all the way down to the ground floor. He'd also had pressure pads inserted under the first three steps that led to his floor. These things were meant to give him time to call the cops. He'd been attacked by a businessman's thugs a couple of years back, and he didn't intend spending another month in hospital.

Those precautions were why the faint sound of scratching on the apartment's steel-lined door took Joe completely by surprise. He looked at the screens showing the landing and staircase. They had gone blank. He immediately grabbed the phone; no dial tone. By the time he'd located his cell and started pressing buttons, it was too late. There was a dull crump and smoke billowed in from the shattered door. Joe slid beneath his desk, catching his broad shoulders in the narrow space.

"Please, Mr. Greenbaum, do get up."

Joe was amazed on two counts—the voice was cultured and it was female.

"We're not going to shoot you. At least, not to death."

Joe pulled his Colt Anaconda from its holster under the desk. He leaned forward and loosed off three shots. It suddenly occurred to him that he hadn't yet sent the information he'd just gathered to his secure server.

"Not even close," came the woman's voice—she sounded very young. "Have a pleasant evening, sir."

Joe heard another voice in the background, this one deeper—a man's. Then there was movement toward the door.

After a short time, the reporter crawled backward from under the desk and got to his feet, holding his weapon in a two-handed grip. Then he saw the black box by the door, a red light flashing on its side. He grabbed the data stick from his computer and rushed to the rear window. After he'd opened it, he hardly had time to breathe before his life was blown to fragments.

I spent an hour in a different café in central D.C. There were no references to Larry Thomson on any sites apart from the North American National Revival's. I went through what there was for Woodbridge Holdings, aware that Joe would have done so, too, by now, but maybe something would jog my memory about the camp. All I found were endless details about the company's interests, none of which pointed directly to the depths of the Maine wilderness.

A little bleary-eyed, I decided to give Joe a call and see how he was getting on. A voice said the subscriber had turned off the cell—I sent him a text in case he turned it on again soon. After ten minutes I grew impatient. I left the café, found a pay phone and called his landline. Again, unobtainable. I began to get a bad feeling. Joe had said he would stay at his computers until he found something. He hadn't been intending to go out and, besides, it was nearly midnight. I hailed a passing cab and told him a street behind Joe's place. I didn't have to risk using the front entrance—I could approach via the yards, as we'd done a couple of nights back.

I heard the sirens as soon as I got out of the cab. Jesus, what had happened? I jumped a low fence and ran across the unkempt gardens. As I got nearer to my friend's building, the smell of hot dust became more intense. I could see a cloud of smoke and steam in the air ahead. Shit, what had I got Joe into? It was only when I saw the firemen in the yard behind Joe's apartment that I stopped and took cover. They were directing hoses at the windows on the second floor. In their shouts the word *bomb* came up more than once.

I retraced my steps and cautiously turned the corner to his street. I needn't have worried about breaking cover. A crowd had gathered in front of the fire trucks and police cars. I joined it and pushed toward the front. Beyond men in heavy clothes, carrying oxygen tanks, I made out the solid form of Clem Simmons. I didn't have his cell-phone number so I had no option but to attract his attention. After he'd finished talking to an attractive red-haired woman, I managed that. Looking away from me, he bent under the barrier tape and walked down the street. I gave him a minute and then followed. He was waiting for me at the corner.

"What happened?" I asked breathlessly.

"We're pretty sure it was a bomb." His eyes lowered. "A powerful one, too. There's nothing left of Joe's apartment. The fire chief has taken his men out as he thinks the whole building might come down."

"Any human remains?"

He nodded slowly. "Small pieces. No identification possible yet."

I knew it had to be Joe. "Fuck," I said. "I'm responsible for this."

"What do you mean?"

"I got him into this, didn't I?"

"You're saying that a reporter with his track record wouldn't have gone after these creeps if you hadn't been involved? Don't be so goddamned conceited."

I thought about that. He was right. Joe was already on the ball about Woodbridge Holdings, and he would have looked out for me and Karen even if I hadn't gone to him. It was a slight to my friend's memory to suggest otherwise.

"You want to come in, Matt?" Clem Simmons asked, his expression softening. "If they got him, they'll be after you, too."

"Let them come," I muttered.

"I don't suppose you've got any clearer idea of who they are yet?" He knew I wasn't telling him everything, but it didn't seem to be bothering him unduly.

"Put it this way," I said. "We've been looking at a company called Woodbridge Holdings. Heard of them?"

He nodded. "They own the *Star Reporter.*"

"As well as a range of other companies—logging, property, pharmaceuticals—you name it, they're into it."

"Got any evidence linking them to Joe's death? Or to the other murders? Or to what happened to you?"

"Watch this space," I said. "Or rather…" I took out my cell phone. "Give me your number." I saved it. "I'll be in touch."

"Don't do anything illegal, will you?" The words sounded more like an invitation than a warning.

I snorted and turned away. Typical cops. They wanted you to do their dirty work. Then a picture of Karen rose up before me. She was in the Metropolitan Police uniform she rarely wore and she was smiling, one hand on her gently convex belly. I swallowed a sob and turned away.

The blonde woman span round and emptied the magazine of her semiautomatic pistol into a life-size human target twenty yards away. The man in gray next to her took off his ear-protectors and clapped slowly.

"Very good," he said, watching as the target was pulled in. "Three to the head, three to the chest and three to the abdomen. I don't think he's going anywhere."

The woman nodded and handed the weapon over. She had only started target shooting five days before and she had been surprised at how proficient she was. She had impressed the instructors at judo and karate, too, and had taken to knife-fighting with alacrity. At first she had been worried that the baby she was carrying would slow her down, but that hadn't been the case. The doctors monitored her every day and the little boy was doing well. She wished she could remember who the father was, but it didn't matter. The people in the camp would look after her and her child. They were a real family.

"They're waiting to take you to the lab, Karen," the shooting instructor said, pointing to the door.

Karen followed the other personnel in gray uniforms down the passages to the place where she had recently spent so much time. The machine was ready for her, lights flashing and tubes pulsing above the bed. At first she'd been frightened by it, worried that its close proximity to her body would harm the baby, but now she looked forward to the daily sessions. She could never remember what happened when the humming got louder, apart from a feeling of deep satisfaction and belonging. The music, which she had originally found discordant, now brought her a calm desire to participate, to strive for something glorious; and the rhetoric that she had once found disturbing now in-

creased her devotion every time that she heard it. As for
the images of men in field-gray and women in white
blouses and black skirts, they inspired her.

She was one of them, and always would be.

In time, her son would join the movement, too.

Thirty-Six

I went back to my hotel across the river, and ate the burger and fries I'd bought. The food tasted like nothing, but I needed to keep my strength up. I was down, hit badly by Joe's death, but I knew I had to keep searching, had to find Karen. But how was I to do that without Joe's help? I had received e-mails from him with useful material, but nothing that broke the case. He had hinted he was on the brink of discovering something hot, but the bomb would have destroyed all his equipment and records.

Or would it? I thought about that. Joe had security cameras and a warning system. They must have been disabled to enable his killer or killers to get in, but he might still have had time to react before the explosion. I tried to put myself in the dead man's place. The obvious thing to do would have been to call the police. Or me. Clem would have told me if Joe had contacted him. Perhaps Joe realized it was too late for that; perhaps his landline had been disabled, too. So what other options did he have? I found it hard to believe that he would have waited patiently for death like an animal in a slaughterhouse, even if it had only been a matter of seconds. He was proficient with computers, but they had all been atomized, as had his cell phone. He no doubt had an off-site backup facility, but he hadn't given me access. What else could he have done? I had a vision of Joe in the bar, his keys on the table by his glass. There were two memory sticks attached. Could that be the answer? Could he have tried to get a memory stick out of the apartment?

I pulled on my jacket and left the room in a rush. Joe's place was on the second floor. His office had windows to the front and rear of the building. Was it possible he had got a window open and thrown a stick out?

I ran across the bridge and caught a cab in Georgetown, getting the driver to let me off at the street behind Joe's. I walked to the corner and looked round cautiously. The barrier tape was still up and police personnel were in evidence, despite the late hour. But the firemen had gone, and they had been the ones in the yard out back. I decided to try there first.

I moved silently over the low fences and made it to the space behind Joe's apartment. There was tape around it, but no one was on watch. I took in the area. I reckoned Joe would have thrown a stick as far as he could, so I started at the rear of the yard, using the flashlight I had brought with me. The surface of the area was broken and covered in rubble from the walls, so I had to run my fingers through each handful. After ten minutes, during which I kept looking toward the building in case someone approached, I had found nothing. Before I moved closer to the source of the blast, I looked over the wall that separated Joe's yard from the one on the parallel street. Bingo. Hanging from a tattered shrub was a black memory stick. I grabbed it and made my exit.

I tried to contain my excitement on the journey back to the hotel. Maybe the stick wasn't even Joe's. If it was, it might not contain anything significant. But I remained hopeful. If Joe had made the effort to dispose of it during what he probably knew were the last seconds of his life, it had to be of some importance. I examined the small plastic-covered device. It didn't show any signs of damage. Better, it looked very like the ones I had seen on Joe's key ring.

I booted up my laptop impatiently and put the memory stick into a USB port. There were a few seconds of extreme tension, then an icon opened. It contained two files, one titled "NANR" and the other "Woodbridge Holdings."

And felt icy fingers walk up my spine. Joe had discovered that *NANR* were not just the initials of the relatively mild-mannered North American National Revival. That had been deliberately chosen to obscure a group with a much more chilling name—the North American Nazi Revival. Joe had found an obscure civil-rights Web site run by an elderly Jewish couple in South Dakota. They had been threatened by a businessman who had been trying to buy their land. When they turned him down, he had let slip the alternative significance of the letters. They had reported the incident to the local police, who said that the man was just a well-known drunk.

I sat back in the hotel room's uncomfortable chair and thought about that. The gray-uniformed bastards at the camp in Maine certainly behaved like Nazis. The place itself was redolent of concentration camps—I had a flash of the man who had been summarily shot for helping me over the fence. So, was this what was behind everything? Far-right supremacists with a taste for Hitler? How did that square with the occult killings in Washington? The first victim had been a neo-Nazi himself.

I looked at Joe's other file. He had certainly been busy. I would definitely have bought champagne because what he had in the Woodbridge Holdings file was vintage investigative research. He had tapped a source who used to work in the CIA. Apparently Woodbridge had been set up in 1972 and had originally only been involved in property—primarily the acquisition of Maine forest land. But gradually it had acquired interests in a pharmaceutical firm that it eventually took over in 1982. Woodbridge had bought its first newspaper, a local rag in Massachusetts, a year later. Logging and paper production soon followed, as did a major expansion into news media, including the supermarket tabloid *Star Reporter* in 1987. The paper was almost defunct, having been badly hit by the thrusting style of its rivals. But soon it became the most imaginative of them all in its coverage of showbiz scandal and outlandish news.

What was most interesting was the near impossibility of identifying the main shareholders of Woodbridge. They had hidden themselves behind a raft of other company names and were always represented by lawyers at meetings. It was indisputable that Woodbridge had been highly profitable from the start, but it was unclear who was banking the proceeds. That in itself was hardly unusual in the financial world, but Wall Street gossip said that the directors were nothing but placeholders, that the real power was wielded by people who remained resolutely behind the scenes. The final entry in Joe's file was that one of those individuals was none other than Larry Thomson.

So where did that leave me? Woodbridge Holdings was run by a man who was also in charge of an organization that purported not to be racist, but seemed to have a Nazi alter ego. *Nazi* meaning what? People tended to use the term to suggest anti-Semitic and anti-federal government tendencies, or just anyone who was really strict. But what if there was a real Nazi involvement? My memory, now firing on more cylinders, came up with Operation Paperclip—I had read about that when I was researching a still unfinished novel set during the Cold War. Operation Paperclip had been the CIA's plan to bring Nazi scientists illegally to the U.S.A. Could Woodbridge Holdings have been set up by scumbags like that? The camp in Maine suggested that was within the realms of possibility. But that would mean people in high places, in particular the CIA, knew about the people behind the company—and Joe's contact had worked for the Agency. My stomach flipped as I realized that I wasn't only up against the FBI. Had Joe been blown up by some shady branch of his own government?

I decided to follow the Nazi angle further. I did an Internet search and found a site that claimed to have an encyclopedic coverage of German history from 1923 to 1950. But what was I looking for? I typed in Woodbridge. Predictably, there was no data. I went to another site that offered translation to German and came back with *Holzbrücke* and several variants. No data. This was going nowhere. For want of a better idea, I typed in North American Nazi Revival. Zilch. I got up and walked around the room, my head pounding. I told myself that I was wasting my time, that I'd never find Karen this way. But what alternative did I have? I could spend weeks combing Maine for the camp and, even if I found it, I would be seriously outnumbered by the gray-clad guards. And I didn't even have any evidence that Karen was there.

I sat down again and played with the keys. Without giving it much thought, I deleted all but the initials *NANR*. No data. I looked closer. There was a hyperlink to another site, one which listed significant Nazi party members. I went there and tried NANR again. This time I had a hit. NANR were the initials of one Nikolaus Andreas Nieblich Rothmann—party number, 1925670; date of birth, September 30, 1915; place of birth, Berlin; date/place of death, unknown. I went back to the site I'd bookmarked and entered Rothmann's full name. I got another hit. As I read, my stomach went very queasy indeed.

* * *

Even though the place smelled bad, the floor was uneven and the furniture was cheap, the rented room suited. The name on the agreement was Marlon Hyde. The owner never came upstairs if the rent was paid on time. Hyde had fixed a heavy padlock to the outside of the door and two bolts and a chain to the inside. No one could get in or out without doing a lot of damage.

The crumbling walls were decorated with cuttings from the newspapers. They concerned the so-called occult killings. The death-metal singer Loki's demise covered one wall. The space around the single cracked window was covered with stories about Monsieur Hexie. Behind the bed were clippings about Professor Abraham Singer, while opposite were pages about the last victim, the tarot reader Crystal Vileda. Hyde had put those up earlier in the evening. It was interesting that the FBI had found prints incriminating the Englishman Matt Wells at Monsieur Hexie's apartment.

There were books piled high on the floor, old books full of strange pictures. They showed demons and witches, priests and zombies, Norse gods and Jewish mystics. There were also a Washington, D.C., Yellow Pages and several local maps. In a box under the bed, the killer had collected numerous pairs of weapons—skewers, knives, pieces of piping. There were even chopsticks. They had proved unexpectedly effective.

But Marlon Hyde was tired and dispirited. This wasn't the way it was meant to be, this wasn't what all the training had been for. There was a greater purpose, one for which every sacrifice was justified. But could that really be right? Most human beings were worthless, that was indisputable. But what about family? Was it ever acceptable to take the lives of parents, of siblings, of children? As time passed, that had become harder to take. It had been emphasized that no one was innocent, that even the children of the enemy had to be wiped out, so there would be no future for their kind. But what of the children of the just? What of siblings who failed the test? Did they deserve to be discarded—no, that word was a lie. Why did they have to be *executed* by those closest to them?

Hyde remembered the scenes in the Antichurch—the hyena-headed celebrant and the cloaked figure with features of stone, the chanting of the naked faithful, the mist of blood from the victims' opened throats. Those had been ecstatic occasions.

It had been a long time before the horror came, and the realization that the death of a brother had to be mourned; that blood would have blood, no matter what else had been taught; that nothing could ever justify the murder of a loved one.

Killing came easy. It always had done for Marlon Hyde. The hard thing had been to feign respect for human life; respect for the poor and needy; respect for the vulnerable. The tarot woman could have been a problem. The gross Loki, the pathetic Monsieur Hexie and the Jew professor hadn't raised a qualm. In any event, neither did Crystal Vileda. Using chopsticks had added an incongruous element that helped, and the need to hurry had removed any lingering doubt. But now, what was left? The pull was still there, the urge to submit to the coffining. Hyde had been fighting it, but confusion sometimes prevailed. To make things worse, Matt Wells had stolen the glory for two of the murders.

It was getting harder and harder to keep up the facade. Marlon Hyde knew that time was running out. Soon the ultimate victims would have to be taken out.

Clem Simmons came into the diner with a scowl on his face. Given that it was four-thirty in the morning, I forgave him. He looked around before spotting me in the booth at the rear.

"This had better be good," he said as he sat down opposite me. "Just coffee," he told the dull-eyed waitress.

"Oh, it's good," I said, rebooting my laptop. I had downloaded the contents of Joe's memory stick.

I spent the next ten minutes taking the detective through the findings. He scribbled notes, his brow furrowed. Finally, he raised a hand.

"Hold up, Matt. Where exactly is this going?"

"I haven't reached the best bit yet," I said, gulping coffee. "Look at this. Nikolaus Rothmann was an *Obersturmführer* in the SS."

"What the hell's that?"

"*Obersturmführer* or SS?"

He raised an eyebrow at me. "I know what the SS was, you fool—the Nazis' private army of madmen."

"Right. *Obersturmführer* is the equivalent of captain."

"Shit, is that all? I thought you were going to say the guy was a general at least."

"It doesn't matter because the rank was largely honorary in this case. You see, Rothmann was a doctor. A specialist in neurosurgery." I gave him a meaningful stare. "As in brain surgery."

"Yeah, yeah, I watch *ER* like everybody else. Keep going before I keel over."

"The point is, Rothmann spent two years at Auschwitz—working under none other than Josef Mengele."

The detective scratched his head. "Mengele? Didn't he escape after the war?"

"He eventually drowned in Brazil in the late seventies. In Auschwitz, they called him the Angel of Death. He carried out horrific experiments on people—on kids, as well, in particular twins. And our friend Rothmann helped him."

Clem Simmons put down his pen. "What is it you're saying here, Matt? That this Rothmann is in the States?"

"He might be, but he would be nearly a hundred. He had kids, though. It looks like the three of them were brought over here secretly after the war. There's no mention of his wife."

"All this because the old guy's initials happen to be the same as a minor organization that might have Nazi connections? It's a bit thin, man."

"Is it, Clem? The man who runs that organization also seems to be involved with Woodbridge Holdings—"

"Who you think set up the camp in Maine where you were imprisoned." The detective shook his head. "Like I say, it's pretty fucking thin."

"I told you, Clem, they messed with my head. My memory was screwed for days. It still isn't functioning normally. And get this—Woodbridge is into pharmaceuticals and chemical research. I reckon they're carrying on Rothmann's work."

"All right, Matt, all right. It's not like you need pharmaceuticals to mess with people's heads. But even if you're right about all that, what has Woodbridge Holdings got to do with the killings in D.C.? Some of which you're in the frame for, don't forget."

I'd seen a news flash saying that my prints had been at the scene of the Crystal Vileda murder.

"Only two of them," I said, realizing how dumb that sounded. "You can't seriously suspect me of the latest murder. You saw me outside Joe Greenbaum's not long after it."

He shrugged. "It's not me you have to worry about, Matt. The Feds have taken that case, too."

I caught his eye. "Who do you think is the killer?"

Clem frowned. "That's what we'd all like to know."

"No, I mean, what kind of person would commit the occult murders?"

The detective gave a hollow laugh. "A crazy person?"

"Really?" I countered. "A pretty organized crazy person. One capable of planning and executing four murders without leaving any traces—except mine, which are obviously a diversion. One who's got a carefully planned agenda, as the diagrams show."

"And one who's violent as hell."

"True. But has it crossed your mind that this could be the behavior of someone whose mind has been tampered with, like mine?"

The detective held my gaze. "Still doesn't explain why he's choosing occult targets."

I slumped in my seat. "You've got me there. The only thing I can think of is that Heinrich Himmler, the leader of the SS, was fascinated by the occult."

Clem grunted. "You will definitely have to do better than that, Matt."

"I'm working on it. By the way, what about the body in the river? The FBI is treating it as one of the series."

"Yeah, they are, even though there were no drawings found on the vic. The guy was a farmer from Iowa whose twins went missing here last winter."

"Twins?" I repeated.

"Yeah… So?"

"Jesus," I said, hairs rising on my neck. "Twins could be the key."

"You mean, the twin weapons?"

"Maybe, but not only that. Nikolaus Rothmann didn't just experiment on twins with Mengele. He had twin children of his own."

That made the detective's jaw plummet.

Thirty-Seven

Peter Sebastian got to the office not much after six in the morning. He'd had a call from his boss late the previous night that had disturbed him. He wasn't used to being pressured from above, and he didn't like it, especially since he'd been told that there were to be no more occult killings if he wanted to keep his job. He had spent hours with the case files before sleep finally overtook him, and he'd woken long before it had any beneficial effect. His wife just shook her head and turned in the opposite direction when he was getting dressed. He knew this had to be the best day's work he had ever put in and he'd asked all the members of his team to come in early.

Dana Maltravers appeared at the open door, carrying two mugs.

"Come in," Sebastian said, with a wave. "I need you."

"Hot and fresh," his subordinate said, handing him a mug. Not for the first time he wondered if she had designs on him, but dismissed the thought.

"Anything on the tarot murder?" he asked.

"The medical team did the postmortem overnight. The report's on its way, but I'm told there are no surprises."

"So the chopsticks were the murder weapons?"

Maltravers nodded. "They did some major damage to the brain."

"What did the crime-scene technicians come up with?"

"You mean, apart from the Matt Wells prints? Nothing conclusive. Some fibers and some soil traces, but they're unlikely to give us a big break—standard clothing and local dirt."

"Canvassing?"

"The team's on it as we speak. So far, nothing, apart from the not-very-brave citizen who lived below the vic."

Sebastian ran a hand across his limp hair. "What about document analysis?"

"Similar ink and paper. They reckon the drawings were done by the same hand. They still haven't any idea about the meaning or meanings."

"Jesus, Dana, who is this guy? The Invisible Man? Somebody has to have seen him."

"Sir?" Maltravers said, her eyes on the wall above him.

"What is it?" Sebastian said, recognizing the tone. She thought he had screwed up.

"Do you think we should have taken the D.C. detectives off the cases?"

He frowned. "Given that the order was mine, yes, I do. Obviously."

"Yes, but…they have local knowledge."

"So do our people, Dana." He looked at her and realized she hadn't finished. "Go on then, spit it out."

"Well, I spoke to a contact in MPDC last night. He reckons that Simmons and Pinker are still working the cases in their own."

Peter Sebastian's face flushed. "Are you sure about that? Chief Owen assured me they weren't."

Maltravers raised her shoulders. "I can't be a hundred percent certain, sir. Anyway, they might find something we could use."

"They'd better not. We'd look like major losers then. Now sit down. I want to run through all the murders and update my orders."

He did so, Dana Maltravers writing copious notes and giving her thoughts. The problem was, neither of them thought that the new orders would result in anything earth-shattering.

"What about Matt Wells, sir?"

"Keep the full alert in operation."

She nodded. "I agree."

Sebastian eyed her dubiously. "At the very least, we have to rule him out."

"Right, sir. About Richard Bonhoff—how much do you want to release to the press?"

"Everything."

"Including the fact that he was looking for his missing children here?"

"What?" Sebastian peered at the relevant file. "I didn't see anything about that."

Maltravers gave a thin smile. "Oh, sorry, sir, that report mustn't have got through yet. The wife confirmed it yesterday evening. Gwen and Randy are their names. Apparently they're twins."

"Do the D.C. detectives know about that?"

"I don't know." The young woman looked surprised at the question.

"Find out." Sebastian stared at her. He could see she wanted to know why he was so interested, but she didn't have the nerve to ask why. He watched her leave, then closed the door behind her.

Peter Sebastian needed to make some rather delicate calls. Roasting the Hate Crimes department for their slow response to his inquiry about the Antichurch of Lucifer Triumphant's threatening of Professor Singer was one thing. Trying to discover why the CIA was putting the

Paul Johnston

squeeze on his FBI boss was another. And finding out just what Clem Simmons and his partner were doing was the last. Then he could get back to catching the killer.

I was in the back of Clem's car, keeping my head down.

"We should be working on the explosion," Pinker said, glancing over his shoulder at me blankly. He had made it clear that he didn't approve of me being involved.

"We know who's responsible for that," I said, even though I knew I wasn't expected to speak.

"So where are their names, addresses and contact numbers?" Pinker demanded. He shook his head when I didn't answer. "Asshole."

"What Matt means is that the same people who don't want him to get any closer killed Joe Greenbaum, Vers," Clem said, keeping his eyes to the front. We were parked on a roadside in northwest Washington.

"Oh, excuse me," his partner said sardonically. "I forgot that the Secretary of State had ordered diplomatic immunity for limey number one here." He turned to Simmons. "Jesus, Clem, have you lost it completely? This guy's a suspect in at least two murders."

"Back off," the big man said. "We're not investigating those cases now, not officially. I'm only interested in making sure there are no more murders in this city."

"And exactly how is cozying up to *this* shithead going to achieve that?"

I leaned forward. "We're going to ask your friend Gordy Lister some awkward questions, Versace." Clem had told me about the newspaperman. I reckoned he must know plenty about Larry Thomson's and about Woodbridge Holdings's activities.

The detective turned his head toward me. "You don't get to call me that, jailbird. You gotta earn the right."

I smiled. He reminded me of my friend Dave, small of

frame but large of spirit. That could only be to my advantage—if he didn't cut my balls off first.

"There he is," Clem said.

I watched as a skinny man in a brown leather jacket and cowboy boots came down the steps of a town house. Apparently Lister rarely used the place, but he'd been keeping clear of his usual haunts.

"Oh, shit," Pinker said, reaching for his weapon.

Three men built like top-weight wrestlers came out after Gordy Lister and formed a defensive wall around him.

"We still going for it?" Pinker asked.

"Oh, yeah," Clem said, a smile on his lips.

They both got out. I stayed where I was—as they told me—but I had a feeling I wouldn't be there for long.

Clem walked behind the group as they headed for a large black SUV. When he called out Lister's name, the group stopped and Lister's face appeared between the solid sides of two of his bodyguards. I couldn't hear the discussion, but it was pretty obvious Lister wasn't interested in cooperating. The big men closed around him again.

That was when Pinker made his move. Holding his pistol in a two-handed grip, he ordered them all to stay where they were. They did so, for about ten seconds. Then one of the gorillas lunged at Pinker with unexpected speed, knocking his gun away. Another of the men bore down on Clem. I got out of the car, my heart racing.

By the time I was across the road, Lister was climbing into the SUV.

"Hey, assholes!" I yelled.

That got their attention. Two of the men stayed on the detectives. The third moved toward me. I glanced past him at Lister. The newspaperman had screwed up. Instead of driving away, he'd stayed to watch the fun. I was about to make him regret that.

My man had a crew cut and a face disfigured by steroid-induced acne. There was also a bulge in his jacket under his left armpit. I made a move for that. As the gorilla tried to grab my arm, I stepped inside and landed the toe of my boot in his unprotected groin. "The vomit shot" my friend Dave had called that, and he'd been sent off more than once for using it on the rugby pitch. As the gorilla went down, I slipped my hand inside his jacket and grabbed a large semiautomatic. I thumbed the safety off and turned the weapon on Gordy Lister.

"He'll be dead before you can aim at me," I said over my shoulder to the others.

Lister looked like he'd been caught in the lights of an eighteen-wheeler. My eyes told him I didn't have any qualms about shooting him and he wasn't prepared to take a chance on my shooting skills. Good move.

"Let them go," he said to his men. "Let my friends the detectives go."

Out of the corner of my eye, I saw Clem and Pinker clap handcuffs on the gorillas. Then Pinker went to check on the guy I'd kicked.

"Clear," he called, after pocketing a set of knuckle-dusters.

Clem went over to Lister and grabbed him.

"Let's go."

Pinker got in the back with Lister and I took the front passenger seat.

I turned to the rear. "So, can I call you Vers now?"

Gerard Pinker stared back at me and then grinned. "Guess you can at that. Long as I can call you Field Goal."

I shrugged. I'd been called worse.

Gordy Lister followed our exchange with the expression of a small boy who had inadvertently walked into a lions' den.

The woman was sitting in the back of a Jeep Cherokee, holding on tight. The driver had been told she was pregnant and he was driving carefully, but the track between the tall pine trees was deeply rutted. Still, she wasn't worried about the child. The doctors had assured her the journey wouldn't affect her son's well-being.

Before she left the camp, she had dressed in a black trouser suit that fitted her very well, the elastic in the waist expanding to accommodate her swollen belly. Apparently the clothes had belonged to her before she had been introduced to the teachings of the party. They had been ripped and made dirty. Her story was that she had been kidnapped by rough men who had kept her locked up in a dark room, giving her enough to eat but never talking to her.

Her face and hands had also been smeared with dirt, and it had been rubbed into her hair. She didn't mind. She wanted nothing but to hear the praise of her superiors after she returned from the city. They had promised that she would have every comfort for the birth, and that a top-level obstetrician and midwife would be in attendance. The child was precious to them—her son was the future and he would grow up surrounded by love and respect. And they had finally told her who the father was. She was looking forward to meeting him. She had to speak to him, but there would be little time. Maybe it would be best that way. Men didn't respond well to rejection.

Her equipment had been easy to hide about her person. No one would find it suspicious in the least, so she would be allowed to keep it.

The pine trees gradually became smaller and the track softer. They passed through clearings, leaving small huts behind. It struck the woman that this wilderness would be a wonderful place to bring up her son. The rest of the world was full of degenerates and the weak, people who had been brainwashed by television, fashion and pop music. They needed to be woken up.

* * *

We left the gorillas to play with their handcuffs and took Gordy Lister to a remote parking place in Rock Creek Park. Gerard Pinker jumped out and blocked the access road with a couple of police cones to make sure we wouldn't be disturbed.

"What's this all about, guys?" the newspaperman said, blinking in extreme nervousness. "I mean, you took us by surprise back there...."

"Yeah, it looked that way," Pinker said. "You didn't think we knew about that extra place of yours, did you?"

Gordy was looking at me. "Who's he?"

"Oh, you know me," I said, with a pleasant smile. "At least, you should do. I've been all over the *Star Reporter* recently."

Lister squinted. "What?" Then he must have remembered the photo of me that they'd been running. "Matt Wells," he said, turning to Simmons. "Why isn't he under arrest?"

"A good question," Clem said, looking over his shoulder. "But a two-timing piece of shit like you doesn't get to hear the answer."

"What do you—"

Lister broke off as Versace jabbed him in the midriff with his fist. "No more questions from you, Gordy. Only answers. Where shall we start?"

I had an idea about that. "Larry Thomson," I said, watching the newspaperman's reaction. As I'd expected, he looked very apprehensive.

"I see you know him. So tell us what he does at Wood-bridge Holdings."

The three of us held our eyes on him. He seemed to shrink, but nothing came from his mouth except a damp tongue that flickered like a snake's.

Vers applied his fist to the prisoner's belly again. This time he let out a yelp.

"All right, Gordy," I said, smiling expansively, "let me

make it easy for you. I'll tell you what I know about Wood-bridge Holdings." I gave him an outline of what we knew about the NANR, the camp and their links with Nazism.

"What's that got to do with me?" he whined when I'd finished. "I don't know anything about this Nazi revival."

"Is that right? Do you know a reporter called Joe Green-baum, Gordy?"

He avoided my eyes and raised his shoulders weakly.

"Is that a yes?" I demanded.

"He…he was blown up, wasn't he?" Lister said in a small voice. "I saw it on the news."

"What do you know about that?" I leaned closer. His eyes stayed down, which made me suspicious. "He was my friend, Gordy. And he told me a lot about Woodbridge Holdings."

I glanced at Clem Simmons. It was time to put the squeeze on Lister big-time. We'd talked about doing it, but he hadn't been sure it would work.

"How do you think Larry Thomson's going to feel about you when he hears you've spilled your guts to us?"

"What d'you mean?" Lister squealed. "I haven't said anything!"

"Yet." I smiled at him, this time malevolently. "Your people killed my friend. You're going to tell me everything you know or I'll stick something a lot sharper than a fist in your gut." I laughed bitterly. "Don't forget—according to the *Star Reporter,* I skewered Monsieur Hexie's kidneys and shoved chopsticks up Crystal Vileda's nostrils." I pulled out a pair of chopsticks that I'd got earlier from a Chinese restaurant.

Gordy Lister's eyes bulged, then he collapsed forward. Versace pulled him up and made him face me.

"All right—all right. Mr. Thomson will never trust me again anyway."

And then he told us his tale.

Thirty-Eight

Gavin Burdett was sitting in a deep leather armchair facing a large antique desk. A nondescript sedan had set him down on a parallel street after a two-hour drive from Washington. He glanced at the Havana he'd allowed to go out in the ashtray and decided against lighting it again. Larry T. tolerated cigar smoke, but he wasn't really a fan. Now that the pressure was on, the Englishman didn't want to make things worse for himself.

The door opened and the tall man walked in, followed by a thin-faced bodyguard wearing a well-cut suit. Burdett immediately stood up, disguising the pain in his knees. He smiled uncertainly.

"Larry, I'm very glad to—" He broke off as the bodyguard walked around the room. He moved a thin rod up and down, scanning for surveillance devices. After a nod from him, the tall man pointed to the door and waited till he and Burdett were alone.

"I'm sorry, Gavin," he said, in a low, smooth voice. "We can't be too careful. It appears that one of my confederates has been arrested."

The Englishman was immediately apprehensive. "*Really?* How much does he know?"

Larry Thomson smiled. "About you? Absolutely nothing at all."

"Thank God." Burdett reached for the crystal glass containing fifteen-year-old malt whiskey.

"He does, however, know rather a lot about other aspects of our operations," the tall man said, walking behind the desk and sitting down. He waved to Burdett to sit, too.

"Will he talk?"

"Almost undoubtedly." Thomson took a cigarette from his silver case and lit it. "It's very difficult to find completely loyal men these days. Particularly as regards what one might call dirty work."

Gavin Burdett raised his hands. "I don't want to know."

Larry Thomson gave another tight smile. "I wasn't going to tell you. What you know about our overseas interests is enough." He filled a glass from a carafe of water. "Not that I've told you about all of those."

The Englishman took a large sip of whiskey. "So, what now? Is the woman ready?"

Thomson looked at his guest with pale blue, unwavering eyes. "Apparently so."

"And you're going to go ahead with the plan?"

"Have you acquired cold feet?" The tall man's tone was mocking. "I seem to remember that you were the one who wanted her...how shall I put? Removed from the equation?"

Burdett nodded. "Of course. She declared a personal crusade against me."

Thomson swallowed water, his Adam's apple becoming even more prominent. "Why so anxious, then?"

"Because...what if the process isn't entirely successful? What if she remembers who she is?"

"That's very unlikely. Our procedures are highly effective."

Gavin Burdett dropped his gaze. "Not in Matt Wells's case."

"As you well know, his treatment was incomplete. Besides, he may still act as planned when the time comes."

"And what about the occult killings?"

"What about them?" The tall man smiled. "If anything, they have added to the general state of panic in Washington. Our forthcoming operations will make the most of that."

"What are you going to do about Wells?"

"He'll be caught. The FBI is fully committed to that."

The Englishman looked across the desk. "You're sure?"

"I've told you before—we have friends in the Bureau."

Gavin Burdett drained his glass. "You'd better be right. A lot of people in the City of London have invested deeply in Woodbridge Holdings."

Thomson raised his eyebrows. "Have any of them lost money?" He got up and took the decanter round to his guest. "No, they haven't. And that's all they care about, isn't it?"

Burdett watched as his glass was filled over half full. "Yes, Larry," he said, with a widening smile. "Indeed it is."

I was in the back of Clem Simmons's car in southeast Washington, about fifty yards down the road from a large building that had originally been a warehouse. Now it was used by junkies and crackheads.

"We shouldn't have let that little rat go in on his own," Gerard Pinker said, looking through binoculars at the building's entrance. The streetlamp near it gave off only a dull glow.

"He'll come," Clem said, stifling a yawn. "He's told us too much. The shitheads at Woodbridge Holdings will crucify him if he goes back."

"That's if he told us the truth," his partner said.

"It squares with what we already knew," I said, leaning forward. "The camp, Woodbridge's activities, the twins."

Pinker shook his head. "It's all just hearsay, man. Gordy hasn't been to the camp. He doesn't know anything about Larry Thomson's past. All he's admitted to is talking the dead Iowa farmer's kids into coming back to D.C."

"Let's see what they say," Clem said, eyeing him dubiously. "You ever have an optimistic thought, Vers?"

"Me? No way. Your problem is you're far too charitable, big guy." He raised the binoculars again. "Movement. Well, I'll be damned. Gordy's bringing out two kids, one male and the other not."

We watched as the trio approached. The twins looked tired, their clothing dirty and crumpled. I wondered if Lister had told them about their father. For all we knew, the newspaperman was involved in Richard Bonhoff's murder, though he had denied that strenuously. The same applied to Joe. I wasn't happy about making deals with the guy who might have been behind my friend's death.

Versace got out and opened the back door for the twins. I could now see that they looked very alike, apart from the boy's longer hair. They were also attractive, despite their sunken cheeks and the heavy rings round their eyes. They were obviously junkies, their skin sallow and their fingers moving incessantly.

"There you go," Lister said triumphantly. "So I can split now, yeah?"

"You keep your cell on at all times," Pinker said, his tone harsh. "If we call, you do exactly what we say, got it?"

"Sure. I'll be keeping my head down, anyway."

"Gordy?" I said, leaning across. "I haven't forgotten Joe Greenbaum. If anything ties you to that bomb, I *will* seek you out."

He looked nervous for a moment, then bounced back. "I told you, Mr. Wells, I don't do that kind of thing."

"Yeah, I believe you," Versace said, closing the door after the twins had got in beside me.

I watched as Lister walked swiftly into the darkness.

"Gordy's okay," the young man next to me said. "He looks after us."

"Randy," I said, extending a hand. "Gwen. I'm Matt Wells."

"Oh, we know who you are," the girl said, squeezing my hand gently. Her palm was damp, her smile slack. "Gordy said you're a writer. You going to write about us?"

"Maybe. But we need to talk to you first."

"You guys cops?" Randy said to the men in the front seats.

"Yup," Clem replied.

"Thought as much," the young man said. "We learned how to spot you the first week we were here."

"Is that right?" Clem said, accelerating on to the freeway. "You want to tell us what you've been doing since you got here?"

I'd thought they might be reluctant to talk, but that wasn't the case. Gordy had told them to answer all our questions, and they did. Before we reached the house over the Maryland state line that Versace had borrowed from his absent sister, they'd given us a full rundown.

Gwen and Randy had spent the first week in D.C. seeing the sights and being wined and dined. Then came the modeling work that Lister had arranged for them. There was nothing tasteless, just fashion shoots and the like. Then Gordy had told them about a residential course Woodbridge ran that would be useful in their future careers. The twins hadn't given it a second thought, though they knew enough not to tell their parents. It struck me that they were as naive as five-year-olds and their permanent smiles began to grate. I wondered if they'd always been like that.

They didn't know where they'd been driven as the van had darkened windows. Randy thought it was up north because of the cold. From the descriptions they gave of the barbed wire and low buildings, as well as the pine forests and snow-clad mountain ridges, I reckoned that it was the camp where I'd been held. The alternative, that there were several such installations, was too depressing to consider. You'd have thought the twins might have objected to being put into uniform—gray, with badges bearing the letters *NANR*—and taught how to handle rifles and pistols, but apparently not. I asked if they'd been given any drugs or if their memories had been affected, but they claimed not. They were vague about the timeline of all this, though, which made me suspicious. They claimed they'd been back in Washington for a couple of months, having escaped from the camp during a power failure.

Then I hit pay dirt. I had asked if they knew Larry Thomson. They said no, so I showed them the photo on my phone.

"That's the Führer," they said in unison, their eyes wide.

I struggled to conceal my shock. "What?"

"The Führer," they repeated.

"He visited us at the camp," Randy went on. "We were greatly honored. He's a very busy man."

The combination of servility and corrupted innocence turned my stomach. What had been done to these kids?

"He talked to me for nearly a minute," Gwen said eagerly. "He asked me about Nazi ideology. Of course, I knew everything by heart."

"Nazi ideology?" Versace said, in disbelief.

I raised a hand. "Just what are the aims of the NANR?"

"The North American Nazi Revival is dedicated to the eradication of Jews and all other under-races from the U.S.A., whatever the cost," they recited. "We obey the Führer and his officers without question. We fight for the Greater Germany, of which the U.S.A. will become part after the global conflict is won. We are dedicated to the extermination of all existing religions, under the instruction of the Antichurch of Lucifer Triumphant."

The twins sat back and beamed at us. It was as if a death sentence had been read out by preschoolers.

"I guess under-races includes blacks," Clem said slowly.

"Oh, yes," Gwen replied, with a smile.

"Well, pardon me, darling," said Versace, "but shouldn't you be trying to eradicate and exterminate my partner here right now?"

Randy and Gwen exchanged anxious glances.

"We…we aren't…aren't authorized to act without orders from our superiors," the young man said, lowering his eyes.

"Well, that is a relief," Clem said, with a hollow laugh. "Tell me, if you liked these people so much, why did you escape from the camp?"

Again they looked at each other, but it was impossible to tell what passed between their dead eyes.

"Well…" Randy began.

"It's all right," his sister interrupted. "I'm…I'm almost over it." She licked her lips repeatedly. "They…some of the comrades…they took advantage—"

"They raped her," Randy said, his cheeks red. "Men and women. With gun barrels. They made her—"

Gwen touched his arm. "It's over. We're free of them."

I wasn't sure if that was really the case, given that Gordy Lister had known exactly where to find them. They'd been taken advantage of and terribly abused, but they still seemed to admire the man they called the Führer. What did that say about the power he exerted?

The atmosphere gradually lightened, but I still felt like I was sitting next to a pair of highly sensitive explosive devices. Then I thought about the Antichurch of Lucifer Triumphant. The twins may have seen human sacrifices at the camp but, given their condition, I could hardly just ask them that straight out.

"How about the Antichurch?" I said. "Did you go to services?"

"*Rituals,*" Gwen corrected. "Of course we did. We all did." Then her expression went blank, as if a shutter had suddenly been closed.

Randy's gaze stayed down. Versace swore under his breath.

"The Führer," I said, involuntarily lowering my voice. "Did he have anyone with him when he visited the camp?"

"Of course," Randy said. "The professor was always with him."

"This prof got a name?" Versace growled.

The twins shook their heads.

"What did he look like?" Clem asked.

They both smiled.

"No," Gwen said, "the professor is a woman. She's tall, like the Führer, and very distinguished. In her sixties, I'd say. Like him." She gave a sudden laugh. "Of course she is like him. After all, they're twins. They were plenty of our kind at the camp."

Now we were getting somewhere. Thomson—the leader of the NANR and éminence grise behind Woodbridge—had a twin sister. Nikolaus A. N. Rothmann, Mengele's helper, had twin children, a boy and a girl, who would be in their sixties now. But did that mean they were responsible for the murders? I thought about the diagrams, the squares and rectangles that had been left on the victims. Something was stirring in my memory, something I'd seen in the camp.

Then I thought of someone else. Gavin Burdett. Not only was he in Washington, but I'd tailed him to the occult supplies shop in East London. He was a dishonest investment banker with an interest in underage girls. Could he also be responsible for the murders in Washington? If so, how much were the Rothmann twins involved?

Pinker showed the twins into their rooms at his sister's house—we had decided to use it in case anyone tried to find the detectives at home. Clem told Gwen and Randy that they would be put in a drug rehabilitation program as soon as possible. They seemed happy enough and showed no sign of wanting to be anywhere else, though that probably meant they didn't need a fix yet. The house had high-security windows and doors, so they'd find it hard to break out when they did, and Versace would be playing nursemaid. Then again, they had been trained how to use weapons at the camp. I didn't feel good about leaving the detective there on his own, but Clem and I had work to do.

"Hey, Field Goal," Versace said, as we headed for the door. I looked round.

"You look after my partner, yeah?"

I nodded. "And you watch yourself with the twins, Vers."

"Don't panic. I've seen *The Boys from Brazil.*"

That didn't reassure me much. I couldn't remember if the movie had a happy ending or not. As we left, it struck me that the twins maybe didn't know about their father's death yet. We would have to tell them later. Considering how dedicated they still seemed to be to their Führer, I wasn't sure they'd even remember who Richard Bonhoff was.

New York State Trooper Reggie Swan yawned and took a slug of cold coffee. He was on his own in the station in the small town of Grantsville thirty miles from Buffalo, and he was bored rigid. He had always hated the night shift. It was all right in a city, with the hookers and pimps, the drunks and brawlers to keep you busy. In the boonies, it was about as much fun as a teetotaler's wake.

Then the door opened and Reggie Swan became an overnight celebrity.

"Help you, ma'am?" he said, as the statuesque woman turned to face him.

Her face and clothes were dirty and torn, and her breathing was heavy. "Ma'am?"

The trooper caught her as she fell. He pulled her as gently as he could to a chair and got her some water. After she'd taken a few sips, she was suddenly much more in control of herself.

"I'm Karen Oaten. Detective Chief Superintendent Karen Oaten of the Metropolitan Police, London."

Reggie Swan stared at the blonde woman and remembered a photo that showed a much cleaner face. It had been in the FBI mis-pers bulletin for weeks.

"Are you all right, ma'am?" he asked, checking her for obvious injuries. He saw none.

"I'll make it," she said, with a weary smile. "I need to make some phone calls."

"I should think you do. I need to make one myself." He went back to the desk and called his sergeant. The old shithead never liked being disturbed at night, but this time he said he'd be right over. Screw him, Reggie thought. He's not getting any of my glory. To make sure of that, he called the local TV and radio stations, as well as the Buffalo papers. Then he watched as the woman whom the whole of the FBI had been looking for made her calls from the sergeant's desk.

For once, the night shift had been a knockout for Trooper Reggie Swan.

Thirty-Nine

"**Y**ou think we screwed up letting Gordy Lister go?" Clem Simmons asked as he drove toward central Washington.

I shrugged. "Maybe. We had to make a deal with him to make him talk. And he did give us the twins. He's not stupid. He'd have understood if we made empty promises."

The detective nodded. "I guess so. I'm not sure we'll be seeing him again, though."

I felt the same, but I'd meant what I said to the newspaperman. If we found anything that linked him to Joe's death, I would get to him, no matter how long it took.

"You sure you want to do this?" Clem asked.

"It's our only option. You're never going to get a warrant to search the Woodbridge building."

"Nope—not unless we find something that ties Thomson or his people directly to the murders."

He grunted. "Know what I think? Larry Thomson's got someone in the FBI."

"Are you serious?"

"Wouldn't be the first big-ass businessman to buy his way in."

I thought about that. It squared with the finding of my

fingerprints at the two murder scenes. The FBI had taken my prints after Karen's disappearance. Some asshole from the Bureau could have planted them at the scenes.

"It's not like they've made much progress with the investigation, is it?" Clem said.

"Is their agent in charge trustworthy?"

The detective raised his shoulders. "Peter Sebastian? They call him Dick, as in Dickhead. I'm not sure. He *is* the deputy head of Violent Crime, so he *should* know what he's doing."

"That's not what I meant."

He grinned. "I know that. Look, I've no idea, man. He's a conceited bastard, but most of those guys are, even the straight ones."

We fell silent as we approached the center, the illuminated dome of the Capitol shining like a huge beacon. My heart began to hammer. What we were about to do was as unconstitutional as it got.

Clem parked the car on the street about five minutes' walk from the Woodbridge building. It was after ten, so there weren't many people around. I took the bag I'd filled at Versace's sister's house and joined the detective on the pavement.

"I could do with a weapon," I said, still regretting that I'd left all of mine at the hotel.

"You're not getting my piece." I was pretty sure he wouldn't have gone ahead with the scam if I'd been armed with anything more than a handful of screwdrivers. After all, I was still officially under suspicion of murder. "I'll do the talking," he said, as we approached the steps outside the building.

"Okay," I said, smiling nervously. "I'll just sneak."

The glass doors were locked. Clem showed his badge to the security guard inside, while I loitered by a pillar. When the door was opened, I kept behind the detective.

"You've got a breach in your system," Clem said.

The guard, an earnest-looking young man, whose jacket almost obscured his heavy biceps, frowned. He went over to his desk and checked the console. "There's nothing showing here."

"Well, you've got an even bigger problem than I thought," the detective said. "Downtown, we're showing an entry at the rear of the building."

The security man looked as if he'd been asked to solve a complicated piece of algebra. "I didn't even know you guys were connected to our system."

"Of course we are," Clem said impatiently. "You're a few minutes from Congress. There's nothing we don't know." He stood with his arms akimbo. "Are we going to check the rear with your help or on our own?"

The guard's hand was hovering over a phone. Clem's tone convinced him to play ball. "All right," he said. "This way."

I followed them as far as the elevators and then hung back as they went down to the lower mezzanine. As soon as they were out of sight, I slipped through the door leading to the stairwell—I wasn't going to risk meeting someone in the confined space of an elevator. I checked the dimly lit stairs and started to climb. There were helpful signs on each landing. The first four were marked "Star Reporter" and the next five were different departments of the holding company—Accounts, Property, Personnel and so on. Things got interesting on the tenth floor. It was marked "Group Management," as were the next three. I was heading for the very top. There was no reason Woodbridge Holdings would be different from every other hierarchical business building—the bosses would be in the penthouse suite. Except that, when I got there, I discovered that there was no sign at all. It seemed the Führer wasn't ready to make himself obvious, even in his own headquarters.

There was a Plexiglass window in the door. Through it I could see a wide passageway, with artwork on the wall.

I shrank back as a man with biceps even larger than the main guard's walked past with a menacing gait. That was both good and bad news: there was someone worth guarding up here, but I had to figure out a way of getting at them. I took a long screwdriver and a chisel with a narrow point from my bag and waited for the gorilla to pass again. He did so two minutes and fifteen seconds later. Assuming he was regular in his actions—something you would guess a boss who called himself the Führer might demand—I had that long to get in and hide myself; assuming there was only one guard. I decided to go for it.

I knew more than most people about breaking locks thanks to my friend Andy, who learned at the sharp end on the streets of New Jersey. My on-off memory also obliged by coming up with the main points. One—ensure any alarm system is disabled: I was relying on Clem to have done that during his time with the guard downstairs. Two—ensure no obvious damage is left. I jimmied the door with the screwdriver, trying not to leave any scratch marks—I didn't want to land Clem in trouble if everything went to hell. The only problem was, the door was resolutely not opening. That was when I saw the pressure pad between the jamb and the top edge. Shit. It was electrically controlled from the other side. I had no choice.

I looked around and saw a fire extinguisher on the landing. Checking my watch, I waited for the guard to appear again. Then I gave him another minute to make sure he wasn't close. The door gave way with the first blow of the extinguisher. Unfortunately, the noise was enough to wake the dead. I sprinted down the corridor and took refuge behind a desk that was set in an alcove, not bothering to conceal myself. The gorilla was on the other side soon afterward. He saw me immediately.

"Get up," he said gruffly.

I did what I was told, putting the bag on the desk between us.

"What's in there?" he demanded, his eyes locked on mine.
I smiled. "A bomb."

His eyes immediately dropped, as I knew they would.
I punched him hard on the side of his jaw. I was in luck.
The other side of his face smashed against the wall and he
dropped to the floor. I dragged him behind the desk and
secured his hands and legs with the plastic restraint cuffs
Clem had given me. I was home free—as long as there
weren't any more goons on the loose.

I took the bag and walked to the end of the corridor.
There was a set of double doors there, the only entrance
I'd seen since I broke in. I hoped the birds hadn't flown
after the noise I'd made.

Just as I was about to slide the screwdriver into the
lock, there was a loud click and the doors opened inward.
I stood there like a schoolboy outside the local brothel,
unsure whether to stay or go. Then a female voice put me
out of my misery.

I went in to meet the woman who called me by name.

Peter Sebastian was still at his desk, having told his wife
that he wouldn't be home till further notice. He was sink-
ing in quicksand, and everything he did seemed to make
things worse. He'd even bawled out Dana Maltravers for
the first time ever, and sent her home. He wasn't sure if
she'd be speaking to him in the morning and he couldn't
blame her. He'd been treating her as if she was his slave,
rather than a special agent on the fast track to the very top.

He drank from a bottle of water. Soon he would have
to draft a report for his boss, and the FBI director himself
wanted to be copied on it. That didn't make him feel good
at all. The simple truth was that he didn't have anything
significant to report about the occult killings. The only
progress his team had made regarded the dead man in the
river. Richard Bonhoff's wife, Melissa, had been inter-

viewed. She had come to Washington and Sebastian had met her, though it was Maltravers who took her statement. He'd been surprised by the woman's coldness—she hardly seemed to care that her husband had been murdered. At least she'd supplied a lot of information about her twin children, Randy and Gwen, who didn't come home three months ago, having been on a trip to D.C. last winter. She had demanded that the Bureau find her children, something that Sebastian could hardly prioritize. It didn't help that the newspaperman Gordon Lister, who had looked after the twins when they won a competition in the *Star Reporter,* was nowhere to be found. The people at the paper seemed to be as much in the dark as anyone as to his whereabouts.

At last the people in Hate Crimes had woken up, but they hadn't been any use. As far as they knew, the Antichurch of Lucifer Triumphant had been defunct for decades. They were of the opinion that some far-right lunatic or lunatics had dug the name up as cover. As for the investigations on the ground, all witnesses had been questioned again, all medical and CSI reports had been collated and double-checked, and all leads had been followed—without a hint of the murderer's identity. Sebastian simply had nowhere else to look.

He got up and went over to the conference table. Maltravers had taken out books from the Bureau library on satanic thrash metal, voodoo, the kabbalah and tarot, as well as ordering up reports on previous occult investigations. They had been through them all, examining illustrations, comparing themes and motifs, trying to make connections. They could have spent years doing that and been none the wiser about who the killer was. He wondered if they were being too subtle. Maybe their man just hated the paranormal; maybe he was just a sad fuck obsessed with the number two—though even that wouldn't explain the drawings attached to the bodies.

The only thing that Sebastian knew for sure was that the twin weapons used in all the murders were significant in some way. If he'd been able to talk to Richard and Melissa Bonhoff's kids, maybe he'd have gotten some insights. As it was, the Bureau psychologists had given him a standard briefing about the complexities of didymous children, as they called them. What was he meant to do now? Go out and arrest every set of twins he could lay his hands on?

After a few minutes of such thought, the phone rang. Wearily Sebastian picked it up. It was the supervisor of the Document Analysis Unit. She'd had an idea about the diagrams.

At last.

The woman was young—around thirty. She had short brown hair and a face that I would have found alluring if she hadn't been pointing a matte black pistol at my chest. She was wearing a black trouser suit and a white blouse.

"Matt Wells," she repeated. "Welcome. We've been expecting you." She waved me inside with the gun. "Please don't do anything stupid. I'm one of the best shots in the country."

The air of certainty with which she made that statement struck me. Did she shoot professionally?

The small hallway opened into a huge room that must have taken up half of the penthouse. The lights of Washington spread across an enormous picture window. Pieces of antique furniture were dotted about the carpeted floor like elephants on the savannah. The works of art on the walls were large and looked both genuine and somewhat familiar.

"Over there," the woman said, pointing to a pair of sofas arrayed in an L-shape by the window. As I approached, another woman got up and turned to face me. She was tall and gray haired, with a striking aquiline nose. I caught the resemblance to Larry Thomson immediately.

"Mr. Wells, what a pleasure," she said, with old-fashioned politeness.

"I wish I could say the same, Ms. Thomson." I sat down without being invited.

The woman smiled humorlessly. "I don't use the surname my brother decided on." She offered me a cigarette from a silver case.

I raised my hand to decline and saw the younger woman's pistol follow the movement. "Don't worry, I won't bite," I said, reaching for the open bottle of red wine on the table and pouring myself a glass. The last thing I was going to do was show these Nazis any respect.

"That is debatable," the Führer's sister said, sitting down opposite me. She was wearing a gray trouser suit that was considerably better cut than the uniforms at the camp. "We have read your books and done additional research. We know exactly what you're capable of. You have escaped from us once already." She raised her glass. "Bravo."

The young woman smiled. "I can assure you that you won't escape again." She moved behind the older woman and I saw that the line of her jaw was almost identical, but she had escaped the beak of a nose.

"Mother and daughter," I said. "Where's Larry, to complete the happy family?"

"Otherwise engaged," the seated woman said. "You can call me Irma if you like."

"I don't," I said, swallowing what was a very good Merlot. "You were born Fraulein Rothmann and that'll do for me. Or did you take your husband's name?"

They both laughed.

"I do not have a husband anymore, Mr. Wells," said the concentration-camp doctor's daughter. "A necessary phase so that I didn't remain childless, but he is long gone. He had the right breeding, but he was weak. Of course, I never took his name."

I hoped the poor guy had survived the encounter. "What about you?" I said to the younger woman. "I'm guessing you have an anglicized name."

"Correct."

I waited, and then laughed. "But you don't care to share it with me. All right, let's try a different tack. You're comfortable with that pistol and by your own admission you're a champion shot. The Glock semiautomatic is standard law-enforcement issue. So what are you? A local cop or a Fed?"

"Everybody hates a smart-ass," the woman said, aiming the pistol at my groin.

"It's all right, Dana," the older woman said. "There's no reason to be coy." She turned to me. "Mr. Wells, this is Special Agent Dana Maltravers of the FBI violent-crime team. She's been working very hard to find you."

I remembered Clem having mentioned that name. "You work with Peter Sebastian?"

The young woman looked surprised, which was what I wanted.

"Could it be that you're the one who made sure my prints were at two of the occult-murder scenes?"

I seemed to have scored another hit, though the FBI agent was still as cold as a glacier. I needed to antagonize her more, make her drop her guard. "Interesting name," I said. I had always been fascinated by what people were called and used to spend hours with encyclopedias on the subject. Fortunately, that part of my memory seemed to be accessible. "Dana is the feminine form of Daniel, isn't it? Rather a Jewish name for your sort, don't you think?"

"It was chosen deliberately," she said, glancing at Fraulein Rothmann. "To divert suspicion."

"It certainly worked for me," I said, with an ironic smile. "As for Maltravers, well, *mal* is evil, so that seems appropriate." Their faces were stony. "And *travers* means a crossing, doesn't it? Particularly an oblique one."

"You'll soon be wishing you never crossed me, Wells," the young woman said, raising the Glock to my face.

I tried to ignore that. "Oblique as in underhand or askew," I continued. "Like your sense of ethics?"

"That will do!" Fraulein Rothmann had finally showed some emotion. "What we need from you is a list of all the people with whom you have shared information about Woodbridge Holdings, my brother, the camp or anything pertaining to it." She laughed sharply. "And if you're waiting for your Negro detective friend to rescue you, don't bother. He has been restrained and will shortly be on his way to the river."

My stomach pole-vaulted.

Jesus, Clem. What had I got him into?

Forty

Karen Oaten sat back in her seat in the FBI helicopter, swallowing hard as the machine took off. She had her hands over the bulge in her midriff, worried that the safety belt and the movement of the helicopter would disturb her child. Then she relaxed as the lights of the small town below faded into the night. All would be well. Her leaders had given their personal assurances.

"Everything okay?" The voice in the headphones was tinny.

"Yes, Levon." She smiled at the occupant of the seat next to her.

"So, do you want to give me a rundown of what happened?"

Karen paused. Levon Creamer was the FBI man who had looked after her when she had arrived in Washington. He was chief of the financial-crime department, a thin, balding man in his mid-forties, whose manner was more that of an accountant than a law-enforcement agent. She was confident enough about the story that she had learned in detail, but she wasn't sure recounting it in the helicopter would do it justice.

"I don't really know, Levon. I came round on a roadside and started walking. I suppose I was lucky there was a policeman in that place."

"Your captors may have put you in the neighborhood deliberately. Hey, Karen, are you sure you're feeling all right?"

His concern touched her, though she knew he really only wanted to know the details of her kidnapping. A doctor had checked her before the helicopter arrived, so Creamer knew her medical status. Maybe he was worried about the baby.

"I'm fine," she said. "And so's the little one."

"Good. You've had a hell of an ordeal. Tell me about it."

"To be honest with you, I don't remember very much. I was lying down in the Shenandoah Valley and suddenly everything went dark. Some kind of hood was over my head. I was carried to a vehicle and driven for a long time—I'd say at least four hours. I tried to talk, but a male voice told me to shut up if I wanted…if I wanted to keep my baby." She paused for effect.

Levon Creamer waited silently for a respectable time. "Was the guy American?"

"Yes, but I couldn't tell you what accent he had."

"Then what?"

"Well…I'm sorry to say, I got very frightened. Eventually I…I couldn't control my bladder any longer…they laughed when they saw what I'd done. There were two…two men."

"The bastards."

"Yes. Finally the vehicle stopped and I was hauled out. The hood stayed on my head until I was inside. After a time, I realized I was on my own and I took it off." She paused again. "I actually laughed when I saw where I was. It was like a bedroom out of a Doris Day film, all frilly bedcovers and pastel wallpaper. I went to the door. Of course, it was locked and very solid. At least there was an en suite bathroom, but the door had been taken off. It didn't take me long to spot the cameras in every corner of the bedroom and bathroom."

"Jesus."

"It wasn't so bad. I held a towel in front of me when I used the toilet. If they wanted to watch me in the shower, too bad."

The FBI man looked up from the notes he was writing on a clipboard. "Brave lady. And that was where you were all this time?"

"Yes. The windows had been boarded up, so I had to rely on my watch to tell the time of day. The date function meant I knew how many days I'd been in captivity, though, to tell you the truth, it still went into a kind of blur. There was no TV or radio, so very soon I felt totally cut off from the outside world."

"They feed you all right?"

"I got three meals a day. It wasn't great food, but adequate. I was even given fresh milk twice a day. They would tell me to go into the bathroom and then open the door to leave a tray. The same in reverse when I'd finished. The cutlery and dishes were always plastic and they checked that everything was returned. I know that because I kept a knife once and they realized immediately."

"Did they ever talk to you or come inside your quarters?"

"Apart from the instructions at mealtimes, which came through a small speaker on the ceiling, no. I didn't see anyone all the time I was there. At least there were some books to read. I've become a great fan of Ayn Rand, not least because she wrote very long novels."

"You didn't have any blackouts or times when you woke up feeling woozy?"

"You mean, did they drug me to find out what I knew? No, nothing that I'm aware of."

Creamer smiled encouragingly. "And how's your memory?"

"Fine." She smiled back at him and tried to act like a normal human being. "Is Matt okay?"

The FBI man kept his eyes off her. "Um, yes, I think so. The deputy director will bring you up to speed."

Karen nodded blankly. She'd been told before she was taken from the camp about her former lover's involvement in the awful murders in Washington. It had been a shock that her baby's father was a killer, but she would make sure the child never knew. Matt Wells belonged to the past—that had been made very clear to her.

"I presume all my files are secure," she said.

"Uh, yeah, they are," Creamer said, reestablishing eye contact. "We picked them up from your hotel the day after you disappeared. It didn't look like anything was missing."

"Good," Karen said enthusiastically. "I need to get back to work first thing tomorrow morning. I presume my meetings with the Bureau and the Department of Justice will be rescheduled?"

Levon Creamer looked surprised. "We assumed you'd need time to recover."

"Am I giving you that impression now?"

The FBI man shook his head. "No, ma'am."

"Please make the arrangements, Levon."

She watched as he changed to another channel and started talking animatedly. Everything was running smoothly. She was sure the meeting she most wanted would also be scheduled soon.

I sat on the sofa and took another slug of wine, trying to keep my face unreadable as my mind went into overdrive. What were my options? I could give Fraulein Rothmann and her gun-toting daughter a list of invented names, but I had the feeling they were in the loop enough to rumble that plan. Telling them about Pinker would condemn him to death, as may have already happened with Clem. Shit, what was I doing debating the issue? I needed to act right now.

I gagged on the wine, then sprayed it over the table and floor. I coughed hard and started gasping for breath, my hands on my throat. I hoped my face had gone a dark enough shade of red to convince them that I was having some kind of seizure.

"Oh, for God's sake," I heard Irma Rothmann say. "See if you can help him, Dana. Give me the gun."

That was progress—she had to be less proficient with firearms than the FBI agent. I kept up the act, pumping my chest up and down like a man who was at death's door. Then I felt the daughter's hands under my arms as she tried to turn me onto my side on the sofa. I had my eyes wide-open, but I didn't focus on her face as she leaned over me.

"Bring some water, *Mutti*," Dana Maltravers said, as she kept trying to get me into the recovery position.

This had worked out better than I'd expected. I waited till the mother's thin form had moved away, then grabbed the younger woman's shoulders and flipped her onto the table. By the time I made to jump on top of her, she had already rolled away on to the floor. Maltravers knew how to look after herself in a fight. The angled foot that I took on my chin emphasized that point.

"Fuck you, Wells. You just made a terminal mistake."

Her right leg shot out and the foot hit me again, this time on my cheek. I reeled backward. As I tried to pull myself up, I caught a glimpse of Irma Rothmann.

She had her arms crossed, the pistol pointing toward the floor. It was obvious who she had her money on.

Dana Maltravers stepped onto the table and launched her foot at me again. This time, my reactions were sharper. I leaned to the side and grabbed her knee, then pulled hard. She managed to flatten her hand and deliver a decent chop to my neck as she flew past. I crumpled onto the sofa and then was just quick enough to take her by the hips and shove her over the back. There was no carpet there and I heard a satisfying thud as her head hit the floor. Her mother suddenly looked alarmed and raised the weapon. I scrambled over the sofa and landed on top of Dana Maltravers. She was still conscious but looked dazed. I twisted one of her arms behind her back and then hauled her to her feet, making sure her body was shielding mine.

"Dana!" Irma Rothmann screamed. *"Let her go!"*

I was fighting for breath. "Drop the gun!" I gasped. "Now!" I looked round my captive's head.

The older woman was still pointing the pistol toward us.

"No, Mr. Wells," she said, her eyes colder than a polar bear's. "If my daughter must be hurt, so be it. The cause is more important than any single person."

"Mutti!" Maltravers croaked.

"That'll be your caring Nazi ideology, I suppose," I said, keeping my head behind my captive's. "Don't you just love it, Dana?"

"Let her go!" Fraulein Rothmann screamed. "If I hit her, the bullet will go through to you, as well."

"So what?" I said, with as much bravado as I could muster. "At least there'll be one less Nazi in the world."

I heard a crash at the far end of the room and risked a look. The older woman's aim was wavering. I shoved her daughter toward her, keeping a tight grip on her. We all three clattered to the floor and I scrabbled for the gun that the impact had driven out of Irma Rothmann's hand. I got hold of it just as a large pair of men's shoes appeared in front of me.

"Here," Clem Simmons said, extending the hand that wasn't holding his service weapon—its muzzle was directed at Dana Maltravers.

I took the hand and was jerked to my feet. I turned to the two women who were sprawled in front of us.

Clem had taken quite a beating and his jacket was torn. He wiped blood from his damaged lips. "This *is* a surprise, Special Agent Maltravers," he said. He glanced at the older woman. "Who's this?"

"Her mother. Irma Rothmann, Larry Thomson's twin sister." That made me think. "Where's your brother?" I asked her.

She didn't respond. She was too busy cradling her daughter's head and speaking to her in German. No doubt she was trying to reassure her that she wouldn't really have sacrificed her for the cause. It didn't look like Dana Maltravers was buying it.

"We'd better get out of here, Matt," Clem said, looking over his shoulder. "I took out three of the fuckers, got them restrained, but there may be more of them around."

I nodded. We secured the women's wrists behind their backs with plastic ties and pushed them toward the door. "Did you call for backup?"

He shook his head. "We need to get this shit in order before I get my people involved."

I nodded. That was the way I wanted it, but we were taking a chance.

In the hall by the exit, there was a small table covered with keys and cards.

"Which one operates the executive elevator?" I asked.

Irma Rothmann looked away, so I jammed the muzzle of Dana Maltravers's gun into her belly.

"If you prefer, I can drop your daughter down the stairwell," I said savagely, remembering what had been done to Joe Greenbaum.

The woman swallowed and then pointed to a yellow card. I inserted it and the elevator doors opened. We got in and moved downward rapidly. As we reached the entrance-hall level, Clem muscled Fraulein Rothmann in front of him. I did the same with Dana Maltravers. When the doors opened, we moved out cautiously. To my relief, there was nobody around.

"The alarm system suffered a catastrophic failure," Clem said.

"Something to do with that screwdriver you had in your pocket?" I asked.

"Something to do with the rounds I had in my service weapon. Let's hit the sidewalk."

We did so, then walked up the street to the car. A passing man in a sharp suit peered at us, but was satisfied by a flash of Clem's badge. Irma Rothmann started talking in a loud voice, but stopped when the detective squeezed her forearm hard. We made it to the car. I got in the back between the two women.

We headed for Vers and the twins. I could tell that Clem was tempted to floor the gas pedal, but he restrained himself. Gwen and Randy had been calm enough, but what would happen when they were confronted with the woman they called the professor, their Führer's ice-veined twin sister?

Peter Sebastian's eyes were fixed on the TV screen in the corner of his office. One of his team had called from home to alert him. There were live pictures of Detective Chief Superintendent Karen Oaten of the London Metropolitan Police climbing out of a Bureau helicopter at Reagan airport, followed by Levon Creamer of Financial Crime. The news channel was making much of the fact that the woman was unharmed from her kidnap ordeal, as well as stressing that the FBI had not yet given any details of how it had ended.

Sebastian knew Creamer, but he'd never worked with him. The bastard should at least have let him know what was going on. Then again, it had never been established that the British policewoman's disappearance was linked to that of the suspect Matt Wells. Sebastian would have to talk to Creamer, but he had the feeling that now was not the time. The sight of the deputy director meeting Ms. Oaten and escorting her to a waiting car reinforced that suspicion. He would have to wait till morning.

In the meantime, he'd decided to call Dana Maltravers and make his peace with her. She deserved to know about the Document Analysis Unit's ideas, too. But, to his great surprise, she didn't answer her cell phone, which rang until the messaging service cut in. It wasn't the first time that had happened recently.

Peter Sebastian wished he hadn't behaved so offensively to his assistant.

Forty-One

I tried to get the women to talk on the drive to the safe house, but Maltravers was semiconscious, or was pretending to be, while Irma Rothmann just stared at me vacantly. I gave up and spoke to Clem instead.

"Call Vers," I said. "Check he's okay."

The detective nodded and opened his phone. "Yo, man, you alive?" There was a long silence, which didn't do much for my nerves, then Clem laughed. "Keep some for us. Be there in ten." He looked at me in the rearview mirror. "The dog! He got the twins to cook dinner. Chili."

"My favorite," I said, noticing that Fraulein Rothmann suddenly looked curious. "Yours, too?"

She snorted disdainfully.

Then it clicked. "Ah, it's the twins you're interested in. They remember you.

"By the way, what are you a professor of?"

Irma Rothmann looked reluctant to answer. "Neuroscience," she finally said.

"Have you by any chance been working on guinea pigs in the depths of Maine?"

This time she kept quiet. I would be following that angle up later.

When we got to the house, I asked Clem to take Dana Maltravers in first and see if the twins knew her. I waited in the car for his call.

"Nope," he said, after a couple of minutes. "No obvious signs of recognition."

"Okay, I'm bringing in the Queen Bee." I opened the car door and pulled Irma Rothmann out.

"What is this ridiculous game you are playing, Wells?" she demanded, as I led her toward the house.

I wanted to mess with her—maybe the twins would lose their respect if they saw her in a distressed state.

"You have no idea how much shit you're in," I said, my lips close to her ear. "If I find out you had anything to do with Joe Greenbaum's death, I'm going to strangle you with my bare hands."

Her face went even paler than it normally was, but she held her nerve. "Greenbaum?" she said, twisting her lips. "Is that a Jew name?"

"It's a German name." The woman was trying to rile me, too. I smiled. "Rothmann. That sounds quite Jewish, too."

She looked away. I reckoned I'd won that round, and pressed the bell. Versace opened the door.

"So this is what a Nazi looks like," he said, in a low voice. "Welcome to hell."

I frowned at him.

"Sorry, Field Goal," he said, stepping back. "My best friend at high school was a Jewboy. His grandparents were gassed by pieces of shit like her."

I pushed the women in after him, wondering in how many states *Jewboy* was an acceptable term.

Pinker led us into the dining room. The table was laid with plates and cutlery and there were large bowls of chili, rice and salad. The smell was enticing, but the reaction of the twins to Irma Rothmann made me forget the food immediately. In the seconds before they saw her, they were sitting quietly at the far end of the table. The instant they took in the tall woman, their backs straightened and their expressions became ultraserious.

"No introductions necessary," Clem said.

I was studying Gwen and Randy. They still hadn't spoken, but I had the impression some sort of silent communication was under way. I turned to Irma Rothmann. Her expression was pinched, her eyes flicking from one twin to the other.

"You can talk to them, if you like," I said.

For a few moments, she didn't respond. Then she moved her bound hands upward slowly and said, "We are not in camp now."

Gwen and Randy relaxed slightly, then looked at Dana Maltravers.

"Who's she?" Randy asked.

Fraulein Rothmann glanced at me. "She is my daughter."

The twins stiffened again. It struck me that they gave no sign of fear, for all the talk of the horrors they had experienced at the camp.

"Right," I said, "it's time for a question-and-answer session. Where can I take contestant number one?"

"Upstairs," Versace said. "Use any of the bedrooms, but don't you dare make a mess."

"I'll come with you," said Clem.

"Better not. Let's not leave your partner alone." There was a strange aura about the twins and the professor.

Clem nodded, though it didn't look like he was tuning into the vibes I was getting. I took Irma Rothmann upstairs and pushed her into the nearest bedroom.

"Can you unfasten my hands, please?" she asked.

"No chance." I had Dana Maltravers's gun, but I'd seen the emptiness in her mother's eyes at Woodbridge Holdings and I wasn't going to give her the slightest opportunity. I sat her down on the bed.

"I'm not going to talk," she said, before I opened my mouth.

"So you say." I took the pistol from my belt and laid it on the bed next to her.

She gave a contemptuous laugh. "You don't frighten me. You are very far out of your depth, Matt Wells."

I raised my shoulders. "All right. I'll go and get Dana."

She frowned. "What for?"

"Do you think the Gestapo had a monopoly on extreme methods of torture?" I was thinking of Joe again, and of Karen. I told myself again that she hadn't been the woman I'd seen sacrificed; I willed myself to believe that was the case.

"She's hurt," Fraulein Rothmann said, more animated now. "You can't—"

She broke off when I touched my groin. "Good-looking woman, your daughter," I said, licking my lips ostentatiously. "I'm looking forward to giving her everything I've got." I was not proud of this strategy.

"You're disgusting," Fraulein Rothmann said, spittle flying from her lips. "There are policemen downstairs. You wouldn't dare."

"Try me. Have you see any warrants? This is hardly an official operation." I got up and headed for the door.

"Stop!" she said, stretching out her bound hands. "Please! Leave Dana alone!"

"All right," I said, going back to the bed. "But I won't hesitate if I think you're lying."

She kept her eyes off me as I sat down next to her and picked up the gun.

"Where's Karen Oaten?" I asked, my heart suddenly thundering. "I hope for your sake she's still alive."

"I don't know."

"But you do know who I'm talking about."

"Of course."

"I suppose you just saw the news reports of her disappearance."

Her eyes burned into mine. "Don't be ridiculous. She was in the camp, the same as you. I don't know where she is now."

I rocked back at the unexpected admission.

"Why was she there?"

"For the same reason you were. To learn the error of her ways."

"What the fuck does that mean?" I demanded—I wanted her to spell out what she and her brother were doing.

Irma Rothmann sighed. "She was getting too close to an associate of Woodbridge Holdings."

"Gavin Burdett."

"If you know, why do you waste time asking?"

I let that go. "Has something been done to Karen's memory?"

"Oh, I think so," she said, with a tight smile. "Don't you?"

I forced myself to move on. "The occult murders. Who's the killer?"

"What makes you imagine I know?"

It was my turn to sigh. "We know of Woodbridge Holdings's links to the North American Nazi Revival and the Antichurch of Lucifer Triumphant. You decided to make examples of occult people you didn't approve of, didn't you?"

She gave a harsh laugh. "Oh, come now."

"Loki was an embarrassment to your puritanical movement. He made Nazism ridiculous."

She pursed her lips.

"And Monsieur Hexie was black, Professor Singer was a Jew and Crystal Vileda was a Hispanic. *Untermenschen*, all of them."

"I cannot argue with that characterization."

"So who killed them?"

"I'm not sure," she said, looking away.

She wasn't sure, but she obviously had suspicions. The murderer had to have some relation to the Rothmann twins and their activities—the pairs of murder weapons, the choice of victims, the way I'd been framed as soon as I left the camp, Woodbridge Holdings's timber and newspaper businesses—everything was connected.

Then I thought of the diagrams that had been attached to the victims: squares and rectangles in four different arrays—what did they mean? Lights flashed before me and I heard an echo of martial music; something I'd seen when I was under the machine in the camp, something that had started as shots of fences and guard towers, a gate with German words above it, rows and rows of huts…and then was mapped from above, into a composite picture…a familiar map of hell:

"Auschwitz," I said, my voice faint.

A smile spread across the woman's thin lips. "Ah, the maps," she said slowly. "You understand them.... Bravo."

I kept silent, my mind in a frenzy. Why had the killer deliberately left clues pointing to a Nazi link?

"You aren't in complete control of the killer, are you?" I said at last.

"You're not as clever as you think, Matt Wells. You have overlooked something much more important."

The tone of her voice warned me that I was in danger, but I didn't know how to react.

Before I could do anything, she screamed, "Barbarossa! The policemen! Barbarossa!"

She said the words twice before I got a hand over her mouth. As I restrained her, I felt a strange mix of emotions—shock at the virulence of her screams, but also a pressure that was being brought to bear on me and an urge, frightening in its intensity, to comply with some immutable authority.

Then the rational part of my mind kicked in. *Barbarossa*: it was the code name for the Nazi invasion of the Soviet Union—the greatest act of aggression in human history. I realized that it was a trigger and pushed myself away from Irma Rothmann. As I crashed down the stairs, images cascaded before me—twin weapons puncturing flesh and organs; twin weapons, held by the hands of twin murderers; twins from a farm on Iowa, whose father had died trying to bring them home; twins who had now been ordered to attack.

Gavin Burdett was sitting in front of the TV in a house on the outskirts of Baltimore, his trousers and boxers round his ankles. Despite the pair of muscle-bound guards downstairs and the open door, he had been zapping between porn channels. There was a bevy of women pretending to be lesbians that almost got him going, but then he had found a spoof horror movie that featured a zombie orgy. It was one of the best climaxes he'd had in months.

After he cleaned himself up, he surfed the normal channels. A cold stiletto of fear had entered his gut when he saw Karen Oaten getting out of a helicopter. What was the bitch doing free? Larry had promised him she'd never be seen again.

Burdett got up, stretched for his cell phone and was brought down by the clothes round his ankles. He finally reached the device and called Thomson's private number.

"What the *fuck's* going on?" he screamed. "Oaten's free."

"Of course she is."

"But…but you told me she was finished. What about the case against me?"

"Oh, Gavin, how can you be so selfish?"

"What do you mean? If I go down, so do you."

Larry Thomson laughed. "That's not exactly true, you know," he said smoothly. "There are other eventualities."

The connection was broken.

Gavin Burdett threw the phone down and caught sight of the men in the doorway. The one in front was carrying a length of rope with a noose at one end.

The last thing the investment banker thought of was the tarot card depicting the hanged man. He knew more than he should have of the occult world, and now he was paying the price. The hanged man meant relinquishing control, different priorities and readjustment. But, as he was only too well aware, it also pointed to a necessary sacrifice.

By the time I got to the dining-room door, the twins had already struck. Clem and Versace were both motionless on the floor; a table knife protruded from Pinker's bloody chest. Nearer to me, Gwen was sawing frantically at the plastic ties on Dana Maltravers's wrists and Randy was turning my way with Clem's pistol. I had already racked the slide on the FBI woman's weapon and I got a shot off before he did. Randy took it in the upper abdomen and crashed backward into the empty fireplace.

His sister shrieked and turned the knife on me. I brought my free hand down hard on her forearm. The knife carved an arc through the air and landed on the opposite side of the table, out of Maltravers's reach. The agent stood up and charged at me with her head down. I was driven into the door frame, but I managed to keep a grip on the gun. The blow stunned me and I could hardly move, but something else was holding me back, a force I couldn't resist…

"Leave him," I heard Irma Rothmann say from the hall. "He won't harm us now. I can drive. I cut myself free with these nail scissors—we'll free you in the car, Dana."

The FBI woman slammed both her elbows into my belly and then stumbled out. Gwen went with her, eyes wide. Then I threw up on to the carpet and tried to get a grip on myself as the pressure in my mind lessened.

I saw Clem Simmons's head. It was lying in a pool of blood. I let out a roar and crawled into the hall, my vision clouded. The front door was open and I saw Clem's car being reversed onto the street. Lying flat and trying to hold my hand steady, I fired at the car until the clip was empty.

The vehicle slewed into a bush and stayed there. Its horn was blasting repeatedly as I dragged myself up and staggered outside. Steam was rising from the bonnet and the front windscreen had shattered. My gun was empty, but I kept going—it had occurred to me that the fuel tank might explode. Then I got to the front door and looked in.

Irma Rothmann was lying back against the headrest, blood coming in gouts from a hole above her right eye. Her daughter Dana was unconscious and I hauled her out, feeling her shallow breath against my arm. She had taken a bullet in the right side of her chest. I got her clear and went back for Gwen. I found the back door on the other side of the car open—no sign of her, no blood on the seat. By the time I looked again, there was no spurting from Irma Rothmann's entry wound. She was no longer alive, but I didn't have it in me to care.

As I got back to the house, I heard the sound of sirens between the horn blasts. I checked Clem and found a pulse after rolling him on to his side. Versace was alive, too—just. Randy was still breathing. They would all have a chance, assuming paramedics were on the way. I picked up Versace's gun and cell phone. There was a number in there that I'd be needing. Staying on-site was not an option.

I headed toward the back of the house. As I went through the sitting-room, I thought I was dreaming. The TV was on and there was breaking news coverage showing pictures of Karen, my Karen, stepping out of an executive jet. She was smiling and looked in good health. I felt a surge of joy, but it was short-lived. I was turning tail, leaving the cops who had been helping me in critical condition—but I couldn't stay, even though it meant not watching Karen. Perhaps I'd never see her again, but she was well. That was all that mattered.

Meanwhile, I had to finish things with the surviving twin from Auschwitz.

Forty-Two

The lights of central Washington stretched out beneath the window of Karen Oaten's suite in what she assumed was the highest and most luxurious hotel in the city. There was an FBI agent on guard duty outside and a team patrolling the building, but she was alone with her thoughts on an antique sofa, her legs drawn up beneath her.

So far, everything was going smoothly. The deputy director of the FBI had been taken aback by her insistence that she resume meetings immediately. He had assumed she would go straight to the hospital for a thorough checkup, but she assured him that would not be necessary and that she would arrange things herself with the British Embassy doctor.

After eating a late dinner from room service, Karen had taken a shower and settled down to review her case files. At her request, they had been brought over from FBI headquarters. The Gavin Burdett investigation would come to nothing now. She'd had a brief conversation with her boss in London. He told her that she would be all over the morning papers and that numerous journalists would want to interview her. She wasn't planning on giving any of them access, at least not yet.

Sipping chamomile tea, Karen leaned back and took in the view again.

America, she thought, land of the free. Or rather, land of the corrupt, the pleasure obsessed and the spiritually vacant. Its people needed discipline, a new set of ideals, just as they did back in Americanized Europe. Now that her eyes had been opened, she knew there was another way.

Matt Wells's face flickered before her, like that of a fading ghost. It had been amusing how difficult the supposedly hardened FBI men had found it to bring up his alleged crimes. She hadn't been surprised when she'd first been told of them at the camp. Matt had shown signs in the past of unbridled fury and had trained himself well to become a murderer, even though he'd made out that he was only interested in self-defense. She hadn't realized how close he'd come to stepping over the line throughout their relationship. Her disappearance must have made him leap into the abyss. He had certainly seen enough violent crime firsthand to be fatally tempted. The irony was unavoidable. After standing up to the worst the White Devil and the Soul Collector had thrown at him, he had become one of their number. Earlier tonight, she'd learned, he had been responsible for the death of yet another person and the wounding of several more. He wouldn't be at liberty for long. It was just as well—her son would never know his father.

Karen didn't feel tired, but she knew she should lie down. Although she was in perfect physical condition, her body needed attention because of the cargo she was carrying. The day that would soon be dawning was set to be the most momentous of her life: a new beginning for her and the whole world.

The last thing Karen did before she went to bed was to check her briefcase.

Everything was in order, including what she had brought on her person from the camp.

***

I found a taxi on a main road about half a mile from the house where I'd left Clem and the others, and directed the driver to Georgetown. There was blood on my clothing, but I'd taken off my jacket and turned it inside out, and was holding it over the other stains. I had Dana Maltravers's, Clem's and Versace's guns under there, too. I was a walking armory, but I had the feeling I would need every round.

The news came on the radio and I asked the driver to turn up the volume. The top story was about Karen and how she'd appeared at a state troopers' station near Buffalo. She was said to be unharmed and had been brought to Washington by FBI helicopter and jet. Deep down I'd never believed she had been the sacrificial victim, but I was relieved—enormously so—to have that confirmed. But I was also frustrated—I wanted to see her, I wanted to make sure that she was as well as she looked and that our son had not been adversely affected, but I had to stay free until I laid hands on Larry Thomson. Without him, I was a fugitive, a suspect for at least two of the occult killings and—if Clem and Versace didn't come round—a suspect for the mayhem tonight. But the alternative was worse: as long as Thomson, or Rothmann as he'd been born, was free, Karen and I would never be safe—and neither would our son.

I got out of the cab on M Street and slipped into the back streets before crossing the bridge to Rosslyn. I stopped on the corner before my hotel and checked for surveillance. Nobody knew I was staying there, but I couldn't be sure of anything anymore. After waiting for five minutes, I walked down the street and into the hotel. The night porter nodded at me with indifference as I went to the elevators. I had my hand on one of the pistols all the way to my room. This time, I needn't have bothered.

After holding my head under the cold tap, I took Versace's phone out of my pocket and clicked into Contacts.

Assuming the entry "GL" was Gordy Lister, I called that number. It rang for a long time before he answered.

"Talk to me, whoever you are."

"This is Matt Wells."

There was a pause. "What d'you want?"

"Get this, asshole. Those twins you gave us attacked Detectives Pinker and Simmons, maybe fatally. If you want me to keep your name out of it, do exactly what I tell you."

"Shit! All right, man. Shit!"

"Larry Thomson—I need to meet him before daybreak. He can name the place."

"He…he won't come alone."

"I don't care if he comes with a division of the SS. Fix it and call me back on this number. Oh, and Gordy?"

"Yeah."

"Tell him I shot his sister. Dead."

"What?" Lister's voice was suddenly higher than a schoolboy's.

"You heard me. I killed Irma Rothmann. And her daughter Dana's badly hurt, too."

"Jesus, man, he's gonna rip your heart out."

"You reckon? Just make the call."

I broke the connection, my palms damp with sweat. Sounding tough on the phone was all very well. Now I had to work out a way to get Larry Thomson away from his bodyguards on his turf. Killing him would be easier, but that would mean sacrificing myself, and I had reasons to live now that Karen and the child she was carrying were safe. I needed to bring Thomson in if I was to have any chance of clearing my name. There was only one thing in my favor. He would be enraged by the news of his twin sister's death. Unless he had a heart colder than the thickest glacier in Antarctica, that meant he'd be desperate to nail me. And desperation, as my friend Dave used to say, caused people to take their eye off the ball. Then again, Gwen

Bonhoff was at large. She would be gunning for me, too, given that I'd shot her brother. If she showed up at the meet with Thomson, it really would be the O.K. Corral all over again.

Peter Sebastian was standing by Clem Simmons's hospital bed. There were machines beeping and numerous tubes coming out of the detective, and he was conscious. Gerard Pinker was not; he was in intensive care.

"So you're saying it was Matt Wells who shot this Irma Rothmann, as well as Dana Maltravers?" the FBI man asked, trying to keep the disbelief from his face.

"Yeah," Simmons croaked. "Had to be. And the boy Randy. I don't know what happened to his sister, Gwen."

"There's no sign of her. Randy's in surgery."

"How about Maltravers?"

"Took a bullet to the chest, but she'll live."

"You know your princess is dirty?"

Sebastian frowned. "So I'm beginning to understand. The twins, Randy and Gwen, you think they did the occult murders?"

Clem Simmons coughed and then winced. "Seems a distinct possibility."

"What about Matt Wells's prints at the scenes?"

"Think about it."

After a few moments, the FBI man's eyes widened. "Dana?"

"Who else?"

A stern-looking nurse bustled into the room. "You'll have to leave now, sir. We're going to do a CAT scan."

"About time," the detective said, with a slow grin.

The nurse's expression slackened. "There's been a run on the machines this evening. So much for law and order in this city."

Sebastian leaned closer. "One more thing, Detective. Larry Thomson. Are you sure about him?"

Clem nodded, his eyes closing. "Oh, yeah. Woodbridge Holdings is a hotbed of fuckin' Nazi…" Suddenly his head slumped to the side and one of the monitors sounded a continuous alarm.

Peter Sebastian was pushed out of the way by a doctor and watched as Clem Simmons's bed was wheeled out of the room, nurses pulling the monitors alongside. Turning the pages of his notes, he shook his head. Karen Oaten had returned safely, but all hell had broken out. And the cherry on the cake was that Matt Wells hadn't been the occult killer after all.

The FBI man heard the sound of his career crashing all around him. He needed to do some major ass-covering, both on his own account and on that of his secondary employers, the CIA—they would be very unhappy if the Agency's protection of Nazi doctors was made public after all this time. Fortunately, Dana Maltravers would be the perfect scapegoat.

I had done what I could to prepare my stash of weapons when Lister called.

"Anacostia Marina, 7:30 a.m.," he said. "If you look at a map, it's northeast of the John Philip Sousa Bridge—a couple of miles before the Anacostia River meets the Potomac. He's got this big black-and-silver motherfucker of a cabin cruiser. It's called the *Isolde*. Oh, and he's coming alone."

"Yeah, right." I grabbed my D.C. map and spotted the place.

"That's what he told me, man."

"All right, Gordy. Did you tell him about his sister?"

"Yeah."

"How did he take it?"

"He didn't start yelling and screaming, if that's what you mean."

"Cool as a cucumber, eh?"

"More like icy as the berg that gutted the Titanic. I gotta go, man."

"You're tainted goods with your employer, Gordy," I said, unwilling to let him off the hook. "New Mexico might just be far enough."

"Bullshit. Larry knows I'm okay."

"Or maybe South America," I continued. "There's no shortage of Nazis there."

"Hey, haven't you noticed? There are Nazis everywhere. Get over it."

He cut the connection. He'd said that Thomson knew he was okay. I would remember that. I still wasn't convinced that Gordy Lister was in the clear over Joe's death.

I looked at my watch. I had just over two hours. That should be enough time to reconnoiter the location and make the kind of preparations that I'd learned from Dave Cummings. I had the feeling Thomson might screw up—unless his trap was already in place. I put my weapons into a handyman's bag and went down to reception. The guy wasn't impressed when I asked him for some resealable plastic food bags from the kitchen, but a couple of twenties cheered him up. I put the bags in my pocket and went out onto the street. Round the corner, I picked up a cab.

The driver dropped me on the Anacostia side of the bridge. It was still dark and there weren't many lights in the strip of parkland below. I went down and walked along the bank until I was opposite the marina. I couldn't see any sign of a large cabin cruiser, which suited me fine. Squatting by a bush, I put a loaded Glock 17 into a plastic bag, sealed it and then slipped it into another bag. Then I took off my shirt and, using the roll of insulating tape that had been part of my tool kit, I strapped the bagged pistol onto my chest. After removing a long strip, I put the insulating tape into another bag and sealed it. That bag, I also lashed to my chest. Then I stripped to my boxer shorts and attached the sheathed combat knife to my belt, before putting the latter round my waist. I could have walked across the bridge and taken my chances with whatever kind of security there was at the marina, but I wasn't going to risk being caught—at least, not before I'd given myself a fighting chance. I took a deep breath and lowered myself into the water. I wasn't the greatest of swimmers, but I was in reasonable shape. The problem was going to be the water temperature.

And, I realized after I'd taken a few strokes, the current. I'd not considered that. Fortunately the river wasn't much more than a hundred and fifty yards wide, though I must have swum a lot more than that and my feet and hands were tingling in the cold. I made it to one of the wooden piers and looked around. There were enough lights for me to see that the pier I was at was the only one with clear space at the end. That was where Thomson would have to moor his cruiser. I clambered up the stanchions, breathing heavily and stood on the one beneath the end of the pier, the wind chilling me even more. With fumbling fingers, I managed to cut strips of tape and attach the bagged pistol to the underside so it was within reach if I lay on the decking above. Now all I had to do was swim back.

Because I was tired and cold, that proved to be a much harder job. At one point I thought I was going to be swept down to the Potomac, but somehow I kept going, flailing my arms and legs. I heaved myself out and used hotel towels to dry myself. Then I got back into my clothes and put on my watch. I had plenty of time to get dressed, making sure there was no dampness in my hair. I put Clem's service revolver in my pocket—Thomson would no doubt

expect me to be armed. I would hand it over with fake re-
luctance when he searched me.

I started walking around to get myself fully warmed up.
During that time, I considered the name chosen for the
boat, presumably by Larry Thomson—maybe his sister
had her say, too. Tristan and Isolde were mythical doomed
lovers and the Nazis' favorite composer, Richard Wagner,
had written an opera about them. It struck me that Thomson was taking a chance using a name that pointed so
directly to his German roots. Maybe he was so arrogant
that he thought he could get away with anything because
he'd taken on a new identity. Then again, it was a fact that
all sorts of people who maybe should have known better
attended performances of Wagner's work and openly proclaimed their admiration for it.

The lovers Tristan and Isolde: I wondered if there was
some incestuous bond between the twins. I thought about
Thomson's sister. I hadn't meant to kill Irma Rothmann,
but my mind had been all over the place and I'd had a rush
of blood when I acted. Although it wasn't the first time I'd
killed, the death of the Soul Collector's sister had been an
accident and I still regretted it. With the woman whose
father had worked at Auschwitz, I seemed to be curiously
unmoved. Thomson's twin was a Nazi whose activities
had probably led to many deaths and plenty of suffering
at the camp, but I would still have expected some kind of
emotional backlash.

Instead, I started thinking about the trigger that turned
Gwen and Randy into vicious aggressors. All it had taken
was the single word *Barbarossa.* I seemed to have a lot of
information at my fingertips about it. My memory was
still behaving very unpredictably—had this stuff been
planted? Barbarossa, or Redbeard, was the nickname of
Fredrick I of the Hohenstaufen dynasty, Holy Roman
Emperor from 1155 until his death in 1190. He was a great

general and natural leader, and an inspiration to future generations of Germans, particularly those driven by dreams of conquest—whence the use of his nickname for the Nazi operation to attack the Soviet Union.

I twitched my head and came back to the real world. The point was that hearing *Barbarossa* had made Gwen and Randy act in a way that was obviously preconditioned. Their escape from the camp was just a story. They were playing parts in some devious plan, pretending to be junkies, perhaps unaware or only partly aware of what was happening. Which led to another thought. Exactly why had they been hanging out in a disused warehouse in D.C.? Gordy Lister knew, I was sure of that. Letting him go was looking even more like a cardinal error. Had the twins been stashed there because of the proximity to the Capitol or the White House?

A siren on the other side of the river caught my attention. I waited till it faded, then hid the bag with my remaining gear under a bush and walked across the bridge. As I got to the other side, I saw a bulky shadow pass quietly underneath. It was a dark boat with silver trim and was showing only running lights. I reckoned that was the *Isolde*. It slowed as it approached the pier. I focused on my plan of action. It was only a few minutes' walk to the marina. The gate had already been opened for early morning business. I went in and walked toward the piers. It was a relief to see the cruiser was heading where I had anticipated. As I approached that pier, two men stepped out of the shadows. So much for Thomson coming alone. I was patted down and relieved of my cell phone and revolver, and an electronic scanner was run over me to check for surveillance devices. Eventually I was pushed toward the boat. Looking round, I saw that the gorillas weren't following me.

I stopped at the end of the pier.

"Thomson?" I called. "I'm coming aboard."

The tall man was fastening a mooring rope at the stern

of the boat. He had a cell phone against his ear, having presumably just been informed by the guards that I was clean. Suddenly fearful of facing him unarmed, I was tempted to scrabble for the pistol under the pier, but I got a grip on myself. Surrendering was the only way I would be able to get close to the surviving twin.

I stepped onto the boat, ignoring Thomson's outstretched hand. He was wearing a black polo-neck and black trousers, and he looked in good physical shape. As he led me into the cabin, I tried to see if he was armed. I needn't have bothered.

He turned toward me and invited me to search him. I did so, and found nothing. He must have been following some weird Nazi honor code.

"Good," he said, with a surprisingly warm smile. "Now we can get down to business. You're lucky that I'm anxious to meet you. I don't normally bother with such day-to-day nuisances."

It was then that the door to the front cabin opened.

Larry Thomson had lied about being alone, all right. Not only that, but he'd invited the surviving occult killer along.

And Gwen Bonhoff didn't look at all forgiving about what I'd done to her twin brother and her Führer's sister.

Forty-Three

"You can use this office, Detective Chief Superintendent."

Karen Oaten glanced around the spacious room and nodded to the female agent.

"I'll be outside if you need anything."

"Thanks." Karen put her briefcase down on the desk. Despite the early hour, there were plenty of people already at work in the J. Edgar Hoover building. Someone had stacked mail on the desk.

Sitting down, she went through the letters. Some of it dated from before her kidnap and concerned the Burdett case. She discarded that. There were also messages from back then, including some from senators and representatives with interests in international crime and policing. Turning to the computer, she saw a sheet of paper telling her how to log on and access her personal e-mail. She did so and was immediately alert.

The first message was from the director of the FBI. He congratulated her on her courage during the kidnapping and invited her to a celebration of her release that afternoon at four o'clock. He couldn't be certain, but there was a good chance that the justice secretary would attend—she had followed

Karen's ordeal with great interest and wished to welcome her back in person, depending, of course, on her schedule.

Karen sat back, a smile on her lips. That was excellent, even more than she had hoped for. She had only to wait until the afternoon. Then she could guarantee that the news programs would have a hot story to report. But, more important, the movement would be fully under way and nothing would ever be the same again.

"She isn't armed," Larry Thomson said, his eyes blue and chill in the soft lights of the cruiser's surprisingly large living space.

I looked at Gwen. She seemed to be having trouble keeping control of herself, her hands twitching and her eyes wide.

"She's got nails," I said.

"Indeed she has." Thomson sat down and waved to me to do the same. "My little tigress." He gave her a tight smile.

I decided to go on the offensive. I needed to get the self-styled Führer talking.

"If you don't mind, I'm going to call you Rothmann."

"Oh, please—do use my first name."

I wasn't going to do his bidding. "Why the change to Thomson?"

He looked at me curiously. "I thought you had everything worked out, Mr. Wells."

"Obviously not."

"You see, Irma and I died in 1972."

"Really? So I killed a ghost last night, did I? A vampire? Yeah, that makes sense. You Nazis share plenty of characteristics with the undead."

"There's no need to be crude," Thomson said, taking a cigarette from a silver case and lighting it. "I'm telling you about my personal history. Are you interested or not?"

I shrugged. He had me there. I needed as much detail

as I could get if I was ever to clear myself—assuming I survived this tête-à-tête.

"We went over a cliff in my sports car."

"Except you substituted the bodies. Who were they?
Some unfortunate college kids?"

He smiled emptily. "Jews."

A wave of nausea washed over me. I took a deep breath.
"What was the point of the scam? Was your family background becoming an embarrassment?"

He frowned. "Let's say that the American establishment was less keen to have links to the Third Reich in the
seventies, even though we were second generation."

"So you reinvented yourselves."

"Exactly. It's the American way. Of course, we kept on
doing what we were good at. My sister—" he broke off and
eyed me with a worrying lack of emotion "—Irma is…" He
broke off and pursed his lips. "Irma was a brilliant chemist,
as well as a world-class neuroscientist. She developed many
drugs and processes that have become world beaters."

"Including the ones that messed with my memory?"

"Yes—though, it would seem, not enough."

"And you provided the business expertise that turned
Woodbridge Holdings into a successful multinational
company." I gave him a harsh glare, trying to provoke him.
"That camp in Maine was just a test bed for Irma's drugs.
And a place for your little Nazi army to grow like fungus
in the forest."

Rothmann nodded impassively. "Irma didn't just work
with drugs, though. She was also involved with some remarkable machines."

I had a flash of the complex mechanical lid that had lowered over me—the martial music, the uniforms, images
from what I now realized was Nazi Germany.

What was it they had called the process?

"Coffining," I said. "What a pretty name."

"Because the subjects died and became ours," Rothmann said, his eyes narrowing. "In most cases."

"You brainwashed me."

"Not just you," he said dismissively. "There are many who came through with substantially better results." He angled his head toward the young woman opposite. "Including Gwen."

I looked at her. She seemed confused, her eyes darting between him and me.

"You bastard," I said. "You turned her into a killer. You made her and her brother carry out the occult killings, didn't you?"

He looked at me and shook his head slowly. "That is where you show your ignorance." His cell phone rang. "Yes, the comrade is expected," he said, after listening intently. "Very well. Send her over."

I wondered who this could be. Another from the Rothmann parade of twin zombies? I heard light steps on the pier outside and a knock on the door.

"Come!" ordered the Führer.

The door slid open and a figure wearing a black rain jacket stepped inside. There was a hood over the head and I couldn't make out the face in the dim light of the cabin.

"Show yourself," Rothmann said. There was a tightness in his voice that hadn't been there before.

I felt my stomach somersault before the features came into view. Could it be that my ex-lover Sara Robbins, the Soul Collector, was behind the killings after all? Could she have inveigled her way into Rothmann's confidence? I didn't have the slightest doubt that she could have.

The hood was pulled back and I felt my gut clench. I'd seen the angular features before. I'd been bound to a wheelchair, surrounded by naked, chanting people—and, up at the front, there had been a pair of prancing figures. One had a hyena's head and the other the stony face of the most depraved gargoyle. The latter was on display now.

"How dare you?" Rothmann said, spittle flying from his mouth. "Take that mask off immediately!"

A hand was raised slowly to the repulsive features—I had a vision of the naked woman, the one I'd feared was Karen, being tied to the upturned cross and then butchered. Then I saw that the person before me was a young woman, red hair pulled back from an attractive face. She dropped the mask to the floor with disgust.

"I know you," I said, as my memory kicked in. "You were at Joe Greenbaum's place with Clem Simmons."

The woman nodded. "That's right. I'm medical examiner for the MPDC, actually—Marion Gilbert's the name. And you're Matt Wells, the so-called occult killer, aren't you? I've seen your photograph."

Rothmann was looking at her curiously. "It's good to see you, Doctor. But I'm rather busy at the moment. Could you perhaps wait? There is very comfortable accommodation that way." He pointed toward the bow of the *Isolde*. "Please take the mask with you. I will need you to explain what you're doing with it. The original is dedicated to the unholy ritual. No copies should ever have been made."

"I made it out of misplaced love." The doctor laughed, but it wasn't a pleasant sound. "I'm not going anywhere, my Führer." She spoke the title as if it burned her tongue. There was a blur of movement, after which I saw she was holding a vicious-looking skewer in each hand.

Rothmann looked astonished. "You!" he gasped. "You're the occult killer? But...but you were one of our earliest subjects, you were trusted with—"

"Stand still, girl!" Marion Gilbert said, pointing one of her weapons at Gwen. "Move backward and sit on the sofa." She glanced at me and Rothmann. "All of you!"

We complied. I tried to move my thigh away from the Führer's, but he wasn't giving me any room.

"What is this?" he demanded. "You are to show respect to me at all times!'

Marion Gilbert stepped closer. "I'm afraid those times are gone. If you speak again, I'll put one of these skewers through your tongue."

Rothmann opened his mouth, but sensibly he made no sound.

Since I hadn't yet been threatened, I decided to act as interlocutor. "Help me out here, Doctor," I said. "You were one of the Rothmanns' guinea pigs?"

She nodded. "There were twenty of us." Then she sighed and words that she had been holding back for far too long were finally spoken.

"We were all at the top of the class in high school. One of the boys and I wanted to study medicine. The rest were going to be businessmen, soldiers, scientists—a range of professions. And we all had a similar racial background— we were white and of German, Anglo-Saxon or Scandinavian stock." She pointed at Rothmann. "This…this man and his vile sister set up a fund, and tempted our parents with scholarships and grants for our studies. The only condition was that we had to spend half of each vacation on what they called research projects. We thought that meant we'd be doing research, but it turned out we were the subjects." She glared at Rothmann. "Guinea pigs is right. We were as expendable as animals. Sixteen of the group were terminated before a year passed."

"Were terminated?" Gwen said.

Marion Gilbert's expression softened. "You're one of us, too, aren't you? I can tell by your eyes. I can also see that your conditioning is in full effect." She smiled sharply. "Try anything and the Führer dies in agony."

Gwen sat back, but her nails were digging into her thighs.

"Were terminated?" I repeated.

The doctor looked at me blankly for a few moments—I got the impression she was struggling to keep focus.

"The people who couldn't take the conditioning were… killed.… If they were twins, which many of us were, the stronger sibling was ordered to execute the weaker."

Jesus. Then I remembered the woman who had cut the man's throat in front of cameras in the camp. Had they been twins, too?

Gwen leaned forward. "It's not like that now," she said, looking at Rothmann earnestly. "I was with my twin, Randy, till…" She broke off and gave me a fierce stare. "Until this man shot him last night." She turned back to her Führer. "Before he killed Professor Irma."

Rothmann's eyes locked with mine. Although there was little trace of emotion, I could see that he intended to make me pay the full price for what I'd done to his twin sister.

"You killed the bitch, Matt Wells?" Marion Gilbert asked, her face suffusing with joy. "That's the best thing I've heard since…" She stopped speaking and peered at the skewers in her hands. "Since Malcolm made the Yale chess team." She took a quick step toward the sofa and buried a skewer to its hilt in Rothmann's thigh, keeping the other pointed at Gwen. "But that still wasn't enough for you. Malcolm…Malcolm." Her voice cracked. "Your sister shot him in the heart."

Rothmann was biting his lip, but he didn't have the nerve to speak.

"I couldn't do it myself." Marion's eyes were damp. "So she made me watch."

I gave her a bit of time. I suspected the conditioning had stopped her grieving for her lost twin until now. I felt a strange empathy for the woman, multiple murderer though she was. I had been struggling enough with what had been done to my brain, but she had obviously been through much worse.

"You've been trying to nail them, haven't you?" I said when she got her breathing under control. "The murders and the drawings—"

That surprised her. "You know about the drawings?"

I nodded. "I've been in contact with the detectives."

Marion Gilbert looked confused. "But you're a suspect."

"Not for everyone. That was the FBI's line, but one of this scumbag's people was messing with the evidence. Dana Maltravers—do you know her?"

The doctor was staring at Rothmann, as if daring him to speak. His face was twisted in pain, his hands clutching the wound, but he kept silent.

"No," she said. "We don't know the identities of the others who have been through the camp. We receive individual assignments and orders."

"And what were yours recently?"

"To keep them informed of the investigations." She gave a strangled laugh. "The investigations into the murders I myself committed." The doctor suddenly looked very tired. She leaned against the walnut-paneled bulkhead, the skewer quivering in her hand. "I…couldn't help myself. Things that happened at the camp started to come back to me…mock executions…sexual abuse. The others turned on us when we refused to commit incest, they beat us terribly…and then I remembered…I remembered Malcolm's death…"

"And you decided to hit back."

She nodded. "The Antichurch…they kept taking us to the rituals, the sacrifices…it's only in the last day or so that I've understood how horrible that side of the process was. They made us believe that Lucifer was rising, that he would reward his faithful servants. So I…I couldn't stop myself choosing people who were apostates, who had chosen the wrong occult path…."

I thought about her victims. "But Loki the singer was a satanist."

"An unworthy one," the doctor said, avoiding my gaze. "He wasn't serious about the faith. It was all a facade. He only cared about drugs and sex."

"So you killed Monsieur Hexie, Professor Singer and Crystal Vileda because the Antichurch didn't approve of their fields—voodoo, the kabbalah, tarot?"

Marion Gilbert still wouldn't look at me. "Yes," she replied, then shivered. "I know about the tarot myself—the Vileda woman was a fraud."

"Hardly a reason to kill her," I said, unwilling to let her off the hook.

The doctor's eyes were fixed on Rothmann. "The fact that they were members of proscribed racial groups was also relevant."

I looked round at the Führer. "Proscribed racial groups? You assholes have such a thing about African-Americans, Jews and Hispanics." I turned to Marion Gilbert. "Let him talk, will you? I want to see how sick he really is."

She frowned at me and then nodded.

"They are all subhuman," Rothmann said, his face still wracked with pain. "Fit only for slave labor or execution."

"Jesus," I said. It was the people who had set up the North American Nazi Revival and the Antichurch who were subhuman. But how guilty were the kids they'd turned into monsters? Were they responsible for their crimes?

I looked back at Marion Gilbert. "So, even though you were trying to avenge your brother's murder, you still chose victims your Führer would approve of?"

She gave me an agonized look. "You have to understand…I've been fighting myself…my mind's been in turmoil for weeks now…it's like there's a sharp-toothed worm, biting and gnawing…I haven't been sleeping…I've been two people fighting for control of one body…"

"Sounds like Dr. Jekyll and Mr. Hyde," I said.

She stared at me. "What?"

I repeated the name of Robert Louis Stevenson's famous doppelganger.

"That's right," the doctor said, blinking rapidly. "That's...that's what I called myself."

"Jekyll?"

She shook her head. "Hyde. Marlon Hyde. The name just came to me. I must have read the book, but I don't remember.... I rented a room and gloried in the killings there.... Oh, God..."

"Pathetic," Rothmann said. "It seems you are even weaker than your brother."

She took a step toward him, but I raised a hand.

"The maps," I said. "Those drawings you left on the bodies. I know what they mean—the camp at Auschwitz."

"Oh, how clever you are," Rothmann said sardonically. "I knew as soon as I saw the first one. How could I forget the huts where the subhumans were contained?"

"It didn't help you *identify* the killer, though," I replied, giving him a scornful smile in return. I looked at the doctor. "Why didn't you just leave evidence pointing directly to the Rothmanns?"

Her eyes dropped. "Because...because I couldn't. Something inside my head stopped me. The process... coffining..." She looked at Rothmann. "I think I even hoped...hoped that you would realize who was behind the killings and stop me...stop me before I did irreparable damage to the movement." She let out a brief scream of frustration, then turned to me. "How did you know the drawings were of Auschwitz, Matt Wells?"

"I...I'm not sure," I replied feebly. My own brain hadn't exactly been functioning normally in recent days. I had a flash of the machine that had been lowered over me in the camp—and the blaring music, the pounding of army boots, the barking voice...

I turned to Rothmann. *"What the fuck did you put in my head?"*

"How should I know? You escaped before the process was complete. Besides, what happens in each case depends on the subject's own mind. Coffining is led by the individual's unique mental structure." He gave an icy smile. "Perhaps, deep down, you are attracted to the Reich's methods."

I wasn't going to let him distract me. I looked back at Marion Gilbert. "Did you do the drawings of Auschwitz because you approved of what went on there, or because you realized it was the Nazis' biggest disgrace?"

She stared at me. "I don't know...I really don't. I was only able to do partial drawings, anyway....they just came from deep within me...."

There were pinpoints of red on Rothmann's cheeks. "Auschwitz was no disgrace. My father did wonderful work there."

"Research on twins, no doubt," I said.

"Of course. That was Dr. Mengele's main interest and my father was his right-hand man. Following their research, my sister found that twins made excellent research subjects. We were able to monitor each sibling's progress during the conditioning process by reference to the other. The unusual complex understanding between most twins—not necessarily identical ones—was highly beneficial in structuring their minds to our purposes."

"Do you know if he ever experimented on you and Irma?" I asked, feeling a strong impulse to hurt the fucker. "Who knows? Perhaps all this is your father's doing, not yours or your twin's at all. Perhaps Irma and you were coffined yourselves, back in Auschwitz."

"Don't speak about my sister," he said, his body rigid. "She was a genius."

"Really?" I said, looking at Gwen. She seemed to be apprehensive and confused. I wondered how deep her conditioning really was. "What about the Antichurch of Lucifer Triumphant? What did two fine Nazi rationalists need with a backwoods cult?"

Marion Gilbert lifted up the mask with the end of the skewer and tossed it onto the Führer's lap. He gave her a supercilious look.

"We understood early on that Americans needed religion, even a perverted one like that. The history of the country shows that. The founding fathers thought they were creating the perfect state for mankind to develop to its full potential." Rothmann gave a scathing laugh. "Unfortunately, they failed to take account of mankind's need for spiritual comfort. If the original state had been atheist, it would have achieved much more. Think of the civilrights movement and those ridiculous Negro preachers."

"You'd just have mown them down, I suppose?" I said.

"Certainly not. There is always a need for research material, even from the base races. Besides, this is not a liberal country. How many people are, to use your words, mown down by the police each year? How many blacks and Hispanics are incarcerated, and rightly so? The subhumans need a firm hand."

I managed not to hit him, somehow. "So you let people wearing gargoyle and hyena masks, the latter with a hardon, into your pantheon?"

He gave me a cold stare. "Whatever was effective."

Marion Gilbert pointed the skewer at the mask. "He didn't just let them into the rituals. He *was* the man in the hyena mask and his sister wore that one. People like them do not lead normal lives in any way." She shook her head. "They think the process blanks everything out, but I remember, after the sacrifice of a young woman, I saw them—incest was no taboo for them...."

Rothmann looked completely unperturbed, glancing at Gwen and holding her gaze for a few moments. My suspicions of incest had been correct, but that only opened a new door into the abyss.

"Dana Maltravers," I said, catching Rothmann's eye. "Are you her father?"

He shook his head. "The research that Dr. Mengele and my father carried out in the camp, and that my father continued after the war, suggested that genetic defects were a danger. No, Dana is not my daughter. With Irma, I always wore a condom."

"What happened to her father, then?" I asked.

Rothmann glared at me. "Are you sure you can handle the answer?"

I held his gaze. "You killed him, didn't you?"

He laughed. "Wrong. Irma did. He was one of the first sacrifices when we reinstituted the Antichurch."

I took a deep breath and forced myself to move on. "What about the blinding of the victims after death? Was that really necessary?"

He raised his shoulders. "The original Antichurch did that. Besides, our father lost his sight toward the end of his life—heavy smoking had damaged his eyes. My sister and I felt that was the kind of commemoration he would have relished."

"I'm sure you're right," I said callously. "That didn't put Irma and you off smoking though, did it?"

Rothmann looked at me evenly. I hadn't laid a finger on him.

"What about Karen and me?"

He frowned. "Surely you have worked out why we abducted your lover. Her investigation into a certain London investment banker was becoming a problem."

"Gavin Burdett of Routh, Ltd."

"I know you saw him recently in Washington." He smiled. "Let's just say he is no longer of any significance."

"What? You killed him, too?"

Rothmann shrugged. "He was expendable, and besides, his personal needs were becoming an embarrassment."

"But Karen's free now."

"Like you, she escaped," he said, giving me a tight smile. "So there's nothing to worry about."

"You better not have harmed her or our child," I said, raising a fist over his bloodstained thigh. He ignored it and kept looking straight ahead.

"I'll tell you something I don't understand," I continued. "Why did the *Star Reporter* pay so much attention to the occult murders? You suspected one of your own people was the killer, but your own rag was full of the story every day."

Rothmann gave me a look that suggested I was mentally deficient. "Woodbridge Holdings owns numerous newspapers. Do you imagine we would censor such a major story from all of them? Murders mean major earnings for papers like the *Star*. Besides, we knew the investigations were going nowhere."

"You had your niece on the spot. Shame about Dana's career."

"She successfully framed you and bought us time. Besides, we have plenty more like her. But *you*, you should have kept quiet after we took your partner," Rothmann went on. "We had no specific interest in you."

"I love Karen. She's carrying our son."

He blinked slowly. "That was what Lister said would be your weakness."

A cold finger ran up my spine. "Lister?"

"You didn't think he was just a pawn, did you?

"Gordy Lister is involved in all our plans. He masterminded the kidnappings, both Karen Oaten's and your own."

We really had blown it when we let Lister go, but I couldn't do anything about that now. "What about Joe Greenbaum?"

"He had long been a thorn in the sides of companies such as ours."

"Lister set the bomb?"

He looked at Gwen again. "No, he did not."

I let my head drop. The sick fuck. "You used her?"

"Yes, we did. And her brother. They have turned out to be excellent operatives. The Jew Greenbaum's work has been atomized for good."

I felt the blood boil in my veins. The bastard was wrong there, but I wasn't going to tell him about the data stick yet. I wanted to get off the boat alive and it might be a useful bargaining tool.

I looked at Marion Gilbert. "The double weapons for each victim referred to you and your bother?"

"And to the…the Führer and the professor, and power of two. They were an inspiration to me for a long time…but not…not anymore." She stepped closer and I realized she had reached the end of her tether—her eyes were wild and her hands were shaking. She raised the skewer high.

"*No!*" Rothmann screamed. "Barbarossa! *Barbarossa!*"

This time, the instant I heard the name, I felt my knees give way. My mind filled with clashing images and sounds, but beneath them I felt a strong will that I could no longer resist. I knew it was foreign to me, I knew it was evil, but I was completely in thrall to it. The clamor ceased and I opened my eyes, ready to defend the man who had spoken the word.

Gwen had advanced on Marion Gilbert, who was bleeding from her right hand. Marion slashed at the younger woman. That was when I realized Gwen was holding a combat knife very similar to the one I had acquired during my escape from the camp.

"Now, my Führer?" she asked, her eyes bright.

Rothmann saw that I had moved closer to them. "So, Wells… Are you ready to do your duty?"

I was looking down on myself, as if I were a spirit floating free. I had no control over the self that was in my body.

"Yes, my Führer," I heard myself say.

"It seems the process advanced further into your brain than we thought."

The disembodied part of me was trying to understand what was going on.

"You see, Marion?" Rothmann was saying. "Things have changed since your time. We are now able to master even the most difficult subjects without prolonged treatment. Sometimes it just takes several repetitions of the trigger to prompt a response."

The doctor took another swipe at Gwen, but the younger woman easily avoided the weak blow.

"You...you don't control him," she gasped. "He got out of the camp, he's been working with the police...."

Rothmann laughed hoarsely, his face white as he clutched his wounded thigh. "If I tell him to attack you, he will do so."

Marion Gilbert looked at me and I saw that she was wavering.

I sensed that my eyes had gone as blank as Gwen's.

"Wells!" the Führer yelled.

I watched as my body immediately tensed.

"Give him the knife!"

Gwen looked at the Führer dubiously.

"Go ahead!" he roared.

I took the blade from her and weighed it in my hand. It felt comfortable there.

"Stop it," Marion Gilbert said, her voice faint. "I can't...I can't take anymore."

Rothmann gave her a triumphant look. "Gut her, Wells," he ordered.

Watching in horror, I saw my body take up a combat stance, knees bent and arms in front of the chest. I tried to take control, but I had no access to the part of my being that was wielding the knife. But my victim was too quick for me.

Marion Gilbert was against the bulkhead, holding the

remaining skewer vertically. The steel shaft was closer to her body than it had been. "I hope all your plans come to nothing," she said in a low voice. Then she took a deep breath and pressed the point against her throat. With a desperate wail, she shoved the skewer upward to its hilt. A few seconds later, she crashed lifeless to the floor.

I felt my separate self slip back into my body and the knife drop from my hand. "Did you...did you make her do that?" I stammered feeling more like myself again.

He grunted in pain. "No, I'm afraid I didn't. Unlike you, she didn't respond to the default trigger word. She was beyond direction... It would seem she may even have regained contact with her conscience."

I felt a surge of anger. "Fuck you."

Rothmann looked up at me, and then smiled. I turned and saw that Gwen had picked up the combat knife. "You know, Wells, I think your reliability is questionable. At the current advanced state of our operation, that is inappropriate." He ran his tongue across his lips. "Kill him, my dear."

I'd been waiting for that. "Gwen, do you know that your father is dead?" I looked over my shoulder and saw that the knife had stopped a few inches from my back.

"What?" Her voice was suddenly that of a child.

"I suppose Gordy Lister made sure you didn't see the papers."

"No newspapers or TV are allowed without authorization," she said emptily.

"Don't listen to him," Rothmann said, his voice was wavering.

"It happened here, didn't it?" I said. I was going out on a limb, but the fact that Richard Bonhoff's body had been dumped in the river was suggestive. "On board the *Isolde*."

"No," Rothmann said, "of course it didn't." But the fear on his face gave him away as a liar.

Gwen stepped up to my side. "Why?" she asked, her

eyes damp. "He loved us. You should have let us contact him. We could easily have reassured him." She leaned forward. "Why?"

"Stop!" Rothmann ordered, edging along the sofa. "Put down the knife!"

"Why?" Gwen moaned again. "He loved us...." Then she pushed past me and grabbed her Führer's collar. "If the river was good enough for Daddy, it's good enough for you," she said, then dragged him forward with surprising strength. When he was clear of the furniture, she put the knife to his throat and hauled him to the cabin door. "Don't get in the way," she said to me, over her shoulder.

I kept my distance, and then followed them out into the pale morning light.

Gwen forced Rothmann along the side of the boat till they were both standing at the bow.

"Barbarossa!" he screamed, then another word I struggled to make out—it sounded like "Gerty." After that, he fell to his knees and screamed for help like any normal person.

I looked to my right. The guards at the gate had heard. Their boots thundered across the deck as they approached. I leaned over the side, reached for the package I'd taped under the pier and ripped it away. I tugged the mooring rope at the stern free.

"Cast off," I yelled to Gwen. "Now!"

"Shoot the bitch!" Rothmann roared, before she clubbed him to the deck with the haft of the knife.

Shots rang out from the pier. I had the Glock unwrapped by the time the men were ten yards away. I fired at their legs and they crashed down. I leaped off the boat and ran toward them, kicking their weapons into the water and then covering them with my weapon.

"Gwen!" I shouted. "Can you start the engine?" I turned and saw that the *Isolde* had already drifted several yards away from the pier. I heard a movement and smashed my boot into the face of the gorilla who had fancied his chances. "Start the engine, Gwen!"

But she stayed at the bow, the combat knife at Rothmann's throat. Looking closer, I saw blood on her chest—a lot of blood. At least one of the rounds fired by the guards had hit her.

I thought about trying to jump on board, but the boat was already too far away.

All I could do was cover Gwen's escape. After all that had been done to her and her twin brother, and their father, it was the least I could do.

There was a curtain of mist on the reach that led toward the Potomac, so the *Isolde* was soon hard to make out. I wasn't sure if I imagined it, or if one of the figures at the bow had gone overboard.

Forty-Four

I let the guys I'd shot look after each other's leg wounds—
they seemed to have had the relevant training—and used
one of their cell phones to call the cops. Telling the dispatcher who I was got me put me straight through to Chief
of Detectives Rodney Owen. He came down to the marina
quickly, several cars in his wake.

"Any news about the boat?" I asked, after the gorillas
had been removed.

"We've got her. She was drifting in the Potomac, but
there was no one alive on board."

"So they both went over the side. I wonder if either of
them is still breathing. The girl looked like she'd been
badly hit."

"Our people are all over the river," Owen said. "They'll
find them soon enough." He shook his head. "Marion
Gilbert's body was on the boat, as you said. Who'd have
thought our medical examiner was a secret Nazi?"

"Not to mention serial killer. She fought against what
had been done to her, but it really screwed her up."

Chief Owen looked at me. "You realize I'm going to
have to take you in for questioning."

I shrugged. "Fair enough. How are Simmons and Pinker?"

"Versace's still in a coma. It looks like Clem's going to make it, though. They had a scare a few hours back, but he's stable now. I spoke to him. Looks like you're in the clear, but there are a lot of details we have to go through. The FBI's on your case, as well. You'll have to talk to them about the occult killings."

I wasn't surprised, but I had another priority. "Karen Oaten. Can I see her?"

"I'm sure you can, Mr. Wells, but I don't know when." He gave me an encouraging smile. "Why don't we just take one thing at a time?"

"Okay," I said. I was too tired to argue.

I followed him onto dry land. I was thinking of Gwen Bonhoff. If she hadn't turned on Rothmann, I would be the one floating in the Potomac right now. I wondered if she had survived to make it ashore, or if the currents were carrying her body toward the sea.

Later it came to me that one of the reasons I hadn't written novels featuring cops was the job's never-ending bureaucracy. The questioning seemed to go on forever, though Chief Owen's team had finished with me by midday. Then I was taken to the FBI building and grilled by Peter Sebastian and his people. Though Clem and Versace hadn't exactly talked him up, I thought he was competent enough—thorough rather than nitpicking, but seriously lacking in a sense of humor. At least he wasn't set against me any longer. Randy Bonhoff had been operated on and was expected to make a full recovery in time—whether he would come round from the coffining would be another story. He was still woozy from the anesthetic and hadn't been told about his sister's wounding or her disappearance from the boat. He didn't know about his father's death, either. I wouldn't be volunteering to be the one who passed all that information on.

"All right," Sebastian said at last, gathering up his notes. "We'll get back to this tomorrow, but right now there's somewhere we've got to be."

I thought he meant the canteen, so I didn't show much enthusiasm.

"Come on, Matt," he said, giving a rare smile. "The Bureau's putting on a party for your Karen."

That was more like it. I'd have preferred to meet her in private, but apparently there were some important people who took priority. I borrowed a clean shirt from one of Sebastian's team and then followed the FBI man to the elevator. When we got out on the top floor, we had to go through another X-ray machine. It seemed the bosses got a higher level of security, as well as a better view.

The party was already under way when we got there. The room was crowded by men in suits and the occasional woman in the female equivalent. I didn't see Karen immediately. She was surrounded by people who were shaking her hand and patting her on the back. She looked calm and collected, as if she'd been at a health retreat rather than in captivity. I wondered if she'd been through what I had and how she'd got out. Then she caught sight of me and smiled, which made me feel better. I started to push my way through the mass of bodies toward her, but a blast of feedback from a microphone signaled the beginning of the formal proceedings. I kept on sliding past bodies toward the front as the FBI director started to talk from a podium.

"Ladies and gentlemen," he said with the smile of a man who finally had some good news to report, "I won't keep you long. I'm delighted to welcome Detective Chief Superintendent Karen Oaten back from her ordeal. I'm also delighted to report that, in accordance with official policy, no ransom changed hands."

There was polite laughter.

"Ms. Oaten is one of the London Metropolitan Police's

most talented officers and we look forward to her completing her work with us."

This time, there was polite applause. Presumably Gavin Burdett's death hadn't come to light yet—Karen wouldn't have much to do in Washington without him as her target. Then again, maybe Rothmann had been lying. I didn't think that was too likely. He was the kind of arrogant smart-ass who didn't bother with blatant untruths.

"Before Ms. Oaten says a few words, I'd like to invite the justice secretary to the microphone."

I craned forward and made out the short figure of the woman who was in charge of all American law enforcement. As she passed Karen, she took her hands and kissed her on both cheeks. She seemed to be genuinely moved to see Karen. As the politician began to speak, I watched my beautiful girl. She was standing next to the podium, her head at the same level as the justice secretary's because of her greater height. She had a cardboard file under her arms and she was fiddling with a pen.

I wanted to be in the front row when Karen made her speech, so I nudged past a couple more bodies. Now I could see her clearly. Karen was looking intently at the politician beside her, but she was still playing with the pen. I didn't recognize it, which struck me as odd because I'd given her an expensive pen for her birthday earlier in the year. I knew for a fact she hadn't had it with her when she disappeared because I saw it in her belongings afterward. Those must have been returned to her by now. Where did she get this one? It looked unusual and was only the length of a finger. It looked like she was trying to make it longer.

Then everything came together. Whatever Karen had said when she reappeared, I knew from Irma Rothmann that she'd been at the camp in Maine. She was in no condition to scale the wire and she would only have been allowed to leave if the Rothmanns thought her ready…for some kind of action. That meant she had been coffined and was under mind control, and she was about to do something disastrous.

I shouted her name and ran forward, colliding with a Secret Service man with very wide shoulders. I could still see Karen as he grabbed at me, then she disappeared from my view as I hit the floor. When I looked up, the pen had disappeared. The justice secretary was peering down at me curiously.

Peter Sebastian came up. "What's going on, Matt?" he demanded. "Couldn't you wait a little longer to see Karen?"

"I thought...I..." I let myself be led away to the side of the room. I was vaguely aware of the speeches being concluded and the noise of conversation increasing. The man who had grabbed me was still holding my arm.

"What did you think?" Chief Owen said, appearing between Sebastian and the big man.

"I thought..." My mind was like mush. I must have been imagining things. Karen was perfectly normal. I looked around, trying to catch sight of her, but I couldn't see her anywhere.

"You need rest," Peter Sebastian said. He turned to Chief Owen. "Can I leave him in your charge?"

Owen shrugged. "Okay. I was heading over to the hospital to check on Simmons and Pinker."

Sebastian nodded. "Why don't you get him checked out, too?"

By the time Owen and I made it to the door, there was no sign of Karen. I asked a woman with a clipboard where she'd gone.

"Ms. Oaten went with the justice secretary and her people, sir." She eyed the temporary pass Sebastian had given me on the way in. "Can I help?"

"That's all right," Chief Owen said. "I'll handle this." He led me toward the elevators.

"But I want to see Karen," I said feebly, tugging against his grip.

"Let it go, buddy. You can't mess with the Justice Department." Owen smiled at me. "Besides, your girl's a London cop. How's she going to feel if you screw up a meet with the justice secretary of the United States of America?"

He had a point there. Karen would not be impressed if I messed with her career. So I let him take me down to his car and drive me to the hospital in the northern suburbs. Just before we got there, he got a call. He listened, then cut the connection and glanced at me.

"They found Gwen Bonhoff's body in the Potomac," he said. "We'll have to wait for the postmortem for the cause of death—and we're a medical examiner short right now—but there's a potentially fatal chest wound, like you described."

"What about Rothmann?"

Chief Owen shook his head. "No sign. Let's just hope the currents sucked him to the bottom. We don't need motherfuckers like him around."

He was right there. But as far as I was concerned, no body meant that the Auschwitz doctor's son was alive and well.

There was good news at the hospital—Gerard Pinker had just come out of his coma. He was still groggy and visitors weren't allowed, but his prospects had suddenly got a whole lot better. We went to see Clem. He looked tired, but he was in good spirits because of his partner's first move toward recovery. They took a dive when he heard about Gwen and Rothmann.

"Shit. That girl deserved better."

"She and her brother stuck a knife in Versace and beat the hell out of you, Clem," I reminded him.

He shrugged. "Those Nazi scumbags screwed with their brains." He glanced at me. "What was that word the queen bitch was screaming? Barba-something?"

My head was suddenly filled with the roar of crowds and the thunder of marching men.

"Hey, Matt?" I heard Clem say. "You okay?"

I managed to push aside the confusion. "Yeah," I muttered.

"Everything you've been through is catching up on you, man," Clem said. "You need to get some rest."

I sat back in my chair. There was a TV on the wall, images flashing but no sound coming. I made out a large silvery-gray building with three imposing towers. Then the camera moved down to the crowd gathered outside an entrance with a Gothic arch. When the camera zoomed in, I saw that many of the people were elderly and in uniform.

"What's that?" I asked. I was aware of a quickening throughout my body and a faint, high-pitched sound like a whistle that would normally only be audible to dogs. "What is that place?"

Chief Owen looked up at the screen. "Washington National Cathedral."

"What about the people?" I said, my eyes locked on the pictures. "Who are they?"

Clem grunted. "They're our heroes, man."

I took in shrunken men in wheelchairs, with military caps on their heads and medals on the chests. They were surrounded by proud families in their finest clothes, and most of them were black.

"World War II veterans from the minorities," Owen said. "The president's taken a special interest in them."

"About time somebody did," Clem said. "They'll all be dead soon."

Chief Owen nodded. "That's why they're having the memorial service—to acknowledge the men before it's too late."

Those last words echoed in my mind—before it was too late. Too late for what? Then I found myself thinking of other things: the gargoyle's head, the Antichurch of Lucifer

Triumphant, Rothmann's hatred of what he called subhumans, the Nazis and their war on civilization, Karen...

I stood up. "Did someone mention the president?"

"Yes," Owen said. "The president and first lady are attending the service."

"How about the justice secretary?" I asked, my lungs suddenly tight.

The chief shrugged, his eyes widening. "I guess she might be there...I think a lot of the government is going."

"Jesus," I said. "Karen." I moved quickly to the door. "Come on," I said, looking round at Owen. "She's in danger, I'm sure of it."

The two men exchanged glances, then Owen headed toward me.

"Has the memorial service been arranged for a long time?" I asked, as I led him to the elevator.

"Can't help you there," the chief said, putting his hand on my arm. "Not my department."

I tugged myself free. "Answer me this," I said, stabbing at the call button. "Can you think of a better occasion for a group of Nazis to strike against this country than a service commemorating the role of blacks, Hispanics, Chinese and I don't know who else in the destruction of the Third Reich?"

Rodney Owen's jaw dropped. "No, I don't think I can," he said. Then he pulled out his phone and started rapidly hitting buttons.

Forty-Five

Washington National Cathedral, the world's sixth largest, was basking on the summit of Mount St. Alban, the city's highest point. The late-afternoon sun was reflected strongly by the blocks of Indiana limestone, causing many of the people on site to wear dark glasses. The trees in the fifty-seven acres of gardens that surrounded the building were a picturesque mixture of russet, yellow and brown. The central tower of the structure topped three hundred feet, giving the Secret Service men and Army snipers a fine panorama. To first-time visitors to Washington attending the service, the cathedral was a surprising vision of the medieval, with pointed arches, rib vaults, flying buttresses and stained-glass windows. There were perhaps not enough gargoyles on the walls to achieve the full Gothic effect, but the plentiful decorative pinnacles made up for that. From every gallery and vantage point, personnel in dark fatigues ceaselessly scanned the cathedral vicinity, weapons at the ready. The president and first lady, accompanied by six cabinet members, were expected in thirty-five minutes.

Inside the building, there was an atmosphere of controlled alert. Clergy from the Episcopal Diocese of Washington, dressed in their most formal robes, moved about their duties with studied calm. They were accustomed to state occasions, even though there were more military and plainclothes security people around than they would have liked. This was the house of God, after all, and the United States' greatest men were commemorated here, with separate bays for presidents and wartime leaders from George Washington to Woodrow Wilson, Abraham Lincoln to Franklin D. Roosevelt and Harry Truman. By the north transept was a bay with a likeness of Martin Luther King Jr., proving that all men were brothers in this, the great stone tabernacle of the nation.

One of the six men in the honor guard flanking the high altar watched as a deacon made his final checks. The cleric took out a handkerchief and wiped a minuscule blemish from the surface of one of the hundred and ten carved figures surrounding the statue of Christ. Nearby, a stone from Mount Sinai had been encased in the floor. The guardsman looked up at the great rose window in front of him, the reds and blues of the glass illuminated gloriously. To his right, ranks of wooden pews led toward another rose window at the far end of the nave. By any standards it was a wonderful spectacle, but the soldier was unmoved. He had no time for a religion that saw all men as equal and gave encouragement to members of the subhuman races. He had seen the carving called *Creation* above the main entrance on his way in, mankind being formed out of chaos. That was a perversion of reality. The overwhelming majority of mankind had never, and would never, rise beyond chaos—that was the destiny only of the chosen few.

The members of the honor guard stiffened even more as their commanding officer approached. Everything had been rehearsed over and over again—there was no need for spoken commands. The organist started to play and service personnel representing all the minorities filtered into the cathedral from various entrances to take up their positions. The guardsman kept his eyes to the front, showing no emotion as various minorities, all the scum of the earth, formed up close by him—no doubt there would be Jews in attendance, too, they got everywhere. But no Germans. They weren't a minority. They had been the U.S.'s biggest immigrant group, but now they were fully integrated—they had become part of the majority. They had even served in their hundreds of thousands against the Fatherland.

That mistake would never be repeated. The Führer would see to that, starting today.

The security checks started long before we got anywhere near the cathedral. Chief Owen's clearance got us through initially, with him vouching for me. But soon that wasn't enough. We were asked to get out of the vehicle halfway up the slope that led to the great church, and I was patted down.

"I'm sorry, sir," the perfectly turned out master sergeant said to the chief. "You and your…friend need special authorization for the ceremony. I can't let you proceed any farther."

"But it's an emergency," Rodney Owen said, taking out his phone.

I briefly considered trying to get into one the cars that were being allowed to drive on, but decided against suicide—the soldiers at the checkpoint had their assault rifles at the ready. I'd spoken to Peter Sebastian and he had said he would spread the word, but I hadn't heard anything more. I crushed my nails into the palms of my hands. *Karen,* I thought. Our son…

"Chief Owen! Wells!"

I recognized Sebastian's voice. I turned and saw the FBI man get out of a car on the other side of the checkpoint. He held up his badge.

"These two are with me." He lowered his voice. "Code Treadstone 23."

The master sergeant called it in and then waved us through.

"Thanks a lot," I said, as we got into Sebastian's car. "I thought we were going to be stuck there. What's going on?"

The FBI man looked round at me from the front passenger seat. "Relax, everything's under control. There's almost as much security up there as there was at the president's inauguration—secret service, army, marines, special forces, take your pick."

I stared at him. "That's the point. If people have been coffined…I mean, brainwashed like Marion Gilbert, they could be part of any or all of those. Did you make that clear to whoever is in charge?"

Sebastian nodded. "Of course I did. It was even passed to the president's people. The man himself said he wanted things to go ahead as planned. The service is very important to him… Besides, it isn't as if we have a lot of hard evidence about Marion Gilbert's state of mind. I mean, I believe you, Matt, but you've got to admit, it's all a bit circumstantial."

I grabbed his arm. "Circumstantial? She killed four people, for God's sake. And Rothmann came clean about the conditioning process."

"To you, and you were a suspect for a while, with a lot to gain by blaming Marion Gilbert," Sebastian said.

"Fuck!" I slammed my head against the seat back. "What more do you guys need? It wasn't only Marion Gilbert who was brainwashed. Gwen and Randy took out the detectives."

"I know, but you can't blame the official channels for some healthy skepticism. Besides, you said that Rothmann got to you, too, Matt. Have you any idea how lucky you are to be here? If it wasn't for Karen Oaten, I'd have left you at the checkpoint back there."

I sat back, thinking about what he'd just said. "If it wasn't for Karen? What do you mean?" He didn't answer, keeping his eyes off me. "You bastard. You don't trust her, do you? You think she could have been conditioned, too."

Peter Sebastian turned to face me. "Think about it, Matt. You've already said that you've been affected by the word that the Rothmanns used—notice that I'm not repeating it. And you were in captivity for less time than Karen."

"So what are you doing allowing her anywhere near the justice secretary, let alone the president."

Sebastian looked away. "It's not my call. I've told the director and he's passed on my suspicions to his counterparts in the other agencies. The problem is, the justice secretary thinks Karen is a hero and we all know how much politicians like to be seen with their heroes. Your woman's also a foreign dignitary. The last thing anyone wants today is a diplomatic incident."

Rodney Owen leaned forward. "I still don't get why you're letting Matt here attend the service."

The FBI man looked to the front. "I'm rather hoping he'll have a beneficial effect on Karen Oaten—maybe put her off trying anything." He shook his head. "Not that I expect her to. She had her chance at the party and nothing happened.... Despite your fears, Matt."

I was about to lay into him for his cynicism, but then I realized it was to my advantage—I desperately wanted to be with Karen, whatever happened.

The car was stopped at the final checkpoint by the cathedral. We got out and I watched as a convoy of heavy limousines swept past. Large men with wires coming from their ears scanned the area and then opened the doors. I caught a glimpse of the president and his wife. They waved and smiled as they went into a side door. I looked up and around. Above the gargoyles and pinnacles, I saw numerous black-clad personnel toting guns. It only took one of those to be a renegade shooter....

"Come on," Sebastian said, heading toward the entrance the president had used. "It's nearly showtime."

My throat was dry and my stomach performing somersaults. I couldn't have had a worse feeling if Rothmann himself had been on the door.

Karen Oaten sat down after the president and first lady had taken their seats at the front of the nave, three rows in front of the justice secretary and herself.

"I'll introduce you afterward," the diminutive woman whispered, with a broad smile.

Karen nodded and looked ahead. There were ranks of veterans in front of the high altar, many of them in wheelchairs, all wearing berets with badges on them. Each was accompanied by a family member and a young soldier with similar unit insignias. The veterans themselves looked bewildered, as if the ceremony was directed at younger selves they had long since left behind.

There was a slight commotion in the row behind her and Karen looked round. To her surprise, she saw people moving along and Matt taking the seat directly behind her. He gave her a smile, which she didn't return. She had assumed, after his behavior at FBI headquarters, that he had been taken somewhere to cool down. What on earth had he been doing? He had put her off something, though she couldn't remember what it was. Fortunately she had regained her composure as soon as the justice secretary invited her to come to the minority veterans' service, saying that her presence would send a message to criminals and terrorists that the kidnapping of a police officer, no matter where she was from, would be given the highest priority by the administration.

And now, Karen thought, here was Matt again. She con-

sidered complaining to the justice secretary, but the ceremony was beginning. Besides, she would have to see Matt
sooner or later to tell him that their life together was finished. She had other priorities for her son now. She knew
a major event was about to change her life irreversibly. She
was ready.

I was only half listening to the readings and prayers as
the service dragged on, so disturbing was the way Karen
had looked at me. It wasn't that she gave the impression
of some horrific intent, or that she showed any signs of
being a different person from the one I loved. But that was
precisely the problem. She was the same woman; she just
didn't seem to care about me anymore. She had glanced at
me as if I was of no greater significance to her than a dust
mite. I began to lose confidence in myself. Maybe I was
the one at fault. Maybe I had never really loved her and had
never wanted a child with her....

I clenched my fists and forced myself to concentrate on
what was going on in the cathedral. From the pulpit, a minister in dark purple robes was preaching about the neces-
sity of sacrifice in wartime and how gloriously members
of the nation's minorities had fulfilled that, particularly in
the defining war against European fascism and Japanese
militarism. I had a flash of the blonde woman who had
been sacrificed by the Antichurch of Lucifer Triumphant
at the camp. Had her death been justifiable in those terms?
In any terms? Then the minister paused and I felt a tremor
of anticipation that I couldn't account for.

"But the regimes you fought against so bravely," continued the man at the pulpit, "despite what you were told,
were not evil. For centuries they were the bulwarks of civilization against the barbarian. As long ago as the twelfth
century, the Holy Roman Empire was defended by the
great German Fredrick I." The preacher stopped again and

looked across the rows of listeners. I was sweating, my heart racing. I knew what was coming—I had seen it in dreams and visions that, deep down, my mind had suppressed and that my conscious will had resisted, until now. "Also known as Barbarossa," the minister concluded.

There were a few seconds of silence and then all hell broke its chains. There was a loud blast from the front of the cathedral, smoke and dust immediately obscuring the altar and its carved figures. Then automatic weapon fire started, shots coming from all directions. People dived to the floor between the pews but there wasn't room for all to find cover and the screams of the wounded and dying filled the air. I rubbed my eyes, my mind clogged by disparate thoughts and images. *Barbarossa*—Rothmann had called that the default trigger and there were obviously plenty of people in the cathedral responding to it. Sweating, I tried to fight the coffining and keep myself under control. Looking ahead, I saw Karen. She was bending over the woman next to her, the justice secretary, and she was brandishing something. Getting up, I saw that it was a pen, but there was a vicious shaft like a small skewer projecting from it.

"No!" I yelled, dashing the weapon from her hand.

Karen turned to me, her eyes wide, and screamed a single word.

I couldn't make it out in the rattle of gunfire and the cries of thousands of people.

She understood that and said it again.

"Gerty?" I repeated, a dim recollection swimming to the surface of my mind.

"Goethe!" Karen screamed back at me.

Immediately I felt my knowing self fly from my body, as it had on the *Isolde*. I was aware that Johann Wolfgang von Goethe, born 1749, died 1832, was the greatest of German writers—the author of novels, poetry and plays, including the incomparable poetic drama *Faust*—and the universal genius of his countrymen. But I also knew that *Goethe* was my personal trigger, the word that activated the deepest level of conditioning that lurked beyond all conscious control.

I watched as my body moved into action, completely indifferent to the bullets flying around—fire was now being returned by army and security personnel against Rothmann's sleeper Nazis. My other self paid no attention to Karen, who was being held tightly by Owen and Sebastian, but pushed his way to the end of the pew. The central passage was crowded by people pushing toward the exits. There was a crush all round as veterans in wheelchairs jammed against current army personnel and guests. Groups of VIPs protected by their phalanxes of guards were unable to reach the cathedral doors.

Then I saw my programmed self catch sight of the scrum of men in suits that had formed beyond the front row of pews. There was a glimpse of the president, his arm around his wife. His mouth was moving, but it was impossible to hear his words.

And then the Matt Wells I didn't know made his bid for glory in accordance with the perverted vision of the Rothmann twins and the Antichurch of Lucifer Triumphant. He smashed his fist into a female soldier's face and grabbed her assault rifle. Switching to automatic fire, he pointed it at the group around the president and charged toward them, screaming like one of the Germanic warriors that had massacred the Roman Emperor Augustus's legions nine years after the birth of Jesus Christ.

The tumult rose to a crescendo.

I was unable to stop my separate self rejoining the body that was intent on destroying the leader of the modern world.

Everything ended in darkness as I tumbled into a deep well.

Epilogue

But after every darkness, until the sun finally consumes itself, there is light.

Well wrapped up, Karen and I were walking across a snowy landscape, the breath billowing from our mouths like ghosts escaping from tombs. In the distance, the hills were covered with pine trees and it was only with difficulty that I could make out the electrified fences marking the boundaries of the FBI research center.

"Not too cold for you?" I asked, squeezing her arm.

She smiled. "Not too cold for your son, you mean."

I laughed. "He's all right. He's in a temperature-controlled swimming pool."

"Yes, well, he'll be out of there in a month, so I hope you're looking forward to disturbed nights." She stopped walking and then shook her head. "Not that there's been a shortage of those recently."

I led her down the path that led to the concrete block we'd been living in for the past three months. It was hardly surprising that the Justice Department had sent us to the facility in North Dakota. Neither of us remembered anything about what had happened latterly in the cathedral. It was calculated that there had been forty-six of the Rothmanns' subjects involved apart from us, the majority in the armed forces and local police. One had been in the honor guard at the high altar and had detonated the bomb that blew him and many innocent people to pieces. Sixteen sleepers had been twins. The subjects had obviously been trained to fight to the death—only three of the forty-six survived, and one of those was in a coma. Neither of the other two said a word to their interrogators. Attempts were being made to reverse their conditioning in secret research centers.

Karen and I had undergone weeks of treatment, too. Unlike the other survivors, we weren't guilty of killing or injuring anyone. Rodney Owen and Peter Sebastian had managed to prevent Karen from stabbing the justice secretary, while I had been floored by a member of the Secret Service as I had tried to get at the president. Fortunately, the M16 I was wielding jammed, so I hadn't been able to shoot anyone. The fact that we were foreign nationals probably helped. We had been visited by staff from the embassy and from the U.K., and given to understand that we would not face charges. But there was no immediate prospect of our release. There was a medical center on site and our son would be born there. Meanwhile, the drug and talking therapies continued, and we both woke up every night screaming.

One hundred and sixty-three people had been killed at the cathedral and over four hundred injured, not counting the attackers. Although the president and first lady had escaped unscathed, the veterans' secretary had been shot dead and a senior White House adviser confined to a wheelchair for the rest of his life. The bomb planted in the floor in front of the altar had destroyed the stone from Mount Sinai, which no doubt had symbolic significance for the Rothmanns. The state of Israel quickly offered to provide a replacement.

The North American National Revival claimed responsibility for the attack, crowing that the bloody disruption
of what it called "the undeserved commemoration of
minority subhumans" was backed by the majority of
Americans. That was called into doubt when, because of
public demand, thirty-six state legislatures immediately
passed bills establishing annual services for minority
veterans. The NANR also stated that the attack was aimed
at destroying "the Jew and Negro controlled regime" that
the recent financial collapse had already shown was failing
America. The tainted logic of the Rothmann twins was
easy enough to discern.

The FBI quickly published documentation proving that
the NANR was a Nazi front and two camps were found,
one in Montana and the other in Texas. The Maine camp
remained undiscovered despite helicopter searches, some
of which I joined. Then one of the psychiatrists working
with me—a strange guy called Ray Iselin—got interested
in the settlement where the Antichurch of Lucifer Triumphant had flourished. Using nineteenth-century maps and
documents, the location of the long-lost town of Jasper was
pinpointed. The camp where I'd been tortured was under
a mile away. I'd like to think that it was immediately shut
down, but no doubt plenty of government bodies and private companies would have been interested in the research
that had gone on there.

"Matt?" Karen asked plaintively. "Do you think I'll
ever get my job back?"

It was the first time she'd mentioned her career since
we'd arrived at the facility. She'd been composed but withdrawn, engaged fully by our son's imminent arrival. I had
slightly more interest in the outside world, but I hadn't
been as deeply programmed as she had. I certainly wasn't
interested in writing books and columns, despite the offers
that my agent kept sending me via the FBI.

"Do you want it back?" I asked, kissing her cheek. "Work isn't everything."

She looked at me solemnly. "Work makes you free."

I felt my abdomen clench. It was impossible to tell if she remembered that *"Arbeit Macht Frei"*—the German version of those words—had been above the gates of the Auschwitz death camp, among others. I wondered if she would ever be free of the coffining. I had no idea if I would ever get over mine—I hadn't forgotten Rothmann's boast, that subjects became his possessions. Even if the experts finally told us we were clean, would we ever be sure that we wouldn't turn into Aryan killing machines at the utterance of some unsuspected trigger word?

That wasn't all. We had asked the scientists if there was any chance that the conditioning could have affected the child in Karen's womb. They didn't think so, but there wasn't much research on the subject. Besides, Irma Rothmann was a brilliant neuroscientist. Who would bet against her having extended her father's research into the unborn fetus? Not me.

Peter Sebastian turned up once a week and filled us in on some things. Predictably, Gordy Lister had vanished—I was sure he would have linked up with Rothmann by now. Dana Maltravers was recovering physically, but she was in deep shit. The FBI is hard on their own who go bad, though her lawyers would no doubt argue that Irma Rothmann—literally the mother from hell, having grown up in Auschwitz—had brainwashed her from an early age. Clem Simmons and Gerard Pinker had both been discharged from the hospital. Apparently Clem was going to take his pension and do some private sleuthing. Versace had been given a commendation and a promotion. Much to Rodney Owen's disgust, Pinker had recently won a contest as the most fashionable detective in the entire MPDC.

Karen stopped about fifty yards away from the building we were forced to call home for the time being.

"Matt," she said softly, "are you going to be a good father to your son?"

"Sure I am," I said, smiling. "Rugby training every evening, two foreign languages before he goes to school, and no arguing with his mother."

She nudged me in the ribs, the first time that had happened for months. The smile faded from my lips. I wasn't going to tell her, but on his last visit Sebastian had passed me an intercepted message from my ex-lover Sara Robbins, the Soul Collector.

Matt, where are you? All that stuff in the press about the Washington murders and then…poof, you're gone. Karen, too. It isn't long now till you'll be a father again, is it? I would swing by sometime, if I knew where you were. After all, we have unfinished business. All right, I accept the challenge. I'll track you down. Don't expect me to be in a good temper when I find you, though. SC

There was a time when I'd have been scared shitless by a communication like that, but not anymore. Rothmann was still at large and it wouldn't be long till he reconstituted the NANR and the Antichurch of Lucifer Triumphant. There would be other camps, other maps of hell, and he would soon find someone else to wear his sister's gargoyle mask.

It was obvious that I'd have to deal with Rothmann, just as I'd have to put an end to Sara. If there was one thing I had learned in the U.S., it was the benefit of nailing your enemies before they nailed you. Actually, it was something I had practiced on the rugby pitch often enough—get your retaliation in first. That was as good a principle as any, though I wasn't planning on passing it on to my son till he was a lot older.

I kissed Karen and we walked into the warmth.

* * * * *

Acknowledgments

Many thanks to Linda McFall, my former editor at MIRA New York, for all her great support and input; and to the new guy Adam Wilson, whose notes on this book were stellar—keep it up!

A champagne-filled glass is raised again to the MIRA teams around the world, especially to my U.K. editor, Catherine Burke, and the brilliant gang at Richmond. My agent Broo Doherty has, as ever, been a font of wisdom. Some very talented doctors have kept me going at close to peak performance—heartfelt thanks to Professor Efstathios Papalambros, and to consultants Yiorgios Pavlakis, Miltos Seferlis, and Alan McNeill.

Huge thanks to Claire Johnston and Chris Miele for generous office provision. And a large blueberry daiquiri to my good friend John Connolly, who drank with me in D.C. and took me to Maine in a Jag. I would call him *il miglior fabbro,* but that would just get me an earful of abuse in which the word *pseud* frequently appeared...

Finally, this undeserving author has been treated with unquestioning devotion and generosity by his wife and kids—Roula, Maggie, Alexander, don't take your love away from me. Oh, and my elder daughter Silje, twenty-one and belle of the ball, wanted a mention, too.

International Bestselling Author

M. J. ROSE

Hypnosis opens the door to the past... but what happens if the truth on the other side is something you can't live with?

A modern-day reincarnationist is hell-bent on finding tools to aid in past life regressions no matter what the cost— in dollars or lives.

Everything rests on the shoulders of Lucian Glass, special agent with the FBI's Art Crime team, who himself is suffering from a brutal attack, impossible nightmares and his own crisis of faith.

If reincarnation is real, how can he live with who he was in his past life? If it's not, then how can he live with who he has become in the present?

The
HYPNOTIST

Available wherever books are sold!

MMJR2675R

REQUEST YOUR
FREE BOOKS!

2 FREE NOVELS
FROM THE SUSPENSE COLLECTION
PLUS 2 FREE GIFTS!

YES! Please send me 2 FREE novels from the Suspense Collection and my 2 FREE gifts (gifts are worth about $10). After receiving them, if I don't wish to receive any more books, I can return the shipping statement marked "cancel." If I don't cancel, I will receive 3 brand-new novels every month and be billed just $5.74 per book in the U.S. or $6.24 per book in Canada. That's a saving of at least 28% off the cover price. It's quite a bargain! Shipping and handling is just 50¢ per book in the U.S. and 75¢ per book in Canada.* I understand that accepting the 2 free books and gifts places me under no obligation to buy anything. I can always return a shipment and cancel at any time. Even if I never buy another book, the two free books and gifts are mine to keep forever.

192 MDN E4MN   392 MDN E4MY

Name	(PLEASE PRINT)	
Address		Apt. #
City	State/Prov.	Zip/Postal Code

Signature (if under 18, a parent or guardian must sign)

Mail to **The Reader Service:**
IN U.S.A.: P.O. Box 1867, Buffalo, NY 14240-1867
IN CANADA: P.O. Box 609, Fort Erie, Ontario L2A 5X3

Not valid for current subscribers to the Suspense Collection
or the Romance/Suspense Collection.

Want to try two free books from another line?
Call 1-800-873-8635 or visit www.morefreebooks.com.

* Terms and prices subject to change without notice. Prices do not include applicable taxes. N.Y. residents add applicable sales tax. Canadian residents will be charged applicable provincial taxes and GST. Offer not valid in Quebec. This offer is limited to one order per household. All orders subject to approval. Credit or debit balances in a customer's account(s) may be offset by any other outstanding balance owed by or to the customer. Please allow 4 to 6 weeks for delivery. Offer available while quantities last.

Your Privacy: Harlequin Books is committed to protecting your privacy. Our Privacy Policy is available online at www.eHarlequin.com or upon request from the Reader Service. From time to time we make our lists of customers available to reputable third parties who may have a product or service of interest to you. If you would prefer we not share your name and address, please check here. ☐

Help us get it right—We strive for accurate, respectful and relevant communications. To clarify or modify your communication preferences, visit us at www.ReaderService.com/consumerschoice.

MSUS10